TALES OF THE
SHADOWMEN
Volume 16: Voir Dire

also from Black Coat Press

TALES OF THE
SHADOWMEN

Volume 16: Voir Dire

edited by
Jean-Marc & Randy Lofficier

stories by
**Matthew Baugh, Nathan Cabaniss, Matthew Dennion,
Brian Gallagher, Martin Gately, Joseph Gibson,
Travis Hiltz, Jean-Pierre Laigle, Jean-Marc Lofficier,
Nigel Malcolm, Xavier Mauméjean,
Christofer Nigro, John Peel, Frank Schildiner**
and **David L. Vineyard.**

cover by
Daniele Serra

A Black Coat Press Book

ISBN 978-1-61227-910-7. First Printing. December 2019. Published by Black Coat Press, an imprint of Hollywood Comics.com, LLC, P.O. Box 17270, Encino, CA 91416. All rights reserved. Except for review purposes, no part of this book may be reproduced or transmitted in any form or by any means, electronic or mechanical, including photocopying, recording or by any information storage and retrieval system, without permission in writing from the publisher. The stories and characters depicted in this anthology are entirely fictional. Printed in the United States of America.

Table of Contents

Advertisement for the 1967 French TV adaptation of The Black Coats

Foreword
The True History of the Black Coats

The remarkable foreword by Francis Lacassin [1] for the recent collection of Paul Féval's *Black Coats* novels in the *Bouquins* imprint mentions the existence of the real life Black Coats, whose trial was supposed to have thrilled the French public in 1845.

Paul Féval himself mentions this trial in Part II, chapter XXII, of Volume 1 (*The Parisian Jungle*) [2] but dating it (by mistake or in order to confuse the readers?) from 1842, and stating that the leaders of the gang were not captured.

The *Grand Dictionnaire Universel du XIXe siècle* by Pierre Larousse provides some additional details under the article *Habits Noirs*:

It would appear that in 1820, three men, named Pernet, Mack and Mayliand, met in a gambling den in Paris. After the closure of said gambling den in 1822, they turned to theft and blackmail. In 1823, Pernet and Mack joined the Vidocq Brigade. [3] (They remained in touch with Vidocq until his death.)

After a series of "about thirty burglaries" committed against various Paris merchants between 1835 and 1837, someone named Gaspard Rivoiron, originating from an "honest family", was arrested and sentenced to 30 years' hard labor. At first, Rivoiron is alleged to have identified some of his accomplices, but later refused to repeat his confession before the Magistrates.

In 1843, it was Pernet's turn to be arrested for the same crimes. He, too, was sentenced to 30 years' hard labor, but turned on his accomplices.

---

[1] (1931-2008). French journalist, editor, writer, screenplay writer and essayist. Lacassin started to work for Jean-Jacques Pauvert's magazine *Bizarre* in 1964. He wrote articles about popular literature in the prestigious *Magazine Littéraire*, worked for *L'Express* and for *Le Point* and was one of the editors of Christian Bourgois' paperback imprint *10/18*. A specialist of pop culture, Lacassin was a founding member of a group of comic book fans who coined the term "9th art" in the early 1960s. He wrote wrote erudite introductions for reprint collections of the works of Eugène Sue, Gustave Le Rouge, Maurice Leblanc, Fantômas, H. P. Lovecraft, and Jack London.

[2] Black Coat Press, ISBN 978-1-934543-03-0.

[3] Eugène-François Vidocq (1775-1857) was a French criminal turned detective whose life story inspired Victor Hugo, Edgar Allan Poe, Honoré de Balzac and Paul Féval. This former criminal became the founder and first director of the crime detecting Sûreté Nationale, as well as the head of the first known private detective agency.

In the subsequent inquiry, some members of the gang were found to have died, others were already serving time for other crimes, some could not be located at all, and thus only nine people were arrested and tried before the Assize Court of Paris, starting on January 10, 1845.

The respectable position of some of them in the high society of the times is what earned them the nickname of "Black Coats."

Mayliand, a former soldier in the French Cavalry, was a so-called "lion of the boulevards," a well-known socialite who also went by the name of "Alfred Cancan." His mistress was a famous actress, Mademoiselle Aldegonde, and they had a lovely daughter, Juliette.

Mack, who used the aliases of M. Labussiere, and "The Marquis," owned a prosperous fashion store.

Among the other accused was a woman, Madeleine, who reminded people of the colorful, eccentric villainess nicknamed *La Chouette* [The Owl] in Eugène Sue's popular *Les Mystères de Paris* feuilleton novel.

Mayliand, the alleged ring leader, was sentenced to 15 years' hard labor; and Mack to 20 years. Pernet (probably because he had snitched on his friends) was let go shortly thereafter. He remained in Paris and, under an assumed name, managed to regain a respectable position.

If Larousse is to be believed, the defendants in the trial of January 1845 represented less than one-tenth of the gang, and, at that time, no fewer than 200 people were arrested for being connected "in one form or another" with the infamous Black Coats.

My friend Vincent Mollet who works as a curator in the archives of the port of Toulon has access to the records of the notorious hard labor camp. If there are no entries for the fictional Jean Valjean and Rocambole, there is an entry for Vidocq, who did some time there.

As it turns out, there is also an entry for Mayliand! Register 1 O 163, registration number 32784, and register 1 O 180, registration 1892: Louis Alfred Mayliand, born in 1798, sentenced to 15 years' hard labor on 16 January 1845.

Because of his dedicated service during the cholera epidemic of 1854 and the typhus epidemic of 1855, Mayliand was pardoned in 1855 and he retired to Rouen. No one knows what happened to him thereafter.

Jean-Marc Lofficier

This wonderful tale by our regular contributor Matthew Baugh draws its setting from H. P. Lovecraft's Dream-Quest of Unknown Kadath, *a classic novella penned in 1926 or 1927, heavily influenced by Lord Dunsany. It borrows its protagonist, Madame Palmyre, from Renée Dunan's (herself a character therein)* Baal *(1924), a novella in which this modern day sorceress encounters the other-dimensional entity Baal, whose octopus-like form is described as the three-dimensional projection of some incomprehensibly vaster entity. (*Baal *is available from Black Coat Press in a translation by Brian Stableford, ISBN 978-1-61227-046-3.)*

Matthew Baugh: *The Peculiar Cats of the Sea of Dreams*

Kurdistan, 1925

"We are very close to Atlaänat," Ishmeddin said in his surprisingly good French. "Before I guide you the rest of the way, I would learn more. How did four *firangī* women learn of the old ruin? And what prompted you to make such a long and dangerous pilgrimage?"

Palmyre smiled, an expression as enigmatic as the Mona Lisa but with a strong note of mischief.

"Our reasons are our own, *effendi*. You do not need to know them."

"Ah, but I do."

Victoria Custer scowled and placed the cup with the dregs of her coffee next to the cooking fire.

"Don't say anything, Madame Palmyre," she said. "I know how these native guides operate. No matter what we tell him, he'll use it as a pretext to demand more money."

The old dervish returned her glare with his own fierce expression. He reached a dirty hand into his even dirtier garment and produced a handful of golden coins, worth several hundred francs. Without hesitation, he flung them into the darkening marshes.

"See what I think of your money, *sayidati.*"

"The cheek!" Victoria said, but Palmyre placed a hand on her arm to quiet her.

"Are you saying that you will not guide us further unless we answer your questions?"

"I hold my curiosity as important as you do yours, *sayidati.*"

"We don't need him," Victoria said. "He said we're close to Atlaänat. We can find it ourselves."

"If God wills it," Ishmeddin replied.

"By the tone of your voice, I gather you think God does not will it," Palmyre said.

The dervish only smiled slyly in reply.

"I suppose there's nothing for it, then."

Palmyre turned her eyes to Mademoiselle Kephra and gave a little nod. The dark woman's expression didn't change as she spoke. Her beauty and stillness made me think of the famous statue of Nefertiti the Berlin Museum had placed on display last year.

"The city is a mystery that I have known of for as long as I can remember," she said. "That is all the reason I need."

"I have a... a lover," Victoria said. "Madame Palmyre said there is a man in the city who may be able to help me find him again."

Ishmeddin turned an inquiring gaze on Palmyre.

"The only man who dwells in Atlaänat is the Dreamer."

"I know," she replied. "He is the one we seek, Mademoiselle Custer to find her lover, and me, because I think the dreamer may be an old lover of mine."

That gave the old dervish pause and he was silent for several moments before locking eyes with me. There was an intensity in those eyes, a sense of strength that made me want to turn away. But Palmyre would think less of me if I showed weakness, so I matched his stare.

"I am Madame Palmyre's assistant," I said.

That seemed to satisfy Ishmeddin, who dropped his gaze and reached into his garment to withdraw a handful of small figs.

"We should fortify ourselves before we go on."

"Go on?" I said. "You don't mean we're going to travel by night, do you?"

"There's no moon," Victoria added. "How can we find it?"

"Twilight is the only time you can find the city," Ishmeddin replied. "Please, eat."

We each took one of the proffered fruit. Victoria popped hers into her mouth impatiently. She made a face, as if surprised by the taste, but kept chewing. Mademoiselle Kephra's face remained enigmatic as she chewed. I sniffed my fig before biting it and found the fruity aroma mixed with an array of spices. There was something familiar about the odor, something that I'd smelled before in Palmyre's Paris rooms.

"Palmyre, stop," I cried. "The figs are drugged."

My friend smiled, as one smiles at a small child who has just discovered that the ocean is wet.

"Of course they are, my dear Renée. Don't fret, I will not let anyone harm you," she said, then bit at her fig greedily.

I stared at the fruit a moment longer. I distrusted the old Afghan, but if Palmyre told me this was safe, I would do it. I took a bite and savored the exotic blend of flavors, then my mind slipped away into a miasma of colors, sounds, and aromas.

When I became aware of my surroundings again, the five of us were standing in a ruined stone vault. There was no roof and the stars stood out with peculiar brightness. Ishmeddin held two lanterns and, as I stared around at the ancient stones, passed one to me and the other to Victoria.

At the far end of the vault stood a massive archway that led into another, darkened, chamber. Someone in some distant age had carved several lines of Arabic script into the capstone.

ميتا ليس الأبد إلى ينام الذي الشيء
أيضا الموت يموت قد الغريبة العصور في

"I wonder what it says?" I murmured.

"It is a warning, or perhaps a promise," Mademoiselle Kephra said. *"The thing that sleeps forever is not dead, and in strange times, death may also die."*

"It is from the writings of an Arab scholar of centuries past," Ishmeddin said. "An American friend translated it more poetically as, *'That does not sleep, which doth eternal lie, and in strange aeons, even death may die.'"*

The words didn't make any sense to me, but hearing them gave me a chill that reached to my marrow.

Taking my lantern, Ishmeddin led us into the chamber, which proved much larger than it had seemed from the outside. It swallowed the light from our puny electric lanterns, yielding only glimpses of distant stone walls decorated with carvings of figures of disturbing aspect.

"Hence lies the Dreamer," Ishmeddin continued. "Before we enter, I ask you again what you seek."

Perhaps it was the drug in the plums, but I no longer felt the need to hide my thoughts from this stranger. Indeed, I felt compelled to pour them out and only the fact that Mademoiselle Kephra spoke first stopped me.

Cleo spoke first, her voice as distant and emotionless as the stars.

Perhaps it was the drug in the plums, but I no longer felt the need to hide my thoughts from this stranger. Indeed, I felt compelled to pour them out and only the fact that Mademoiselle Kephra spoke first stopped me.

"This place is very old," she said. "It may be that its Dreamer is even older than me. Perhaps he can help unravel the secrets of my past and my future."

It was odd hearing this woman imply she was ancient. She radiated a timeless sort of beauty, it was true, but there is a limit to that. It was difficult to credit her as more than thirty.

"What is old?" she replied, her voice dreamy. "I only know that I am weary of life and the suffering it brings."

"You long for death?"

11

"No, for I have already died many times." She stared dreamily into the dark opening before speaking again. "Eight times, I think. Without finality, it offers no relief."

"Then what?" Ishmeddin asked, his voice barely audible.

"I long to reach the scales of Maat, where Anubis waits with a feather to judge my heart."

"And then?"

"Then, I expect I shall be devoured, for my heart is heavy after all that I have seen."

"Wishing that, what do you seek here?"

She sighed and there was such sorrow in it that I wanted to weep.

"I cannot remember my beginning, nor can I imagine my end. Perhaps the dreamer can tell me these things and give me a measure of peace."

The dervish nodded, as if her answer was nothing to strange to him. He turned to Victoria Custer.

"The lover you seek, who is he?"

"He is Nu, the son of Nu," she replied. "He is a hunter and a killer of great beasts."

"And where did you know him?"

"In Africa. We were together only a short while, but I have known him in my dreams since I was a girl."

"What became of him?"

"There was an earthquake."

Victoria crossed her arms and shivered.

"What became of Nu?"

"We were separated." She drew a breath to steady herself. "I did not see him again, only a skeleton that had been dead for a million years. My brother said that was him and that I had only dreamed he was alive, but I knew better. Madame Palmyre said, since he was my dream-lover, perhaps the Dreamer could reunite us."

Ishmeddin nodded again, still looking as if nothing extraordinary had been said. He turned his gaze to Palmyre, and her eyes shone bright and full of mischief.

"Aren't you going to ask Renée your question first?"

"Her answer is obvious," Ishmeddin said. "She cares nothing about the Dreamer, but follows because she loves you."

A blush suffused my face and upper body. Even if such a thing were true, who was this dervish to make such a suggestion? I opened my mouth to protest but both Ishmeddin and Palmyre ignored me.

"You mentioned a lover," the dervish said.

"Not a human lover, but a being from beyond time and space as we understand them," she said. "You would call him a god."

"There is no god but God, and Muhammad is his prophet," the dervish replied mildly. "Perhaps *you* would call him such."

"He is known by many names," she said. "Some call him Azathoth, others Cthulhu, and others Mana Yood Suchai. I knew him as Baal."

Fear rushed through me, chilling my entire body. My mind was filled with the memory of a rift, somehow torn into the empty air of Palmyre's Paris apartments; squid-like tentacles emerged from it to loop around her slender body, threatening to drag her into the chaos beyond, a space of impossible curves and angles. She had scarcely escaped that alien embrace and her flesh was burned where the tentacle touched her. How could she yearn for another encounter?

"You think that the Dreamer is your Baal?" Ishmeddin asked, echoing my thoughts.

Palmyre suppressed a laugh.

"I am certain of it."

"Palmyre!" I cried. "Baal's touch nearly killed you. Why would you want to experience it again?"

"Because, my dear Renée, his love for me is purer than the love of any man or woman could ever be."

That stung me to silence.

"Surely you understand the implications of your plan, *sayidati?*" Ishmeddin asked. "All of us, all the world, everything seen and unseen, are but parts of the Dreamer's dream. If he wakens, we shall disappear into the nothingness that all dreams must return to."

"So say the stories," Palmyre said. "But how do they know?"

"You would dare to test them?"

"If I am right, he will waken and we can be together. If I am wrong and the universe disappears..." Palmyre spread her hands in an exaggerated shrug. "Of what importance is the passing of an illusion?"

Ishmeddin shook his head.

"This is the madness of all you *farangi*. You seek to master what you cannot even understand."

"You are foolish to assume that," Palmyre replied. "Will you try to stop me? I warn you, I control forces powerful enough to blast you where you stand."

"No, *sayidati*. I have warned you. The choice is yours."

Palmyre gave a nod of satisfaction and crossed the threshold into the cavernous room. Victoria, Mademoiselle Kephra, and I trailed in behind her. Our torches revealed a seated figure on a low throne at the far side of the chamber. At first, I thought he was a statue, for he was motionless and covered by a layer of grey dust. As we drew closer, I could see that his chest moved, slowly and steadily.

"I wonder how long he can have been sitting there," I whispered.

"Since before the building of the city or even the foundation of the world," Kephra said.

"Nonsense," I replied. "How could he have sat there before there was a place to sit?"

She shot me a look, her annoyance briefly showing through her sphinx-like stoicism.

"Do you think we should do this?" Victoria asked. "The old dervish said…"

Palmyre smiled and moved close to the dreamer.

"Have you come this far just to run away now?" she asked. "Waking the dreamer is the only chance for you to see your Nu again."

Victoria nodded and Palmyre's gaze shifted to Mademoiselle Kephra, who also nodded. Finally, her eyes fell on me.

"I'm more afraid of losing you than the world," I said.

Palmyre laughed.

"Do you imagine that I would leave you to be with my Baal? No, Renée; wherever he takes me, I shall bring you with me, I promise."

She turned back to the Dreamer and bent until her face was close to his.

"The fairy tales teach the best way to do this, I think."

She pressed her warm, living lips to his dusty and gray mouth. As she did, the room fell dark and silent, and I lost all sense of feeling.

I can't say I woke for I do not believe I had been sleeping, but when I next became aware of my surroundings, I stood in a twilit field. To my right lay a dark and placid ocean, while on the left pretty green hills dotted with quaint cottages merged with the foothills of a snow-capped mountain. Straight ahead stood a city, like something out of a storybook, with gleaming marble walls and burnished bronze gates. Distant figures milled around the base of the city and I wondered if this was the Atlanaät that was, long ago.

"You look quite stunning, Renée."

I turned to see Palmyre standing near me, a small, striped grey cat in her arms. Next to her stood a woman I barely recognized as Victoria Custer. Her dark hair hung around her shoulders, wild and unbound, and her clothes were gone, replaced by a crude loincloth and moccasins made of animal pelts. It seemed to me that her skin was even more tanned, her muscles even firmer than just a few moments before. As for Palmyre, she was taller, slimmer, more goddess than mortal now, and dressed in an Art Deco gown that I recognized from Erté's painting, *Symphony in Black*.

"What…?"

"It is a lot to take in," my friend said. "I believe the Dreamer has sent us to earth's Dreamlands, though I cannot say why. If we seem different here, it is because each person's dream-form is an idealized version of their own self image."

"Where is Mademoiselle Kephra?"

14

As if in answer to my question, the cat sprang from Palmyre's arms, trotted to me and meowed. I bent to scratch her cheeks and she received the gesture with feline dignity.

"That is how she sees herself, it seems," Palmyre said.

"As a cat? But that makes no sense."

Palmyre shrugged.

"How often do the things in dreams make sense?"

"So, Victoria sees herself as a naked savage?"

"Nat-ul!" the fur-clad woman said.

"You're not Victoria?" I asked, startled.

"That is the name I am called by some, but my true name is Nat-ul."

"Palmyre, you said this is only a dream," I said.

"Have you never had a dream that felt truer than waking reality? To paraphrase Zhuang Zi, who can say if our friend is a modern woman dreaming she is a savage, or vice-versa."

I shook my head, not really understanding but feeling the need for more time before pursuing the topic.

The city proved about an hour's walk and we passed many people on the way. The bay was filled with tall ships and galleys, and the more richly dressed travelers rode on horses, elephants, ostriches and other, stranger, beasts. The aromas as we passed through the gates and into the great onyx-paved marketplace were as exotic as the people. The mixture of spices, incense, and cooking meats was so heady that I felt a little dizzy.

Then there were the cats. Every breed, and many I had never seen, in a bewildering mix of sizes and colors. They strode through the market or basked in the waning sunlight with that typical feline panache. But, where in the world I knew, they might have been shooed away, cursed, or chased, here they were regarded with great deference. The butchers gave them the best scraps, the dogs didn't bark, and people ceded them the right of way, often with a reverent bow.

"This is wrong," Victoria said. "We will not find Nu in a place like this."

"There are no coincidences in dreams," Palmyre said. "We can only be here because it is useful for us to be here. Keep your eyes open for something that may help."

I was about to ask what sort of thing to watch for when I saw it. Two lines of Arabic script had been inscribed on the lintel of the door of a small residence on the edge of the marketplace.

ميتا ليس الأبد إلى ينام الذي الشيء
أيضا الموت يموت قد الغريبة العصور في

"If there are no coincidences, I suggest we start there," I said.

Palmyre knocked, and a gaunt but pleasant-looking man in exotic robes answered.

"Can I help you?"

"Perhaps so," she said. "We are dreamers in search of a particular dream."

The man's lean face brightened.

"Ah! You must be the women who my friend, Ishmeddin told me were coming. I am Randolph Carter, late of Boston and presently of Celephaïs."

Palmyre's eyebrows rose at the mention of Ishmeddin, but she did not exhibit any surprise otherwise.

"Greetings, Monsieur Carter," she replied. "I am Madame Palmyre and these are my companions, Mademoiselle Dunan of Paris, and Mademoiselle Custer of Nebraska."

"Charmed, especially to meet a fellow Ameri—" Carter's face froze as he turned his gaze to Victoria.

"This is how our friend sees herself in her dreams. She doesn't mean to scandalize you."

I knew Palmyre's words to be true, but it seemed to me that she was enjoying the man's discomfiture.

"I know that, Madame," Carter replied stiffly. "Nevertheless, as an American, I am mortified to see any white girl—let alone a Custer—in the semblance of a savage Indian."

I suspected that the Indians would be equally mortified, but held my tongue as Carter turned to Victoria. He seemed about to say something, but hesitated when he saw that she held Kephra at her bosom. With a musical meow, the small creature leapt into his arms and he held her with an expression of sheer joy. Carter scratched the cat's head and she nuzzled his hands, even butting her head into his chin affectionately. I could have sworn there was some sort of unspoken communication between them, for when Randolph Carter looked up, he beamed at us.

"It is an honor and a pleasure to welcome you," he said. "Please, come in."

Carter's home was pleasant, if rather untidy and filled with bookcases. I inspected these while he sent Victoria upstairs to find a dressing gown. I saw a number of books there which I was aware of through Madame Palmyre, and some I did not recognize. *Astral and Astarral Co-ordination and Interference*, the *Black Tome of Alsophocus*, the *Seven Cryptical Books of Hsan*, the *Necronomicon...* All told he was a scholar and a man of arcane and eclectic tastes.

"How strange," the old man said as a door shut behind Victoria. "What could compel a sweet-seeming child to see herself as a barbaric primitive?"

"She is in love," Palmyre said. "A hunter from the stone-age visits her in her dreams."

"Ah, love." Carter shook his head in disapproval.

"Haven't you ever been in love?" I asked.

"I choose not to pursue such mundane things." As he spoke he moved to the kitchen where he poured milk into two saucers. "My passions are reserved for my books, cats, and my quest to see the Great Ones in their unknown home of Kadath."

He placed one saucer on the tiled floor, where Kephra began lapping at it. He took the other to the front, opened the door, and placed it on the stoop.

"You are very attentive to the neighborhood cats, Monsieur Carter," Palmyre observed.

"I am a lover of the creatures, both here and in the waking world. They are far superior to dogs, and indeed, to most humans. It was because of your tabby, as much as the message from Ishmeddin, that I welcomed you into my abode." Carter nodded at Kephra, who was now washing her paws with her tongue. "Even among the cats of Celephaïs, she is exceptional."

"I noticed that the people here show the cats a great deal of regard," I said. "Why is that?"

Carter regarded me with a pitying expression.

"If you knew anything about cats, you would not need to ask," he said.

A few moments later, Victoria returned, wrapped in one of Carter's shirts. The old man bade us to take seats around a round table as he laid out candles, a crystal ball, and other familiar trappings I had seen in Gypsy tea rooms.

"You're holding a séance?" I asked.

Carter glared at me.

"It is no such thing! A séance is mummery and prestidigitation, designed to prey on the superstitions of the over-credulous. What I am doing is the channeling of our gestalt of telluric energy in a sympathetic resonance with Miss Custer's mentations. It is a purely rational and scientific process."

I thought of challenging his ridiculous pomposity, but Palmyre gave a little shake of her head and I remained silent. Carter bade us close our eyes, and told Nat-ul to focus all her thoughts on her lover. After a moment, the candles went out and a rush of chill air passed through the room. Carter stood up without any ceremony.

"The message is sent," Carter said, and moved to shutter the windows.

"Nu will come?" Victoria said.

"I cannot say," he replied. "But he knows that you are here and that you seek him."

"Then Nu will come."

"Randolph Carter! Randolph Carter!" The reedy voice came from the front door.

"Could that be him already?" I said.

"That is not his voice," she replied.

The voice continued to repeat Carter's name. He walked to the door and opened it, revealing a small grey cat with long legs and huge ears.

"Hello, my friend," Carter said. "What prompts your visit today?"

The cat strolled in, rubbing against the old man's ankles by way of greeting.

"Hello, Randolph Carter," he said in excellent French. "There is a rumor among the cats of Celephaïs that there is a distinguished visitor in your home."

"I have several visitors," Carter replied. "Madame Palmyre, Miss Custer, Mademoiselle Dunan, this is a distinguished cat of the city. Unfortunately, his master in the waking world has neglected to give him a name."

We offered our greetings to the remarkable animal, but when Kephra, who had been napping on a bookshelf, opened her eyes, he ceased to pay any attention to us. She hopped down, strolled to him, and touched her nose to his.

The gray cat backed up, eyes wide and ears up. A moment later he turned and trotted to the door, Kephra following him closely. When they reached it, he turned to Carter.

"Please open the door for us, Randolph Carter."

Carter did as he asked and the two cats leapt through the door and bounded down the street.

"Where are they going?" I asked.

"I believe he is taking your friend to the Temple of Bast," Carter said, donning a frock coat. "If we hurry, we may see something most extraordinary."

The sun was setting as the cat led our little group down the street of the pillars and past the magnificent turquoise temple of Nath-Horthath. The girl who insisted we call her Nat-ul remained behind lest Nu answer Carter's summons while she was away. Carter was an enthusiastic tour guide and pointed out innumerable details as we went. Palmyre ignored him, so I made conversation for politeness' sake.

"Do all cats speak like humans in the city?" I asked.

"No, my dear. Our little guide is a special case. I'm given to understand that he gained the power in the waking world after eating his master's parrot. Ah, here we are."

We had come to a smallish temple of alabaster veined with purple and the minty aroma of burning catnip issued from within. The entrance was flanked by a pair of statues: women draped in the style of ancient Egypt and bearing the heads of beasts. More specifically, the statue on the left had the head of a house cat while that on the right had the visage of a fierce lioness.

"Bast and Sekhmet," Carter said, the two faces of the great goddess of cats. "As Bast, she is the gentle and helpful—albeit aloof—companion. When roused, she is Sekhmet, Lady of warfare and slaughter."

Gesturing us to remain quiet, he led us into the Temple. I paused at the entrance, noticing that our guide had stopped to wash his paws.

"Aren't you coming inside?"

"I will stay close, for this is an auspicious day for the cats of Celephaïs," he said. "However, as I am in the process of becoming a Jew, my master would not approve of me entering the temple."

A shook my head at the strangeness of his comment, then moved to rejoin Carter and Palmyre. We stood at the back for there was no room to do anything else. All the floor, the rafters, every stair-step, ledge and horizontal surface was covered by cats. I have never seen so many of the little creatures gathered in one place. All of them sat or stood or lay immobile, their gazes fixed on the one circle of open floor in the temple's center where Kephra sat as an old gray cat circled her, sniffing as he went.

After a moment, he sat opposite her, then raised his muzzle and let out a loud yowling. The other cats caught this up and, within a few seconds, the temple was filled with the deafening caterwauling of hundreds, perhaps thousands, of feline voices.

"Oh, this is good!" Carter said, shouting to be heard. "This is very good, indeed!"

"What has happened?" Palmyre shouted back.

"They have accepted her as a great dignitary," he said. "A messenger of their goddess, or perhaps the goddess herself in mortal form, I cannot be certain."

"One of us, at least, has found her destiny," Palmyre said.

When the caterwauling showed no signs of letting up, we returned to Carter's home. To our dismay, we turned into the narrow lane to find that the front window was broken and the door hung from one hinge. We hurried to the door to find the front room in similar disarray and the bodies of two men on the floor.

"Victoria?" I called.

"Nat-ul?" cried Palmyre.

There was no reply. Palmyre and I searched the rest of the house while Carter, who was near to a faint, remained in the front room. We hadn't discovered any sign of the girl anywhere when we were interrupted by the sound of Carter screaming. We raced back to the room and found the old man on his feet holding a small piece of soapstone carved with a strange glyph in front of himself as if to ward off a new intruder.

The man opposite Randolph Carter, was a magnificent savage; I can't think of any other description. He stood several inches over six feet and looked as strong as any three other men. He wore a loincloth fashioned from the pelt of some animal and a bear's hide across his shoulders like a cape. His dark hair had been chopped to shoulder length, I suppose with the flint knife in his waistband, and he was clean-shaven. He held a crude axe with a chipped flint head loosely in his right hand but made no move to threaten us. A fact that seemed lost on Carter, who regarded him with an expression of terror.

19

"Are you Nu?" Palmyre asked

"I am Nu, son of Nu. I have come to find Nat-ul. Where is she?" For all the savagery of his appearance, the man's tone was gentle.

"We do not know," Palmyre said. "We have only just returned to find her missing."

"She was taken by these men?"

The men were dressed in the simple work clothes I had noticed on many of the locals and their skin was burnt dark by outdoor work. One, clearly dead lay on his back, his hands clutching the handle of the carving knife buried in his chest. The other wore a great purple and green bruise on the side of his face. Next to him lay the fireplace poker.

"Our Victoria seems to have dealt this one a telling blow," Palmyre said. "There must have been others and they must have overcome her too quickly for her to have called out."

"Vic-to-ri-uh," Nu repeated carefully. "This is Nat-ul?"

"It is."

Nu scanned the bodies again and nodded with satisfaction.

"Nat-ul is strong. They were foolish to attack her, but they were many. I see the spoor of six. Nu will track them."

"Can you do that?" I asked.

Without a word, the caveman bent low to the ground. Remaining in that position, he moved out of the house and down the narrow lane at a quick pace.

"Go with him, Renée," Palmyre said. "Carter and I will remain to question this man when he wakes."

"Go with him?" I echoed. "To do what? If we run into anything that could hurt that brute, I will be of no help whatsoever."

"If you do, you will run back here and inform us."

Palmyre sounded impatient, the way she sometimes did with the silly housewives and businessmen who sought her services in Paris. She was not one to suffer fools and the last thing I wanted was to become a fool in her eyes.

I ran after Nu and caught up with him at the end of the block. The invisible trail twisted and turned through the winding streets and alleyways, but Nu seemed able to follow it unfailingly. Then we came out into the crowded marketplace and he stopped.

"I never knew there could be so many people in the world," Nu said.

"Can you continue to track her?"

Nu shook his head, a baffled gesture that must have meant the same thing in his prehistoric time as in ours.

"Her spoor is lost among all these others."

"Our kidnapper was not terribly competent," Palmyre said. "He took the wrong woman."

"What do you mean?" I asked.

We had returned to find my friend and Randolph Carter poring over several of the man's many books. There was no sign of the body, nor of the survivor they had planned to question, and I decided not to ask. Madame Palmyre can be pitiless when she needs to.

"I mean that he and his confederates were supposed to kidnap me," she said. "They were told to come to this house and abduct the 'dark-haired woman' so she could become the bride of their master, who dreams eternally."

"No!" Nu said. "She has chosen me and I have chosen her. She shall have no other mate. I will find this Dreamer and kill him."

"How do you hope to do that?" Palmyre said. "The Dreamer is no man."

"Indeed," Carter answered. "He is an eldritch blasphemy of cyclopean stature and unspeakable power; a primordial abomination whose very presence would sunder your sanity."

"I will kill him," Nu repeated. "I am Nu, son of Nu, and I have killed many great beasts. I have killed Ta, I have killed Ur, I have killed Zor, and even mighty Oo."

"I don't know those names," Palmyre said. "But the one we face is not of this world."

"A spirit?" The caveman paled. "No matter, I will fight even the spirits for Nat-ul."

I am not normally an admirer of the muscular and indomitable characters who pass for heroes in fiction, and even less of the real men who seek to ape them. Nonetheless, I found myself touched by the simple devotion of Nu's.

"We must move quickly," Palmyre said. "The man we questioned said that they have taken Vic... Nat-ul to the black galleys, which will take her to her final destination."

"Where is that?" I asked.

Carter took a rolled parchment from one of his bookcases and spread it open on the table. It proved to be a detailed map of the Dreamlands.

"We are here." He touched a point on the map labeled *Celephaïs*. "The black galleys typically frequent the port of Dylath-Leen, where they conduct secretive commerce with the locals, trading great rubies for provisions. From thence, no man knows where they sail; perhaps to lands beyond the edges of the earth, or even to the moon itself.

"The moon?" I said, incredulous.

"If you sail east from Dylath-Leen, you can reach the horizon just as the moon is rising and cross to it."

"Then we must charter a ship," I said.

Carter shook his head.

"None have ever seen the oarsmen of the black galleys, but they can outrow any ship in the Dreamlands and they never tire."

"Carter, is there any way we can get to Dylath-Leen ahead of them?" Palmyre asked.

"A shantak-bird could fly you there," he replied. "Unfortunately, I do not know how to summon their kind."

"Is there anything you can summon?" Palmyre said.

"Not I," he replied. "But we have a friend who may be able to help. We shall see."

"The sound of the cats and their song grew louder as we approached the Temple of Bast. Palmyre seemed fascinated and Carter almost ecstatic. Nu, on the other hand, was clearly uneasy and I sympathized. I have always had some fondness for the animals, but one at a time, and in the comfort of a friendly house."

When we came to the doorway he stared up at the statue of Sekhmet with an odd look on his face.

"What is it?" I said.

"It has the face of Oo."

Palmyre went in and presented herself to Kephra, who lay sphinx-like on the altar. This time, we did not have our translator-cat, but my friend somehow made herself understood. After a few minutes, Kephra hopped down and walked side by side out of the temple with my friend. The great congregation of cats fell silent at this, and followed en masse, feeling the street from edge to edge. Their song ended, they moved as silently as an army of shadows, and their eyes shown in the moonlight like a million torches of unearthly green flame.

When we reached the city gate, the guards opened it without question, such was the influence of the cats in Celephaïs. The eerie procession without at the city and toward the foothills, where a gigantic cat like creature with eyes that shone like spotlights stood waiting for us.

What happened next was so dreamlike that the details are fuzzy in my mind. It seems to me that Palmyre and I climbed inside of the great creature's body, along with Nu, Kephra, and a score of the biggest and fiercest cats of the city. The beast then began to run at impossible speeds, leaving Randolph Carter and his wondrous city behind. Perhaps I napped—if it is even possible to sleep in the Dreamlands—for I lost all sense of time during the trip. In any case, I lost track of our progress until we disembarked at the slender basalt towers of Dylath-Leen.

Though it was nearly midday, a pall of clouds hung over the dark stone streets and buildings of the city, making it gloomy, and a thin, oily fog coiled through the streets. The natives were a smallish people with pale skin who watched our strange group suspiciously. They were in awe of Nu, but seemed most frightened by the cats.

The locals were not inclined to be helpful, but Palmyre and Nu proved most persuasive and soon we were in the possession of a small one-masted vessel. Neither Palmyre nor I had any experience at sailing and Nu had clearly never even heard of a boat before. As for the cats, they were no help at all.

Fortunately, Palmyre had managed to convince a small group of Dylath-Leenians to crew the vessel. I'm not sure just how she did it, but suspected hypnotism, or some other subtle form of mind control. We were soon underway, with Kephra sitting at the prow like a living figurehead and Nu stationed at the rail with a case of seasickness.

Just before moonrise, we spotted the black galley and Palmyre had the captain steer to intercept it. She called to Kephra, who was occupied with washing her face. The cat paused to focus on the distant galley; her tail began to twitch and she made the peculiar clicking sound that all cats use when they are stalking. A stiff breeze sprang up to fill the sails and the little craft raced across the waves. As strong as the oarsmen were, even they could not match us in a good wind. Slowly but steadily we began to close the distance.

As we drew nearer, the crew of the galley began hurling sling-stones at us. The cats ran under cover and, when one of the crew was struck down, I joined them. Nu stood on the deck shouting defiance, and somehow was not hit. Palmyre crouched behind the rail and raised in an arcane pointing gesture I had seen before. A crackle of etheric energy shot from her fingertips and struck down one of our enemies. Three more times she repeated this and three more adversaries fell, the last being the man at the tiller. The galley hove to port and, as the crew struggled to regain their course, we came alongside her.

My first clear sight of the galley crew was a shock. From a distance they had seemed merely men wearing long robes and turbans. As we had come close, they had stripped for battle and were revealed as something very much like the satyrs or fauns of myth. A score of them on deck wielded short curved swords and long billhooks.

"Are they men or beasts?" Nu asked.

"Don't let then frighten you," Palmyre replied. "Carter told me that the men from Leng are only men, despite their strange appearance."

Nu grunted and shifted his grip on his axe. For a man so unused to the sea, he seemed settled and confident now. As the ships came together, one of the Leng-men raised his sword and, with a bleating war cry, leaped onto the deck of our ship. Sounding a cry of his own, Nu met the man. For all his muscular bulk, he moved as nimbly as a monkey, ducking past the creature's sword stroke and striking him down with a single blow of the axe.

The other Leng men were shocked at their champions defeat, but only for a moment. The next, they swarmed over the rail. Nu met them with the axe in one hand and Randolph Carter's carving knife in the other. Behind him, Palmyre sent bolt after bolt of her psychic lightning into the crowd of goat-men. They were fierce fighters, but the odds seemed overwhelming. The ensorcelled crew did not more to help them, and the cats and I remained in our hiding places.

"Hey!" I whispered to Kephra, who had taken shelter near me behind a great coil of rope. "They will be killed! Send your cats to help them."

She blinked at me sleepily and I felt despair. Even if she had helped, what use would cats have been against armed men?

A sound of flutes emerged from the black galley ad had a profound effect on our foemen. They broke off their attack on Nu and Palmyre and backed away to form a semi-circle around them. My friends had been backed up to the main mast and Palmyre leaned against it for support. Her dress was torn and blood ran down her left arm. She looked exhausted but she still wore a mocking smile. Nu was bleeding from many different gashes and I was certain that only his animal vitality kept him on his feet. Around them the bodies of many slain men of Leng gave silent witness to their ferocity.

A small group of monsters emerged from below decks of the black galley. I say monsters for I don't know what else to call them. The closest description I could think of was of bipedal frogs, as tall as tall men and more massive. But that description fails, for frogs have bones in their bodies, and their faces are more than squirming masses of pink tentacles. I wondered if these were the un-seen rowers, or perhaps they were the masters of the galley, for the men from Leng moved aside for them.

Five of the creatures appeared, the last of whom led Victoria on a leash the end of which was clasped to a collar around her neck. When she saw us, her face lit up with hope.

"Nu!" she cried.

"Nat-ul!" Nu straightened with a look of renewed determination. He would have charged the monsters, but Palmyre laid a restraining hand on his arm.

"Wait," she shouted. "You have made a mistake. I am the woman Baal wants. I am the one your confederates were supposed to abduct. Release the girl and I will take her place, gladly."

The frog-like creatures did not respond in any intelligible way but the wav-ing of their face-tentacles became more agitated. One of the Leng men stepped forward.

"My masters bid me to thank you for revealing the mistake," he said. "They will not release the girl, for no one taken in the name of their god is ever released, but they will allow you to join her."

"Your terms are less than inviting. What must I do so that you will let the girl and my friends go free?"

"My masters instruct me to tell you that your companions are all to be killed, but that you will be allowed to surrender to us before this."

"Your masters are terrible negotiators. I see I must be more persuasive." Palmyre raised her hands and pointed her index fingers at the repulsive crea-tures. She frowned in concentration, but nothing happened.

"My masters have negated your ability to harm them," the Leng-man said.

"They have not taken away *my* power!" Nu raised his stone axe over his head. "Come, and see how many more will fall by my hand."

"Too many of my brethren have fallen to you already. My masters will deal with you themselves."

One of the hideous things slogged forward toward Nu. Its body contorted as it moved so that it was sometimes taller and sometimes shorter than him, but as least twice as massive. Nu glanced at his weapons, then seemed to make a decision. He hurled Carter's carving knife end over end to lodge in the wooden deck at Victoria's feet.

"Nat-ul, free yourself!"

Then the monster was on him. With cat-like speed, Nu ducked past the grasp of the flabby arms and struck a powerful two handed blow with his axe. The stone head smashed into the side of the beast's head deforming it. To my surprise, the monster didn't fall, or even act as if it had been hurt. Its flesh sprang back to its original form like a ball after it has been kicked only more slowly.

The creature reached for Nu again and this time the axe struck its forearm, bending it at right angles. The blow should have shattered the bones of the limb, but the arm came back into shape, just as the head had. Nu backed away, scowling in bafflement. He rammed the axe into the center of the thing's chest and ripples ran from the point of impact throughout its grotesque form. It was if the monster were a leather bag of some thick fluid that absorbed the terrible impacts of the cave man's weapon. Too, its rubbery hide seemed too tough for the axe's crude edge to cut or tear.

I chanced a glance at Victoria and saw that she had cut through the leash and now backed away from one of the other monsters, brandishing the knife. I shifted my gaze to Palmyre, who stood, rigid as a statue, her index fingers still pointed and sweat streaming down her face.

A gasp of pain brought me back to Nu. His axe now lay broken on the deck and the monster had caught him around the waist in a powerful bear-hug. He hammered away at the thing's head with fists and elbows, but what good were flesh and bone when stone had failed? Nu might be muscled like Heracles, but in the indestructible monster, he had found his hydra.

Kephra rose then, her ears back and tail fluffed to several times its normal size. She let out a terrible caterwaul and the other cats joined in, leaving their shelter and joining her in her advance, backs arched, legs stiffened, bodies turned sideways.

The effect on the monsters was dramatic. They huddled together, face tentacles writhing furiously and backed away. The men from Leng moved in front of them, swords drawn, to form a defensive line. Only the beast fighting Nu was unaffected and I guessed that it was too occupied to notice the cats. I couldn't understand how such beings could be so frightened by the little creatures, but it gave me hope.

I looked back to Nu, an idea coming to me. Heracles *had* defeated the hydra, but not by himself. Perhaps, I could be Nu's Iolaus. Forcing myself to move in spite of my terror, I scooped up a fallen cutlass and took a swing at Nu's opponent. The impact stung my fingers and I dropped the weapon, but the blow had opened a gash in the monster's side from which a thick, dark, foul-smelling fluid started to flow.

The beast reached toward me with one arm, but that allowed Nu to slip out of its grasp. He fell to the deck, gasping for breath. I scrambled backward away from the monster as it shambled toward me. I ran into the rail and had to stop. I wanted to get up and run, but my fear was stronger than ever and my limbs wouldn't follow my brain's instructions.

As the monster reached for me, a powerful pair of arms caught it around the waist from behind. Nu had recovered enough to resume the fight. With a heave, he raised the massive thing over his head, and cast it into the ocean. I stood and watched the ripples that followed its fall, but the monster did not reappear. I doubted such an alien thing could drown, but at least it didn't seem to know how to swim.

The swearing of the cats hadn't turned into the sounds of battle yet. They stood in a line facing the goat-men, but hadn't advanced into sword-range. Then Kephra let out a new cry, deeper and more terrible than the roar of a lion. As I watched, she grew, becoming the size of a lynx, a leopard, a tiger, and even bigger. When she stopped, she stood more than five feet at the shoulder with foot-long upper fangs.

"Sekhmet," I whispered.

"Oo! She has become Oo, the killer of men." Nu laughed. "No, she is Oo, killer of monsters. Come, great one; Nu fights by your side today!"

Still laughing, the big man scooped up my fallen sword and launched himself into the fray. What happened next was so fast and chaotic that I was not able to keep track of the details. Victoria had made her way back onto our ship and stood by Nu, her knife and his sword flashing in every direction. Kephra tore through the line of goat-men and sprang on the monsters, tearing them apart with claws and saber-teeth. Palmyra, free from the creatures' spell, fired more of her deadly bolts. I even saw the cats fall on one of the monsters and pull it down.

Then it was over. Nu and Victoria embraced, Kephra began washing her paws, and I moved to tend Palmyre's wounds.

"How are you?" I asked.

She smiled.

"Weary in body and soul, but that shall pass."

Half an hour later, we had disposed of all the bodies and cut our ship loose from the black galley. Once we were free, the galley's oars came out and resumed rowing. The moon had appeared, created a path of reflected light that the galley followed toward the rising yellow disc. I had no idea who or what was left alive to pull those oars, not did I want to. We were leaving and that was enough.

I woke, not having been aware of falling asleep. Rising, I saw that I was back in the Kurdish marshes, at Ishmeddin's cooking fire. The old dervish knelt at the fire in the half-light that precedes dawn, making coffee. Nearby, an unwounded Palmyre stirred from sleep and Mademoiselle Kephra—human once more—blinked her eyes as she sat up.

"Ishmeddin, did you bring us back?" Palmyre asked.

"Back? Had you gone somewhere, *sayidati?*"

"Yes, and we intend to return. Take us back to Atlaänat and the Dreamer."

Ishmeddin shook his grey head.

"You speak of legends, *sayidati;* there is no such place. Would you like coffee?"

Palmyre glared at him for a moment, then shook her head and laughed.

"My visit to my lover's world ended as badly as his sojourn in mine. No matter; I will find him again, someday."

"And I will find an escape from this life as well," Mademoiselle Kephra said. "But not today."

"Wait!" I glanced around, looking for a fifth face. "Where is Mademoiselle Custer?"

Ishmeddin made no reply, Palmyre's eyes widened, and Mademoiselle Kephra smiled. I knew somehow that we all knew where Victoria Custer was, and with whom. One of our little group had realized her dream at last.

This story by our regular contributor Nathan Cabaniss is a traditional NY crime thriller, a wonderful homage to the works of Chester Himes and his Harlem Detective, who are featured prominently therein. It is particularly appropriate to add Himes to our gallery of French-American crossovers, since he moved to Paris in the 1950s, seeking a less racially-loaded environment, and also because of his popularity in French literary circles. There, he met fellow expatriate writers Richard Wright, James Baldwin, and William Gardner Smith, as well as Herald-Tribune columnist Lesley Packard, who became his second wife...

Nathan Cabaniss: *Rage of Terror*

New York City, 1955

"What a mess..."

Coffin Ed Johnson and Grave Digger Jones made their way through the backroom of the joint, careful not to get any blood on their newly-shined shoes. The room was a maze of bodies and bullet casings, one that Digger and Ed navigated carefully so as not to disturb anything.

"You think this is our huckleberry?" Ed said.

"Maybe."

"Certainly tracks with the others."

"Yeah, well, try not to get too excited, Ed. Don't wanna tamper with the evidence."

"How dare you. I'm housebroken."

Coffin Ed placed himself at the room's center, and crouched. "Large concentration of casings 'round this spot."

He stood and spun around on the ball of his heel, surveying the room.

"I say a single shooter, and he did most of his shooting right here," Ed said, and mimicked shooting with his fingers. "Two .45 automatics, like in the movies."

"Single shooter?" Digger said. "There's at least a dozen bodies here, Ed."

"That's what the room's telling me."

"The room? What, you some kinda black Sherlock Holmes now?"

"That dude would wish he was the white Ed Johnson, he saw me."

Digger smirked, shook his head. "It definitely lines up with our gambling den shoot-up last night. And the hooch operation before that..."

"I'd stake my paycheck on it."

"Not worth much, that."

"It is to me." Ed tiptoed his way around the remaining bodies towards the back of the room, where wooden crates were stacked against the wall. Outside, a bum played a weepy violin.

"'Course, for this to really track with the others, this would have to be a refuge of vice and ill-repute…"

Ed pulled down one of the crates, pried it open with his bare hands—they were large enough that he didn't need a crowbar. "Well, well… wouldn't you know it…"

He held the crate out. Digger tiptoed through the bodies to get a look at what was packed between piles of straw. "Nice. I'd say Ming Dynasty, 15th century."

Ed pulled a vase from the crate, scattering straw everywhere. "More like a sweatshop on 110th, from last year."

Digger rubbed his chin. "Gambling, hooch and counterfeit merchandise… If there's a connection, I'm not seeing it. Rival outfit wouldn't bother with small stuff like this, 'less they're tryin' to send some kind of message."

"Rival outfit also wouldn't send just one man…"

"You're stickin' with that?"

"Ain't nothin' else to stick to. What the room's tellin' me, like I said."

"Hey," a voice called from across the room.

It was a flatfoot, so young his face looked like a peach, although you could tell he was starting to go bald despite wearing his officer's hat.

"Hey, what the hell are you two doing? Get out of here. This is a crime scene."

Digger raised his eyebrow at the young man. "Really? And here I thought it was a church social."

"I ain't kiddin'. Get out of here before I run your asses into the station for loitering…"

Digger and Ed shared a glance. Digger reached into his pocket, flashed his badge at the flatfoot.

The young man studied Digger's badge closely. "Who—who are you two again?"

"Jones and Johnson. Though folk in Harlem have taken to callin' us Grave Digger and Coffin Ed."

"You're… detectives?"

Coffin Ed stepped towards the officer, making it well known he had the young man beat by a good four inches. He had an acid scar on his face that flared up whenever his temper got the better of him. It was flaming now.

"I know you boys ain't supposed to be smart, but surely you got enough schoolin' for you to read a detective's badge when you see it."

The officer bristled, looked like he might snap back, but Ed's sheer size kept his tongue in check.

"You're outta Harlem?" he said, swallowing. "Long way out of you boys—you guys' jurisdiction..."

"Fits the profile of a case we been workin'," Digger said. "Might be ours, so we had to come check it out."

The flatfoot remained uncomfortable. "I—I think I better call this in..."

"What's going on here?"

The voice travelled on the air, smooth and lilting. The three men turned to the clack of elegant heels against the tiled floor. A white dress sauntered into view, and thick blonde hair bounced against bare shoulders. Even without the heels, she had to be almost six feet tall. She walked as if she knew she was the center of attention of any room she dared to grace, which some may have taken as haughty or arrogant, but there was nothing in her manner to suggest as such— it was simply the truth.

The flatfoot straightened and cleared his throat. "Miss? I'm sorry, but this is a crime scene..."

"I'm here because the crowd outside has caused the traffic to back up, and I'm going to be dreadfully late for a very important engagement."

"You really shouldn't be in here..."

"And you really should be outside handling the crowd, so I can be on my way."

The flatfoot sighed, getting hot under his collar. "Miss, I'd rather not have to ask you again..."

"Listen to me, Officer..." She paused, taking time to peer at the young man's badge. "...Kojak. I make it my business to know every head of every department of every city I visit. If you don't get back out there, I promise you I will let your shift commander know just how badly you've bungled crowd control at this scene, all because you didn't believe these two men were detectives."

The flatfoot looked like he was about to say more, but the blonde woman produced a lollipop from her purse and stuck it in the flatfoot's mouth. "Now why don't you make yourself useful and get back to doing your job?"

Red-faced, the flatfoot left without another word.

Digger and Ed each fidgeted in place, trying their best not to stare with their mouths open.

"Grave Digger Jones and Coffin Ed Johnson. It's a pleasure to meet you both," she said, extending a gloved hand.

Digger and Ed looked at each other, shrugged and shook it each in turn.

"I'm Ellen Patrick."

"How do you know who we are?" Digger asked, raising an eyebrow.

"Hard not to hear of you two after picking up monikers like that. Not to mention your arrest records," she said with a smirk. "My late father was the District Attorney of Los Angeles some years ago. He died under mysterious circumstances. I've since made it my business to keep up with the comings-and-goings of the criminal justice system in every city that I visit."

30

"And what is your business in the city, Ms. Patrick?" Ed asked. Digger nudged him with his elbow. "If you don't mind us asking."

"Not at all. I'm in town for a *soirée* a friend is having," she said, immediately turning deflective. "What's going on here? If you don't mind *my* asking, that is."

Digger stepped towards her, apologetic. "Not to be rude, ma'am, but we're really not at liberty to discuss an ongoing investigation."

"Quite right—my apologies, gentlemen. I suppose I'm naturally nosey. Still..."

Something caught her eye, and she weaved her way towards the back of the room. She stopped at one of the bodies, deliberately crouched and lifted one of its arms.

"Hey, you can't..."

Digger and Ed moved to stop her, but halted dead in their tracks when they saw it beneath the arm, lying on the floor like a lost glove: a sickening mass of hair and flesh, folded over itself into a lumpy pile.

Ellen Patrick studied it for a moment, then reached out and seized it from the ground. She held it up, letting it dangle between two fingers. It was a mask, and an incredibly life-like one, at that.

"That's curious, don't you think?" she said.

Digger grabbed the mask and held it up for he and Ed to have a closer look. It looked real enough to have been skinned from a human body, but it was made of some advanced latex material. Pores had been carefully sculpted into the folds of skin, and the hair and eyebrows were applied in such a lifelike manner, Digger thought it might wink at them.

Digger looked away from the mask and turned his attention back to the woman in white, whose sudden appearance now seemed less and less a matter of happenstance.

"How did you know this was underneath that corpse?"

"I saw it there..."

"You just happened to see it all the way from across the room?" Ed piped in, moving to Digger's flank; blocking any attempt at escape.

Ellen laughed uncomfortably, tried to be disarming. "You both sound like you're interrogating *me* now..."

The faces of Digger and Ed remained unchanged. "You mind telling us exactly what you're doing in town, Ms. Patrick?" Digger asked.

"I already told you. I'm in town for a party..."

"Which is where, exactly?" Ed followed up.

"Gentlemen, surely you don't think I had anything to do with this? I just got into town this morning..."

"It just seems awfully convenient that you'd be passing a run-down bar like this on the way to wherever it is you're going." Digger paused, letting a heavy silence fill the room.

Slowly, Ellen's smile dropped from her face.

"So, where were you going?"

The doors burst in, and everyone turned to see Officer Kojak storm his way back into the room, exasperated. "Lady, I don't know what you're trying to pull here, but there ain't no traffic out... Hey, where'd she go?"

Digger and Ed turned back around. Ellen Patrick was gone. A back door was open and creaking on its hinges from the wind. The detectives shared a glance. They pulled their revolvers and rushed outside after her.

The door led to a back alley, slick from a hot, summer rain. Digger and Ed looked up, caught a billow of white fabric just as it disappeared from the fire escape over the edge of the roof. Digger wasted no time—he leapt up and grabbed the ladder of the fire escape, ascended the rickety stairs one ass-clenching creak after another.

Ed was less enthused. *"Crazy white woman makin' me run,"* he muttered under his breath, before following his partner's lead.

The two were on the roof a moment later. Ed did his best to hide how out of breath he was as he crawled over the rooftop's ledge, gun in hand. "This girl better be worth the chase..."

Digger grabbed his partner's elbow, helped him to his feet. "She ran, so I'm willing to bet she knows more than she lets on."

"She's also rich and white as a spring lily. I'm not keen on the image of the two of us runnin' her down to the station in handcuffs on a *hunch*..."

"Nobody said nothin' about handcuffs. At least, not yet," Digger said. "Besides, I thought you were all about hunches..."

"Not ones that wind up with me losin' my job. Or worse."

They traversed along the rooftop in silence, peering around the corners of brick housings and wooden posts holding up a billboard advertisement for cheap cigarettes. They found her next to an electrical unit, crouched on the ground and with her back to them. Mysteriously, she had added a black cloak around her white dress. Something on the roof had her attention—she worked at it diligently in her white gloves.

The detectives held their guns on her. "Hands on your head, Miss. And no sudden movements," Digger said.

She froze. Her head turned slightly towards them—she had what appeared to be a domino mask covering her eyes. "Detectives," she said evenly, careful not to move a single muscle. "Please do yourselves a favor, and go back down. Forget you were ever here... Trust me: I'm doing you both a favor."

"Uh-huh," Ed replied. "Tell you what: you come down to the station with us, explain that to our captain. I'm sure it'll go over a damn sight better than it would if me and Digger told him instead. Especially wearing that get-up."

"We're gonna need you to drop whatever you're doin', Miss, and stand up nice and slow," Digger said.

"I can't do that."

32

"It's not a request," Ed said, his tone cold as ice.

"I don't have time to explain…"

"So do your best."

"If I stop now, we're all dead!"

Ed looked to Digger, raising his eyebrow. Ed shrugged. "All right. We're gonna take a few steps closer to you. You give us a reason, we'll put you down. Ain't got no qualms in shootin' a lady… So don't give us a reason."

They eased along the rooftop—Digger to the woman's right, Ed to her left. They saw what she was working on simultaneously. It was a bundle of dynamite, with a simple cooking timer connected via a series of wires to the fuse.

"I found it up here. It's set to go off in two minutes." She looked down at the timer. "Correction: a minute and a half. Any more *questions*, or can I get back to work now?"

Digger and Ed turned grey in the faint light of the streetlamps below. They nodded, unsure of what else to do. Ellen pinched the wires and removed them in sequence, trying to keep her hands from shaking.

Twenty-five, twenty-four, twenty-three…

Her mask caught the beads of sweat on her forehead, keeping them from getting in her eyes. *That's handy*, Ed thought.

Fifteen, fourteen, thirteen…

Digger saw himself scattered all over New York, a piece of him for every borough. Ed imagined himself in an oven, basted up like a Christmas turkey; the cooking timer sticking out of his ass and ticking down the seconds 'til he was good and cooked…

Ellen removed the last of the wires as the hands of the timer reached the two-second mark. They all let out the breath they'd unknowingly held back. Ellen pulled herself up and raised her hands for the two detectives.

"You were saying?"

"Who are you?" Digger asked.

"I already told you," she said with a smile. "I promise I haven't lied…"

"But you maybe haven't told us the whole truth…"

She dropped her smile, narrowed her eyes beneath the mask. "I wasn't kidding before. You can still get out. Just go back down and forget I was ever here…" She put a hand up, stopping them before either could speak. "I know what you're going to say. You're good cops, in a city that doesn't have a surplus. I admire that… but all the more reason why you shouldn't get involved. This is a whole other world…"

"Lady, like it or not, we're already involved," Ed said. "And Coffin Ed Johnson and Grave Digger Jones never leave a job undone."

"I was afraid you'd say that," she said, sighing. "I don't even know where to start…"

"How 'bout explaining the get-up, for a start," Digger asked, motioning to her mask and cloak.

"What, you've never heard of the feared Domino Lady?"

This was met with blank stares.

"You two are always so serious..." Ellen shook her head, the corner of her mouth curling in a smirk. "It was supposed to be a joke. Of course you've never heard of me before... I've operated exclusively on the West Coast, until to-night."

Digger put a hand beneath his chin, trying to figure it all out. "So this is, what... some kind of disguise?"

"Oh, come now. New York had its fair share of masked avengers not too long ago. Surely I'm no stranger than any of them..."

"Depends on whether or not you believe in ghost stories and boogey-men," Digger said. "How'd you know about the bomb?"

Ellen shrugged. "It was a guess."

"That's a hell of a good guess," Ed replied. "Only way I'd a' known a bomb was up here was if I placed it myself..."

"Why would I shoot up a roomful of thugs in a counterfeit ring, set a bomb to go off on the roof, and then return to the scene of the crime only to diffuse said bomb?"

"Don't know. But I also don't know why would you dress up in a mask and cape and go runnin' around rooftops."

She sighed, like an older sister explaining the rules of a game too complex for her younger siblings. "Just think of me as a concerned citizen. Look, there's been a series of incidents lately, right? Criminal rackets ransacked all over town? The same was happening in Los Angeles. I was chasing down a lead, and caught wind of a terror plot. Foreign agents sneaking into America and taking the coasts. Someone's coming over here and seizing power, taking control of every major criminal operation in the country. I have reason to believe he's overseeing his operations directly here in New York."

"Who?"

"I don't know his name. I think he's from Europe, maybe England or France. He certainly inspires a great deal of fear in his cohorts. Every agent I've captured winds up biting a cyanide tooth before they can talk." She tried swallowing, but her mouth was too dry. She shivered for a moment. "Whoever he is, he's covering his tracks. He was willing to blow up this whole building just to leave no trace of his actions behind. This is just a preview of what's to come..."

"And we're just supposed to take you at your word on all this?" Ed asked.

"I can understand your unwillingness to believe me," she said through gritted teeth, getting more frustrated with each passing minute, "but we're running out of time. Whoever's behind all of this is ramping up his timetable. Mark my words: an all-out war will break out in the streets, and you can both bet your badges that innocents will be caught in the crossfire."

Digger and Ed shared a glance. They'd spent so much time together that a look from one could tell the other what they needed to know, all without having to say a single word. The woman seemed to be out of her gourd, but clearly *something* was going on.

Digger turned back to Ellen. "Tell you what: how 'bout you lose the mask, come down to the station with us. You tell our captain everything we need to know, and we get the appropriate parties involved. If what you're saying is true, now you're not having to deal with all this by your lonesome."

"You don't understand. There's no time..."

"The only way you're leaving this rooftop is with us. End of story," Ed said.

"I'm afraid I can't give you that chance. The stakes are far too severe..."

She dropped something round from the palm of her hand, like a black marble. An instant later, the roof was covered in black smoke.

Digger and Ed found themselves lost in darkness. Everything was blotted from vision, so dark it was as if they no longer existed in the material world. They coughed, waved their hands in front of their faces to blow the smoke from the air, but it was so thick it may as well have been an airborne oil-spill.

A minute later, the smoke dissipated; thin, black wisps curled above them before disappearing completely. The detectives pulled their guns, waved them around as they found themselves standing on a rooftop once again, but they were the only two there. Ellen Patrick was gone.

Digger holstered his pistol. Ed squeezed the butt of his so hard, a drip of blood slipped between his fingers.

"What you thinkin', Ed?"

"I'm thinkin' it smells like shit, of the variety that usually comes out the bull's ass."

"Sounds about right," Digger said. "But still..."

"But still what? Don't tell me you actually believe that load she tried to sell us..."

"Don't know what to believe. What I do know is that something's goin' on. Something big." Digger reached down, carefully lifted the bundle of dynamite. "This is proof enough of that."

"Woman's outside her mind. Wearin' a mask and a cape, talkin' nonsense about foreign agents and secret plots... You ask me, she's readin' that nonsense they print on cheap paper and charge a dime for at the newsstand."

"You saw what she did with *this*." Digger said, raising the dynamite. "There's gotta be more going on here than we can see with our own two eyes."

"We don't even know if that's real..."

"You willin' to stick it down your pants and dance the Jitterbug?"

Ed grimaced in the harsh light of the floods beaming up the rickety billboard above them, his acid scar turning a shade darker. Digger didn't back away, and the two of them stared each other down on a roof barely forty-feet into the New York skyline. Ed threw up his hands, turned to face the other way. Cooling off, he took a sharp breath through his nose.

"So, what now?"

Digger stopped, turning his head. Something moved at the edge of his vision. Ed saw it, too... A black-clad figure dashed to an adjacent building, its roof roughly ten feet above. It jumped the gap and caught the building's ledge with two hands.

The detectives drew their pistols and yelled. The figure didn't stop, hopped over the ledge as easily as if it were a chain-link fence.

Ed slumped. "*Not more running...*"

"You want to let 'im get away, then?"

Ed sighed. "Lead the way, Tonto."

"*Huh-uh...* You're the strong, silent type. That makes you Tonto," he said, running to the roof's edge and leaping the gap to climb up the adjacent building. He caught the ledge with one hand, dangled perilously for a moment before pulling himself over it.

"Hi-Yo goddamn Silver." Ed followed after his partner, taking much longer to pull his enormous frame over the adjacent roof. He cleared the edge in time to see Digger sprint with everything he had at the fleeing suspect. Gaining on him, but only *just*... the black-clad figure was fast as the devil. Ed sucked in a lungful of air and followed after them, his acid scar practically burning off his face.

They leapt from roof to roof, weaved through pillars and stoops as they chased the dark figure, close enough now to see it was a man dressed in an unusual get-up. It almost looked like a police officer's uniform, but all in black. Shiny-black boots and gloves glinted back and forth as they caught the errant light from floods and lampposts below. Every time Digger and Ed thought they were close enough to take a shot, he would disappear behind another outcropping, climb to an adjacent roof above or make a daring leap to one below.

Just as Ed caught a mental image of his lungs exploding in his chest, a sound fluttered from above. A flap of leather, almost like... a pair of wings. It was enough to halt all three in their pursuit, as they looked up in horror to see a creature descend from black-clouded skies...

Scalloped wings unfurled to their full length as it dove through the air. It looked like a bat swooping down to catch its prey with blood-stained talons, but that was impossible... the thing was roughly the size of a man. A particularly large one, at that.

It landed on the man in front of Digger and Ed, slamming him into the roof's deck with heavy thud. The man had a chance to call out, but the massive wings fell over him—his shriek died in a whisper.

The detectives raised their pistols, unsure of what to do. Unsure of what they were looking at. The thing turned its head towards them—a pair of eyes burned from a heavily-shadowed, demonic face.

Before they could react, a double thunder-crack split the air. Twin jets of flame flashed briefly from within the creature's wings. Digger and Ed's guns went flying from their hands, leaving their fingers feeling like tuning forks that had just gotten a good rap against a metal bar.

The thing stood, and took the shape and dimension of an ordinary man. Getting a good look at it now, they saw the leathery flaps flowing from its back weren't a pair of wings, but rather a scalloped cape. The face wasn't demonic at all, but rather half-covered by a mask. And in its very human hands it held twin .45 automatics, smoke coiling up around their barrels.

"Stay out of my way," he told them, in a voice of gravel and hard whiskey.

"*Your* way?" Digger said. "That's our suspect! You're interfering with police business..."

"Not your business. Not tonight."

Ed could only shake his head. "What the hell is with everybody in this city tonight?"

The fallen man took advantage of the distraction. He jumped to his feet and broke into a run, desperate to escape the roof by whatever means necessary. The mystery man turned, blew off the fleeing man's kneecaps in a quick burst from his automatics. He fell against the wall of the building's electrical room in a bloody heap, screaming in pain.

His prey subdued, the mystery man strolled over casually and picked the other up by his shirt. Digger and Ed could only watch, helpless spectators to a carnival show they didn't understand.

Without provocation, the wounded man began to laugh through the pain—a wild, hissing sound that could have easily been mistaken for hysterical sobs.

"*No*," the mystery man said. "Don't you do it..."

The two struggled over something. Black forms in rooftop shadows, they melted into each other, their surroundings... Digger and Ed approached cautiously, eager to get a better look at what was going down.

"You'll never find us now..."

"Don't you do it, don't..."

"You'll never find us NEVER FIND US NEVEEERRRRrrr..." His breath gave out in a final hiss. He slumped over lifelessly, a hideous rictus grin frozen on his face.

"What'd you do?" Digger asked.

"Cyanide," the mystery man said, letting the thug drop to the roof. "Must have had a fake tooth."

Coffin Ed Johnson couldn't hold it together any longer. The scar on his face flared. His hands shook so hard they almost vibrated. He seized the mystery man by the shoulders, slammed him into the wall of the electrical room.

"I'm about sick and tired of grown-ass adults playin' Halloween..."

The mystery-man was unfazed. "You're an officer of the law, so you get one chance to unhand me before I have to get nasty."

"*You'll* get nasty? How 'bout I just smash your head through this here wall, huh? How nasty you think you'll feel then?"

37

Digger sidled alongside Ed, got in the mystery man's face. "This is normally the part where I pull Ed away before he goes too far. He's got this temper, see. They don't call him Coffin Ed Johnson for nothin'. But I'm not stopping Ed tonight. Because you directly interfered with an ongoing investigation, and we lost a prime suspect as a result."

"He would have gotten away from you. The two of you were barely keeping up."

"Enough!" Ed said, slamming him into the wall again. "You're gonna tell us what's what, or I swear to God we're gonna see if these wings make you fly!"

"We're on the same side here, gentlemen. We all want the same thing."

"Oh, really? And what would that be?"

"Seeing the guilty punished, and having justice prevail."

"You wanna put the bad guys away?" Digger asked. "Take off the mask and put on a badge."

"The law has its limits…"

"I think I've about heard enough," Ed said, "We're runnin' you in. Maybe sweatin' it out in a box down at the station will…"

"*Fantômas.*"

"What?"

"That's who you should be worried about tonight. That's the fiend we're after. I had him dead to rights earlier, but he slipped from my grasp. That dead man was one of his agents, left behind to make sure the building was demolished in time…"

Ed glanced at the automatics in the mystery-man's chest holsters, and shared a glance with Digger. "It was you. You were the one who shot up the back room of that saloon…"

The mystery man nodded. "Fantômas and his goons, although I didn't know it at the time… the devil's a master of disguise."

Digger and Ed shared another glance. The mask…

"You've seen his efforts recently, right? Unsolved murders, scenes of massacre all over town… He's consolidating his power, and he's on the warpath to see it done this very night," the mystery man continued. "You want to stop him? You'll need me…"

Ed hesitated, and finally loosened his grip. The mystery man straightened, nodded his appreciation at the two men deciding to trust him for the moment.

"I suppose you're not gonna level with us and tell us who you are?" Digger asked.

The mystery man stiffened, narrowed his eyes beneath his mask. "Call me the Black Bat."

Ed snorted a laugh, shook his head. "*Of course you are…*"

"Fantômas," Digger said, trying the name on for size. "Who is he?"

"No one knows. He hails from France, and he might as well be the devil. Murder, extortion, terrorism… he's done it, and more. He's been active for the better part of fifty years now. Maybe even longer than that."

"Fifty years?" Ed said. "He's gotta be a geezer, then, 'less he was plotting crimes from the crib."

"I wouldn't put it past him," the Black Bat said, without even a trace of humor. "It could be a relative, someone else picking up where he left off… I don't know. Whoever he is, he's using the name, and he's got the clout to back it up. He's got agents everywhere, a veritable army at his beck and call. But if we find him in time, cut the serpent at its head, then maybe…"

Just then, the rooftop shook beneath their feet. A sound like the sky itself erupting tore the air. An orange light illuminated the three men against the night-sky. They watched in horror as a column of flame shot up in the distance. A building had just blown up.

"What the…?" But before Ed could finish his sentence, another boom shook the building where they stood… a whole series of them. A series of buildings erupted in quick succession, an entire city block exploding as if a wave of fire and smoke had crashed over the skyline and swallowed them in its wake.

The Black Bat ran to the rooftops edge, watched helplessly as an entire city street burned in the distance. "My god. It's already begun…"

He leapt from the roof, disappearing into the night like a shadow cast over an empty black pit. Digger and Ed approached the roof's edge cautiously, transfixed by the tableau of destruction in the distance. Even from here they could already hear screaming and shouting. Sirens began to wail, harbingers of a long night ahead.

"*What the hell is going on…*" Digger let slip in a low tone.

Ed didn't respond, could only watch grimly while firelight danced over the two men's faces, painting an incomplete portrait.

Coffin Ed Johnson and Grave Digger Jones burned rubber against the asphalt, their siren blaring its warning song like the mythological creatures of old. Neither man spoke, each keeping their eyes on the road as Digger steered through traffic like a man possessed.

People were already gathering in the streets: businessmen tying one off before going home, women in bathrobes with their hair in curlers, young people out on the town enjoying their evening—they crawled out from their apartments and their cars, united in confusion and panic. The smell of fear was rank in the air, no less potent from the smoke and cinders drifting above them all.

The swell of people grew the closer they got to the scene. Digger laid on his horn until they scattered. Eventually they reached the blockade hastily set-up by their fellow officers. Digger pulled to a stop on the street's shoulder, and the two men exited into the crowd gathered at the checkered sawhorses. They didn't need to provide much incentive to push their way through—Digger had retrieved a hand-cannon they kept in the glove compartment; Ed a 12-gauge from the trunk.

The beat cop at the sawhorse turned a few degrees whiter than he was already, gave them flak when they tried to cross the barrier. Digger showed him his badge. Ed showed him the business end of his shotgun. The cop relented, and the two detectives ran headfirst into a landscape that was quickly turning to Hell on Earth.

The smoke and dust congested into a thick fog between the buildings that were still standing, and Digger and Ed could feel the immense heat hit them like a wall. Shouts and machine gun fire danced on the air between licks of flame. Working their way through the detritus, the detectives came upon a few dozen cops huddled against a gathering of squad cars, acting like a fortress between Hell and the living. Flames roared into the heavens on the other side. Men in black uniforms scrabbled amongst the rubble-strewn landscape, firing Tommy guns into the night with glee. Screams and other human sounds too horrid to describe echoed between perverse squeals of laughter. If this wasn't the end of the world, Digger and Ed didn't want to see what was.

Amongst the huddled cops, Digger and Ed recognized a familiar face—Lt. Anderson, of their own 126th precinct. They ran over, joined him in his cover behind a bullet-ridden black-and-white. He did a double-take as soon as he saw both men. His eyes practically hung from their sockets, soot and ash stained his face and clothes. He looked like he was barely holding himself together.

"Jones? Johnson?" Anderson said, his voice a hoarse crackle. "Damned if you boys ain't a sight for sore eyes…"

"What's the situation?"

"I wish I could tell you," he replied. "We're trying to clear a path to get the fire-trucks in, ambulances for the wounded, but it's a certified war-zone. We thought it might a' been an accident at first—I mean, how does a whole city block go up like *that?*" He snapped his fingers. "Then these storm-trooper lookin' goombahs arrive on the scene, shooting up everything in sight. No idea where they came from, what they're after… They've had us pinned down for the last half-hour. I swear to God, there's gotta be a hundred of 'em, at the least."

Digger narrowed his eyes at the lieutenant. "We may have some juice on that…"

"How's that?"

"You know the shoot-ups we been tracking? If our leads are lining up right, then all of this is connected. Some kinda massive, coast-to-coast gangland takeover. It sounded too impossible to believe, but now…"

"Gangland takeover? Jesus… who's got the moxy to pull something like this?"

"It sounds like something out of a pulp magazine, sure," Ed continued for his partner, "but we had two unconnected sources confirm it earlier tonight. If what they've got is accurate, then we're lookin' at the work of a foreign agent."

"Foreign agent? What, like a commie invasion?"

"Don't know about all that. They said his name was…"

"*Gentlemen!*"

The voice boomed above the commotion in the street—deep, hypnotic and distinctly French. The machine gun fire ceased at once. The huddled cops all risked a glance above their makeshift battlements, saw that several of the storm-trooper-esque soldiers were standing in perfect formation around the remains of an overturned Studebacker. Posing atop the vehicular corpse was another black-clad figure. He wore a hood that covered his face and shoulders like some kind of Medieval executioner, and he was holding a megaphone.

"*Not another one…*" Ed whispered under his breath.

"I hope you're enjoying the fine evening's entertainment that we've provided for you, my dear New York," the figure said, his voice carried by the megaphone. "But alas, I am afraid the curtain is calling, bidding us off our current stage. Do not fret, however, for we are but the opening act in our grand show… For those of you in the audience wishing to join us on stage, well, now's your chance. Let's rise and take back the night…"

His laughter echoed through the megaphone, chilling the night in spite of the fire raging all around. On cue, half of the cops huddled behind the barricade attacked the others, shooting them coldly at point-blank range or slipping thin stilettos in necks and ribcages. The officer next to Anderson lifted his gun to the lieutenant's head. Ed didn't think twice about it: he pumped a load and blew the copper off his feet.

Vastly outnumbered by the turncoat flatfoots, Digger and Ed grabbed Anderson, hopped into one of the black-and-whites and started the engine. The bullet-ridden heap coughed and sputtered, but the engine turned over all the same. Digger put it in reverse and sped away, the dark laughter fading in the distance.

In the backseat, Anderson was still shaking. "You just shot a cop, Ed…"

"You gonna write me up?"

"*Jesus,*" Anderson said, at wit's end. "They just turned on us, like it was nothing. I've known Solomon for almost ten years, and he was gonna plug me… What the holy hell is going on?"

"We're gonna need to call in some serious back-up," Digger said.

"Who? The chief of police, the commissioner… they're all stuck in that mess. Every copper in the city's on the scene, and it looks like half of 'em ain't on the level anymore…" Regaining his composure, Anderson made up his mind. "We need to get to a phone. Call the Governor, get the National Guard in… Christ, am I the ranking officer now?"

"You sure as hell outrank Ed and me…"

"*Christ,*" Anderson said.

Machine gun fire pelted their vehicle, causing Digger to swerve. Muzzle flashes licked the darkness all around them. The engine caught flame. Digger screeched to a stop, and the three men poured out from the vehicle with their heads down. The heap went up in a plume of flame and smoke, illuminating several black-clad figures filling the street. Digger and Ed returned fire, to little effect—within seconds they were surrounded, looking down the barrels of a dozen or so Tommy guns.

"Drop the guns," the lead storm-trooper said. Digger and Ed complied, seeing no other way out of their current predicament.

"All right," the lead continued. "We're gonna take you to the boss. He'll decide what to do with you from there. Although I have a guess at what that'll be..." He drew a hand up to his neck, made a chopping motion. The storm-troopers all laughed, except for the lead—he froze where he stood. His face twitched, as if he'd just been stung by a wasp. A syringe stuck from the side of his neck, held in place by a white-gloved hand.

His Tommy gun went wild. Digger and Ed dropped to the pavement with their hands over their heads, pulled the still shell-shocked Anderson with them. Within seconds, the *rat-tat-tat* of the Tommy ceased, and the three men dared to look up. The storm-troopers were all down, replaced by a vision in a white dress. Although the dress wasn't as spotless as before—Ellen Patrick was looking much the worse for wear as the night dragged on.

"Detectives," she said, retrieving one of the fallen Tommy guns from the ground. "Good to see you fellas again."

"Good to see you, too," Digger replied. "Considering we'd be dead as ducks, otherwise."

"Charming as ever," she said with a smirk.

"Who are you?" Anderson said, staring slack-jawed at her mask and cape.

"I'm the Ghost of Christmas Future. I tried to warn these two Scrooges what we were in store for tonight, but apparently my warnings fell on deaf ears. I suppose I should have pulled out my crutches and done my Tiny Tim act, instead."

"It's not polite to stare, Sir," Ed said. He turned back to the woman. "Guess we shoulda listened to you after all. It woulda helped your cause if you hadn't given us the drop earlier, though..."

"We can share the blame later. Right now, we need to get a fix on the madman responsible for all this..."

"Fantômas..."

She looked away, nodded.

"That's gonna be tricky," Digger said. "He's got a bonafide army at his beck and call, and there's only the four of us."

"He puts on a big show, but that's all it is. We take the ringleader out, and the circus around him will fold like a house of cards."

"You got a plan to get to him?"

"Maybe," Ellen said. "I have it on good authority that Fantômas will be staging public executions shortly, in the center of the street where he blew up the buildings. My ride's nearby... if we charge them when they least expect it, then maybe we'll take the bastards by surprise." She threw Digger her keys, lifted her Tommy gun with a smile. "In other words: you do the driving, I'll do the shooting..."

Digger and Ed grinned as well, their blood rising in the chill night.

"Call in the troops," Digger told Anderson. "We'll do what we can to hold 'em back in the meantime."

"I... I can't let you do it," Anderson said weakly. "It's gonna be suicide."

"So remember that when you're handin' out raises at the end of the year," Ed said.

Anderson shook his head, grinned in spite of himself. He shook hands with the detectives and tipped his cap at Ellen, before he ran off into the night.

Digger shook the keys. "Well, gentleman and lady: our chariot awaits..."

"Bring forth the next one..."

Another from the long line of cattle was dragged forward. He protested, kicked and screamed with all his might, but the storm-troopers had a firm grip on him from both sides.

The guillotine stood out in stark relief from its hellish surroundings, its blood-stained blade flickering from the fires still burning around them. At the base of the guillotine, a hooded figure sat on a makeshift throne of rubble and debris, overseeing the grim scene like a perverse judge of Hell.

The roar of an engine halted everyone dead in their tracks. A gleaming roadster powered through piles of smoldering rubble. A blonde woman in a mask and cape sat in the open window on the passenger's side, brandishing a Tommy gun. On the other side, a large black man pumped a shotgun, took aim at the nearest black-clad storm-trooper...

The night erupted in a hail of bullets. The gathered masses lined up for public execution scattered to the four winds. The storm-troopers returned fire, pelting the roadster with lead, but it was too little, too late. The vehicle shot forward like a missile, and there would be no stopping it until it reached its final destination.

"Get back inside," Grave Digger Jones called out from behind the wheel, to his companions. "I'm gonna ram this rig right up that hooded jokester's ass..."

Ellen and Ed slid back into the roadster, braced themselves. Digger steered right at the guillotine. The hooded figure leapt from his throne of debris, desperate to get out of the way...

The roadster plowed into the guillotine, causing it to splinter into a hundred shards. The blade spun loose from its housing, spiraled through the air in a gleaming arc, heading straight for where the hooded man was now standing. It implanted itself in the concrete with a heavy *thunk*.

For a moment the three in the roadster thought that maybe he'd been split right down the middle, but he stepped out from the other side, wholly intact. Only his hood had been caught by the guillotine's blade—it hung off his face in tatters, barely clinging on.

He tore the remnants of the hood off. The three in the roadster gasped. Underneath was an inhuman face with an unsettling green pallor; a featureless, gargoyle visage that looked as if it had just come to life and stepped down from its rocky perch. His eyes were distinctly human, burning in the darkness of the night with a fire greater than any currently raging about him. The thin slit of his mouth broke into a grin. He drew a knife from his belt and disappeared from sight. Fantômas was on the hunt...

Digger, Ed and Ellen exited the roadster, careful of their surroundings. The line of civilians was still dispersing. Chaotic faces ran past in a blur; it was impossible to tell where the enemy would strike next.

A silver spiral hissed through the air, and Digger dropped his hand cannon—a knife stuck out of his wrist. Ellen was next—a thin stiletto found its way into the barrel of her Tommy gun, and she was quickly backhanded by a black-gloved hand. Before Ed could pump another load into his shotgun, something flashed in front of him—the shotgun came apart in his hands, spilling buckshot all over the pavement as it split into two pieces. He stumbled back and away as sharpened metal cut the air in front of his face. Fantômas now stood before him, a knife in each hand.

"I wonder," he said with a grin, "does your kind bleed red, as well?"

"Come on over and find out, Slick..."

Fantômas laughed and twirled his blades. He approached Ed casually, before ducking and lashing out with both blades like a tiger. Ed felt the cold bite of sharpened metal at his wrists, his side, but Fantômas left himself an opening...

Ed saw his opponent's next move before he made it, caught him directly in the face with a haymaker. Fantômas was lifted off his feet, knocked flat on his back. A trickle of blood appeared at the corner of his thin mouth.

"You bleed red enough..."

Fantômas' eyes went wide, overflowing with anger. He grabbed Ellen's fallen Tommy gun and pulled the stiletto from the barrel. Coffin Ed Johnson had a split-second to imagine lead cutting through him as easily as a hot knife through butter...

Twin gunshots echoed through the night. Fantômas' Tommy gun went wild, spraying the pavement and surrounding rubble. A figure descended, bat-like wings flowing out from behind. The Black Bat laughed maniacally as he let loose with his automatics. Fantômas dropped the Tommy, now leaking blood from a bullet-hole in his shoulder.

Digger and Ellen both got back to their feet as the Black Bat joined them. Fantômas was outnumbered four-to-one. He seemed to calculate the odds in his head, must not have liked whatever figure he came up with. He ran off into the night, tail firmly between his legs.

"Come on," the Black Bat said. "We've got him on the ropes!"

He disappeared after Fantômas, cape billowing behind him. Firing his automatics as he laughed wildly.

Ed moved to follow him, but his partner put a hand on his shoulder. He was going to ask what the hell was the matter, but that's when Ed saw it. Ellen must have, too, as her gloved hands went immediately to her mouth.

A young boy stood over the bodies of a man and woman, red holes painted over their torsos.

Digger, Ed and Ellen all traded glances. Ellen moved her hands from her mouth. "I'm so sorry…"

"Tell that to them."

She looked as if she might say more, but turned and ran off in the direction Fantômas had fled.

Sirens pierced the night again. Fantômas' army now scattered, the firetrucks and the ambulances were able to get through and help, after all. For those who still needed help, anyway.

In the distance, two dark figures battled each other. One of them laughed wildly, oblivious to the horrors left behind in their wake.

Coffin Ed Johnson and Grave Digger Jones went over to the boy, trying to think of comforting words. For the life of them, they couldn't find any.

Matthew Dennion, one of our regular contributors, has already penned several stories featuring Colonel Bozzo-Corona, the secret, all-powerful master of the Black Coats, into whose mouth his creator, Paul Féval, inserts the following speech: "I had a strange dream the other night, I saw myself a hundred years from now, speaking to a man whose father has not yet been born, but who was already sporting a grey beard, and telling him that there are only two things that shall not die: God, who is Good, and I, who am Evil!" Matthew's story provides us with yet one more illustration of the Colonel's true evil...

Matthew Dennion: *Dwelling in the Dark*

New York 1990

The lawyer looked down at his watch as he entered the building where the man he was going to meet lived. He grunted when he noticed that the timer indicated that it had only fifteen minutes until it reached zero. In his mind, he chided himself for not finding a quicker method to reach the man he was meeting with in order to give himself more time, but that couldn't be helped now.

Finding out about the meeting between Frank White and Joey Dalesio and its contents had been difficult enough. He then had to divert Dalesio to another location after his meeting with Arty Clay in order to take his place in meeting with White without generating any suspicion. Setting up that scenario had taken a great deal of time and subterfuge. All of this consumed precious time from the ninety nine minutes he had in daylight.

When the elevator door opened, the man walked out and approached the door of the notorious gangster Frank White. A quick look at his watch showed twelve minutes remaining. He felt a surge of anger course through his mind and he nearly smashed the door to pieces before he was able to calm himself down.

He whispered to himself, "Hold it together. You've nearly reached the top. This is the last stop to determine where Durant was getting his orders from."

The man took a deep breath and knocked on the door.

It swung open to reveal two burly men standing there with Frank White waiting behind them. One drew a gun while the other stepped forward as White spoke:

"Sorry, Joey, but even my lawyer needs to be checked before meeting with me."

The lawyer nodded and let the thug check him. Once it was clear that he was unarmed, White ordered his bodyguards to leave. After the hired muscle had left, he gestured toward a chair.

"Take a seat Joey, would you like something to drink?"

The lawyer shook his head.

"No," he replied in a gruff voice. "I got a sore throat. It's screwing my voice up."

He glanced down at his watch and saw that it had passed the ten minute mark and was still counting down. He looked back at White.

"Mr. White," he added, "I met with Arty Clay and ran your proposal past him. He was not happy about it and said that a move like that couldn't be made on your authority alone. He said he needed to know that it came from the very top. He said that there was only one man who could authorize it, and he needed to know that it came from him."

The lawyer took a step closer to White, and continued:

"He said there was a guy who was above him, above you, even above Robert Durant, who made all of the big decisions, not just for the city, but around the world..."

"That stinking fool doesn't think I have the clout to make a call like this!" White started screaming. "He thinks I can't decide how to redistribute the profits in this city?"

The lawyer looked at his watch to see that it now read seven minutes. He realized that he would have to take a gamble if he was to get the name he wanted—and a location.

In his war with Robert Durant, he had only once heard the name of a possible criminal organization that connected all of the crime bosses around the world. He had been unable to verify if the name he had heard was real, or just a myth. With his timer running down, he decided that now was the chance to take that gamble and drop the name. He knew that gaining access to another crime boss who could point him in the direction of the man who had ordered Durant and Louis Strack to ruin his life would take time that he didn't have.

The lawyer took a step toward White and said:

"Clay said that one member of the *Black Coats* would never move against another without the go-ahead from the top guy. He said, if you just give me the name to bring back to him, that will be enough, because that name would never be spoken unless it was authorized by the man himself."

The anger in White's face faded and a small look of fear crept into his eyes. He rubbed his hand over his face.

"Dammit, I didn't realize that Clay was a member of the Black Coats too." He shook his head. "We don't want to get on his bad side. We're going to need to set up a meeting with the head to make this work."

The lawyer glanced at his watch; it read five minutes. He took a step closer.

"Just give me the name. I'll take it back to Clay; then he will know everything is on the up and up. We can set up a meeting then and keep this guy from coming after either one of you."

White shook his head.

"Clay actually wants me to say his name? He knows that even speaking that name can lead to getting whacked! What is he thinking?"

The lawyer placed his hand on White's shoulder.

"He's thinking he may be in higher standing with the Black Coats than you are. If you want to avoid him making a power play, give me the name to take back to him before he calls the guy himself."

"You're right," White nodded. "It's risky but Clay hasn't given us a choice." He shook his head. "Damn it, how did I not know that Clay was also part of the Black Coats?"

The lawyer looked at his watch and saw that it was closing in on three minutes.

"Mr. White, maybe Clay didn't know you're a member of the Black Coats either. I'm your lawyer, and I never even heard of them until today. This could be some kind of test... The sooner you give me the name, the sooner I can run back to Clay and stop him from reaching out to the guy before you do and getting the authorization to make a move on you."

Frank White looked his lawyer in the eyes. '

"Knowing about the Black Coats is dangerous enough, but the name I am about to give to you, if you even whisper it to your wife, it can get us both killed."

As the timer passed two and half minutes the lawyer squeezed White's shoulder.

"Then tell me before Clay sends this guy after both of us!"

"Colonel Bozzo-Corona," whispered White, sighing. "The name he is looking for is Bozzo-Corona. Now go back and tell Clay while I reach out to the Colonel to keep the Marchef from coming for all of our heads."

The lawyer nodded and quickly left White's penthouse suite. He ignored the elevator and ran down the stairs.

When he reached the ground floor, he saw the real Joey Dalesio walking into the lobby of the building. The man who had been masquerading as Dalesio turned and ran through a side door out into the alley where the hotel stored its garbage. He reached up and tore off the face of Joey Dalesio and looked down to see it bubbling and melting in his hand.

The scarred, disfigured face of Doctor Peyton Westlake smiled as he popped up a vent to the subway system and dropped down into it. When his feet hit the tracks, he pulled a roll of gauze out of his pocket and wrapped it around his face as he said:

"Colonel Bozzo-Corona. Now that I have a name, enjoy what little life you have left because Darkman is coming for you."

Over the next several months, Darkman worked his way through other members of the Black Coats. He used both his skills as an infiltrator to gain access to key members of the gang, and his enhanced strength and reflexes as a cloaked vigilante to beat information out of those whom he couldn't trick as he tried to find his way to the infamous Colonel.

Darkman traveled the country, clashing with the like of Marsellus Wallace, posing as a fixer for Keyser Söze, but it was following the money that ultimately gave him access to the Colonel.

By donning the identity of various employees at Jackson Steinem & Co., over the course of several weeks, Westlake had gained valuable information on Gordon Gekko, implicating him in various financial crimes, as well connecting him to the Black Coats.

Westlake had first tried to approach Gekko by donning the guise of FBI Special Agent Aloysius Pendergast, but the business tycoon had refused to break despite the charges that could be levied against him. He then went to Gekko as the famed report Carl Kolchak and threatened him with publishing a story about his dirty dealings, while agreeing to spike it if the banker was to throw him a bigger story regarding Colonel Bozzo-Corona. At the mention of that name, Gekko had become terrified and told the man he thought to be Kolchak to leave at once.

When that second attempt to gain the information he needed from Gekko failed, Westlake's fragile psyche snapped. He screamed in anger, tore off the false face of Kolchak, revealing his horrific visage. He then thrashed Gekko to the point where the man was barely conscious. Darkman laughed maniacally as he dragged Gekko out onto his patio.

When the banker awoke, he found himself leaning over his fire pit with the flames just below his head, as Darkman held onto his shirt. He looked up to see Darkman's face staring at him and he screamed.

"What do you want from me?" he begged.

Westlake smiled and held his hand to the flames of the fire. The vigilante showed no concern as the fire burned his fingers.

"I can't feel any pain and my hands are already burnt nearly to the muscle," he snarled. "You're afraid of the Colonel, but I am going to make you even more afraid of me." He leaned in closer to Gekko. "Either you're going to get him to come to New York in a place where I can meet him, or I am going to hold you in those flames until the fire scores every inch of skin off of your body."

Darkman pushed the financier a little closer to the flames. Gekko's eyes went wide as the heat from the flames causes the skin on his back to burn and blister.

"He's in the US!" Gekko shouted. "On the East Coast even. I can have him in New York by tomorrow! Where do you want him?"

Darkman looked back toward Gekko's house.

"Here. Have him come here tomorrow night. Until then, you and I are going to spend every second together, and if I even think you are trying to warn the Colonel we are coming right back to this patio."

49

He threw Gekko against the wall.

"Right now, you and I are going to go on a little trip back to my lab."

As night fell, Westlake prepared himself to finally meet the man responsible for making him into the deformed and psychologically unstable man he currently was. He had placed his newly-made Gordon Gekko mask over his face and turned off the lights in the house. The longer that he was able to stay in the dark, the longer his false face would last. This was an encounter that he did not want to rush. He wanted answers from the Colonel before he tore the man apart with his bare hands.

Darkman was sitting in Gekko's study when he heard the door open. The vigilante was surprised that he had not heard a car pull up to the driveway. He was even more surprised when an old man entered the study with only a giant wearing a mask over his face behind him. Given the amount of wealth and power this Colonel Bozzo-Corona wielded Westlake thought he might have had to fight through a virtual army of thugs to reach him.

Westlake started to stand up when the Colonel motioned for him to remain seated.

"No need to get up, my dove. I will walk over to you," the old man said.

The Colonel sat down in the chair across from Westlake and the giant known as the Marchef stood behind his master.

The old man stared at the man posing as his financier in silence for nearly a minute, before Westlake broke the silence.

"Colonel, let me get to the point about why I asked you here so abruptly..."

Once more the Colonel held up his hand to stop Westlake from speaking.

"Let us not begin quite yet. I am still admiring your work." He leaned in closer. "You are to be commended, Dr. Westlake—or do you prefer Darkman these days?" He shrugged, "Either way, your artificial skin is nearly flawless. Had I not known better myself, I would swear I was looking at Gordon Gekko."

The Colonel extended a long and bony finger toward Westlake.

"Tell me, have you made any progress in the duration the skin is viable in the light, or are you still stuck at ninety-nine minutes?" he asked.

Westlake was stunned by the amount of information the Colonel knew about him. He could feel the anger welling up inside of him and he yearned to leap out, knock the giant unconscious, and strangle the Colonel with his bare hands, but he restrained himself. Above all else, he needed to know why this man had thrown him into the living hell that was his life.

Darkman reached up and grabbed his false face. He pulled it off and held it in his hand. Typically, the sight of his deformed visage made people uneasy, but neither the Colonel nor the Marchef flinched. Clearly, these two men had seen much worse than the horrible burns that covered two thirds of his face.

The vigilante held the face out to the Colonel.

"Would you like to examine it more closely?" he inquired.

The Colonel nodded.

"Yes, very much so."

Darkman leaned over and handed the face to the Colonel. As he moved the fake face of Gordon Gekko around in his hands, he asked:

"Is the real Gordon still alive, or did you kill him like you have so many other members of my organization?"

Darkman smiled.

"He's still alive and stashed somewhere that only I know. I figured that, when dealing with a man of your power, having an ace up my sleeve in the form of the man who launders a large portion of your wealth would be beneficial."

The Colonel held the fake face up in front of his eyes.

"You have been creating a good deal of trouble for my organization over the past few months, just in order to set up this meeting, between the two of us." He placed the false face down into his lap and looked into Darkman's eyes. "Can I assume you wanted to meet me in order to find out why I had you attacked in the manner that you were?"

Darkman gritted his teeth and dug his fingers into the armrests of the chair.

"I've learned a good deal about you over the past few months as well. Whatever the reason, it had to be more complicated than a mere real estate deal."

The Colonel smiled and nodded.

"Indeed it was. The real estate that Durant could have helped us to acquire would have meant but a modest increase in our finances; it wasn't the real prize." He leaned in closer to Westlake's charred face. "That was you."

Westlake shook his head in disbelief.

"You're trying to say that your plan all along was to turn me into Darkman? That's ridiculous! I nearly died in the explosion. How could you possibly have guessed that I would be thrown free from the fire? Even then, what possible benefit am I to you? I have done nothing but hurt your organization?"

The Colonel leaned back in his chair.

"Robert Durant had always been a rather blunt instrument, as opposed to a surgical weapon. He was supposed to make sure your face was disfigured and your body burned. We needed you in a situation where you were personally motivated to complete the work on your on the synthetic skin. Durant was supposed to hurt you, but he was instructed to keep you alive. Luckily, you proved to be more resilient than we ever would have thought. The medical procedure for cutting off your ability to feel pain, while increasing your strength, speed and agility, was something I have wanted to test for a long time.

"Combine that with the suspected psychological effects of the explosion, and it became a very intriguing operation. A few bribes to doctors willing to risk performing such a radical surgery, and I'll have the means to create an army of super-powered assassins that I can use to benefit my organization." The Colonel shrugged. "Yes, your activities as Darkman have caused us a few minor set-backs, =but that's nothing compared to the potential benefits we might reap."

Westlake could feel anger welling up inside of him as the Colonel admitted to what he had done. He dug his fingers deeper into the armrests as he continued:

"You said the benefits *we* might reap?"

The Colonel nodded.

"Of course. I meant, you and I."

He stood up and began to walk around the room.

"Think of it Westlake, I have unlimited funds at my disposal. I can provide you with a state of the art laboratory and specialists to help you with your research. With that kind of support, how long do you think it would take you to perfect your synthetic skin? Within a year, your research could reach the point where it is sustainable in daylight. Through our legitimate holdings, we could patent it and gain untold wealth by becoming the sole provider of replacement skin for burn victims. We can become rich, all the while helping people."

The Colonel's eyes seemed to glow as he laid out the second part of his plan.

"Even more important than wealth is the power we would gain. If our agents had the ability to become anyone, imagine the access they would have. We could infiltrate political offices, the inner circles of other criminal organizations, replace any person with a member of our team."

The Colonel looked back at Westlake.

"Now, I am sure that, to a man like yourself, those benefits are not nearly as rewarding as taking your revenge on me. So let me point out other benefits of you joining forces with me..."

He walked over in front of Westlake and stared into his eyes.

"With the formula perfected, you will no longer have to live in the dark. You can have your old face back. Additionally, I can provide you with the best psychological care on the planet to help control your anger and depression. With these changes, you can live out your life with your beloved girlfriend, Julie Hastings. Not only that, but you can do it with undreamed of wealth.

"But if you so desire, you can even continue to fight crime as Darkman. The only stipulation would be that, from this point on, you avoid interfering in my affairs. But there are plenty of other, rival criminal empires towards which you can direct your efforts..." He shrugged, "I know that my actions have caused you a good deal of physical and mental pain, but look at the gifts I have given you in return. The motivation to be fully committed to your work. You are now one of the most physically gifted men on the planet, and you feel no physical pain. You have the opportunity to become wealthy beyond your wildest dreams, and you can still help countless people with your synthetic skin and through your crusade on crime.

"You are already a ruthless murder, and you even dress yourself in a long black coat. You are virtually already one of us. Embrace your destiny, join the Black Coats, come work for me, and realize all of your dreams and more."

Darkman's tormented mind was swirling with all the Colonel had just laid out before him. Riches, his face back, the ability to help burn victims, and most importantly, Julie. It was all that he had ever wanted—and more.

For a brief moment, he considered the offer; then, an immense sadness overcame him as his thoughts reverted back to Julie. He had to accept that she was lost to him forever. The first time that he had brutally taken a life, the first time he had become Darkman, he had closed off any chances to ever have a normal life of happiness with the woman he desperately loved. She could never live with what he had done, no matter how luxurious an existence the Black Coats might make for them.

The sadness within him began to turn to rage as he stared at the Colonel.

"I had a life with everything I wanted. I had a woman I loved, work that was meaningful, and that would have helped people. I would have perfected the formula on my own had you not turned me into the monster I am!"

As Darkman stood up, the Colonel took a step back and the Marchef moved to stand in front of him.

"You took everything from me!" Darkman screamed. "They say you are immortal, and I hope that's true because I don't want to kill you! I want to make you feel like you are dying over and over again until I feel that you have experienced as much pain as I have!"

Darkman rushed forward as the Marchef sprang out. The giant drew a large knife from a sheath and swung it at the vigilante. Darkman leaned back to avoid the weapon and then struck the assassin in the face with a blow that would have rendered any normal man unconscious. But while the executioner's knees buckled, he remained standing.

Darkman took a step closer and delivered another blow, this time to the Marchef's ribs that shook his foe's entire body. He was preparing to kill the executioner when the Marchef connected with a thrust kick to the vigilante's abdomen that sent sent him falling to the floor.

When Darkman felt his body hit the floor, he rolled backward. As he was halfway through, he saw the Marchef's knife flash down and embed itself into the spot where he had been laying only a second ago. He quickly stood up and delivered an uppercut to the assassin which caused the giant to take several steps back. Darkman looked down at the knife still stuck in the floor.

The vigilante than leaped toward the Marchef and wrapped his arms around the giant. With his enhanced strength, he was used to easily overpowering his enemies, but the Marchef was stronger than any man he had ever encountered. The assassin powered out of Darkman's grip, grabbed the cloaked avenger, and then tossed him to the floor.

Darkman rolled once more and sprang to his feet. He was about to attack the Marchef again when the Colonel called out:

"That will be enough. I have seen all that I needed to." He nodded at Darkman. "I am impressed Doctor Westlake. You were able to hold your own against my Marchef." He looked at his executioner. "I believe that the last person who was able to do that was the Nyctalope." He looked back at Darkman. "Either way, you have confirmed that the process you underwent is capable of giving me operatives who will be physically superior to any of our enemies. You were wise to take Gordon Gekko as an ace up your sleeve, but I am too old not to have one too…"

A devious smile crept across Colonel Bozzo-Corona's face as he finished his sentence. Darkman's eyes went wide.

"Julie," he whispered.

The Colonel nodded.

"Indeed. Can we agree that within the hour, we will exchange Mr. Gekko for Ms. Hastings at this location?"

Darkman nodded silently.

The Colonel smiled.

"Good. Then let us also agree that after said exchange, we shall no longer seek each other out, since we both know the location of individuals who are of high importance to us?"

Darkman nodded again, and then slipped out into the night to retrieve Gordon Gekko.

As the vigilante left, the Colonel pointed to the facsimile of his face on the floor.

"Pick that up and place it in a dark bag. We shall take it our scientists. It will take us longer to perfect his formula without Westlake, but time is something that is most definitely on my side."

Brian Gallagher committed to chronicle the adventures of Marie Nizet's Captain Liatoukine—from her ground-breaking 1879 novel Captain Vampire *(Black Coat Press, ISBN 978-1-934543-01-6)—moving forward in time with each story. While each installment can be read independently, the sequence is most impressive, starting with "City of the Nosferatu (Vol. 10), "The Trial of Van Helsing" (Vol. 11), "The Stake and the Sickle" (Vol. 12), "The Berlin Vampire" (Vol. 13), "The Death of Von Bork" (Vol. 14) and "The Skull of Boris Liatoukine" (Vol. 15). Here is the final chapter of that thrilling series...*

Brian Gallagher: *The Vampire President*

Moscow, 8 March 2024

Boris Liatoukine always felt uncomfortable in church. Given that he was a vampire, this was unsurprising. He occasionally attended church for the sake of appearances. He could not stay for too long sustained exposure could be fatal. He was in a church office, but it was still on the grounds. Still holy.

The man sitting opposite him was a priest. They had made some small talk, but now it was time to get to the reasons they were here.

"Father Joseph, I am honored to be invited here to your church. However, spiritual matters aside, I believe you wish to discuss with me political matters?"

Father Joseph stroked his long beard.

"Of course, but all in connection with the church. You are a candidate in these elections to become President. I wish to know more about you and your attitude to the church. Although you are seen as a nationalist, a number of people consider you a liberal, and more inclined towards the European Union than Bezukhov—a man who respects the church. It must be said that you are hardly a frequent visitor to the church."

Liatoukine understood that he had to be careful in what he said.

"My belief in God is in my soul; I appreciate I should attend church more often, but many pressures mean I work long hours—my businesses continue to be successful because of this and thus keeps many Russians in work and taxes paid to the government which benefits all. In this way I believe I carry out the work of God."

Liatoukine took momentary pleasure in having said that with a straight face. Father Joseph looked incredulous, but the Russian vampire pressed on before he could recover.

"As for being a liberal? Yes, perhaps I am. I believe in democracy, just as Vladimir Putin does, a man I take great inspiration from. As for the European

Union, I would certainly like a closer relationship; it would be good for our industry. Certainly it should be easier for Russians to visit the EU."

That was more truthful, thought Liatoukine; freedom of movement in the EU had been most convenient in order to conduct his affairs—both legitimate and otherwise.

Father Joseph had managed to compose himself. It was clear to the Russian vampire that the priest had not bought into anything he said—and he sensed that this went beyond the usual cynicism about politicians. What was going on here?

Father Joseph spoke. "This is most interesting. Let us have some vodka in order to deepen our conversation."

Liatoukine could detect the man's heartbeat—it was going fast.

From a bottle already on the table, he poured out to the drink into two tumblers and gave one to Liatoukine.

"*Za zdorovye!*" they both said and drank the vodka.

The priest drank it down straight and looked back at Liatoukine. The man had frozen, his tumbler in his raised hand, but not quite near his mouth. He stared at the priest, and the priest suddenly noticed that his eyes appeared to resemble those of a cat. Father Joseph felt fear—fear, as he had not felt before.

He knew it was over.

Liatoukine put his tumbler back down.

"Why is this vodka so warm? I can feel it through the tumbler?"

He touched the top of the liquid with his finger. He sucked his breath, smiling at the priest and then showed him his finger. It looked burnt, with steam coming off it. The priest said nothing. The Russian vampire then resumed speaking.

"Holy water mixed with vodka. An old trick to poison vampires. It would have burnt my throat severely, incapacitating me somewhat. However, whatever made you think I would not detect it before it got to my lips? Ah, perhaps you believe that in this church my powers would be blunted enough to not notice? Yes, my powers are blunted—but not to that extent."

Liatoukine rose. *Time for a quick interrogation*, he thought. In that moment, the priest regained his wits and courage. He leaped over to nearby cabinet and out of it grabbed a Heckler and Koch MP5 machine gun.

Before he could raise the weapon to fire, the Russian vampire's hand was around his neck and he was lifted aloft. The machine gun fell harmlessly to the floor.

"Silver bullets?" he asked.

The priest said nothing; he just stared at the vampire—terrified, but also defiant.

"Who provided you with this weapon? Someone in the West?" Liatoukine asked the priest.

Again, the same look of defiance.

"Hell awaits you!" he managed to say.

Liatoukine nodded. "Yes, Yes. I know that—in fact, I expect to be given a position of some authority when I get there."

The vampire laughed. Father Joseph did not.

Liatoukine realized that time was not on his side. He could break the man, but his powers were lessening the longer he stayed in this church. It would not look good to leave here with a dead priest left behind. Letting him live would be risky, but who would be believe this man? However, it was now clear why Father Joseph had insisted on such secrecy; Liatoukine would just have disappeared with no trace back to this church. That secrecy would now seal the priest's fate.

He stared into his eyes, and drained him of energy—which the vampire needed right now—but stopped short of complete absorption. He dropped the body of the priest onto the floor.

He opened the door to the main church. Sitting a short way away was a layman of the church, entirely oblivious to what had happened. He walked over to him and they man stood up. Before he could say anything, the vampire had fixed him with a glare. They layman could only see the cat-like eyes of Liatoukine. The vampires started to speak:

"You will go to see Father Joseph in ten minutes. You will find him dead, and then you will contact the authorities. You will forget any memories of me or Father Joseph meeting anyone. He was simply working in his office."

The layman sat back down.

Liatoukine left, and left unobserved with his head bowed. He walked over to his car and got in the back. The car moved off. Next to him in the car, was a raven-haired woman wearing a smart business suit.

"We used electronic jamming to catch any recording devices we have missed," she said, "as well as making sure the security cameras were scrambled, in addition to those we already disabled. How did it go?"

"Very well, Natasha," Liatoukine replied "He wanted to kill me; so I killed him. One less threat. I assume he had intended to record my death. Given the secrecy, perhaps it was a recording for a select audience to prove my death, or it could be he wanted to release it to the public if he felt it was convincing enough. No doubt this is linked that network around the Countess Petrovski."

"We should certainly retaliate," said Natasha.

She was fully aware of Petrovski's network—as a vampire herself, she could not afford not to. Her original, true name was Polly Bird. She has taken many names, forms and identities since, including that of the notorious criminal Irma Vep when she herself spent many years as a famous jewel thief. Now she was Natasha Rostova—a name suggested by Liatoukine, based on someone he vaguely remembered meeting in the 19th century. Her role was that of a well paid political advisers to Liatoukine; a post that secretly involved a security role, which given her criminal past she was well suited for.

"Yes," replied Liatoukine, "but not just at the moment, there are too many eyes on me at the moment due to this election. Let it be as planned."

Natasha nodded. "We have the St. Petersburg rally to plan for," she said.

The Russian vampire nodded as the car continued its journey to their electoral HQ.

Paris, 9 March

The Countess Irina Petrovski looked around the table. Seated around the table were some of the individuals most feared by what was left of the supernatural community. Feared due to their effectiveness in eliminating many of the most the hostile elements to humanity—especially vampires. Here there were aristocrats like herself and millionaires, policemen, spies and others including descendants of people who had fought supernatural evil. She was one such descendent as well as being a Countess and millionaire. Everyone was here. She decided to open the meeting.

"Ladies and gentlemen, how good it is to meet again."

She was immediately interrupted.

"Could we not have done this online? The secure technology exists. I had intended to attend an important debate this afternoon at the European Parliament in Brussels. And putting us in one place does make us a target."

The accent was Germanic and came from a well-dressed man right at the other end of the table. The Countess understood that he was making a genuine point—but also that this was a unspoken, although minor, challenge to her authority as chair of the meeting and de facto leader of the group.

"My dear Baron Vordenberg," she replied, "we all recognize the important work you do at the European Parliament. Your dedication in promoting links between the old Hapsburg states within the European Union is most commendable—and something still greatly needed after the ravages of communism. However, meetings by electronic means are too prone to being tapped. We don't keep written minutes for similar reasons."

Another voice spoke up. The Countess saw with pleasure that this was her old friend Karl—a senior member of the BND[4].

"Technology can still be hacked. We have to use it sometimes but not for a meeting like this. It would be unfortunate if a recording of a meeting were made public—technology can still be hacked. Discussing the destruction of supernatural beings? Vampires? The press would have a field day portraying us all as deranged fantasists. The days of official groups dealing with such creatures are long gone—you of all people should know that."

The Baron knew what he meant.

---

[4] Germany's Federal Intelligence Service.

"Yes, one of my ancestors did command the Austro-Hungarian Empire's department for dealing with dark forces. The dissolution of the Empire saw the end of that. My ancestor, however, would certainly have been in favor of using modern technology today, especially to defend ourselves against the Russians, let alone the supernatural"

The Countess saw her chance to end this diversion.

"Technology, Baron, that our subject today may well have the capability of intercepting. He is the ex-KGB officer now turned oligarch Boris Liatoukine, also known to quite a few people as 'Captain Vampire.' He has eluded our efforts at eliminating him over the years. Now he has a candidate in the Russian presidential elections in which Vladimir Putin can no longer stand due to constitutional term limits. This has caused great concerns among many of us. How can we deal with the situation? I have asked Karl to give us his view—his work at the BND gives him an insight."

The Countess noted that the Baron clearly did not press his points over and above her introduction.

Karl proceeded to give his views, not giving the Baron any opportunity to interrupt him.

"Boris Liatoukine is of course known to us all as a vampire, a role he has been active in for quite possibly over 300 years. His main motivation is power— but from behind the scenes. However, he is also a proud Russian—which may seem strange given that his country has a strong religious objection to his identity. It would seem that Liatoukine simply ignores that part of it. He is also a survivor and a pragmatist. We believe he joined the KGB—then the OGPU—in the 1920s. He fought the communists as a White officer and was tracked down by the Soviet spy Von Bork, whom I believe gave him little choice but to work for him. Subsequently he managed to replace von Bork in 1979 by killing him. With the end of communism, he took full advantage of the changes and became an oligarch."

"We know all this," said the Baron, taking advantage of a pause.

"We indeed do," responded Karl. "However, I wish to make a point. Liatoukine has survived many threats. He has had setbacks, but always finds a way ahead. He certainly can be destroyed, but any attempt now would likely fail. His long experience almost gives him a special extra sense. As a presidential candidate, his security will be more heightened than usual. A failed—or even successful—attempt now at assassination by us would be exposed as a Western plot, which would be essentially true. That could have dangerous international repercussions. It is not worth it, not least as Liatoukine is not expected to win. He is slated to come third, behind the Communist candidate Kuragin. He is only there as nationalist candidate to drain votes from those unhappy with Putin's candidate—Kirill Bezukhov—rather than seeing them go to any potential real rival. Bezukhov is determined to win outright in the first round, and

Liatoukine is to ensure that. We should wait until the election has passed, then consider how to proceed."

There were murmurs of agreement around the table.

"I must agree with that assessment," said the Countess. "We cannot act now, but after the election we must certainly prioritize his destruction. Before we take a vote, are there any other views?"

She was not surprised when the Baron spoke up.

"As has been pointed out," he said, "Liatoukine has survived many attempts on his existence over the decade—centuries even. Unorthodox methods should be considered. This election gives us a special opportunity to neutralize Liatoukine. If we do nothing, then he will have more influence than ever as a reward for helping Bezukhov. The election of Bezukhov will be a disaster for the West—the advancement of Liatoukine within the Kremlin court would be catastrophic also. He will use his influence to promote Russian aggression even further."

The Countess knew well that the Baron's distaste for Russia rivaled—if not exceeded—that for the supernatural.

"I am well aware of Russian behavior which I directly fought during the Cold War," she stated. "Even then, we had to make sure not to provoke them too far."

The Baron knew he needed to be careful. The Countess's record was well respected and, despite her age, she was she still sharp and looked younger than her years. He himself was not old enough to have played the kind of role she did in the past.

"Of course, we are all aware of your achievements, Countess," he said, "but please allow me to outline my plan."

She made a hand gesture indicating he should proceed. He then outlined his plan. When he had concluded, the Countess spoke:

"That plan—assuming it would even be successful—would have the very real effect of inflaming tensions between Russia and the West with unpredictable consequences. Exactly the sort of thing we are trying to avoid as we have just discussed." She was clearly irritated. "Let us proceed with a vote. All in favor in not making any attempt to neutralize Liatoukine during the Russian elections?"

All bar Vordenberg raised their hands.

"I think that settles it," the Countess said, not wanting to proceed with those against.

"I bow to the wisdom of the group," Vordenberg said, smiling.

He was aware the Countess was much too influential and respected to be easily defeated. Now, it was best to change the mood.

"With the business out of the way, it is time for refreshment. If we move to the adjacent room, a buffet has been prepared. I have also brought along some wines from my personal wine cellar."

The mood immediately changed, and even the Countess smiled.

Later, after the buffet, Baron Vordenberg got into his chauffeur-driven BMW 8.

"My apartment, Jacques," he instructed.

As the car moved off, he took out his mobile phone and switched off the intercom on the soundproof partition between him and the driver. He wished privacy. He dialed a number.

"The meeting, as predicted, did not go well," he said. "We will proceed to Zagreb. It is time to talk to Lady Ruthven. "

Meanwhile, Karl had driven the Countess back to her Paris residence. As he saw her to the door, his mobile phone rang. He looked at the caller's name and took it. The Countess waited; she sensed this was important.

Karl finished the call. He looked at the Countess and said:

"Irina, there is bad news about Father Joseph…"

10 March

Baron Vordenberg was on his private jet en route to Zagreb. He was reading news of the death of Father Joseph, a respected figure in Moscow, in an Austrian newspaper. There was no hint of this being a murder; the priest was reported to have died from natural causes. But the Baron knew better. He had, along with the Countess, tried to discourage him from attempting to kill 'Captain Vampire.' They knew the vampire would not be so easy to kill. The weapons they had supplied him were for defensive use only.

"Unfortunate news regarding Joseph," said his aide.

"Yes", replied Vordenberg. "We had warned him. Now we have lost the best contact in we had in Russia." He looked at the newspaper again. "Natural causes it says here. Given that he was an admirer of Putin, no one will think he was murdered. How ironic; he was killed by the very creature the West thinks of as a lesser evil than Bezukhov."

His aide looked puzzled. "If Father Joseph was a Putin admirer, how did he come to work with the network?"

"The network is dedicated to eliminating vampires and the like," the Baron replied. "Father Joseph understood that, and set aside his politics. Our network being informal helped this; we do not even have a name. With the supernatural fading away, there are less and less experts to deal with the matter, and fewer still in Russia. Why? Because we think Liatoukine had them eliminated—at least those he could not recruit. We have few people left in Russia now. It becomes ever more important to neutralize Liatoukine."

The Learjet soon landed at Zagreb's Pleso airport, where a car was already waiting for the Baron to take him onto his next destination.

At her Paris residence, the Countess took a call. Her phone indicated from whom it was: Boris Liatoukine. They had spoken in the past, making vague threats against each other. She picked it up and spoke in English:

"How can I help you, Mr. Liatoukine?"

The voice on the other end replied in English. "How kind of you to offer to help me, my dear Countess. I will come to that in a moment. I just wished to call to give my condolences over Father Joseph, who died very recently. He was well known in my country. I believe you were friends?"

"We had met a number of times," the Countess replied icily.

Liatoukine continued, "Yes, I thought as much. His death was... a waste. He had much to offer the world. It is in his spirit that I propose that relations between Russia and the European Union—and perhaps our British friends as well—should change. We could have relations based on 'you leave us alone, we will leave you alone.' We could solve many conflicts. What would you think of such a proposal? I know you have great influence in certain circles."

"You seem very certain of victory, Mr. Liatoukine," the Countess replied. "I had read that you are likely to come third, and indeed that your candidature is merely to ensure that voters none too keen on Bezukhov will vote for you, thus ensuring that votes will not go to any possible real challenger."

Liatoukine laughed. "Of course I intend to win! However, if God decrees I should lose..." the Countess winced as no doubt the vampire intended, "...then I am sure that my advice on many matters would be highly sought after."

"Thank you for calling me, Mr. Liatoukine. I will consider what you have said."

She hung up on him. She understood very well what he meant. He was after some kind of truce between himself and the network. Surely, this indicated some kind of weakness? Regardless, it could not be countenanced. And yet, it was true that, whilst they had come close to eliminating him in the past, they had not been able to do so. Liatoukine was certainly capable of eliminating some of the network—as clearly he had done with Father Joseph.

She had never been too keen on the priest's Russian nationalist views, especially his views on her beloved Poland. However, they had both put that aside in order to cooperate against the supernatural, and she had respected him for that. He had been told not to attempt an assassination—he was frankly not capable of dealing with a vampire of Liatoukine's stature. She was sure that this was what provoked Liatoukine to murder him. His death—amongst many others—should be avenged.

Liatoukine had proved to be someone very difficult to kill. A truce could well be exploited by him to continue murdering his opponents. No, there could be no truce. However, this was still a sensitive time. Effectively, there was a truce due to the decision not to go after Liatoukine during the election. What to do next? She hoped that Baron Vordenberg would do nothing foolish.

In Moscow, Liatoukine switched off the phone. With him was Natasha.

"Do you think she is interested?' she asked.

"Probably not at the moment," he replied. "However, she and the others may well reflect over the death of Father Joseph and finally realize that co-existence is the best option. After all, have they not virtually won? There are but a handful of vampires in existence now. Yes, I seek power in the form of influence, but it is very much on human terms."

"You seek power, but this is an election you wish to lose," said Natasha, teasingly.

"Indeed it is. The powers that be want someone to make sure that those electors who want a slightly 'gentler' nationalism, but not a Western stooge. This is a favor to the Kremlin. I do not appreciate the limelight, but not doing it would make me enemies, and given that I have been promised influence and a free hand for my business activities, this is good for me. The polls have Bezukhov first, Kuragin some way behind in second position, and myself a bit past that in third place. So far, the plan goes well."

"Just as well for you—if you won, the scrutiny from home and abroad from the intelligence agencies and the media would soon find out that you are not quite human," Natasha said.

"Yes," laughed Liatoukine. "Not that Bezukhov has a clue. It grates having to do this for him. He affects an aristocratic air. I knew his ancestor, a Count—Bezukhov was descended from one of his illegitimate son. Even the name was taken decades after Count Bezukhov's death. He doesn't mention that when he talks about his aristocratic heritage in his campaign rallies!"

She joined in with his laughter.

"Now," he said, "have you made security arrangements for the rally in St. Petersburg?"

She nodded and started to give him the details.

Baron Vordenberg's car arrived at its destination in Zagreb. It was an old building in central Zagreb near Ban Jelacic Square, dating well back into the Austro-Hungarian Empire when it was used for military purposes. The Baron took pleasure in the fact that this building was still in use. In his soul, he was an Austro-Hungarian; his family had served that Empire for generations. One ancestor had commanded the Empire's division that dealt with supernatural threats, using this very building. Then, the Great War had come and that had been the end of the Empire—an empire which had certainly been better than the fascism and communism which had followed it—of that Vordenberg had no doubt.

A private security firm now used the building. The Baron was pleased with this company; he owned majority shares in it and it made money—enough money to be able to provide security for the secret basement.

He and his aide went down the stairs to the basement, and through the security doors. A guard escorted them. The structure was clearly old, but supplemented by modern reinforced doors and various technological devices. It was a prison.

"You know, Boris Liatoukine himself came here in the past as a visitor?" the Baron said to his aide.

The aide looked startled.

"Oh yes," continued the Baron. "He came officially as a Russian officer. A record of his visit was made. A vampire held here died during his visit. Somehow, he avoided suspicion, no doubt using his powers. The Hapsburg's supernatural department ran this place. Now, that department has gone, but the values of the Empire are still with us, and now we maintain this place privately."

His aide was used to this; Baron Vordenberg was well known for his Hapsburg nostalgia.

They swiftly came to one particular door. A security guard was there waiting for them. He opened the door—which on the inside was lined with silver and had a crucifix on it, with garlic hung on it for good measure. Ahead of the door was a further door constructed entirely of a reinforced plastic. Behind it, seated in a chair, was a beautiful young brunette, seemingly no more than twenty. Behind her, there appeared to be the fashionable room of a larger apartment.

The Baron and his aide sat down in chairs opposite her.

"Good evening, Lady Ruthven," said the Baron.

"Good evening, Baron," Lady Ruthven replied in a cut-glass English accent. "I was told to expect visitors. No doubt you want more information from me? Over the years, I rather think that I have told you everything I know."

"Not information this time, but rather a favor, shall we say," the Baron replied. "It would see your freedom—for a time."

Lady Ruthven was slightly startled by this—although she did not show it. What did this Austrian aristocrat mean?

"Go on," she said.

"You have cooperated with us before. When we captured you, you gave us information regarding other vampires and others, enabling our network to locate and eliminate them."

She interrupted him.

"Oh yes, I don't have any loyalty to other vampires. My husband killed me and then abandoned me, not bothering to see if I returned from the grave. I took the name Lady Ruthven—perfectly legally, given that he was a Lord. We are fellow aristocrats, you know."

He ignored her comments.

"In return for your cooperation, we allowed you your continued existence," he stated.

"And in luxury too," she replied, waving her arm at the rooms behind her.

The Baron resumed talking.

"The information you gave us has helped reduce the numbers of vampires to an even lower level than there were previously. However, our holding up our end of the agreement demonstrates that not only are we not genocidal in intent, but that we can be trusted."

Lady Ruthven nodded her head cautiously.

"We want you to help us neutralize Boris Liatoukine," he said.

"Thank you for visiting me, Baron Vordenberg. I really must get back to watching something on the television," she said and then got up to go.

The Baron was ready for this.

"Fail to cooperate, Lady Ruthven, and you will find many of your privileges curtailed."

Lady Ruthven got back in her chair.

"You said that you could be trusted. I see now that is not true."

"Your privileges and existence were dependent on telling us everything you knew about your fellow vampires. Upon closer inspection, it seems that those you did provide us information on those who happened to be enemies of yours. We know that, in the early 2000s, you had business dealing with Liatoukine in London. You never mentioned this to us. As such, we feel that some curtailing of your privileges may be in order, if not a stake through your heart."

The vampire did not like the sound of that. What he had said was perfectly true. She had refrained from mentioning her dealings with Liatoukine—which were both amicable and profitable—not out of any loyalty, but purely due to the fact that the notorious 'Captain Vampire' was both powerful and hard to kill. She did not want the remotest chance of making an enemy out of him. She would not give in to the Baron just yet.

"I am immortal, A few years here will hardly affect me. Just moments in time."

As soon as she said it she realized just how weak that comment was. The Baron smiled and responded:

"First of all, if we liked, we could destroy you at will." He pointed upwards to the ceiling on her side of the wall. "The fire sprinkler system is linked to a supply of holy water. We turn it on—no more Lady Ruthven. Or we could just starve you by denying you the animal blood we supply you with. Alternatively, you help us and your privileges shall remain intact. More importantly, you get to see the outside world again, and if it goes well you will get to go on other missions."

She could see she was defeated.

"Very well," she said. "Tell me how I will not simply escape you the moment I am let free for this 'mission' of yours?"

It was the Baron's aide who answered. He opened a briefcase he had with him. Inside where two small capsules nestling in foam.

"These implants will be placed in your neck and stomach," he explained. "They are lead-covered and contain holy water and shards of silver. They have small explosives contained within them which we can detonate via a satellite signal. Once you have concluded your mission, we will remove them. They will be triggered if tampered. Further, the devices will receive a regular signal. If they do not get that signal, say, because you decided to enter an area where such signals are blocked, they will detonate after a certain time."

"How long?" Lady Ruthven asked.

"That is for us to know," the aide replied, smiling. "It could be seconds, minutes, hours... Probably best for you to simply make sure that you do not 'accidentally' enter a signal-free zone, such as a metro station for example. Although, if the mission does require it, we will make sure it won't go off in any such circumstances. Provided we know beforehand, that is. We will implant a communications device also. This all being said, your body will eat at them, to purge them from your system. The capsules have a coating made to a certain formula which will hold out for about ten days. When it eats through, the anti-tamper mechanism will be triggered. However, if you complete your task, the capsules will be removed well before then."

Lady Ruthven did not like any of this. However, she gave the only answer she could.

"Very well," she said.

St. Petersburg, 13 March

Boris Liatoukine stood in front of the monument of Tsar Nicholas in St. Isaac's Square. This was familiar ground. He had been here when the monument was being constructed. In fact, he knew Nicholas I personally. Tonight's rally for his candidature would play on Imperial nostalgia. Although, of course, the audience would not know just how nostalgic Liatoukine was, or rather why. He thought back to those times. They had certainly been better for him. A long period of power and status, and Imperial adventure. He remembered in particular his operations in Rumania. Crushing the locals was always something he had enjoyed. He had found some kind of accommodation with the Soviet regime, but he was happy enough it was over. The Imperial age was gone—but the compensation of being an oligarch was reasonable. He even had a wife for a while. He had divorced Magda fairly recently, most amicably. She had played her part well, and there was no need to liquidate her. He would have kept her on for the election had he known he was going to be a candidate. Still, she gave excellent comments about him to the media when they contacted her.

His thoughts were interrupted by his cellphone ringing. He answered, and recognized the voice immediately—his contact in the GRU[5].

---

[5] Russia's external military intelligence agency.

"Greetings, Boris. I take it the preparations for tonight's rally are to your satisfaction?"

"There are indeed," said the Russian vampire, looking at the workmen putting up the last of the crowd barriers.

He had ensured that the rally would take place in the evening—when he had more power. It was best to seem as invigorated as possible at such events.

"Excellent, Boris. We notice that the West is increasingly interested in your candidacy. You are being spoken highly of amongst human rights groups. Perhaps you should cultivate these contacts?"

Liatoukine knew what he meant—trying to cultivate them for GRU purposes. This would be going too far in their arrangement. The last think he wanted was to be associated such groups, a sure way of being portrayed as a stooge for the West, something that could be easily used against him in the future.

"No, my friend," Liatoukine replied, "I have no desire to encourage such elements. Furthermore, if I were to be seen as working for the West, I am sure I would lose the votes of those patriots who are not happy with the leading candidate for any reason."

"Of course, of course, Boris. We would not wish to do that. We are keen to have your candidacy to be a success. We will be in touch again soon."

The caller rang off

Natasha approached the Russian vampire. She had been looking over the preparation for tonight.

"Our GRU friends again?" she inquired.

"Yes," he replied. "It is fortunate that we have others on our side from within the Kremlin. The GRU never really forgave the KGB—or rather myself and Von Bork—for monopolizing supernatural affairs. However, with the general skepticism towards such matters that has grown over the years, that antagonism should have gone, and yet the GRU are still a little unfriendly."

"There are still people around who are aware of the reality of the supernatural—or rather what's left of it," Natasha replied. "Perhaps there are such people left in the GRU?"

"Perhaps. In the time before leaving the KGB, I had eliminated a few such people. It could just be coincidental—general antipathy towards an ex-KGB man. Whatever, I think our GRU friend will have to shock his colleagues and die young, just as soon as this election business is over."

He changed the subject.

"Is my speech ready?"

She nodded. They moved away from the monument and towards the nearby parked campaign bus. On its side it had a picture of Liatoukine, looking stern, with the slogan "To a better Russia" on the side. Liatoukine liked the slogan—it could mean anything to anyone.

Once on board the bus, they looked over the speech.

"We will need to make some amendments here. A little more criticism of the West. Given the GRU's behavior, it is best to make any attempt to portray me as in the pay of the West look absurd. Here, it should say…"

He stopped suddenly, looking around. Natasha was suddenly on alert too. They had both sensed something…

Lady Ruthven put her binoculars down. If she had had her sniper's rifle, she could have taken a shot there and then. However, that was not the plan. Clearly, Liatoukine and his lackey had sensed her presence—and the element of threat, simply by her looking at them. It is possible they would take further security precautions.

She decided not to tell Baron Vordenberg that piece of information. Best not to upset anyone who could destroy her at the touch of a button. She had broken into this room; it had a perfect view of the monument. Unfortunately it also had a perfect view of the St. Isaac's Cathedral which overlooked the moment. It was far enough to do her no harm, but it made her feel uneasy. Her target was a lot closer to the Cathedral, although clearly it did not entirely inhibit his powers. She would return later—fully armed. She would fire the shot—a silver bullet—and then she would leave rapidly. Her vampiric speed should get her out of danger quickly. Furthermore, she had changed form—she was now a bit taller and blonde. Lady Ruthven thought this prudent; it would be unfortunate indeed if Liatoukine somehow saw her and recognized her before she completed the operation.

The doors to the apartment opened—two Moscow police officers walked in. They saw the petite woman in front of them and kept their guns holstered.

"What are you doing here?" one of them asked.

Lady Ruthven bluffed. "I am looking after the property for the owners," she said.

The officer replied, "No, you are not. They have said nothing about you. Are you foreign?"

He put his hand on his pistol. His companion started to talk on his radio. They were clearly checking the area ahead of the rally. And as good as her Russian was, she could not hide her English accent. She had to act fast.

She ran towards the officer with the radio. At high speed she covered his mouth and switched off his radio. She stared into his eyes.

"Silence!" she hissed.

She had the power of mesmerism, and she only needed it to work for a moment whilst she dealt with the other officer.

The other one was astounded. What was he seeing? She moved so fast—like a blur. Whilst she was in front of him, dealing with his colleague, he grabbed at her, but she knocked him flying.

He smashed to the ground, but still had his wits about him. He pulled his gun out of the holster and aimed it at the woman in front of him. She was smiling, and looking at him. Her eyes seemed to bore into him.

"Fire, then," she said.

He looked fearful—and then pulled the trigger. And then realized his gun was missing. The woman had it. She was tossing it up and down in her hand.

"Get up," she said.

She then spoke to the other officer, still standing there.

"Get onto the radio. Tell them all is well, the person was just an employee on the stairs."

After he had done so, she spoke to both of them.

"Why are you here?" she asked.

They both answered at the same time.

"Quiet. Just you," she said, pointing at the officer who had tried to shoot her.

He responded, "The occupants downstairs had seen you on the stairs and did not recognize you. They called the police. We were checking on the area and were able to respond swiftly."

"Very well," Lady Ruthven said. "As far as anyone was concerned you only came across another employee. The people who made the call—where are they?"

"Downstairs" came the answer.

"Please invite them in," she said.

They did as instructed, and a man and a woman came in. The vampire swiftly mesmerized them. It transpired they were the only ones who had noticed her.

Excellent, she thought. *And most convenient.* The man had made the call. She said to him:

"It turns out the person you saw earlier was in fact your colleague here, who had business on this floor—that would be plausible, wouldn't it?"

They both nodded. She continued:

"Good. Make up something more detailed if anyone asks, but say nothing if no one does. Forget me, and any other sightings of me. Off you go now."

They went off.

"And you two," she said to the policemen, "will ensure that this area is regarded as fully checked—and you will respond to any calls or commands from me, whilst telling no one of me. Resume your duties."

They did so.

Splendid, thought Lady Ruthven. Her mesmerism powers were strong as ever, despite her ten-year incarceration in that Zagreb dungeon. She liked little tricks such as taking a gun off someone whilst they were under her influence. Their bemused looks when she took them out of their trance were also amusing.

Now she had two policemen to help her with tonight's events... that would make things a lot easier.

No wonder Baron Vordenberg wanted her for this job—such powers were most useful for an assassination. The Baron would not doubt affect to disapprove, if she told him, but he should be grateful that she had killed no police or members of the public—as he had demanded.

As she left, she noticed a window was tinted slightly green. It was an occasional giveaway for some vampires. It could be controlled, she had done so for many years, but it seemed that being let out meant some lapses. She would need to concentrate more on that—which was difficult given the intensity of her task.

St. Isaac's square was crowded that evening. Boris Liatoukine was pleased. He was less pleased about St. Isaac's Cathedral being lit up as well—but there was nothing he could do about that. He decided not to keep them waiting. He stood on the platform, and began his speech.

A distance away, Lady Ruthven was looking down her telescopic sight. She could see him making the speech. She could hear him through an earpiece connected to radio coverage. It was up to her when she should take the shot. She settled on firing when he said something particularly irritating.

Liatoukine was thinking that the speech was going down well. He had spoken of the need of to maintain defenses, to preserve Putin's achievements, and to stand up to the West. It was now time to differentiate himself from the leading candidate, and make a gentle gesture towards the West—but not too much.

"We must take a new approach to the West. Yes, they do accuse us of interfering in their elections. They even blame us for Jeremy Corbyn becoming the British Prime Minister!" The crowd laughed. "I will look into the matter, but I also expect them to look into their interference in our own elections—the funding of 'activists' and radio stations..."

The crowd roared wildly. Now, however, for the fig leaf to the West.

"However, whilst the West are most certainly guilty of human rights violations, can we honestly say we could not do better? Even in the KGB, I was always concerned about the well-being of our citizens. Now, I see our society must develop further. Russians must not fear voicing their opinions. Please believe me, the cause of human rights is very dear to my heart."

He clasped his hands over his chest. The crowd applauded. Lady Ruthven rolled her eyes and then pulled the trigger.

Liatoukine heard the crack of the rifle in the distance and, due to his heightened vampire senses, saw the bullet coming straight at him. He moved slightly, and the bullet missed his head and smashed into the set behind him.

For a moment there was silence and bewilderment in the crowd. Natasha leapt onto the stage, along with FSB[6] bodyguards. They grabbed Liatoukine to move get him off the stage. But he used his strength to move them back. He spoke into the microphone:

"My friends, please leave immediately and in an orderly fashion. Your safety is paramount."

He then let himself be rushed off the stage.

In the back of a police car, still listening to radio coverage, Lady Ruthven laughed at Liatoukine's attempt to play the concerned candidate. The car was driven by the policemen whom she had mesmerized earlier. They thought they were driving a lost British journalist to safety, rather than helping an assassin escape.

Later, in a secure location in St. Petersburg, Liatoukine awaited a report from Rostova. She came in.

"The would be assassin has of course got away. The Police and FSB seem to have no idea as to who it was. However, the bullet has been retrieved."

She showed Liatoukine a picture on her phone.

"A silver bullet?" he asked.

"Yes," she replied. "It seems this is an attack against you as a vampire. Unfortunately, someone has seen fit to decide it would be good to quickly reveal this to the press."

Liatoukine grunted. "It looks like my nickname of 'Captain Vampire' is going to be wheeled out to a greater audience than ever. This is the Countess's work."

"Are you sure? Could it not be the GRU?"

"No, they would not dare, given Bezukhov is my ally. Now, I must be seen by the public, no matter that I do not intend to win—I must not be seen as being weak. However, first I must make a call."

The Countess was watching television coverage of the incident, with news coming in constantly. Already, the Russian vampire was being portrayed as a hero for his telling the crowd to leave. Despite the late hour in St. Petersburg, it appeared that Liatoukine was going to make a press appearance. She wondered if he had set all this up for himself. Did he really want to win? Her phone rang. It was Liatoukine.

"My dear Countess! Another failure of your group, it seems."

"I have no idea what you are talking about," she replied.

---

[6] Federal Security Service of the Russian Federation, the internal successor of the KGB.

"Yes, you would say that," he responded. "However, I think the silver bullet used was a clear enough response to my offer of good will. I will send my own message back in good time."

He hung up.

A silver bullet? The Countess realized what must have happened.

"Vordenberg!" she spat.

In St. Petersburg, Liatoukine switched off his phone. He and his entourage were on board his campaign bus. They got off outside the Mariinsky Theatre, its neo-renaissance façade making an excellent background for media pictures as intended. The press had already been alerted. They jostled around him Liatoukine. The vampire was pleased—he had made clear his instructions that the journalists were not to be pushed away. He must be seen to be fearless, not so much for the election, but more for not showing any public weakness to his enemies. Many questions were being thrown at him. He was able to create a small space in the crowd by raising his hands. His power as a vampire was largely responsible, although the assembled throng believed they were showing respect.

"My friends! I am pleased to be with you. I am delighted that my supporters only suffered minor injuries rather than anything more serious in their rush to avoid this would-be assassin. I expect the authorities to do their job properly and apprehend the criminal. For too long this kind of thing has gone on in our country, with the perpetrators getting away. Well, no more! When I become President, yes, I will stand up to the West, and yes, I will promote Imperial Russia's values. But I will also insist on human rights in our country, for the ordinary Russian to not live his life in fear. I will set up a commission to defend human rights and investigate corruption. I will not take a penny from the West for this. Now, I must return to my headquarters—my staff are frightened and distressed, and I must see to their well-being."

As he moved back to the bus, journalists shouted questions. He ignored them, but then one pushed forward, sticking her microphone under his nose.

"The police say that the bullet used was made of silver. What do you say about that?"

Another journalist shouted from behind, "Is it because you were known as 'Captain Vampire' when you were in the KGB?"

Liatoukine smiled. "If a silver bullet was indeed used, this can only point to the mental health of the perpetrator. We all know from the cinema that silver bullets work only on werewolves, not vampires!"

The crowd burst into laughter, allowing Liatoukine to get back on board the bus.

"How little do they know," said Natasha as he sat down.

"Quite," he replied, laughing.

In Paris, the Countess was controlling her fury. Had Vordenberg gone mad? She knew he advocated extreme methods against the network's foes, in particular vampires. Furthermore, he had a particular animus against Russians. She sympathized to a degree; but communism had been defeated, and they still had to cooperate with a few Russians in dealing with supernatural forces.

She took a call. It was Karl.

"I've made checks on the Zagreb detainment center. The prisoner we are interested in is officially still there. However, one of my sources in the prison has informed me that Vordenberg met with her and subsequently, she left. Orders were given that no one was to report her departure for security reasons. It is clear that he is proceeding with his plan."

The Countess knew that Karl maintained certain informal sources in the network. A good intelligence officer, he did not simply take the word of people.

"Karl, " she said, "We have to stop Vordenberg. Where is he?"

"He is in St. Petersburg as a member of a European Parliament election monitoring group. He was a last minute addition to the team. I am having the whole team monitored, but beyond that I cannot do more. To target him with resources would invite many questions—he is very well respected. Trying to suggest he is involved in an assassination would not go down well—let alone discussing the... particulars of things."

Despite the secure line, Karl was still circumspect with his language.

"Berlin would have me removed," he concluded.

"Do you have any suggestions?" she asked.

"You could try and talk to him. Bluff that you will expose him. Or reason with him. It might work."

"I have tried to call him, Karl. He did not answer. I am disinclined to continue."

She had certainly been displeased by having been ignored. She was not accustomed to that.

"I will continue to monitor the situation," Karl continued. "I will see if there any other avenues to pursue. However, I fear we may be able to do nothing. It could be that we have to hope that Vordenberg succeeds completely in his plan, with no trace back to us... Irina, there is one thing that plays in our favor. It seems that western diplomats and some of the non-governmental organizations they back are now seeing Liatoukine as the candidate to back, despite his known KGB past, his dubious dealings as an oligarch, and his nationalism. His talk of human rights and rapprochement with the West has convinced them that he is probably the best option. Even though it is known he is simply trying to drain support from the communist candidate in order to for Bezukhov to get more votes—they are even trying to doubt this."

"Please tell me you're joking? No, I can well believe it—their hypocrisy and naiveté is nauseating. How on Earth does this help us?" she asked, exasperated.

"It means that it less likely that the attempt to kill him will look like a Western plot," Karl answered, "but more possibly a business rival—or some lunatic, given that a silver bullet was used. Even the Russian state could now be blamed. However, I can certainly push the idea of a business rival. I will brief some of our friends in the media. I am, of course, looking into helping us increase our own security, given Liatoukine's threats to us."

"Thank you Karl. That is most considerate. Goodnight."

She put the telephone down. The Countess was unused to feeling powerless. What could be done?

15 March

In Moscow, Baron Vordenberg was meeting with Lady Ruthven in Alexander Gardens, near the Kremlin. She had some concerns about the location.

"Baron, as a member of the EUP monitoring team, are you not aware that the FSB are monitoring you?"

"Of course, they are! That is why we are meeting here. I also have an electronic device on my person which will interfere with any devices pointed at us. Furthermore, there is nothing suspicious. You are a journalist from the *New York Times*. Why should I not be meeting you?"

Lady Ruthven was grateful that, at least, he was being discreet in conversation, not mentioning the fake ID she had been given. She had also used her powers to change her appearance. A little taller, with blonde hair and changed features. She had not changed accent however; it would sound fake whatever she tried.

The Baron looked over to a couple also walking in the park. He gave them a cheery wave. They ignored him.

"They are FSB. Are you deliberately trying to antagonize them?" asked Lady Ruthven.

"What does it matter? They would not dare to arrest us!" he exclaimed.

Lady Ruthven was none too sure about that.

"Will you be at the TV debate on Friday night?" he asked, knowing the answer.

"Yes," she said. "I will be reporting on it for my paper."

"Security will be tight of course," he said. "After the attempt on Liatoukine's life, and the failure to capture his assassin, there is some nervousness. You know, Putin did not bother with debates back in 2018—his stature and poll popularity meant he did not need it. Bezukhov does not quite have that lead, despite being ahead in the polls. He is attending this final one in order to show he doesn't fear the other candidates. Not in the least due to Liatoukine looking like a hero after the attempt on his life."

Lady Ruthven nodded. "Liatoukine has taken a few votes off Bezukhov. But he has taken rather more off the communist. He may even come second in the polls, but Bezukhov will come well ahead. With Putin's endorsement and his anti-Western rhetoric, I can't see him losing. If Liatoukine really is Bezukhov's man, he is doing the job we expected."

The Baron smiled. "And I certainly expect you to do yours. Perhaps you could deal with these two? I will see you after the debate."

He strode off.

Lady Ruthven strolled over to the FSB couple. She spoke to them. And then she left, knowing that the FSB records would show that Baron Vordenberg had met with a journalist from London's *Daily Telegraph*. He would not be linked to a fake *New York Times* reporter. However, she was unhappy with having had to meet him at all. He was too confident and reckless. He just wanted to remind her he was in control, regardless of the risk o the FSB observing. This whole plan was dangerous. However, she had no choice but to go through with it. She had everything planned —her powers should see that she came out of this well. The world would be hunting a fake *New York Times* journalist with blonde hair. She would not be resuming this form again. Still, she knew much could go wrong—but she had no choice. Vordenberg's devices implanted in her body had seen to that.

Liatoukine sat in his campaign HQ. He and Natasha were in an office. Through the glass doors they could see the campaign workers outside in the open plan area busily concerning themselves with election matters. They were preparing for the big event tonight.

"Bezukhov will be there tonight. His first and only of these debates," said Liatoukine. "It seems the polls show that the public want him to do so. He's not quite as popular as Putin was, which must annoy him. I am not to outshine him tonight. Irritating, but I should be able to manage it."

"You will need to be careful, Boris," said Natasha. "You've appeared in all the debates, cultivating your 'democratic' credentials. You did well, and the polls place you a close third. You need to tone down the performance—we cannot have you suddenly chasing down Bezukhov."

"I will deliver my part of the bargain," he replied. "In any event, I can't see any great polling change. Bezukhov will win, Kuragin will come second, and I come third—with the Kremlin owing me a lot. Perhaps the first favor I shall ask is the liquidation of a member or two of the Countess's network? A couple of unfortunate accidents perhaps, if not any poisonings. Perhaps I could request the GRU does it? That will teach them to treat me with more respect."

"We've been assigned further FSB agents for security reasons. No doubt this is genuine after the attempted assassination and so on, but they must have orders to keep an eye on us in a more political fashion."

Liatoukine nodded. "Yes, Bezukhov is no fool. Still, I have my friends in the FSB which has allowed us to oversee security. However, there have been renewed attempts to look more deeply into my—and your—backgrounds. This also includes efforts by foreign services such as MI6, the CIA, the BND and all the rest. It has been ensured that they only received the material we wish them to have. Decades upon decades of practice will mean our covers will withstand a degree of scrutiny, but not much more. The sooner this election is over, the sooner I can fade back into background—or at least what is possible. Wealth and a degree of influence is all a vampire can achieve; too much power and profile means more scrutiny from the world, and in this new era of social media, that could be dangerous to one's health."

Natasha smiled, "If you do win, we could always say that claims of vampirism are 'fake news,'"

Liatoukine laughed. "Yes—but that won't work with the intelligence services who may get so suspicious that they may take any information from people such as the Countess's network seriously. Another good reason to kill a few of them."

There was a knock on the door.

"Time to head for the studio," Natasha said.

Lady Ruthven arrived at the Russia TV studios in central Moscow. She was part of a small group of western journalists permitted to cover this last of the debates. She was accredited with the *New York Times International Edition*. It was known that this was Liatoukine's favorite international newspaper. No doubt Vordenberg thought it amusing to associate her with the newspaper. It could draw Liatoukine's attention. It had not done so, but this again showed how reckless the Baron was.

Now, it was time for her to get through security. A matter made easier by her vampiric powers. In that, at least, choosing herself as the assassin made sense. She had a firearm in her bag, next to her laptop. It was made out of a plastic that would resist electronic detection, but would certainly not elude the eyes of the police searching through her bags.

She approached the security gates. She could see that there was a queue for the bag search. She waited for her turn. The police officer at the search desk started to open her bag. She immediately used her mesmerism.

"All perfectly safe," she said, looking directly into his eyes.

Without a beat, he looked into her bag, took out all the items, bar the gun, and then nodded her to the next stage.

She quickly put her items back in the bag. *That was easy*, she thought. Clearly Liatoukine had not used his influence to place people more resistant to mesmerism here, assuming he had any that is. He probably thought that it was a human assassin who was after him—as the Baron had reasoned.

She then set to placing all her items in a tray for the electronic scan. She left the gun in the bag, with her laptop. The tray went through. She walked through the metal detector and scan on her body. No problem there. She was waved through to where the other journalists were collecting their things from the trays that had passed the scan. She felt nervous. Had her tray not gone through yet?

It did not come out from the machine. A policeman from behind the machine stood up. He held up her bag.

"Whose bag is this?" he asked the journalists.

"Mine," Lady Ruthven said.

She moved towards the police officer. She was prepared to get out fast. If the policeman had spotted the gun, he had probably already alerted his colleagues. She would have to use whatever supernatural violence to escape, and just hope Vordenberg won't detonate the devices in her.

The police officer handed her the bag.

"It contains your laptop. The instructions on the notice in front of the machine are clear. You must go back, and place the laptop into a separate tray."

"Yes, of course. My apologies, officer."

She went back to the end of the queue for the machine. Vordenberg's gun would not doubt pass security again, she thought. Where did he access such weaponry, she wondered, as well as her impeccable credentials? He may be reckless, but he certainly had resources.

Finally clearing security, she proceeded into the studio. Here, she would carry out the assassination. Her escape plan was crude and simple: After firing the weapon, she would use her strength and speed to exit the studio. The first moment she was unobserved, she would change form into someone else. Someone older, with short black hair. Her jacket was reversible; she would look wholly different. Shorter even. To all intents and purposes, the assassin would have disappeared into thin air. Any bullets fired into her by the police would be disintegrated by her metabolism.

She took her seat. Despite being coerced into it, she was excited by what she was going to do. As far as she was concerned, Liatoukine's fate was sealed.

The press and studio audience were mostly seated now in the TV studio. Final checks were being made on the set. Natasha Rostova walked around the set, consisting of seven podiums for the seven candidates. She looked at each of the bottles of water as she walked around. She sensed nothing from them. No holy water in them.

The communist candidate, Kuragin, had sent a young representative today, rather than himself—one Boris Drubetsky, claiming a lack of respect from others. He had a glass of water thrown into him by a woman candidate in a previous debate and used this to back out. Natasha thought that his ego was indeed damaged by this, but also that his debating skills were not up to the level of the others. He would lose votes for that. Probably to Liatoukine or Bezukhov. Either way, it would help Bezukhov to get over the 50% and win the first round.

Her thoughts returned to security. She could not notice anything wrong, and the water bottles were safe. Hopefully, the police and FSB had done their jobs—they seemed competent.

She went backstage. Liatoukine was waiting his dressing room.

"Is all well?" he asked.

"As far as I can see," she replied. "Still, be ready for anything."

"I always am," he replied.

He pointed to the grey streaks in his black hair and beard. "Does this look alright? I am probably the only candidate who dyes his hair to look older. Unavoidable given that I am known to be old enough to have been in the KGB. However, do I look distinguished or just older?"

Natasha knew he had a vain streak.

"You look fine," she said. "Very distinguished indeed. Just don't try to over-shadow Bezukhov."

Liatoukine nodded—perhaps a little reluctantly thought Natasha.

"*The New York Times* wants an interview with you," she said. "They are very keen on your liberal values. Perhaps straight after the debate?"

Liatoukine smiled. He had been reading the international edition of that newspaper since it was founded in 1887 as the *Paris Herald.*

"Is the journalist here tonight?" he asked.

"Yes, he is," she replied. "The press list also shows a freelancer for the same newspaper; she is doing more general coverage of the election, apparently."

"Of course. The newspaper understands Russia is a great power and needs extensive coverage," he said.

Natasha noted the vampire's strange patriotism. If the Russian people found out what he was, he would not last very long.

An electronic buzz came on.

"Time to put on the show," Liatoukine said.

Lady Ruthven watched the candidates take up their positions on the podiums, formed into a semi-circle. She was glad that they had come on at last; she was getting tired of the journalist next to her, from a British broadsheet.

"You are from the *NYT*? You must know Jim then? He's got an interview for Liatoukine for your paper, he says."

"We don't really know each other; we are working independently on our own stories," she said.

Her neighbor seemed to accept that, then started to gush about Liatoukine.

"Isn't it wonderful what he is saying about human rights? Imagine if he could win!"

"He was in the KGB," she replied in a bored tone of voice.

"Oh, yes, but that was long ago! Look what he says now!" he replied, not put off by her attitude.

She could not believe the stupidity of this man. She was relieved when, at that moment, the candidates came on. To applause, they all went to their individual podiums, laid out in a semi-circle. The moderator, a well-known Russian TV political correspondent, started to introduce the proceedings.

Lady Ruthven felt into her handbag for the gun. It was a handgun; there was no way a rifle could be used. However, as a vampire, she knew her senses would enable her to hit her target accurately. She could take the shot now; but no, she wanted to watch them speak for a bit.

Also watching—albeit on TV—was the Countess. Her phone rang. It was Karl.

"I am in Zagreb, Irina. I have used my contact in Vordenberg's security firm to find out more. Explosives are implanted into Lady Ruthven which will release silver and holy water, and even bits of garlic, if detonated. This can be done by a signal from here. I think I can get into where their control room is."

"Do so immediately," she replied. "Detonate the device. Even if she is in the audience for this debate, better she blows up there than carry out the assassination."

"Agreed. I will proceed."

He hung up and walked into the building. Time was against him; perhaps he should not have wasted time calling the Countess, he thought.

In Paris, the Countess continued to watch the debate. They had no choice but to kill Lady Ruthven. She had no real sympathy for the vampire, but the network had given their word that they would permit her continued existence. It was Vordenberg who was forcing her to do this. However, an assassination tonight at the debate would have destabilizing effects for Russia. They had no choice. Vordenberg would also somehow have to be dealt with. She watched the screen intently.

In the studio, Lady Ruthven continued to watch the candidates giving their opening speeches. All dull. However, they were now arguing with each other. This was amusing—the assassination could wait for a short while.

In Zagreb, Karl entered the prison. The guards knew him; after a cursory security check, they let him through. They had no problem with his pistol.

Karl was pleased; he had ensured in the past that his clearance with this company permitted him to carry a firearm in the building, as a defense against the creatures kept prisoner. Waiting for him, was his contact, one of the Baron's security analysts.

"Which way, Vojna?" he asked.

Wordlessly, she pointed up a flight of stairs. They rushed up onto the first floor. There was a guard by a door.

"I'm sorry sir, no one can enter this room. Direct orders from the Baron."

"I have clearance to go anywhere in this building," Karl said, in perfect Croatian. "Given to me by the Baron himself."

"Except in here, sir," the guard replied.

Karl had no time for this. He pulled out his pistol from his shoulder holster.

"Open the door," he said, pointing the weapon at the unfortunate guard's head.

Karl's man took the guard's weapon from his belt and gave it to Vojna. The guard wisely let them in.

The room was small, but there was a communications set-up complete with live TV coverage of the debate on a large screen. There were two technicians seated by it. There were startled to see Karl waving a gun at them and one of their analysts holding a gun at their guard.

In Moscow, Liatoukine was making a point.

"People say that I have sold out to the West in the last few days. This is not true. Yes, I accept some criticisms from the West..."

He was cut off by hisses from the members of the public in the audience.

"...but I do so only on our terms. I will also bring back Imperial codes of honor! I will mix the best of the past with the future!"

"A future determined by the West," shouted Drubetsky.

He was a man in his 20s with no experience of the ideology he believed. Clearly, thought Liatoukine, he was going to try and make a mark for himself whilst his boss was too proud—or rather too cowardly—to turn up tonight. However, his implication of treachery could not go unanswered.

"Boy," said Liatoukine clearly trying to patronize, "I proudly served Russia in the KGB for years, risking my life for the motherland. I saw your ideology from the inside. It failed Russia in the end and was worthless. Like you."

Liatoukine had surprised himself; there was real anger in his words.

Drubetsky spluttered. "How dare you! Stalin saved us from the Hitlerites! The world feared us! You insult the dead who fought the fascists! I will treat you how we have been treated!"

He flung his glass of water at him. The audience laughed. Liatoukine took out a handkerchief and slowly dried his face. He was truly angered now. He simply glared at Drubetsky. The audience fell silent—they could sense something.

The young man could see nothing but Liatoukine's eyes, which suddenly looked like those of a cat. He was consumed with fear, yet did not know why—except that he knew he had provoked something terrible.

He started shaking, and then walked off the stage at speed without saying anything.

Liatoukine turned to the camera that was on him and smiled.

"I suppose that's why some people call me *Captain Vampire!*"

The atmosphere broke and the audience laughed again. Liatoukine had turned a potential humiliation into a triumph.

Bezukhov decided he had better weigh in—he was displeased that the limelight was off him. He was also annoyed that Liatoukine had just made a big impression, and that he was being overshadowed.

"Only one person can maintain and increase the strength of Russia," he said. "He is before you. Unlike the two bickering candidates we have seen, I respect everything that makes us strong. I am no communist, but I recognize their achievements in defeating Hitler, putting the first man into space—and most of all, keeping the West at bay!"

There was applause. None of the other candidates interrupted. Not even Liatoukine. He knew his role—and it was not to try and win this debate. However, it rankled that he had to give way to this man—someone who was nothing more than the illegitimate descendent of a Count he had had little time for.

"However," continued Bezukhov, "there was much to be said for the Imperial age, especially in regards to the monarchy. I will set up a commission—perhaps we can restore something of the aristocracy—in a purely ceremonial role of course."

The moderator, who himself had felt a little sidelined, intervened:

"Are you suggesting the establishment of a new Tsar?" he asked.

"There are no living relatives," Bezukhov replied, "but we could perhaps establish something from the surviving relatives of aristocratic families, who knows?"

Liatoukine could contain himself no more.

"You mean yourself, don't you? What, the country will crown you Tsar?"

As he said it, he knew the deal for influence was over.

Bezukhov took this challenge on.

"My dear Liatoukine, I have my duties as a politician to consider—such a thing would not be on my mind. Perhaps you are thinking of such a role?" he gestured to Liatoukine's hair. "With your talk of Imperial honor, perhaps you can remember those years?"

The audience laughed. As did Bezukhov, who shot a glance at Liatoukine at the same time. The vampire was unnerved—did Bezukhov know what he was? A joke at his expense—or something more?

He then noticed something on one of the studio monitors near him. It was an audience reaction shot—of laughter—but there was a strange tint of green. It seemed to be more intense at the edge of the screen, especially on one woman, whose features he could just make out. A technical hitch or the presence of a vampire?

He scanned the audience and spotted the woman. Lady Ruthven sensed his eyes. She looked at him. They made eye contact. All this happened in a moment, during the laughter.

Time to do the job, she thought.

She stood up and pulled out her firearm from the bag and pointed it right at him.

In Zagreb, Karl knew he had to act fast.

"Detonate the device," he said to the men at the table.

They did not move—they were calling his bluff.

"The red switch," said Vojna.

Karl moved forward.

In Moscow, Liatoukine leapt from the stage into the audience—he would not run from her, but would take her on directly, even if that meant his own death. He would use his powers to elude the silver bullets.

Then she moved her arm away. And fired at Bezukhov.

The FSB were already hurtling towards the candidate to protect him. They were too late. Bullet after bullet—not silver, this time, Liatoukine noted—smashed into his body. Bezukhov was propelled backwards, and then the last bullet hit his head, blowing the back of it off onto the set and the unfortunate moderator's face.

There was pandemonium, screaming and shouting. Liatoukine pushed passed the audience, even stepping on some of them to get to the assassin.

Lady Ruthven herself had already been on the move, heading along her row to a side exit. She looked back, and saw Liatoukine racing towards her. She was surprised. She and Vordenberg had expected that he would have allowed himself to be taken to safety by the FSB. However, she was prepared for any encounter with him. She did a high kick at him.

The end of the heel caught his face—burning him. He staggered back slightly and then realized the stiletto heel had silver at the end of it.

Lady Ruthven did not press home the attack, but decided to take advantage of his momentary hesitation to head for the door. Liatoukine was even faster. He managed to grab her arm and pull her around. She seemed familiar.

"Who are you?" he demanded.

She looked him right in the eyes and opened her mouth.

Then she exploded.

Liatoukine was flung back. He could feel bits of sliver and even holy water burning on his face. It burned badly, but not enough to kill him. His vision became blurred, but in front of him, he could still see the assassin, now a skeleton, writhing in white flame, somehow still screaming.

She collapsed over two rows of seats. The flames died out and there were just bones, then ash.

Liatoukine stared. He knew what had just happened. The bullets were aimed at Bezukhov, but they may have well just been stakes to his heart.

The FSB got to Liatoukine and pulled him away.

In Zagreb, Karl's finger was still on the depressed switch. He was staring at the screen, which had gone to a news studio with a newscaster relaying what had just happened, already showing slow motion of the assassination.

One of the technicians had grabbed his arm as he tried to press the switch. Karl had shot him in the leg. In the ensuing melee, the assassination had taken place. Karl had hit the button too late. The fight had distracted him from the screen in those precious seconds; he had heard the shots, but was firing his own gun at time. It was only the replay that confirmed that he had been too late. Baron Vordenberg's insane plan had succeeded. Now, he could only pray.

At the EU's observer headquarters in Moscow, Baron Vordenberg was watching what had happened. All the staff were in shock at what they had just seen. The Baron, however, was well pleased. He would find out later what had happened to Lady Ruthven—his intention had been to honor his part of the bargain with her. Despite her death, he was delighted. The plan had worked, as he knew it would.

Paris, 17 March. Election Day

The Countess and the Baron met in a Paris Gardens of Luxembourg. Anywhere indoors would have been too risky, due to possible surveillance. They started walking together. The Countess said nothing; she was going to let the Baron start to explain himself.

"After the assassination," he started, "all the EU observers were kicked out promptly. Some Russians think the West was behind it."

The Countess looked at him coldly.

"They are not wrong," she said.

Vordenberg laughed. "Not officially! The EU—and Washington—did not do this, and indeed have no idea of who was responsible." He laughed again. "One popular theory is that rogue British elements are responsible." He grinned at the Countess. "Perhaps we can push that theory through your friend Karl? It would teach the British a lesson. That would be a splendid bonus!"

The Countess could barely contain her fury.

"What you have done is create international tension, and it looks like Liatoukine will become President, thanks to your turning him into a hero!"

The Baron was not concerned with her anger.

"The tension will blow over. You fail to see that many objectives have been achieved. We have neutralized a dangerous Russian nationalist. Did we need another Putin? And yes, Liatoukine will become President. The scrutiny he will be under will soon see him found out for what he is—and neutralized. There will be a renewed belief the supernatural—at the very least amongst the intelligence services. That will be invaluable in dealing with the remaining such creatures that exist."

"And what might be the consequences of all this? The ones we cannot foresee? We could have dealt with Liatoukine in time," the Countess said.

"In time?" the Baron looked incredulous. "We—and others—have spent years trying to eliminate Liatoukine, and have consistently failed. You saw what happened when Lady Ruthven took a shot at him. I knew it would fail, the point being to ensure everyone—especially Liatoukine—would think there was a threat against him, rather than Bezukhov. If Bezukhov had won, the vampire would have had even greater power. No, action had to be taken! He will be disposed of, very likely by his own countrymen. The GRU are not fond of him. He is beyond our reach, but not theirs. He can't mesmerize or kill them all. And when he is gone, Russia will be weakened. Let them try and interfere with our elections then!"

"You are wrong. You should be held to account," she replied, not accepting anything he said.

"For what? For defending Europe against Russia? I would be applauded as a hero. Further, although you voted against my plan, you and the others all knew about it. And without the resources of the group, I could not have achieved what I have. If there is any accounting in the way you think, you and all the others will go down with me. " He paused. "Perhaps it is time for new thinking at the top of our network."

The Countess looked at him. He was reckless. However, his plan had worked—on its own terms—so far.

"I think not. Good night, Baron."

With that, she strode off.

The Baron was pleased. He had no doubt his plan would continue to succeed. His fellow Hapsburgians in the EU parliament would be horrified by his actions if they knew—but he did not need them. The others in the Network would come round to him. With their support, he knew he could achieve much more.

Moscow, Election night, 17 March

Boris Liatoukine looked out onto the stage from the window of the room next to it. He would have to go out there very soon to address his supporters.

Natasha Rostova was in the room. For the last few minutes, they had been watching TV coverage of the final vote counting.

"They all think you are a hero," she said. "It's not every presidential candidate that tackles an assassin and suicide bomber."

"That is the only story that makes any sense," said Liatoukine. "However, whilst that is the current speculation, many aren't quite believing it. I spoke to my FSB contacts today. Whilst they are briefing the public that it was some kind of incendiary device that she had on, they themselves do not accept that as fact. They are pouring over this. The TV footage is repeated endlessly around the world, blurred and green tinted as it is. The world does not know what happened, and unfortunately, they are not going to brush it under the carpet either. They are determined to know. One theory is that I was responsible!"

"Not surprising," said Natasha. "The security devices in this room will block any listening devices—our team did find a couple earlier. Whether that is the usual sort of listening or something of greater interest, I cannot say."

"Oh, I am sure it was," he replied. "It has been made known to me that there will be a delay in providing me with the nuclear codes and so on. They claim to be updating systems. Perhaps they are. Such matters are in the hands of the GRU. Bezukhov leant towards them, and after that debate, I wonder if he knew something."

"I thought all the files of your old department were destroyed? You had seen to that?" Natasha asked.

"Those in the FSB and SVR[7], yes. Or rather I appropriated them. However, I had rather less influence in the GRU. Stalin had our Vampire City destroyed with an atomic device in 1953. It is not likely that the GRU had no information about that. I was kept out of that operation, but such information would be evidence of the supernatural. GRU, FSB, SVR, the western intelligence agencies. Eventually, they will put it all together. The discrepancies in my past will no longer be overlooked. The medical checks and so on. And what kind of Russian President tries to avoid the church as much as possible? My time is limited.

"The FSB and SVR insisted that the election should go ahead as planned, believing they can control me. However, they are looking very hard at the circumstances of the assassination. And if some supernatural files do still exist, they may no longer dismiss as them as lunacy."

"You could run," said Natasha.

"Like you plan to? I am aware of flights to London in your original name of 'Polly Bird' in a few days' time. Don't look so surprised; my FSB friends are always on the lookout for certain names I have given them. A bit sloppy, using that name?"

"I can be a bit nostalgic. Or rather, I had no time to create a new identity for myself," she replied.

"Do not concern yourself over it. You may leave; but I expect you to resign, saying that your job is over and you have had other offers. Not overly convincing, but rather better than you simply disappearing. As for me, running? No.

---

[7] The Foreign Intelligence Service of the Russian Federation, the external successor to the KGB

I will not run away. I doubt it would be possible now, anyway. After me, they would come after you."

"They will never catch me," Polly Bird replied.

Liatoukine's cellphone rang. He looked to see who was calling.

"Our friend, the Bolshevik Kuragin. I assume he is calling to concede defeat." He switched him off. "To Hell with him."

He looked up at the TV coverage. The figures on the screen were clear; he had won outright with 54% of the vote. There would not be a second round.

The crowd outside had seen the news. "Boris! Boris!" they were chanting. He walked out of the room. He strode by himself onto the wings of the stage and walked straight on. The crowd roared in a frenzy.

No, he would not run away. The impersonal forces of history had crushed the supernatural. And now, those same forces had come for him. He would face fate right in the eye. Whatever else, he had made his mark. For however short a time, he would be ruler of Russia. Now, he would tempt the fate that delivered him here, and to the Devil with the consequences.

"My friends!" he said to the crowd, "I am so pleased to have been elected your President. You know, they once called me 'Captain Vampire.' Well, now they can call me 'President Vampire'!"

For several years now, as with Brian Gallagher with Captain Vampire, Martin Gately has been building a corpus of stories featuring Gaston Leroux's indomitable journalist sleuth, Joseph Rouletabille. Usually, each story can be read independently, but this new tale is a direct sequel to the one published in last year's volume. The chronological sequence of the stories is "Rouletabille Rides the Horror Express" (TOTS 13, 1906), "Rouletabille at the Old Bailey" (TOTS 14, 1909), "Rouletabille and The House of Despair" (TOTS 15 & 16, 1909), "Leviathan Creek" (TOTS 8, 1916), "Rouletabille and The New World Order" (TOTS 11, 1926), "Rouletabille vs. The Cat" (TOTS 10, ditto), and finally, "Rouletabille on Mysterious Island" (TOTS 12, 1927).

Martin Gately: *Rouletabille and The House of Despair (2)* *(The Yellow Terror)*

London, Summer 1909

The great iron gate of Newgate Prison clanged shut behind Dr. Rupert Grierson making a sound eerily like that of a single toll from a lonely funeral bell. Before the resonance had died, Grierson showed his credentials to the guard and then was swiftly admitted to the inner courtyard. Grierson confidently assured the guard that he would be easily able to find his way to 'A' Wing North from previous visits, and would require no escorts. The guard recognized this little, bald-pated, gnome of a man to be a prominent medical practitioner—the head of Leytonstone House Asylum for the Criminally Insane, but his breadth of knowledge was insufficient to know that Grierson was also one of the foremost forensic psychiatrists in the country. He would therefore have been surprised to discover that Grierson's entry papers were complete forgeries, and he had no legitimate business to conduct within the geol. on this day. But the guard had no reason to suspect any of this, so he retreated back to his little wooden sentry box, where a chipped enamel mug of hot tea rested on the shelf, awaiting his return. He perched back on his stool, took a swig of tea, and then went back to reading the latest issue of the *Police Gazette*.

Grierson tramped his way up the steel stairway on the north side of the gloomy courtyard. He could see that the building work around the condemned cell area to repair the bomb damage was now largely complete. That was where he had made his abortive, and rather desperate attempt to free Schellenberger just before his execution. Schellenberger had been killed by the French journalist, Rouletabille, during the break-out. Grierson gave an audible bark of cynical laughter. It was quite plain now that this Frenchman was merely using his position within the fourth estate as a cover. He was obviously one of France's top intelligence operatives. Rouletabille's interference during Schellenberger's trial for the murder of his wife had proved fatal to Grierson's plan to have the killer certified insane. An insane man is not placed on the gallows, he is locked away in an asylum. And in this case, it would have been all too easy to make Leytonstone House Schellenberger's place of incarceration. Later, no-one would have known if the German had been replaced by a similar looking street derelict and spirited back to the Fatherland. Yes, Rouletabille had seemed dangerous from the very beginning—his deductive reasoning matched, or perhaps even exceeded that of the legendary *Great Men of Baker Street*—those four consulting detectives who had now been joined by the irritating American neophyte, Harry Dickson. Dickson too had become embroiled in the Schellenberger affair at an even earlier stage than Rouletabille, since the American had been hired by Frau Schellenberger to investigate her husband's odd behavior. The reason for his odd behavior was simple enough, Schellenberger was a German spy tasked with finding out as much technical information as possible about the new British triplane being tested out on the military proving grounds of the Wanstead Flatlands.

And so, the German spy neglected his wife and his job—and was ultimately forced to murder his spouse when she revealed she had put a Baker Street detective on his trail, such sleuths were infamous for their close contact, nay allegiance, with the upper echelons of the British Government. Schellenberger then fell back on a standing protocol used by his spy ring: when the authorities are closing in, feign insanity. He beat Reginald Scott, the owner of the fruit and vegetable stall where he sometimes worked, to death in the *Salmon and Ball* pub in front of witnesses, and also killed Edward Cookson, an acquaintance after spreading rumors that the man was having an affair with Frau Schellenberger. In the end, it was perhaps Schellenberger's own over cleverness which carried him to the gallows. No madman would be able to think of procuring a weather balloon and using it to carry off the dismembered remains of his murdered wife. On this point the Old Bailey jury had agreed with Rouletabille—especially after the brilliant young French detective calculated the likely landing area of the balloon and had its shredded remnants and bloody cargo recovered by his colleagues in the International News Service bureau in the Netherlands. Yes, without the involvement of Rouletabille and Dickson things would have looked very different.

Grierson reached the North Wing and the heavy door was opened by a prison officer to admit him to the landing. After an even more cursory check of his documents he was directed to Cell 19, where Klaus Eschmann was incarcerated. The prison officer opened the small metal viewing slot near the top of the door and called through.

"Visitor for you, Eschmann."

The only response was an animalistic grunt.

The door swung open and Grierson entered without hesitation. He looked Eschmann up and down, insofar as was possible in the gloom of the cell. He seemed like he had lost even more weight—his skin was tight across the bones of his face. Yet still, it was obvious the man was highly dangerous. It was so very apparent to Grierson who had seen many caged men that this specimen would kill to escape the moment the opportunity presented itself.

"I hope you have good news for me," rasped the prisoner.

"A point of culmination has been reached. The mission of your team—the mission you failed to complete, will soon be brought to a suitable conclusion by two individuals I have corrupted. They are very close to the *Yellow Terror*—closer than your agents with their note books and stopwatches, making futile attempts trying to ascertain the plane's secrets from hundreds of yards away by means of schoolboyish observation."

"Have a care, Grierson. I am well thought of by our superiors, my long history of covert action against the Fatherland's enemies speaks for itself. You know it is true or you would not be here. Now what are your orders?"

"Naturally, I am to help you escape. You are to be broken out of prison before you stand trial," said Grierson.

"Well then, I hope that you are of greater assistance to me than you were to Schellenberger. Personally, I can't think of a more idiotic plan than trying to rescue someone from jail a split-second before they were due to be executed."

"It was a daring plan, and it would have worked but for the interference of Rouletabille and Dickson. The former is a dangerous genius, and the latter a young bumbler with the luck of Satan himself," said Grierson.

"What have you done to ensure that the genius and the bumbler are well and truly out of the picture?"

"It has not been easy. If I had taken direct action against Harry Dickson—had him killed—it would immediately have attracted the involvement of the *Great Men of Baker Street* en masse. Can you imagine such a situation? They would have descended on us like enraged furies to take vengeance on whosoever had harmed their protégé. Instead, I neutralized Dickson by placing him in the tender care of a woman I believed to be one of my top operatives—Judith Fraser, also known as *Vinegar Judy*. I had previously schooled her extensively in the practice of hypnosis. And so, with the American kept permanently half-drugged with a mild scopolamine derivative it was possible to use hypnotic suggestion to prevent him from recalling his relationship with Rouletabille. This state of affairs continued for some weeks, and perhaps I was overoptimistic in thinking that it would remain the case until the conclusion of the espionage mission," said Grierson.

"I expect your so-called 'bumbler' broke through the wall of his hypnotic conditioning."

"That would have almost have been too predictable. No, Dickson's salvation came from a rather more unexpected quarter. I arrived at Dickson's Baker Street lodgings one afternoon to find that his temporary housekeeper had gotten the better of *Vinegar Judy* in a rather brutal physical confrontation. She must have given herself away through some inadvertent slip, possibly while administering a dose of the drug. I could not see any way to rescue Miss Fraser inconspicuously from Dickson's rooms without placing myself in severe danger of arrest. I therefore drew my repeating air pistol and shot the girl once in each eye, before retreating out of the front door and hailing the nearest hansom cab. I had hoped to prevent her from revealing anything during interrogation. But only today I discovered that a surgeon at Marylebone Hospital had served her life, though not her sight. It can only be a matter of time now before she recovers sufficiently to tell everything she knows," concluded Grierson.

"Your catalogue of incompetence grows ever longer. To be honest, I am having difficulty keeping track. But if you could not stymie the bumbler, I daresay the 'genius' Rouletabille was able to outwit you. Pray, what became of him?" asked Eschmann.

"I had another of my female agents drug Rouletabille while he was at large in an East End pub conducting his investigations. The drug induced symptoms similar to the sudden onset of psychosis. So while he raved and foamed at the mouth, my men were called from Leytonstone Asylum to cart the lunatic away. He had only been incarcerated in the asylum for a few hours when he almost managed to escape. I ordered him restrained in a straitjacket, and he escaped the straitjacket twice. The second time he absconded from the grounds completely, though precisely by what means I am yet to discover. If I did not know better, I would suspect that he had assistance from someone within the asylum. Yet I am sure none of my men would risk such a betrayal—they all know the medical interventions I have planned for those who dare to oppose me," said Grierson.

"I shall not bank too heavily on being rescued by your machinations, Grierson. I would be better advised to steal a spoon from the refectory and commence digging a tunnel.

"Your sarcasm is understandable, but misplaced. We are arriving at the end game, the final reckoning. Before very long, all of the secrets of *The Yellow Terror* will be ours, and you, my friend will be back in your beloved Berlin—making plans for that technological hierarchy which you are so keen to see running the world. The zenith of my achievement will be the final destruction of Rouletabille and Harry Dickson. They will be drawn to their doom by the single thing they cannot resist—an impossible mystery. Already the trap is primed, and once it is sprung, we will see not only the end of this pair of nauseating meddlers, but of all of the *Great Men of Baker Street* too," said Grierson.

Eschmann looked hard at Grierson's face. Yes, there was confidence written upon it. But the eyes stared a little too wildly, the grin was inhuman—almost shark-like. Grierson's reputation as an infallible master-planner had taken some near-fatal hammer blows since he went up against these two young men. He did not doubt that Grierson was capable of anything, and was also fired up to get the better of adversaries he had underestimated. Yet, Eschmann wondered at Grierson's levels of mental resilience—knock back and frustration at his defeats had affected him. And would it not be a supreme irony if a man in charge of an insane asylum was tipped over into insanity himself?

Inspector Hopkins approached the door of Theydon Grange House's little lodge keeper's cottage with some trepidation. He knew that Joseph Rouletabille and Harry Dickson were now fully recovered and impatient for action. He used the knocker to rap loudly, and within a few seconds the door swung open. Mrs. Bardell's face broke into a welcoming grin as she recognized the veteran Scotland Yard detective who has assisted Sherlock Holmes himself in the *Case of the Three Music Boxes*. She showed him into the cottage, which was filled with a most delicious aroma of baking. Bread, cakes and sausage pie were Mrs. Bardell's particular areas of expertise. In the small sitting room, Rouletabille was in an easy chair gorging himself on a great slice of chocolate cake. The gauntness caused by his imprisonment in the asylum had now vanished, and the roses had returned to his cheeks. Harry Dickson was neglecting a great slab of steaming hot sausage pie which was sitting on a plate on the dining table. Instead, he was sawing off the long barrel of a shotgun with a hacksaw he had purloined from the garden tool shed, in order to make it into a more effective close-quarters weapon. Hopkins looked on this activity with growing horror.

"Good God, Harry! That's one of the Lord Chancellor's Purdey shotguns. Have you any idea how much those things cost?" asked the Scotland Yard man.

"Nope. And I don't care. We're spoiling for a fight and hit by cabin fever. When are we going to raid the asylum and grab hold of Grierson?" demanded the American.

"When Special Branch executes warrants to search Leytonstone House and arrest the offenders within, I'm sure you will be informed. But as a private citizen with an interest in the matter you most certainly will not be invited to participate. Nor will you be allowed to take possession of other people's firearms," said Hopkins, assertively relieving Dickson of the sawn-off shotgun.

"You know I am perhaps not so hot-headed as my American friend," began Rouletabille. "But this long delay is equally incomprehensible to me. Why is Dr. Grierson allowed to retain his liberty when we know that he is an agent of a hostile foreign power? Even if you do not believe that, he unlawfully imprisoned me and attempted to kill Miss Judith Fraser."

"Grierson is being kept under extremely close surveillance. Why just today he was followed when he made a visit to Newgate Prison to see Klaus Eschmann," said Hopkins.

"And what more proof do you need? Eschmann is to stand trial for espionage at the Old Bailey later this month," barked Dickson.

"His guilt has not yet been established. And a state of war does not yet exist between England and Germany…perhaps it never will. For the purposes of diplomacy we must tread carefully and avoid exacerbating the situation," said Hopkins.

"If Grierson has been to see Eschmann it can only be because he intends to break him out just as he tried to do with Schellenberger," said the Frenchman. "We foiled him before and we must stand ready to do so again."

"The primary reason for holding off action against Grierson is that the remnants of the Schellenberger spy ring are still at large. We have no idea where they are. But, if he makes a move to contact them, we can round the lot of them up. At the moment, no one has come near the secret AVRO workshops close to here on the Wanstead Flatlands in the way that Schellenberger and Eschmann did," said Hopkins.

"They have merely changed their tactics. They'll be lurking around here somewhere…," said Dickson.

And then Rouletabille realized that he had been struck with a sudden headache. He had suffered from these a lot since his escape from the asylum. Somehow, it was the mention of the AVRO workshops that had brought it on. He had thought that all of his memory had come back to him in a flood—but this was not entirely true. Something was still being held back, and he was not sure what. Something had happened to him immediately after his escape. After he had said goodbye to the boy, Alfie, and trying to bring it to mind was like trying to grasp wisps of smoke. Every time it eluded him and sent a knitting needle of pain probing into his frontal lobes.

A few hundred yards away, Captain Oliver Treadwell arrived at Theydon Grange House and pulled hard on the doorbell. The eagle-eyed would have noticed that Captain Treadwell's smart Royal Engineers' uniform bore an unusual shoulder flash—a modest black badge with red lettering bearing the legend 'Pilot.' Treadwell was one of handful in that vanguard of officers who were learning to fly in the British armed forces. In the years, and then decades, to come, that cadre of officers would become the Royal Flying Corps, before finally taking pride of place as the Royal Air Force. But right here was their point of genesis, brave, yet inexperienced men testing the limits and capabilities of highly experimental aircraft built in the wake of the Wright Brothers' triumph at Kitty Hawk, North Carolina. Naturally, such dashing and valorous men were almost irresistible to women, especially perhaps to the daughters of judges raised in the rarified atmosphere of the Lord Chancellor's judicial lodgings within the Snaresbrook Crown Court Campus.

The door swung open and a beauteous vision met Treadwell's eyes. This was his fiancé, Berenice Munro, the only daughter of His Honor Judge Aloysius Munro, that ogre of the assizes who ate inexperienced young barristers for his breakfast, yet had taken such a shine to this handsome captain. She practically dragged him inside the hallway and after a quick look behind her to see that no servants were in sight she delivered an intimate and arousing kiss. And while she could've easily done the same within the comparative privacy of the drawing room, part of the thrill was the possibility of discovery.

"Surely, you do not wish your father to happen upon us and think that I'm here to take your virginity before our wedding night!" chided the young captain.

The girl laughed coquettishly.

"Since we are to be married in less than a month, it would hardly seem to matter what anyone thinks. Besides, I would hear the creaking of my father's wheelchair a mile off, and I know for sure that he is locked away in his study reading the case papers for that awful murder trial he is presiding over next week."

They moved into the sitting room where her slim hands moved to his waistband and began to unbuckle his belt. At this, he lost his temper and slapped away her hand.

"Cool your ardor, my dear. You are like a bitch in heat," said Treadwell.

Berenice dropped herself onto the couch in mock anger and crossed her arms, her desires frustrated for now.

"Very well. I suppose you want to talk about that silly little toy aeroplane of yours instead," said the girl.

"The Empire's greatest and most secret weapon is hardly a toy. There was a nasty cross-wind over the Hackney Marshes this afternoon, and I nearly ended up in the sewage treatment works, instead of my refueling stop near the cricket pitch. I daresay I'd have been court-martialed for damaging government property, but if I'd splashed into that noisome morass I'd probably still carry the stench, and that might be enough to keep even you away!" said Treadwell.

"You may be sure of it. I'd have had Jenkins the gardener hose you down in the yard before you were admitted," teased the girl. "But whatever is the point of all this? I hear the interminable drone of your engine overhead...I hear the clatter of your dismal guns as you reach the proving grounds—typically disturbing my afternoon nap. And the next day it's the same. Will you be testing the plane here forever? I, for one, certainly hope so. I have no desire for you to be posted elsewhere following our marriage. I would get so...lonely."

"There are some things which must remain secret. As it is, I tell you far more than I should. Let's just say that I will be around here for at least a little while longer. And now, before you call for tea in the conservatory, I really must pay some attention to your dear mama. I have been rather neglecting her of late. Is she upstairs in her room?" asked the young officer.

"Of course, the old dear is suffering dreadfully with her hay fever. She sniffles and sniffles both day and night. I will be the most enormous relief to her when summer is over. What a martyr she is..."

Treadwell ascended the stairs and on the landing encountered another of the young beauties closeted away in the judicial lodgings, Lara Haining, the younger child of His Honor Judge Thomas Haining, her elder sister had just recently married and she was beginning to find life on the Snaresbrook Crown Court campus stifling and isolating. She was a pleasant enough to him, but she could be haughty and aloof when the mood took her. A keen horsewoman, he often saw her exercising her mare on the Wanstead Flats while he was piloting his plane. There was something rather unobtainable and imperious about her, he mused for a moment that the chase had been rather too easy with Berenice. Perhaps he had gone after the wrong girl, though there was little he could do about it now, gentlemen were still sued sometimes for breach of promise when they failed to follow through on their stated intention to marry a young lady.

Lara put her fingers to her lips.

"You'd best be quiet up here, Captain. My father has just reprimanded me for disturbing him while he was studying papers for his new Old Bailey case."

"I was just going into see Berenice's mother, and wish her well. Why don't you join us in the conservatory for tea in a few minutes?" he more or less whispered.

"Yes, I'll be down shortly," she confirmed.

He moved silently down the corridor and rapped ever so gently on the third door he came to. A quiet feminine voice asked him to identify himself and when he did he was bade to enter.

Treadwell entered Mrs. Munro's bedchamber and could not help but smile. Berenice often made reference to her mother as if she were an old woman, while, in fact, she was barely forty, and looked much younger. Her youth had somehow been mysteriously preserved, she was just as vibrant and lovely as her daughter. A pang of illicit desire rose within him and he quashed it, this was no time for dalliance, but there was always time for flirtation.

"How lovely to see you again, Oliver," said Mrs. Munro, huskily, her throat much affected by the terrible hay fever which always afflicted her at this time of year.

"And you are looking as radiant as ever," he flattered. Though, in truth, it was the bedchamber in which the woman lay which seemed radiant. It was illuminated by every conceivable means, a cluster of incandescent bulbs in a newly installed modern style chandelier on the ceiling, the flickering gas lamps on the walls as well as a host of candles. The room seemed as bright as it did in daytime, light from those various sources seemed to bounce off the multiplicity of mirrors, including the enormous gold framed one which hung over the marital bed.

"Sit down a moment, why don't you?" urged Mrs. Munro, patting the side of her bed. He needed no further encouragement and placed himself down on the edge of the bed. Now there was the usual fight he had with himself to look into her remarkable hazel eyes instead of at the contents of her extraordinarily sheer negligee. Her full breasts were exactly like those immortalized in those rather filthy dog-eared French lithographs which were constantly being re-circulated around the barracks back when he was a cadet.

"I wanted to ask if you were feeling well enough to join us in the conservatory for tea," said Treadwell.

Mrs. Munro's hand strayed onto his thigh. His whole body tensed. Now was not the time...now was not the time. His inappropriate dalliances with his future mother-in-law could not be discovered now, that would ruin everything. He was struck by a powerful premonition that as soon as his finger tips caressed Mrs. Munro they would be walked in on. His mind played out in vivid detail the embarrassing aftermath of such an occurrence, and Mrs. Munro interpreted his sudden qualms as a lack of interest; the expression on the older woman's beautiful face hardened somewhat.

"If it is my daughter you wish to be with then go to her."

"Only if you are sure you do not desire to join us," he said.

She kicked back the bedclothes suddenly and rather lasciviously, revealing her long legs as well as the fact that the action had caused her negligee to ride all the way up her smooth flat belly. She was exquisite.

"I cannot imagine you will find anything of greater interest on offer in our conservatory. But if you do, then I am disappointed," she chided, waspishly.

The display had been crass and unladylike, yet monstrously tempting.

He got up to leave.

"Do not pursue me onto the landing and create a scene. Judge Haining is hard at work reading his papers," said Treadwell.

A few minutes later in the conservatory, the Earl Grey tea had been poured and Berenice was sitting with arms tightly folded, unappreciative of the presence of Lara Haining. But now that he was back downstairs Treadwell was starting to feel more relaxed. While Berenice stared out of the window into the darkening garden, his mind wandered too. He was a slave to his own desires, he wanted to strip practically every woman he met of both clothing and inhibitions. He wished to could somehow hypnotize both Lara and Berenice and make love to them both right now, wiping clean their recollection afterwards like a wet sponge across a slate. Such feelings had grown and grown in him recently, like some kind of weird addiction. And the more he tried to satiate them the more they increased.

From somewhere outside and faraway came a persistent whine. It was the sound of a straining engine.

"That sounds like the noise of your...," began Berenice.

Immediately Treadwell cut her off.

"It can't be...it just can't be," he got up suddenly and then stood stock still, waiting, listening. Then came the clatter of machinegun fire, and the high caliber bullets started to rain down on the house.

Inspector Hopkins almost battered down the door of the lodge cottage, fortunately Mrs. Bardell unlatched the portal before his fists burst through the wood.

"C'mon, you two! If ever you were needed it is now," shouted Hopkins. "Get your coats and hurry. You must have heard the shots!"

Although it was not late, Rouletabille was laying on his bed resting. Dickson was smoking in the living room and reading a Dickens novel. Perhaps this would not be the precise clarion call to action they had desired, for they were both desperate to participate in a raid on the insane asylum. But they had been cooped up in the cottage for so long that any diversion was a blessed release.

Rouletabille skidded to a halt at the bottom of the stairs and demanded to know what had happened.

"It's the AVRO experimental plane—*The Yellow Terror*. We thought it had been stolen since not ten minutes ago Theydon Grange House was attacked from the air, and Judge Haining killed. But the Special Branch officers guarding it have just told me that the plane is still in its workshop-hangar," explained Hopkins. "There is no other plane in England armed with machine guns. How did the perpetrators steal *The Yellow Terror* and replace it without being discovered?"

"If you are certain of this plane's uniqueness, then that is a mystery indeed," said Rouletabille. "Fortunately, impossible mysteries are our trade."

Outside the Gatekeeper's lodge cottage were two armed constables with bull's eye lanterns. They guided Rouletabille and Dickson through the gloom to the far side of the Crown Court campus towards Theydon House, with Hopkins dragging along behind. Truly, the two foreign detectives were in their element— like a pair of terriers being led to a rats' nest. As they walked they reminded each other in hushed tones that a man had died, and after that their levity became muted; their mood deliberately made somber. Nevertheless, it was a blessed relief to be outdoors in the warm summer night and away Mrs. Bardell's rather stifling benevolent supervision.

As they neared the rather grandiose regency dwelling that was the Judges' lodgings the two constables shone their lamps onto the upper storey to pick out the damage they had seen earlier. It was evident that the bricks and rendering around one of the bedroom windows had been hit by a volley a high caliber bullets - deep, precisely circular pockmarks abounded. The glass and mullions of the window itself had also been struck. Hardly any glass remained, and a dark green curtain flapped occasionally in the breeze, like a restless spirit.

Without further ado, Hopkins led them directly upstairs to the scene of the murder while the two constables stood guard outside. Their eyes began drinking in every detail from the moment they crossed the threshold. Every scintilla of information would be absorbed and cross-referenced by Rouletabille's extraordinarily analytical mind, and this made Dickson feel slightly competitive. The Frenchman had solved numerous mysteries and had well and truly made his name in the annals of detection. While he was under the wing of *The Great Men of Baker Street* he also had to become 'his own man'—and perhaps this was the case in which he would be fully able to demonstrate his acumen, especially if he could beat his friend, Rouletabille, to the punch. But when Dickson found himself starting to visualize newspaper headlines celebrating his success he was forced to rein himself in—now was not the time for counting his chickens, there was work to be done.

The two detectives stood in the doorway to Judge Haining's combined study and bedroom and surveyed the scene. The body had been covered by a spare sheet, and the still fresh blood had soaked through in numerous crimson patches that were even now trying to amalgamate themselves into a single awful stain. The Frenchman's keen eyes scanned the floor of the room and settled on a scuffed area of partially coagulated blood over by the desk.

"What has been removed from the floor over there, Inspector?" he asked, pointing.

"The Judge was reading confidential case papers for his forthcoming trial at the Old Bailey," replied Hopkins. "They were dropped to the floor during the attack, and ruined by the amount of blood that was over them. I picked them up and disposed of them in the basement incinerator."

"Nothing should have been removed from the room before our arrival - Nothing!" rebuked Rouletabille in hushed tones.

For another ten minutes, Rouletabille examined everything in the room— the carpets, the furniture, bullet strikes on the internal walls, and most particularly, the bloodstains and spattering of blood. Dickson was no slouch at detective work, but here he learned, as if at the feet of a master, lessons he would remember for the rest of his life. Finally, Rouletabille announced that he was ready to meet residents of the house (not servants) who had been present during the attack. Hopkins informed Rouletabille that Lara Haining, the judge's daughter, had been in such deep shock she'd had to be sedated. Judge Munro's wife, Adelaide, was in a state of extreme hysteria—due to a bullet passing through an internal wall and hitting the chandelier in her bedroom. She had refused sedation and was currently being comforted by her husband. This left available for interview the couple's daughter, Berenice, and her fiancé, Captain Oliver Treadwell, who was also - by coincidence—the test pilot of *The Yellow Terror*. In fact, this suited Rouletabille, because though it was of primary importance to interview these firsthand witnesses, he was extremely impatient to get to the 'real' scene of this impossible crime—the nearby railway arch workshops from which the aeroplane had been stolen and then returned without raising the suspicions of the uniformed Special Branch officers assigned to guard it.

Inspector Hopkins ushered Rouletabille and Dickson into the conservatory where Miss Munro and Treadwell were waiting. Her face was tearstained, and his pale and bloodless. Hopkins explained to the traumatized couple that these two private detectives had been temporarily seconded to Scotland Yard's Special Branch.

Dickson utilized his gentle charm to put them at their ease and then encouraged them to relate exactly what had happened.

"We were sitting here with Lara just about to have tea," began Berenice. "When suddenly I heard the sound of the plane's engine, but it was much louder and much closer than it normally is. Usually, it's just a far off whine."

"And I was perhaps even more shocked when we heard *The Yellow Terror's motor,* for I know I am currently the only person authorized to pilot it," stated Treadwell.

"And to fly it presumably takes a great deal of skill?" asked Rouletabille, somewhat rhetorically.

"Why, yes. I suppose this is not the time for false modesty. It is a tricky beast to fly. It takes some practice, particularly because it is easily blown off a precise trajectory by crosswinds," said Treadwell. "And the thing is, I would balk at flying it in twilight or nighttime conditions, but that is precisely what the pilot who has stolen it has done."

"What is so unusual about this plane? What makes it so secret?" asked Harry Dickson.

"Am I allowed to reveal technical details to these two foreign gentlemen?" asked Treadwell.

"You are," said Hopkins. "I have written authority from Whitehall which allows them access to all secret information relating to the German spy ring…and in my estimation this murder and the espionage case are inextricably connected."

"Very well then, *The Yellow Terror* has twin front mounted machine guns which fire *through* its propeller. This allows the pilot unparalleled ability to aim, and then shoot with pinpoint accuracy. After the attack I ran outside and it was obvious to me that only *The Yellow Terror* could have fired on the house with quite such accuracy. Most of the shots hit the Judge's window or the area of brickwork just around it," said Treadwell.

"So you actually saw the aeroplane still above the house?" asked Rouletabille.

"No, not really. It had pulled up and was starting to execute its turn— already quite a long way away. But Miss Munro did see it too," replied Treadwell.

"Yes, I did. And I could still hear its engine quite clearly," she said. "I was very worried it would return, but it just kept on drifting away."

"Something should be done immediately about the men who say that the plane was never stolen, for that is quite impossible," demanded Treadwell. "They must be in league with the German spy ring. That plane could only have been stolen and returned by an expert pilot. And there is absolutely no way to remove it from the workshop hangar, let alone replace it, without someone outside noticing."

"It is certainly pretty darn perplexing," said Dickson. "I guess we'd better go and see for ourselves."

Dickson hastily concluded the diagram of the house and environs he has been drawing in pencil in his notebook. He noted that the plane had approached from the west, and that the conservatory was built onto the eastern side of the house.

As they left, Rouletabille whispered to Dickson, "We are not done here by a long way. I have an instinct that we should return to search the bedroom of the hysterical Mrs. Munro. Something is not right here."

Hopkins and his two uniformed officers led Rouletabille and Dickson beyond the confines of the grounds of Theydon Grange House for the first time in a few weeks down towards the railway embankment a few hundred yards away where *The Yellow Terror's* hangar had been constructed inside a large brick archway which was part of the support structure for the railway above. It was a common in London for the spare space in a bridge or embankment to be utilized by local businesses in this way—nearer to London there were car repair garages or machine shops housed in railway arches, and on the approach to the country it was sometimes a blacksmith's forge. Typically the railway arch was bricked up at the far end, and a set of wooden or steel doors fitted at the remaining opening. Additional ventilation or chimneys were added as required. The uniformed officers' bull's eye lamps illuminated the locked steel doors upon which were painted in letters almost ten feet high the legend 'AVRO'—short for A.V. Roe, the embryonic aviation company which would one day go on to become a major force in the world of aircraft construction.

"The workshop has been left unguarded," judged Rouletabille as he strode forward. "Let us try to imagine how the miscreants were able to remove the plane from the archway without alerting the watching officers."

"Have a care, m'sieur," warned Hopkins. "You take your life in your hands by approaching this facility unannounced. It is indeed guarded, by my fellow Special Branch officers, and they have instructions to open fire on anyone who is not known to them personally."

Rouletabille was aghast, but now he saw there were figures in the shadows of railway embankment archways, and lurking in the undergrowth, as well as in the shelter of nearby trees. There were perhaps seven men in all, and they were all armed with heavy Webley revolvers.

Then Hopkins raised his voice and shouted, "This is Inspector Hopkins with constables Willis and Matthews. Also with us are two private detectives seconded to Special Branch: Joseph Rouletabille and Harry Dickson. Please allow us to approach."

The men guarding the AVRO workshop stepped out from cover and holstered their weapons.

"Get the doors opened quickly," ordered Rouletabille. "There may be some trick or illusion in place, making it look as if the plane is in the workshop, when in reality, it has been stolen."

At a nod from Hopkins, Rouletabille was obeyed and the great doors swung open. Inside, *The Yellow Terror* was most definitely still in its home. The tri-plane was delicately constructed, yet it looked positively vespine in its yellow and black painted livery—a lethal and gargantuan wasp ready to spew forth death. Instinctively, Harry Dickson put his hand to the barrels of the machine guns and then onto the engine housing.

"Cold," said Dickson. "The plane hasn't been used for hours, and the machineguns have not been fired."

"I suppose that could be achieved by means of deception," mused the French detective. "Perhaps cold, wet rags could've been applied to the engine cowling and the barrels of the guns."

"I am more interested in how the plane was removed," said Dickson. "We need to check if an aperture has been created at the rear of the railway arch—maybe all the bricks were cut away and then replaced. It wouldn't be possible to do that without leaving at least some sign, surely?"

But the two men looked for such an opening without success. More out of desperation than conviction, Dickson suggested that the railway ties above the workshop had been removed and the plane craned out of its home. This caused a little confusion because in England railway ties are known as 'sleepers.' Nevertheless, whatever you call them, a close examination of them—following a climb to the top of the embankment by all of the investigators—found no indication at all that they had been removed and replaced.

"All these men guarding the workshop hangar could not be in the employ of a foreign power," ruminated the Frenchman. "That would be ridiculous. And yet not one of them saw the tri-plane removed. However it was removed there would have been some sign...some noise. To do the job invisibly and inaudibly it is either the work of phantoms or angels."

"What if each of them had a relative or loved one held hostage by this gang of Teutonic spies?" wondered Dickson. "They could have been compelled to assist by means of blackmail."

"And what would be the point? If you wish to steal an experimental plane, then why not just steal it? Why use it to commit a murder and then replace it as if nothing has happened? Who exactly were they trying to fool?" questioned Rouletabille, almost ranting.

"Can we even be sure that this is the real *Yellow Terror?*" asked Dickson. "If it is merely a good facsimile how could we know? We need Captain Treadwell to take it aloft and test it out in the morning, to see if it handles and performs exactly the same as the genuine tri-plane."

"If a burglar breaks into your house and replaces all of your possessions with exact duplicates, are you the victim of a crime or not? Is the perpetrator a criminal genius or a performance artist?" laughed Rouletabille hollowly. "This is a similar conundrum, my friend. This unique vehicle is used as a murder weapon in circumstances that are quite literally impossible. My head is starting to hurt—and I do not mean that metaphorically—it does not hurt from the effort of thinking, but rather because something is gnawing away at the inside of it. Painful thoughts and recollections summoned up by the plane itself...I am reminded of the torture I suffered at the hands of Dr. Grierson, and parlous mental state in which I found myself in the aftermath of my escape from the asylum. Something from that time still eludes me. There is a memory that would make sense of this whole narrative if only I could access it."

"Come now, we have taken this as far as we can tonight, surely. Let us return to the Lodge Keeper's Cottage and rest," advised Dickson.

Rouletabille had anticipated that he would wake up early the following day, at the first crack of dawn. He surprised was when he picked up his borrowed pocket watch from the bedside table to find that it was five minutes after nine. Mrs. Bardell had allowed him to sleep in, and the delicious aroma of frying bacon was wafting up from the kitchen. He took his dressing gown from the back of the door, pulled it on and padded down the stairs.

"Good morning, Mrs. Bardell," called Rouletabille cheerily, as he looked about the cottage. "Where is Harry?"

"Oh, he made himself some toast hours ago, and then went out for a walk. I think he was just going to Theydon Grange," said Mrs. Bardell.

The Frenchman was not entirely sure what to make of this. Had Harry decided to solve the case on his own, or was he just giving Rouletabille additional opportunity to rest? Either way, he had enjoyed the extra couple of hours sleep. The nocturnal ramble to the railway arches had taken more out of him than he really wanted to admit. He took a leisurely breakfast, followed by a long soaking bath on the basis that this mystery was not the sort that would take flight and elude him. No, its various constituent components were anchored here in the court buildings, their environs and a comparatively small envelope of the surrounding countryside.

The day was already very warm as Rouletabille set off on the short walk to Theydon Grange House from the cottage. The machinegun damage to the side of the house seemed somehow worse in the day time, and a carpenter was just arriving to board up the window. The police must've felt that all of the available clues had been identified. Although neither of the two uniformed constables guarding the property had seen Rouletabille before, they had a clipboard upon which was a typed a list of people with permission to enter the house, and he was gratified to find that his name was third on the list after Inspector Hopkins and Harry Dickson.

Once inside he went straight to the conservatory on the far side of the house which was where the occupants seemed to congregate and drink their tea. There he found only Berenice Munro—her face pale and tear-streaked. And while he had very little to go on, it did not seem to him that her suppressed sobs were being caused by the death of Judge Haining. Some other force was at play here.

"Hello Miss, I am very sorry to intrude," began Rouletabille. "Is my American associate, Mr. Harry Dickson, here in the house?"

She took a moment to compose herself and then said, "Yes, he is upstairs, examining where the bullet went through the wall of my mother's room."

"Then your mother is with him?" asked Rouletabille.

Miss Munro had to force from her mind the image that was so powerfully scorched there. The image of what she had seen when she suddenly walked into her mother's boudoir, and found her mother engaged in a shameless and filthy act with Captain Treadwell. Her mother had fled the house almost immediately upon discovery leaving the Royal Engineers Officer to refasten himself and mouth hollow apologies. It was strange that she might never see her mother again. Even stranger that she would never kiss her, and had no desire so to do.

"My mother has gone. Somehow I doubt if she will ever return. My father does not yet know his marriage is over. He went to his chambers early to study the papers for the case he's had to take over from Judge Haining."

Then anticipating the Frenchman's next question she said with some venom, "Captain Treadwell is not here. He is no longer my fiancé, and I have no interest in his whereabouts."

And with that she threw herself down on the conservatory's chaise longue and emitted a maelstrom of howling sobs such as Rouletabille had never heard. He withdrew.

Upstairs in Mrs. Munro's bedroom, Harry Dickson had turned on the electric light, lit all of the myriad oil lamps and was examining the great mirror which hung over the head of the bed and a slightly odd angle, as is tipped forward. Upon even closer examination he noticed it was the surface of the wall itself that had been built at the strange angle.

"She liked it very bright in here. I wonder why?" said Rouletabille, looking around. His eyes lighted on the dressing table and he walked over and yanked open one of the drawers. He was taken aback to find drug taking paraphernalia hidden beneath a small, neatly folded pile of lace handkerchiefs.

"I am forced to make the conclusion that Mrs. Munro is a hopeless cocaine addict," said Rouletabille. "A strange state of affairs for a judge's wife. She was caught *in flagrante delicto* with Captain Treadwell, and that is doubtless the only reason the equipment and powder is still here. In her haste she fled without it."

"What do you make of the mirror over the bed?" asked Dickson. "Why is it at that weird angle?"

"Let's see, shall we?"

Rouletabille picked up the poker from the small fireplace and wielded it like a sword at the mirror. The glass immediately started to break apart, and some of the jagged reflective dagger-like fragments fell down onto the cotton sheets of the bed, while others dropped noisily to the floor of the secret space - too small, surely, to be called a room—which was hidden behind the mirror.

Gingerly, Dickson stepped up onto the bed doing his best to avoid the glass.

"Yes, it's a moving picture camera, angled to be able to film whoever was in the bed. There's not really enough space for a cameraman. Oh, I see. There's a concealed switch allowing her to activate the camera from within the bed," said Dickson.

"And so, what we thought was merely a lodging place for itinerant judges for this legal term is instead a den of debauchery and corruption. Blackmail too must be part of the equation, with Treadwell as the victim," decided Rouletabille.

"Treadwell's involvement links it back to *The Yellow Terror*. There is only one villain of this piece, and that is Grierson—all roads lead to him," said Dickson. "To control the pilot of *The Yellow Terror* is to control the machine itself."

"Where is Inspector Hopkins?" asked Rouletabille. "We must tell him what we have discovered here and what it has led us to suspect."

"I saw him here first thing this morning, but he has gone now to make the arrangements for the Eschmann trial. The trial will take place here at Snarebrook Crown Court instead of the Old Bailey," explained Dickson.

"Why? Why is that?" demanded the Frenchman, suddenly horrified.

"Well, the trial is now allocated to Judge Munro following the death of Judge Haining, and this is his primary residence. It's all easier for him here because he is wheelchair bound."

"My God, the pieces of the puzzle have finally dropped into place. What incredible arrogance Grierson has to think we would not see through his plans. And the appalling sleight of hand distraction he planned for us—that whole business of *The Yellow Terror* being stolen and impossibly returned all seems so transparent now."

"Is it? Well then I sure wish you'd explain it to me," laughed the American.

"The 'impossible' mystery concerning the theft of the aeroplane was merely flypaper. We were supposed to devote all of our time and mental energy to solving a conundrum that did not, in fact, have any substance to it at all."

"Well, I guess the removal and return of the plane did bother me from the first. Captain Treadwell was *The Yellow Terror's* test pilot. He must've logged dozens of hours flying over the flatlands and testing the weapons. But he was also hesitant to fly at night, and thought it was a tricky beast to keep in the air. Also, he was present here in the conservatory during the attack which killed Judge Haining, so he can hardly have been the one who piloted the stolen plane. Even if he is being blackmailed he must be innocent of the murder," reasoned Dickson.

Rouletabille creased his face and momentarily shut his eyes as he tried to summon up every fact, every contradictory impression connected with this affair and assemble them into something resembling the truth.

"My friend, that is not true. I strongly suspect that he is guilty of that murder—I just cannot prove it—yet. Don't forget how he insistently led the women to the conservatory for tea. The conservatory is precisely on the opposite side of the dwelling to Judge Haining's bedroom study. Treadwell knew of the attack and was attempting to take to comparative safety those who were not its intended victims. In the case of Mrs. Munro he tried and failed. She was supposedly confined to her room with a case of hay fever, when in reality, she did not wish to stray far from her drugs; such was the state of her addiction," said Rouletabille.

"Which begs the question, what did attack Theydon Grange House? Is there a duplicate of *The Yellow Terror?* And, if so, what is the purpose of the espionage ring, for if they can build a duplicate then there is no good reason to spy on the original," said Dickson.

"No, no. The question is not what attacked the house, but rather why?" started Rouletabille. "And now we know the reason. Quite plainly it was in order to change Eschmann's trial judge, for changing the judge changed the trial venue. We must turn our minds back to Grierson's failed attempt to rescue Schellenberger. He personally undertook the jailbreak just moments before the man was due to be hanged and failed—barely escaping with his own life. We know of his monstrous ego, and he will have been bruised by this failure. Now he will undertake a similar rescue, but he has given himself more time, and he will act at a distance through his agents and those under the influence of his blackmail. In this endeavor he will perhaps take a backseat—be the spider at the center of the web—he is not willing to risk his personal liberty this time."

"We need to return to the cottage to properly plan our next move and to arm ourselves," said Dickson.

"And also get word to Inspector Hopkins," agreed Rouletabille.

Suddenly the two men became aware that Miss Munro was standing in the doorway to the bedroom. Curiosity about the source of the sound of breaking glass had overridden her emotions and now she saw the shattered mirror and the moving picture camera that had been concealed behind it. They eased past her in the doorway without attempting to engage her in conversation. They were partway down the stairs when they heard the sound of her retching, it had only taken her a few moments to realize the significance of the camera and its positioning.

Back at the Lodge Keeper's Cottage, the two detectives considered their best course of action. Rouletabille noticed that at some point Inspector Hopkins must have replaced the sawn-off shotgun Dickson had created back in the gun cabinet. He took this for himself and secreted it under his jacket, then filled his pockets with cartridges. Dickson settled on a beautiful double-barreled Purdey.

There would be no time to take a saw to it and he had little desire to invoke the Lord Chancellor's wrath, now that he knew who the weapon's belonged to.

From the sky above them they could hear the persistent drone of *The Yellow Terror's* engine. Treadwell was already in the air. Ostensibly it was just another day of flight tests, but this was also the first day of preliminary hearings in the Eschmann trial which meant that the prisoner would be present, having been transported in a secure wagon from Newgate Prison. Rouletabille was insistent that *The Yellow Terror* comprised a vital part of the plan to spring Eschmann. After all, it would be capable of mounting a devastating attack on the prison wagon.

"Yet still we have so little real evidence," bemoaned the French detective. "I am more reliant on instinct and guesswork than in any case I've ever been involved."

"Sometimes you just have to play your hunches," smiled Dickson. "I know I haven't been a detective for long, but it seems to me that instinct can be just as valuable as brainpower."

"Well then, my instincts tell me this. I should go out onto the flatlands in an effort to catch Treadwell at a refueling stop. If I capture him there then the attack will be over before it begins. You, my friend, just warn Hopkins and protect the wagon," said Rouletabille.

"I think it would be much better if I went with you," said Dickson. "I am not sure we should split up."

"I originally thought that my memory had fully come back, but I am increasingly aware there is a single piece of it missing. It is lost like a physical object—dropped somewhere on the rough grass of the flatlands like a pocket watch or a ring. I am convinced that if I go looking for it alone, I will find it," said Rouletabille.

"I'm sure you will, Joseph," said Dickson. "You're the one person I know who can do anything you set your mind to."

They shook hands, and then Rouletabille put on a borrowed hat Mrs. Bardell had obtained for him previously. He walked out from the cottage with a feeling of dark finality, as if he would not be coming back this day, or any day. He was headed for a reckoning with Dr. Grierson—or at least his machinations, and it would be a very great pleasure indeed to thwart them.

After walking in the hot sun for just forty minutes, Rouletabille regretted not bringing a canteen of water, or one of the stone bottles of fiery ginger beer Mrs. Bardell was always trying to force on him. But ahead of him was a small copse of just a handful of trees, if he lay down there for just a few minutes in the shade it would serve to revive him. During his recuperation in the cottage he had kidded himself that he had completely recovered from his dreadful incarceration in Leytonstone House, but it was not really true. He was still much weakened. As he wearily trudged his way into the middle of the small copse he encountered a strange, camouflaged barrier. There was canvas and netting into which had been interwoven leaves and twigs—the general purpose of all this was to mask a sort of tent or den. Rouletabille poked his head into the den's opening and looked inside.

"Oh, hello Mr. Frenchie. Would you like some lemonade?" asked Little Alfie.

Rouletabille glugged at the sweet cloudy liquid while the rotund boy made his explanations.

"I didn't really realize planes were all that exciting until I saw that one chase you and try to kill you. That was very good. I'm glad you got away though. Mind you, I didn't tell anyone. Nobody believes what I say anyway. I'll always remember it though," assured Little Alfie.

This was the event Rouletabille could not recall—being pursued by *The Yellow Terror* and ultimately running into one of the Wanstead Flatland's little lakes. It made sense, but still the memory was locked away and seemingly irretrievable.

"I made a den here because this where they pull the other plane into the sky," and then, before Rouletabille could ask for further details. "Hush. They're coming."

Two men in mechanic's overalls and flying helmets approached. They stopped about fifty feet away and with practiced efficiency lifted up a series of concealed and camouflaged sections—they were effectively trapdoors in the ground. They then started to lift out the components that would go to make up a modestly sized one man glider, albeit one with a generous wingspan. They swiftly bolted and screwed the components together and then fitted at the very front of the cockpit a pair of machineguns identical to those which fired through the spinning propeller blades of *The Yellow Terror*.

So this was how it had been done. Treadwell had towed the glider into the air, and then it must have circled in the clouds for ages—allowing him sufficient time to get to Theydon Grange House—before commencing its diving attack with guns blazing. Then Rouletabille remembered that Miss Munro had heard an engine during the attack, this must have been just trickery, for surely the glider had no engine.

Moments later, Rouletabille heard the whine of *The Yellow Terror* as it came in to land, and then rolled close to the glider's assembly point. Treadwell extricated himself from the plane, resplendent in his glossy, horse chestnut brown leather flying jacket and blindingly white silk scarf. He looked every inch the hero—but the Frenchman recognized him for precisely what he was.

"Hurry and attach the tow cable," ordered Treadwell. "It is almost time to free Eschmann."

And while one of the mechanics hefted the tow cable the other topped up *The Yellow Terror's* fuel tank from a jerry can.

"Is the glider's machinegun fully reloaded?" Treadwell demanded to know.

"Ja, all is as it should be," said the mechanic who was refueling Tread-well's plane.

Rouletabille cocked the twin hammers of his sawn-off shotgun.

"Then get into the glider and prepare for take-off," ordered the English-man, to the German who was obviously both a mechanic and pilot.

"Ein moment, I must relieve myself first," confessed the German.

"Oh for God's sake, hurry," admonished Treadwell. And to Rouletabille's horror the German started to make his way directly towards the copse where the French detective and Little Alfie were crouching in the den.

"I wonder how Grierson is getting on with his bomb to destroy *The Great Men of Baker Street?*" wondered the second German mechanic.

"All I know is that he hired a delivery wagon from a local business and filled it with high explosive, he set off for Baker Street a while ago now. You never know, we might even hear the explosion—you'll certainly see the smoke plume from the air," said the first German just as he reached the copse.

Until this moment, Rouletabille had thought that when people referred to their blood running cold it was mere hyperbole, but now his blood was freezing in his veins at the prospect of some of the world's greatest minds being elimi-nated en masse. Nevertheless, he had an idea as to what he should do about it.

A couple of minutes later, *The Yellow Terror* jerkily pulled the glider and away from the flatlands, And then, at about one thousand feet, the towing cable connection was released and the glider started to soar even higher. Rouletabille was going to have to figure out the controls pretty quickly. While being towed it hadn't seemed to matter much what he did—it was as if the controls were locked off. But now he placed his hands around the joystick and found it highly respon-sive, likewise the rudder control pedals, upon which he was now exerting exper-imental pressure. It was undoubtedly the case that Treadwell would've expected the real glider pilot to participate in the attack to free Eschmann, but Rouletabille was incapable even of pretending to take that course of action. He felt lucky that he was even able to keep the glider in the air. He dipped the nose of the glider slightly with a view to opening fire with his machineguns on Treadwell's retreating plane which was moving fast out of sight, then he pulled on the triggers, but nothing happened. Whatever the means was for disengaging the safety he couldn't figure it out. Perhaps that was for the best. He would not be able to defeat so experienced a pilot in aerial combat. At the moment, Tread-well had no idea he had knocked the German pilot-mechanic unconscious once he reached the copse, exchanged clothing with him and taken his place. Tread-well would probably assume the glider wasn't taking part in the attack due to some technical malfunction. In fact, Rouletabille had now resolved to do his best to fly the glider towards Baker Street and warn of the bomb.

Rouletabille found himself in a cold sweat with an extremely elevated pulse rate and fizzing with adrenalin which would avail him little in the circumstances. He must calm down and he must start to think. It was nauseatingly ver-tiginous to look down out of the cockpit at the parched Wanstead grasslands and the streets of terraced houses where London's suburbs began, but really he had no choice. He had to orientate himself and then commence to fly this craft straight and level. Baker Street was in Marylebone, roughly southwest of his current position. He could only guess the distance since there were no maps on board. Dredging up from his memory all he knew of the geography of the me-tropolis he would say it could not be much more than ten miles away. The ques-tion was—did he have enough altitude to undertake such a journey? He wasn't sure. He pulled up gently on the joystick and the glider spiraled upwards like some dark and malevolent gull.

It all looked very different from the air, but within minutes he was passing over a London park, the thin dirty ribbon of a canal nearby led him to think this was Victoria Park on the edge of Bethnal Green. He was heading roughly in the right direction and still managing to keep this thing in the sky. Yes, he has start-ed to relax a little, but a creeping dread about the descent and landing. How in God's name was he going to land the glider in a built up area like Baker Street? He dismissed the idea of attempting to land on rooftops—it would be suicide. Or was this whole thing just suicidal? What had he been thinking?

As St. Paul's Cathedral and the River Thames came into view he realized he needed to correct his course—there was no compass, so it had all been guesswork, but he was now much too far south and was rapidly losing height. He dismissed the idea of crash landing in the river and made the necessary cor-rection. The open spaces around Lincoln's Inn looked too small to land the glid-er in. If he survived a landing that far from Baker Street he was bound to be questioned by the police, and it would take time to establish his bona fides. All of this would slow him down. He had to land as close to home of the *Great Men* as possible for he had no idea how much time he really had. He craned his neck to see that he was just going over the British Museum, there was still no open space to land in—just little square parcels of green—and he was far too low. In another couple of minutes he would be skimming the roof tops. Then, finally, his hoped for landing space came into view over to the North West. He had not remembered that there was a public park so near to Baker Street. What was the name of it? He strained his memory. It didn't matter. It didn't matter. He wres-tled with the joystick. Then he noticed for the first time an odd brass handle on the right hand side of the cockpit. He turned it swiftly just in case its function was connected with landing the glider. In fact, it was a kind of siren, adjusted to emit a sound like the noise of the *Yellow Terror's* engines. The Germans really had thought of everything.

He lined up the glider to the park's emptiest open space and pointed the glider's nose slightly downwards. No! That was too much. He adjusted, but was still coming in too steeply and too fast. He pulled back and the glider made as if to ascend then simply belly-flopped onto the grass before cart-wheeling. The cockpit split open like an egg and Rouletabille was hurled out onto the ground—injuring his right knee, and wrenching his only recently healed shoulder joint. Every bone in his frame ached from the jarring impact. But after only a few moments he leapt up and commenced a limping run in the direction of Baker Street. It was imperative that he not get caught up in a crowd of gawkers, nor be arrested by the police. Where was he? Regents Park! He was within yards of Grierson's intended targets. He had used up the luck intended for a whole lifetime in a single morning.

Rouletabille limped his weary way along the pavements of Baker Street looking for Grierson. His only clue was that a business local to the asylum had hired him a horse drawn wagon. When he saw the delivery van it looked so ordinary, so mundane, that he discounted it. But then he saw the dwarfish figure who was bundled up with a scarf around his face on such a very hot day.

The French detective did not hesitate. He pulled the sawn-off shot gun out from inside of his overalls and fired at Grierson as he was parking the wagon which bore the legend "Hitchcock Greengrocers, High Road, Leytonstone. The wagon's horses reared up momentarily at the sound of shot then settled back down making dismissive snorts. The unbelievably wide spread from the sawn-off peppered Grierson with buckshot, and some innocent passersby into the bargain. He cried out in a strangulated mixture of surprise and agony. He was bleeding from multiple small injuries, but not too badly hurt.

"You! How can you be here? How can you know of my plans?" he screeched, while yanking his lethal air pistol from his coat pocket.

Grierson loosed a couple of rounds at Rouletabille which hit him in the forearm and leg.

"Run you fool! It is only a matter of moments until the detonation..." shouted Grierson, as he himself quit the wagon's driver's seat and fled away from Baker Street.

Reeling from the fresh injuries, Rouletabille staggered to the doors at the back of the wagon. There was a heavy padlock which he set about with the only weapon he had to hand—the sawn-off. He dare not attempt to shoot off the lock in case it triggered the explosives. Holding the shotgun by the remaining section of its barrel he beat down on the lock repeatedly until it finally gave way. Flinging the doors open he saw a multiplicity of perhaps a dozen slow burning fuses. Grierson had lied. The explosion would perhaps have been two full minutes away. Rouletabille pulled the sputtering fuses out of the blocks of explosives.

Climbing out of the wagon to continue the pursuit, the Frenchman suddenly realized he had no strength, no energy, left. He was too badly hurt. One day he would catch up with Grierson, but today was not that day. He collapsed onto the pavement.

The Yellow Terror swooped down and unleashed a series of staccato bursts of crimson tracer fire at the armored prison wagon transporting Klaus Eschmann. The shots ricocheted off the vehicle's steel plates even as the driver and guard jumped away to cover. As the plane made a banking turn to attack again, Harry Dickson and Inspector Hopkins stood up from their positions of concealment behind Snaresbrook Crown Court's low boundary wall and opened fire—Dickson with his shotgun and Hopkins with a heavy Webley service revolver. This was followed by a fusillade of further pistol shots from the uniformed Special Branch constables.

A line of oily smoke started to trail from *The Yellow Terror's* engine, as it swiftly lost height. Anticipating where it would come down, Harry Dickson set off at a sprint, reloading his shotgun as he went.

Treadwell was already extricating himself from the crumpled plane's cockpit as Dickson approached. The American could see the traitorous pilot was holding a Mauser pistol in one hand as he jumped free of the plane.

"Going somewhere, motherfucker?" enquired Dickson. "Drop that pistol before I shoot you in the face."

Treadwell dropped the gun and momentarily reflected on the fact that he'd not had the guts to use it on himself. They'd hang him now for sure.

Epilogue

Naturally, it was Mrs. Bardell who was again give the job of nursing Rouletabille back to health at the Gatekeeper's Lodge Cottage. She limited the visitors and well wishers as best she could, but most of the *Great Men of Baker Street* made the pilgrimage to his sick bed to give him grapes or books with which to pass the time.

Dr. Watson had calculated that he and Holmes would both have been killed instantly by Grierson's bomb since the greengrocer's wagon was parked adjacent to 221B. By coincidence—or perhaps not knowing Grierson's intricate plans—Blake had just returned from his case in Scotland, he would likely have been killed or seriously injured. Begg was away on vacation in his beloved Paris. The mysterious Drago's whereabouts are unknown, but his assistant, Spencer, is believed to have been in residence in Baker Street at the time of the attempted atrocity.

Little Alfie Hitchcock was also a regular attender. One afternoon, Rouletabille lay in bed, unable to concentrate on the latest issue of *Strand Magazine* and a thought struck him so he called out to his nurse and housekeeper.

"Mrs. Bardell? Could you go around to Theydon Grange House and get the moving picture camera from Mrs. Munro's room? I'm sure she has no further use for it, and I'd like Little Alfie to have it. Making films would be a most marvelous hobby for a boy like him."

We normally discourage writers from using film or TV characters, but the charm of Joseph Gibson's story, which admirably succeeds in blending the Falcon and Fantômas from the movies with Georges Franju's Shadowman, *the 1965 TV series* Belphegor *and other similar sources, could not be resisted. In French popular fiction, the 1970s were a turning point between the old myths of the 30s, the 40s, the 50s and the 60s, and the new, more modern and more brutal, heroes and villains that followed. The protagonists of this story are only trying to adapt to a new and even more fantastic world...*

Joseph Gibson: *The Other Vampires of Paris*

Paris & its surrounding area, 1968.

The screams of Subject #41A2 would have pierced the night around the outwardly nondescript French manor had they not been buried under at least a foot of reinforced soundproof steel. They came from a mixture of pain and fear, but the Shadowman in his red hood was not interested in emotional response tonight. Instead, his eyes were fixated on the subject of his experiment.

The woman was tied on an altar while two of the Shadowman's masked servants, dressed in black, wearing goggles, were piecing her body in various places with long gold needles. The needles were connected by wires to a box, looking like a Geiger counter, held by a third man, who also spoke softly into a microphone, taking notes and checking its readings.

The goal of the experiment was to perfect a process that was known to transform certain humans into something... *more*, while, hopefully, keeping these specimens bound to the Shadowman's will. That was the larger goal, at least—in more singular terms, the goal tonight was for #41A2 to exhibit the regenerative faculties or extraordinary strength that had been exhibited by earlier subjects.

The Shadowman watched from behind a protective glass window until the man holding the "counter" turned and looked at him, shrugging in a very gallic manner. On the altar, #41A2 collapsed in exhaustion, evidently unable to move, let alone protest.

Ah well, thought the Shadowman, as he turned off the lights and coldly ordered that #41A2 be taken back to her cell. *Better luck next time.*

Tom Lawrence first noticed that something was amiss towards the end of his transcontinental flight.

At first, he welcomed the slight foreboding feeling, as the Derek Carson paperback he'd picked up at the airport was particularly uninspired, even by that hack Larker's standards. But the welcome respite from its awkward prose and contrived scenarios was quickly overshadowed by the bizarre nature of the event.

It all began when, before Tom's eyes, every man, woman and child onboard the plane, stewardesses and infants included, seemed to freeze at the same instant. Bites of airplane dinners paused halfway between tray and mouth, gestures were interrupted in mid-air, a book dropped to the floor of the cabin… Then, everything started again, as if an invisible projectionist had just restarted the film, but this time, the passengers seemed to be moving like clockwork automata, unaware of their surroundings.

Only the Falcon and two other persons sitting next to him (even though a minute ago, he could have sworn that these seats had been empty) appeared unaffected—one was a charismatic individual, balding, with piercing black eyes; the other was a slim brunette with a strong face, and large grey eyes who seemed to gaze unfocused into empty space.

"Tom Lawrence, alias The Falcon," said the bald man. "Amateur criminologist. Wealthy playboy. Moderately successful lothario. Now a past-his-prime former adventurer."

"Yes, and what is it to you?" replied Tom.

"My name is Boris Williams," said the man. "May I ask you what brings you to Paris?"

Not sure at first if he should answer, Tom eventually opted for the less awkward option of honesty.

"A message," he said. "From my older brother Gay. He said I was to meet him in Paris as soon as I could. Since I haven't seen or even heard from him in years, I jumped at the chance."

Williams nodded as if he had already guessed the answer.

"You see, Mr. Lawrence, my, er, little group has its eyes on many of your, shall we say, fellow travelers—amateur sleuths, detectives, crimefighters. Quixotes. And when your comings and goings intersect with your potential usefulness, a message goes out, and, hopefully, a disaster might be averted. Now, if you please, look behind you, towards the rear of the cabin. Aisle seat, third from the back. A woman is sitting there. A blonde."

The woman, a blonde, as Williams had said, sat in her seat in the same dazed, out of focus posture as the rest of the passengers. But with her, the effect was strangely pleasing, as if she was uniquely suited to being seen frozen in space or time. She appeared at a glance to be approaching 40, although a closer look would have shown her to be closer to 60.

Who in the hell is she? thought Tom.

To his surprise, his thoughts received a direct answer:

"Her name is Ellen Patrick, Mr. Lawrence," said Williams."Also known as the Domino Lady. Like you, her heyday was in a bygone era. She fought for justice in the days preceding World War II, using her formidable charisma as well as her iron will and keen flair. She sought to avenge her father, former District Attorney Owen Patrick, who'd been murdered by racketeers. You probably don't remember him; he was before your time.

"Ellen's skill set, as well as her chosen avocation, makes her a subject of great interest to, shall we say, a significant rival of mine. Because fate has placed you on the same plane as her, it behooves me to request your services in making sure that she does not fall into the wrong hands. You see, there are limits to my powers, and in situations like this, it is often better to seek safety in numbers, at least when dealing with wolves of his caliber."

"Wolves?" Tom asked. "What exactly are you asking me to get involved with here?"

Williams' response was chilling. Tom thought he was going on a Parisian vacation to catch up with his brother; he was not expecting to get involved in some bizarre new mystery.

"Nothing more than you have already gotten yourself involved in, Mr. Lawrence. Stay close to Madame Patrick, I shall be in touch." Then Williams turned to his companion, and said: "You may release them, Stéphanie."

"Yes, Grandmaster," replied the woman with grey eyes.

The lights flickered briefly and everything went back to normal inside the cabin. And the two seats next to the Falcon were suddenly empty again, as they had always been.

Tom scratched his head, wondering what was going on, when a stewardess approached him and handed him a white card on a small silver tray. On the front was a message in graceful, feminine cursive, directing him to come to the plane's lounge for a word with the sender. On the back, a printed statement read: *Compliments of the Domino Lady.*

Tom walked through the cabin and into the passengers' lounge. One could use many words to describe this mostly bygone relic of a more elegant age of air travel, but the one that most immediately sprang to mind was "swanky." With bright blue molded chairs of space-age plastic, dangling psychedelic light fixtures, and oblong, pop-art-inspired windows, it resembled a newfangled fashion magazine spread rather than an airplane lounge.

Tom was in no mood to appreciate the airline's exercise in swinging 60s style. That was because, among other things, seated in one of the amoeba-shaped chairs, was Ellen Patrick, a.k.a. the Domino Lady, who had beckoned him to come, and was obviously mixed up in this strange business in some unknown way.

Ellen smiled at Tom and offered her hand in a charmingly old-fashioned greeting.

"Hello. Tom Lawrence, I presume," she said. "We haven't been formally introduced, but we appear to have a few shared acquaintances."

Tom distractedly took her hand.

"You have the advantage of me, Madam," he said. "I gather from your words that you have also been contacted by the mysterious Mr. Williams. Just what can you tell me about him? Who is this rival he mentioned? And what are we supposed to do?"

Ellen smiled.

"I expect he delegated the task of filling you in to me. How typical!" she tsked-tsked, which may have been annoying coming from anyone else but her. "Boris Williams contacted me a month ago in New York. From what I gather, he is the leader of a small group of men and women who are interested in the next stage of human evolution. Five years ago, he worked with a remarkable woman, Laurence Borel, gifted with extra-sensory perception and superhuman strength... It all ended rather badly, and sadly Laurence died, because they ran afoul of the French Police. Williams believes that ordinary humans can't but hate and fear people like Laurence; some even call them 'vampires' or some other monstrous names, but some day, humanity will be on the same level as they are—evolutionarily speaking, of course."

"That seems rather far-fetched," said Tom.

"After what you just experienced, I'm amazed by your skepticism, Mr. Lawrence," said Ellen. "The woman who sat next to Williams is Stéphanie, Laurence's sister, who, while weaker, is still capable of amazing feats, like plunging this entire plane into a trance, for example."

Tom wasn't sure where to begin, but before he could respond, the light from one of those bizarre lamps hanging from the ceiling began to move, coalescing and crystallizing in an entirely unnatural way. The light flowed from the fixture to the lounge's entrance, guiding both Tom and Ellen's eyes to the orchestrator of the light show: an outwardly serene red-haired young woman with freckles, dressed in loose hippie threads and sunglasses, her eyes closed in deep concentration.

"This must be another 'friend' of Boris Williams," said Ellen, as much to herself as to Tom.

The young woman opened her eyes and, in an instant, the pulsating river of light hovering between them vanished, and the lounge seemed to snap back to its relatively mundane appearance.

"Sorry to show off," she said, "but it's usually the best way to convince skeptics. Assuming they don't lose their heads and try to kill me, of course."

"Why would they want to kill you?" asked Tom, nonplussed.

"Because I'm as vampire," she replied smiling. "My name's Solange."

An hour later, the plane landed at the Orly Aérogare, and the flight's closing spiel from one of the flight attendants crackled over the PA:

"Thank you for choosing Oceanic Airlines," she said nearly unintelligibly. "If Paris is your destination, please enjoy your stay. If you're continuing on to

114

Lugash, please wait until the other passengers have exited the plane to stretch your legs, and we will be continuing on shortly."

Both Tom and Ellen as well as Solange had gone back to their seats, after a somewhat awkward conversation during which the red-haired girl had explained that she was their escort, tasked to take them to Boris Williams (whom she called the "Grandmaster"), who would explain everything then.

They were naturally skeptical, but they both agreed that they had seen enough strange things already to want to know more, and their natural detective instincts remained dominant, even a few years past their prime.

The plan was for them to collect their luggage and meet outside the airport, where Solange would take them to her car and drive them to meet Williams at his castle in Médan. After they talked to him, she assured them, all would become clear. But Tom had his doubts about that.

Tom first sensed that something was wrong, or perhaps more accurately, that something *else* was wrong, when they were waiting to collect their luggage at the baggage claim area.

Ellen was chatting with Solange about all and sundry, but Tom sensed a more malignant presence amongst the milling throng; nothing he could isolate specifically, but a worrisome, threatening presence all the same.

As he tried to pinpoint the source of his feelings, a bullet whizzed by his head, singing a bit of his hair.

"Ellen! Solange!" he shouted

The three ran from their unseen attacker, baggage forgotten.

It was Ellen who spotted the stairs leading up to the pier, or jetty, where only a handful of men knew that a time traveler had been shot four years prior. There, hopefully, they would be able to duck away without being seen by whomever had tried to kill Tom.

At this time of the day, the jetty was almost empty, with just two businessmen making awkward small talk. Tom was desperate to figure out the best way to flee the airport, but nobody in the trio felt comfortable talking in front of the two strangers. Once again, it was Ellen who took action, approaching the gentlemen with deliberate, methodical poise.

Tom watched her whisper something to each of them, and they both looked at each other startled and quickly left, leaving the three unlikely companions alone. Tom's curiosity got the best of him:

"What the hell did you say to those two men?" he inquired.

Ellen seemed to smirk almost imperceptibly beneath her vaguely out-of-fashion Veronica Lake hairdo.

"Let's just say a woman has her ways and leave it at that," she replied. "Hopefully you have a way to get us out of here?"

"I can help with that," said Solange. "I know this place like the back of my hand. It was undoubtedly a member of the Grandmaster's rival's gang who attacked us—an evil brotherhood led by a masked man known only as the Shadowman, or the Faceless Man, waging constant war against us. We thought this pickup could happen without a hitch if I managed to get a seat on your flight, but evidently, they knew where I was all the time. Do either of you have any idea how they might have managed to acquire that information?"

Tom and Ellen looked at each other helplessly, when all of a sudden a police officer came up the staircase. A uniformed gendarme, he was a youngish man with fashionable sideburns.

"You there!" he barked. "We're looking for any suspicious characters. There's been some kind of attack in the baggage claim area. Shots were fired. Did any of you see anyone trying to get away?"

"No," replied Ellen in perfect French. "We've been here for almost an hour watching the planes take off and land. I hope this doesn't mean we'll have any trouble getting to our hotel?"

"Afraid so, ma'am," answered the gendarme. "There'll be checkpoints outside. Cars will be searched. The airport will be completely shut down until the source of the attack is found. Standard procedure."

Ellen approached the gendarme, having palmed something from her purse. With a lightning-fast movement, she plunged a small syringe into the officer's neck, causing him to fall unconscious at once.

Tom didn't know what to say, but Solange seemed to catch on immediately.

"We'll have to swipe his credentials and use them to get out of the airport" she said. "We don't have time to wait around while an investigation takes place, especially if the Shadowman is counting on us being trapped here. You do the honors, Tom; you look more like a *flic* than either of us."

Fifteen minutes and one anxiety-wracked exchange with another police officer later, the three adventurers were in Solange's small burgundy Citroen on their way to meeting the mysterious Boris Williams.

Tom wondered which of his many questions he would ask first. Then, just as had happened on the plane hours earlier, the light seemed to flicker and Williams appeared to all three passengers, somehow reflected in the car's numerous mirrors without actually being visible inside. It seemed he had a real flair for the theatrical.

"Good afternoon to you both, and to you, Solange," he said. "I trust your flight was pleasant. As you can see, with you being safely on the ground, it's easier for Stéphanie to create a shared psychic link between us. I'm relieved that you've safely escaped from the Shadowman's clutches. I understand he had a man waiting for you at the airport? Any idea who it was, Solange?"

"None," the young woman answered. "I don't think it was anyone we've crossed paths with before. The psychic pattern was unfamiliar to me, and I think I would have picked up if any other vampire was in the airport."

Williams scowled in consternation.

"Very troubling. The Faceless Man seems to be growing more and more proficient at finding, and perhaps even creating, these uniquely talented individuals.... Ah, I see you're approaching my château.... I shall see you shortly and explain what we should do next and your role in all of this. *À tout de suite.*"

Sure enough, Tom noticed that they were now approaching a massive country estate.

Solange pulled the car into a detached garage and they all exited and proceeded towards the chateau.

Tom looked around before going up the steps to a set of great, oaken double door, which creaked open by themselves upon their arrival before they had a chance to knock.

He remembered what Solange had said about her people being seen as vampires by the human race, and wondered if he was about to be offered immortality through blood drinking, and whether he would be able to turn such an offer down with his bygone youth as the carrot.

He and Ellen looked at one another and seemed to swallow their fear together. They stepped into the large entrance hall of the château together, side by side, while Solange led the way.

Inside the hall, a giant marble staircase dominated the view. Solange quickly excused herself and left to go to some unknown wing of the château, but, at the top of the stairs, Tom saw the very last person he ever expected to see there: his brother Gay.

"Good evening. Welcome to the Château de Médan. How good of you to come," Gay said, his famously strong voice echoing through the large hall, an ironic smirk plainly visible as he intoned the melodramatic words.

Tom's brother, better known to the public as the first Falcon, walked down the steps, chuckling at his brother's confused expression as he opened his arms in greeting.

"Gay?" Tom said, more confused than ever. "What on Earth is going on here? How are you mixed up in all this?"

Tom was also unmistakably happy to see his older brother, who somehow still seemed to be the same age as he had been back in the 1940s when he had given up the title of "Falcon" and passed it on to his younger sibling.

"Happy to see me? I invited you to Paris for just this reason. You see, I joined up with Mr. Williams' 'Vampires,' as we now ironically call ourselves, two years ago. Truthfully, I was getting awfully tired of retirement, but couldn't picture myself returning to an endless stream of whodunits and capers. Remember those days, Tom? Remember how you inherited the mantle of the Falcon? You, too, have served our cause beautifully, but I wasn't in a position to recruit you along the Vampires back then, having only just been recruited myself. I hope you'll forgive me, in time."

"The Vampires," observed Tom. "Weren't they some kind of criminal gang around the turn of the century?"

"Yes indeed," replied Gay, "but their last leader, a man known as Venenos, was also a scientist. It was he who first became interested in abnormally gifted humans, like the famous Irma Vep... Eventually, they turned away from crime, and concentrated on the discovery and study of such persons, although they continue to operate largely outside the law—as we did, too. Our current Grandmaster, Boris Williams, a man of remarkable abilities, became entangled in the *Belphegor* affair in '65 and even had to leave France for a while..."

Ellen, increasingly fed up with this impromptu family reunion, barked:

"Excuse me, Falcons, this is all very interesting, but someone better tell me what the hell is going on here, or I'm leaving."

"You're free to go, of course," said Gay. "but you're part of this too, Miss Patrick—or should I call you Domino Lady? You both on the Vampires' shortlist for admission, owing to a variety of factors, but largely stemming from the fact that it's been years, decades in fact, since your activities were the stuff of articles, stories, and even B movies... The Vampires now specialize in recruiting these kinds of personalities, those who have seen their glory days come and go, but still want to be part of something greater than themselves, possibly with immortality thrown in in the bargain if Williams' research pans out."

Before either Tom or Ellen could reply, a bright, loud klaxon sound began echoing through the entrance hall.

"*Alerte intrus. Alerte intrus,*" repeated a smooth female voice in between the almost painful klaxon bursts.

"This means I need to find a dressing room," said Ellen.

The Domino Lady found just such a dressing room, one of the seemingly infinite chambers to be found in this unbelievably massive chateau, and quickly stripped off the faded sweatshirt and grey Capri trousers she had been wearing on the plane and unfolded a white, backless dress, which she hadn't worn in years, from out of her purse.

She pulled the familiar garment over her body, and it felt like a warm greeting from a fondly remembered friend—and that was even before she put on her domino mask.

She looked into the mirror over the sound of the alarm and spared a moment to sigh with disbelief to herself. The Domino Lady, after a hiatus of almost three decades, was back!

Ellen caught up with Tom and Gay as the latter led them to some sort of high-tech monitoring station, with a handful of young people, including Solange, sitting in front of computer terminals.

They looked like a bunch of grey boxes with small screens and random flashing lights to computer-illiterate Tom, but apparently they imparted vital information. Gay conferred with one of the other staff members in front of a green-tinted monitor.

"Our sensors picked up some hostile presence, but they can't figure out who or why," he explained to Tom and Ellen. "Some kind of psychic screen is shielding them from our probes. Were you followed...?"

Gay's question was never completed, because at that moment, some kind of change seemed to take place behind his eyes. To Tom, it looked as if a light had gone out in his brother's head He realized that it was Williams communicating with him in the same manner that he had communicated with them on the plane and in the car.

So that's how it looks from the outside, he thought. *Damn silly, if you ask me...*

He looked back at the monitors and saw what appeared to be a large gray blob lumbering its way towards the entrance to the chateau. Not knowing what else to do, and hoping to impress Ellen, he gave his best imitation of a heroic nod in her direction.

"I'll see what that is," he said, with a dash of the charm he used to display during his cases in the 1940s. And before Ellen or anyone else could stop him, the second Falcon was gone.

Ellen had also noticed the change in Gay's eyes. Part of her wanted to stick around and try to confer with Williams, but the situation seemed dangerous and urgent enough to warrant immediate action.

She pulled the .45 automatic pistol from her purse and made sure it was properly loaded. Bullets may be useless against 'vampires,' but she felt a little more secure with her Domino Lady's signature weaponry in her hand. Then she decided to leave the control room and see if she could help Tom.

Tom dashed through the corridor between the control room and the entrance hall in an attempt stop the blobbish man on the front lawn before it got inside. *Maybe he could convince it to go away peaceably*, he thought, remembering all the past scrapes he'd gotten out of through his wit and charm.

The man was, in fact, not alone. He was accompanied by five other men, also the size of sumo wrestlers, dressed in black robes with a coat of arms on their chest, and wearing a strange, golden mask that covered the upper half of their faces with heavy, sculpted features reminiscent of a statue of the pagan god Baal.

At that point, Tom hit a metaphorical wall as the five impossibly large men fell upon him and quickly battered him into unconsciousness.

Dash it all, he thought before passing out, *I think I've just been captured.*

Ellen was hidden behind a well-placed suit of armor in the entrance hall, and watched as the gang of angry masked men hauled Tom off like a sack of potatoes. It hurt her to see them take her new friend away, but she couldn't think of anything she could do at the moment, and it seemed unlikely that she'd be able to do much damage with her gun, her trusty syringe, or any of her other tactical assets. So instead, she watched in horror as the gang took Tom to a large black truck they'd parked out on the lawn and drove off, just as sunlight began to give way to dusk.

With a little luck and that small motorbike she'd seen in the garage earlier, Ellen thought she just might be able to follow them without being seen.

Tom had remained mercifully unconscious during the roughly hour-long van ride from the chateau, a bumpy voyage along back country roads under the best of circumstances.

Eventually, he came to when daggers of light prodded him back into painful consciousness. He heard a vaguely familiar sound. What was it, he wondered, not being able to place it, but knowing it was from somewhere in his dim, dark past.

Suddenly, the daggers coalesced into a motion picture on a silver screen. Tom realized in confusion that the sounds he had recognized weren't from his own past, but the dramatized version of it featured in the movies devoted to his career, made more than two decades ago. It was *The Falcon in Hollywood,* which, for some reason, his attackers had decided to project on a screen in front of him.

At that moment, he realized he was in no typical screening room, as his hands and feet were bound to the chair in which he sat. Before he could spend much time reacquainting himself with the film, based on one of his old cases, the sound cut out and a maliciously sibilant voice came through the speakers in lieu of the still-unspooling soundtrack:

"Lovely, isn't it? Pure Hollywood fantasy. Based on real life, of course, but how few in the audience ever bother to find out the real facts? And how even fewer yet would believe them if they did? Your exploits, Mr. Lawrence, tended to be relatively mundane, but I've always enjoyed them—even if I did prefer George Sanders to Tom Conway."

Why was this voice talking about these old movies based on the cases he and his brother had solved back in the 40s? What was the point of all this? Could this person sense his thoughts as Boris Williams had?

"You're probably wondering where you are…" (Evidently his thoughts were still his own, Tom thought.) "But the location is unimportant. It is merely one of my many strongholds throughout France. If you must address me, you may do so as the Shadowman, or better yet, Fantômas!"

Fantômas' voice paused for a moment, presumably so that its owner could rejoice in the sight of the once famous Falcon struggling against his bonds helplessly.

Not knowing what to say, Tom remained silent and simply waited for Fantômas to reveal his plans .

"You do not wish to speak? Very wise. I come to you not as an enemy, despite all this, but as a friend, Mr. Lawrence. With a proposition. You see, I only intended a friendly exchange of information between my organization and you and Madame Patrick. But one of my associates, one with, shall we say, a rather hot temper and a very bad aim, grew frustrated when he saw that Solange, the young vampire in the employ of my old friend the Grandmaster, had gotten to you first. He had been on the plane all along. Whatever had gone on during the trip had left my man exceedingly unhappy, so when he saw his chance, he tried to kill Solange—and missed. Very clumsy, of course, but when you work with young people, you become accustomed to certain outbursts of emotion. Fortunately, I was able to enlist the assistance of the Companions of Baal to bring you here. I hope there will be no bad blood between us.

"Since you're here now, I thought it amusing to remind you of your glorious past exploits, in order to better convince you to join me. I am no ordinary criminal, unlike what you might have heard. In fact, my main targets these days are criminals, so we would be an excellent fit for someone with your, er, proclivities. Benefits would include full access to my organization, its vast resources and any future innovations I may develop in my laboratories. I am especially interested in duplicating the Grandmaster' rumored research into immortality…"

Immortality? thought Tom. That was the same thing that Gay had been talking about before everything had gone haywire at the château. *Was it truly possible? Should he become a vampire, too, or consider joining Fantômas?*

While he was thinking this over, a nurse dressed in medical scrubs came into the room and checked on the bonds that fastened him to his seat. After making sure he was still securely tied up, she reached under the seat and pulled a lever, causing it to recline fully so Tom was now flat on his back.

She then inserted an IV into his arm, and checked the pulse on his neck, before leaving as quickly as she'd come in. So quickly, in fact, that Tom almost didn't notice the two items she'd left in his still trapped hands: In one, a bobby pin, which in his younger days he'd used to use to escape situations just like this; and in the other, another card that read, *Compliments of the Domino Lady.*

"Do you remember those carefree days, Mr. Lawrence, when you were young and fast and sharp?" Fantômas continued. "Do you remember when your exploits were the subject of big screen matinees, when you were played on-screen by a movie star, or at least the brother of a movie star? Life was good then, and full of infinite possibilities. As we both know, things are different now, but I can offer you a second chance. Aid me in my plans, take part in my grand scientific experiments! The old ways are gone; today is an age of super-crimes and super criminals, able to see through walls or blow holes in them. Many of us have quietly retired, but Fantômas will never admit defeat, and neither, I suspect, will you!

"I've long been aware of the Grandmaster and his so-called 'vampires,' but the absence of his involvement in my own affairs made him seem irrelevant, until I learned the details of the *Belphegor* affair, and his interest in shepherding the next stage in human evolution, as he calls it. It's something that can be found within many of us, if only we have the courage to look.

"The chemicals you see being fed into your veins are an aid to that kind of search, and if my guess is correct, you will discover their effects sooner rather than later. And if you wish to recapture your early days of glory, and hone your human potential, it is Fantômas to whom you should plead allegiance. Good day, Mr. Lawrence."

Tom was only dimly paying attention to Fantômas' big speech as he carefully manipulated the lock over his right wrist with the bobby pin. With a subtle skill he'd almost forgotten he possessed, the shackle clicked open. When Fantômas signed off, Tom hoped he wasn't still watching him as he now used his free hand to release his other bonds. He then returned them to a closed position so he could spring free at an opportune time. He wondered when he'd see another human being in this weird movie theater, and whether he'd ever get the chance to return the favor to Fantômas by arranging a screening of one o the movies that featured the Lord of Evil.

Inside an adjoining room, Fantômas clicked off the intercom machine. The light from the film projector beamed the old Falcon mystery onto the screen in front of the prisoner, but Fantômas was not watching it or him anymore. Instead, he was looking over case notes from the latest round of experiments, most of which, as usual, had been failures.

It seemed that Fantômas was failing at trying to generate his own "vampires," Anyone less cold-blooded than him probably would have shuddered in reading about Subject #SS02, who had spontaneously combusted, or Subject #BD7K, who had become incurably insane; but Fantômas felt only disappointment that this messy process produced so many errors and so few real successes. He sighed heavily to himself and left the room as the film continued to play—it was time for another meeting with his scientists.

In the laboratory, six of Fantômas' researchers stood in matching red medical garb, complete with surgical masks. He'd always preferred to work with masked henchmen, since it saved him from having to even try to remember to put names on their faces. Instead, he addressed them collectively, explaining how pleased he was by the unexpected capture of the Falcon, particularly after his older brother's disappointing decision to join up with the Grandmaster's gang. Setbacks were a part of life, explained Fantômas, but the key to success was to press on and not let your enemies force you to lose sight of one's goal. As he spoke, he noticed something unusual about Orderly Number Five. Number Five was wearing high heels.

In the split second during which Ellen realized that her cover had just been blown, she retrieved her trusty syringe and jammed it into Fantômas' neck, causing him to hit the floor unconscious before any of the other orderlies could react.

Then, it was a free-for-all, with each of Fantômas' men hoping to be the one that captured the intruder. One of them swung his fist toward her midsection, catching her in the stomach and sending her careening across the lab. She hit the wall and her red medical mask, swiped from the unconscious orderly currently bound and gagged in a utility closet, fell off.

The other orderlies stepped back in deference to her large assailant who crept menacingly across the room for a second blow.

"Fantômas is going to have fun dissecting you, Domino Lady," he said with a sneer, "and I'm going to be there to watch."

At that moment, the door to the lab swung open. It was Tom Lawrence, who Ellen was relieved to see had made good use of her bobby pin and was now here for the timely rescue.

Tom had grabbed a fire extinguisher and was now swinging it with abandon, cracking two of the orderlies' skulls and smashing another's windpipe with the heavy metal object. The slow-moving orderly who had hit Ellen turned, and the Domino Lady took the opportunity to kick him with one of her high-heeled shoes where it was likely to do the most damage.

Tom looked around and wondered who it was who had beaten up all these younger men splashed across the floor.

"What exactly was in that IV you gave me?" he asked Ellen as he helped her up off the floor. "And do you have any more of it?"

Ellen smiled and decided to herself not to tell him that it was a simple saline solution until after they had escaped Fantômas' lair.

The two left the laboratory and Ellen led Tom to the structure's underground parking garage, where she'd parked her motorbike near the exit.

"I followed those masked goons here from Williams' château after they took you," she explained, "but I don't know where they are now."

As if to answer her question, the five Companions of Baal suddenly appeared in silhouette from the moonlight outside, blocking their exit from the parking garage.

"Looking for us?" growled the leader of the pack, rubbing his hands together.

Another one pulled out a gum and started shooting, hitting the motorbike.

They were trapped, thought Tom.

The five Companions marched in lockstep down the exit ramp towards Tom and Ellen, who had instinctively jumped out of the way to avoid the bullets, and now stood pressed up behind a concrete support pillar. Taking out regular henchmen was one thing, thought Tom, but these five seemed to be very experienced in the arts of battle.

Just as the leader began to charge, the moonlight from outside seemed to brighten and strobe, creating a disorienting effect that caused the heavy villain to lose his concentration.

It was Solange, bending the moonlight to her will and using it to distract Fantômas' accomplices.

The one with the gun tried shooting at the young "vampire," but Ellen who had silently crawled out from behind the pillar hit her on the head.

Meanwhile, Tom had his hands full with two of the Companions. Only ten years ago, I would have dispatched them with ease, he thought. But now, he felt his breath shorten, his blow becoming weaker and less accurate, and knew it was only a matter of time before he would be knocked out.

Then, all of a sudden, two gunshots cracked, one after the other, and the two Companions fell to their knees, a bloody circle in dead center of their strange gold masks.

"Dreadful things, guns," said Gay Lawrence, the original Falcon, as he ran down the exit ramp to meet Ellen and Tom, "but sometimes we must use them."

He was joined by Boris Williams and Stéphanie, who placed the two still-conscious Companions into a sleep trance.

"I wish we could appeal to their reason," said Williams, "but we don't have much time to get away from here before Fantômas wakes up. We should go now."

Accompanied by Solange, they slunk out of the garage and into a black Citroën van parked a block away in what turned out to be a deserted factory in an industrial south of Paris.

Solange took the driver's seat as usual, with Stéphanie sitting next to her, giving Boris Williams time to confer in the back with Gay, Tom and Ellen.

"Well my friends," said the Grandmaster, "you now have some idea of what we deal with on a regular basis here. Our group, the 'Vampires,' are constantly at war with Fantômas, the Companions of Baal, and others like them who only seek power regardless of the costs. I wish I could say the events of the last few hours were unusual, but they are actually fairly typical of our skirmishes in service of a society which mostly hates and fears us.

"But it is my sincere belief that eventually, humanity will make peace with its next evolutionary stage, if for no other reason than that it must. That's why I started this group, as a way to try and develop a bond of good will between us and the next men."

"He already convinced me," said Gay. "That's why I asked you to come to Paris, Tom, because I knew you must have been as unhappy as I was since we

Falcons lost our spot of glory in the crime-fighting game. And when Boris found out that the famous Domino Lady was also coming, it was a relatively simple matter to arrange for you to be on the same flight with Solange. Unlike Fantômas, we can offer you a long life of adventure without becoming subservient to his sinister plans. All that we ask in return is that you help us fight evil, just as you did in your younger days. So what do you say, brother? Are you in? Or do we have to kill you?"

Tom laughed, familiar with his older brother's dark sense of humor.

"The Falcon is in," he said, wondering if there were going to be any fraternal disagreements over which of the two brothers would be allowed to continue using that moniker.

Everyone in the van, even Solange who was supposed to be watching the road, waited expectantly for Ellen's answer.

The Domino Lady pulled on her lower lip nervously, wondering if now would be a good time to tell Boris Williams that she had come to Paris to try and steal a priceless necklace from a visiting duchess's hotel room, not to become a crime-fighter again. She thought with amusement that, no matter how many times she tried to use her skills for a more self-serving purpose, her better nature always seemed to win out.

As the continued success of the Pirates of the Caribbean *franchise demonstrates, there's nothing quite as exciting as a good pirate yarn, except maybe a murder mystery within a good pirate yarn! Our regular contributor Travis Hiltz assembles a stellar cast of suspects for Doctor Eric Palmer—a would-be Sherlock Holmes created by Paul Féval Junior—to investigate in this tropical whodunnit...*

Travis Hiltz: *A Pirate's Life*

1903

In any other circumstances, visiting a tropical island would have been considered an idyllic holiday for Eric Palmer.

Instead, the young doctor found himself bound, in a hut, bruised, weak and sweltering in the heat.

He alternated between fitful dozing and mental reproaches for the misjudgments that had placed him in these circumstances.

Palmer had alternated professions between a small medical practice and as a consultant to Scotland Yard. A smuggling case had taken him from the docks of London to the Isle of Bombay.

It was there that things had begun to go wrong.

Palmer ran his tongue across dry, cracked lips, the tiny bit of moisture a crumb of relief.

He was sure that getting free from his bonds would be a matter of a few moments' effort, but once free of the hut that served as his prison, what to do?

He had, from bits of conversation of his captors, learned that he was on an island, possibly off the coast of India.

Unfortunately, bouts of unconsciousness, from both a beating and hunger, had affected his ability to judge the passage of time accurately. He knew they'd been two days out from Bombay when the smugglers had discovered his true identity, and he'd been taken captive. How long he had traveled to reach his current location was no more than a rough guess.

The climate gave him a clue to his location, but that only narrowed his guesses to a quarter of the globe.

On the second day of his captivity, the door of his hut opened, not at the usual mealtime, and Doctor Palmer found himself squinting through the noonday sunlight that poured in, at two figures that stood in the doorway.

Two men in sailors' striped jerseys, coarse cloth pants and bare, calloused feet, scooped him up and, gentler then he expected, took him from the hut.

Palmer, too weak to put up a fight, allowed himself to be dragged along, down a narrow snaking path, through a stretch of tropical jungle.

The jungle opened up into a large, man-made clearing, dotted with two-dozen tents. Some were large, elegant and silken; others made from rough, weathered sailcloth.

Palmer was escorted to the largest tent, set in the center of the makeshift village.

It had a more extravagant air about it, reminding him of his brief stay in Bombay. Two younger men, their uniforms similar, but in a better state of repair than his escorts, one slim and athletic, the other a bit burly and sporting the beginnings of a beard, stood at attention at the tent's main entrance.

They took custody of Palmer, escorting him to a white, wingback chair.

After days of harsh captivity, a comfortable chair seemed blissful enough that it took his focus off his situation, until the fair-haired guard, leaned in.

"Remain here," he instructed quietly. "The Captain will speak with you in a moment."

They quietly exited, leaving Palmer alone in his exotic surroundings.

Allowing himself the briefest of interludes to savor his comfort, he then began to study the interior. The décor was sparse, but retained the mix of nautical and Indian stylings.

Suddenly, the flap at the back of the tent parted and the younger of his two guards entered, holding it open, for two new arrivals.

The first was a robust, middle-aged man, dressed in the uniform of a ships' captain: blue coat, decorated with the appropriate braid and polished buttons, grey trousers and a black-peaked cap tucked under his arm. He sported an impressive black beard and a prominent forehead. His bright eyes studied Palmer with an angry intelligence.

But it was the second man who caught the young detective's attention. He was frail and elderly; his snow-white beard hung down to his chest. His movements were slow and deliberate. He leaned heavily on an ornately carved cane. He, too, wore a uniform: a long coat of bottle-green, black boots polished to a mirror shine and a turban of a lighter shade of green, adorned with a single blue stone, was perched upon his wizened head.

Declining any offer of assistance, he made his slow, steady way to a high-backed white chair, set at a white desk.

He sat, leaned his cane against the desk, accepted a glass of tea from a servant, sipped and then dabbed at his lips.

The other captain and two sailors stood by patiently, while this gentle ritual was enacted.

The old man eventually placed the glass upon a silver tray and, when he turned his gaze upon Eric Palmer, all of his frailness and vagueness melted away.

Palmer suddenly was transported back to his school days, and rather than feeling a prisoner, instead he felt he had been dragged before a rather stern schoolmaster.

"Do you know who I am, Doctor Palmer?" the elderly man asked, his voice dry and sharp.

Palmer nodded. His mouth felt dry and he didn't believe it could solely be blamed on his captivity.

"Captain Nemo," he replied, hoarsely.

The old man nodded, with a satisfied expression that gave Palmer the impression he had passed some test, proving he was a promising student, rather than a delinquent one.

"Do you know where you are?"

Another simple question, but Palmer could feel that this was another test, maybe even one with a trap, hidden within it. It felt less like Nemo was attempting to interrogate a prisoner, and more like a job interview.

"Judging by the few glimpses I've been allowed, and your presence, I would have to guess that I have been taken to Duke's Key."

The standing Captain and servants exchanged anxious glances, while Nemo merely leaned forward and steepled his long fingers together, while continuing to study the young detective.

He then nodded to himself.

"Every fifty years, the pirates of the world gather," Nemo intoned, quietly. "During the course of this conference, territory is marked, disputes are settled and so, amongst our community, peace is kept."

Palmer nodded in stunned understanding. The legendary Pirate's Conference!

And somehow, fate and his own misadventure had dropped him in the midst of one the largest, most infamous gatherings of madmen, cutthroats and rogues in the world!

"I understand that you would have no reason to believe me," Palmer said, focusing on Captain Nemo, while struggling to remain even-toned. "But my presence here is sheer accident. I had no knowledge of this gathering, or any desire to infiltrate it…"

The uniformed man, with the black beard, humphed to himself, while Nemo merely gave another hint of a smile and a nod.

"There is no need to protest your innocence," he assured the young detective. "The intent to have you here, was all mine."

"What…?" Palmer exclaimed, unable to stop himself.

"Circumstances allowed for your capture to occur as there was a need for an investigator."

Palmer found himself blinking as his brain struggled to take in Nemo's words.

"Are you saying... uh... that I was brought here because you need to engage the services of a... er... a detective?"

Nemo merely nodded.

Palmer ran a hand through his matted and tangled hair as his mind raced. It was difficult to formulate any plans when the situation kept spiraling away in odd and inexplicable directions.

"I don't quite know what to say...?" he muttered. "Should my fee include travel expenses?"

"If you are lucky," the standing Captain growled, "your 'fee' will include your continued health."

Nemo raised a bony hand, halting any further exchange between the two.

"Enough, Robur," he said. "We must excuse Doctor Palmer, as he comes to terms with his current... unusual circumstances."

"And you are not encountering me at my best," Palmer added, taking in his ragged attire and ratty beard.

"As I said, every fifty years, there occurs this gathering of those deemed by civilized nations as pirates," Nemo explained. "Amongst ourselves, we settle disputes, form alliances and other such matters. It is a precarious situation, at the best of times."

"I can imagine," Palmer nodded.

Despite his current surreal and hazardous circumstances, he felt strangely calm, as the analytical portion of his mind took over and he began to treat all he saw and heard as facts to be taken in, and mentally sifted through, while he focused on finding those crumbs of information that were essential.

He was on a case.

"In general, a safe harbor is chosen, and one amongst our number is designated as 'host.' He acts as arbitrator, his crew as peacekeepers. There is an added tension at this point in time, amongst my brethren," Nemo continued. "As the emerging number of 'pirates of the air' have joined the conference and wish their community to have an equal voice. So, it was decided that, for this conference, to have dual hosts, one from the sea and one from the sky. Captain Robur and I were chosen from our respective factions."

"So, a crime has occurred, and due to the added tensions between the two pirate factions," Palmer mused, scratching at his unkempt beard thoughtfully, "a neutral party is required, not only to investigate but to, hopefully, negate potential discord between the two parties...? Am I correct in my summation?"

Both Captains nodded in assent.

"Then, I must say, I am at a bit of a loss as to what interest should I have in preventing you from fighting amongst yourselves?"

There was a moment of stunned silence about the tent. The two guards struggled to look anywhere in the enclosure but towards their respective captains, while Robur rumbled like a volcano on the verge of eruption.

Again, Nemo halted any protest with a casual gesture.

"Enough, Robur," he said, with quiet authority. "Doctor Palmer would be no use to us if all he did was parrot back what he believes we wish to hear. This matter requires truth."

He then turned back to Palmer.

"Yes, Doctor, we are pirates: brigands and outlaws. We prey upon the civilized nations of the world," Nemo explained, in a sardonic, conversational tone. "But, it is the accords created during these gatherings that set the limits, the boundaries, of our lawless activities. If our tenuous alliance is pushed to the breaking point, then those fragile borders will drift away like ash in the wind, and the world will become our battlefield, with the teeming masses of humanity mere obstacles in our way. The civilized world may see us as evil, but this conference is a quite a necessary evil."

There followed another anxious pause, as all of the tents' occupants watched the bedraggled detective and awaited his response.

"Yes," Palmer nodded. "I see your point and cannot fault your logic, Captain Nemo."

Robur harrumphed with satisfaction. Nemo merely nodded in acknowledgment.

"I believe," the elder pirate continued, "that there was discussion of your fee."

"Ah, yes, well…" Palmer began.

"Resolve this matter and I shall see to your safe passage to a neutral port," Nemo announced.

"I would also like to request better accommodations than I have, so far, partaken of, while conducting my investigation," Palmer suggested, stroking at his salt and dirt crusted beard and ragged wardrobe.

"It will be seen to," Nemo replied. "Misters Gunn and Haddock will escort you to the scene of the crime. I will join you shortly."

Feeling he had been dismissed, Eric Palmer got to his feet, glanced, at his escort and held out his bound hands.

The young, blond sailor glanced at the two captains for instructions and must have received some signal, as he drew a sword and cut the bedraggled detective's bond, freeing his hands.

Palmer flexed his hands, while they walked, getting the feeling back, as well as attempting to mentally prepare for the task ahead.

He needed to compartmentalize his current situation from the coming investigation.

His situation was deeply worrying and tenuous. Perhaps escape was an option, but currently, it seemed that his best hope was going ahead and trusting Nemos' word that a successful conclusion to this investigation would result in his safe release from the pirates' conference.

"Since I assume you gentlemen will be assisting me, as well as acting as my chaperones," Palmer said. "perhaps introductions are in order?"

"I'm Gunn," the fair-haired sailor said. "This surly fellow is Archibald Haddock."

The bearded sailor's growl, told Palmer that he was not enamored with being referred to by his first name.

"How do you come to be in the service of Captain Nemo?" Palmer asked, keeping his tone light and conversational, as they moved from the sandy clearing and down a gravelly path that ran into tropical foliage.

"My family are seamen," Gunn replied. "And have had our share of encounters with piracy. My Christian name, James, actually comes from a friend of some distant relative. Story goes, he saved my great uncle or grandfather from pirates…"

"Oh blatherskites…!" Haddock muttered. "This story again!"

Gunn chuckled to himself, indicating this was a long running joke between the two sailors. He then gestured and the trio left the main path, onto a narrower, snaky one, crowded by jungle on either side.

"Tell me about the… compound where the pirates camp," Palmer asked, pushing aside grasping, leafy branches, as they walked single file.

The sailors exchanged a glance, then shrugged.

"All ships dock in the bay," Gunn explained. "The Captains bunk in the tent village we just left, while the crews either stay shipboard or camp on the beach. A few of the captains are not what you'd call trusting or social. They set their tents a bit apart."

The path ended at a small clearing, which contained a modest, grey tent.

"Our destination?" Palmer asked, pointing at the canvas structure.

Receiving a nod, Palmer paused and took in his surroundings before proceeding.

"Wait here, please," he said, reaching for the tent flap.

The ceiling was mere inches above his head. There was a cot, a wooden chair, small table, an oil lamp and a corpse.

The dead man, sprawled on the ground, appeared young, slim and dressed all in black, from his boots to the head rag and domino mask.

Palmer stood in the opening of the tent, absorbing every detail he could from this macabre tableau. There was little sign of the furniture having been moved, yet the posture of the course indicated the victim had died by violence. His black silken shirt showed a small, blood-crusted tear on the chest, evidence of stabbing being the cause of death.

"Yet," Palmer muttered thoughtfully. "He must have known his assailant or been caught completely by surprise… Who was this man?"

"That," Gunn said, joining him in the tent opening. "Was… is… the Dread Pirate Roberts."

The sailor's tone was matter-of-fact, but the information it conveyed was as startling to the detective, as if he had said the corpse was Father Christmas!

"Roberts!" Palmer breathed. "That's... impossible... he's a story... no more real than the Flying Dutchman... Besides he'd have to be...?"

"Over three hundred years old," Gunn prompted, his tone not altering. "According to the lore, he's attended every conclave of pirates since the first one."

Palmer shook his head in disbelief, his analytical mind having been given a fact it could not accept. It was like placing a stone on a railroad track. He scratched at his beard, and then without further word, gestured for Gunn to leave.

Once the tent flap had closed, Palmer moved through the dim interior and crouched down, besides the corpse. A fantastic notion niggled at his brain, and with a sigh, he tentatively reached out and parted the dead man's lips.

To his relief, the teeth were, slightly yellowed, but otherwise normal.

"Not a vampire," he muttered. "That's something, at least."

Hesitantly, he reached for the black mask, pulling it off. The face underneath was narrow, with a sharp nose, the hair a sandy blonde.

"Why do I feel I should know you...?" Palmer asked, faintly puzzled.

Not that he had been expecting any major revelation as to the man beneath the mask, but to be on a remote, tropical island, surrounded by pirates and experience the vague notion that he should know the fellow he'd just met, as one does at cocktail parties, was nearly as disconcerting as the notion that this man had died at the ripe old age of three hundred.

Further investigation showed that, for a dread pirate, Roberts had surprisingly uncalloused hands, and that there was no evidence of any object, laying about that tent that could have caused his fatal wound.

"Shape indicates a dagger, more than a cutting knife," Palmer pondered "Or, since I'm dealing with pirates, a sword... more of the fencing variety than the traditional cutlass... I suppose that narrows the suspect list... which I must get around to obtaining at some point..."

Palmer glanced about the room, but nothing else struck him as significant. He'd obtained all he could from the crime scene and needed to extend his investigation.

Captain Nemo awaited outside. The elder pirate was seated on a camp stool and leaning on his cane.

Palmer peered at him, trying to arrange his thoughts, his many questions and concerns. After several moments, he ducked back into the tent, brought out the chair and placed it across from Nemo's. He then sat, and, after a further moment of thoughtful mustache-stroking, began to speak.

"Are the stories about him true?"

"About Roberts?" Nemo mused. "All of them, and none of them. It is the way with pirates in general, and with this gathering in particular."

"Has anyone else seen the face beneath the mask?" Palmer asked.

"The crewmen sent to investigate most likely sated their curiosity," Nemo replied. "But, if you are asking about his true identity, then I would have to say, no."

"I was told the Dread Pirate Roberts had been attending these conferences since they began. Is that true?"

"Are you asking me if the stories of Roberts immortality are true?" Nemo countered.

Palmer nodded in reply.

"What do your deductive skills tell you?" Nemo asked.

"It tells me that if you keep speaking in riddles, then your pirates are going to go to war," Palmer replied, with grim frustration.

For a moment, Nemo's calm demeanor slipped, and a flicker of anxiety flashed, before quickly being stifled.

"I am a detective, not a magician," Palmer continued, in a quieter, sympathetic tone. "I require facts... the solution does not merely spring forth, like Athena from the brow of Zeus."

"To navigate, one must have stars or compass points to guide the way," Nemo murmured, nodding to himself. "I see. I have not recruited you as part of my crew, but rather have entered into a partnership of sorts. What would you like to know? Is there more you need from this 'scene of the crime'?"

"No," Palmer said, shaking his head. "It has told me all I need. The 'how' of this murder is really quite straightforward. It is the 'who' and 'why' which are confounding, as I know nothing, and am given only rumors and legends."

Nemo straightened slightly, his fingers toying with the carved ivory head of his cane.

"Where should I start?" he asked.

"The victim," Palmer replied. "Tell me of the Dread Pirate Roberts."

"There are several, among my pirate brethren, who claim to be immortal," Nemo said, thoughtfully. "A few, I believe, speak the truth, but for most, it is a ruse. The Dread Pirate Roberts was not a man, but a succession of men. Who the original Roberts was, or if it has ever been more than just a title, I cannot say."

"Is this common knowledge?" Palmer asked.

"Suspected, but not confirmed," Nemo replied. "Those of us who have lived a generous amount of years have noticed telltale hints as we've crossed paths with Roberts."

"Do you know anything about the current Roberts or his predecessor?"

Nemo gave a brief, cynical smile.

"The entire idea of the succession is that it is meant to be secret," he explained. "There is no guest book that they sign, no formal paperwork for applicants."

"You've crossed paths with Roberts before?" Palmer asked.

"On occasion. Pirates are not, by nature, a social group. Minor conflicts can... am I a suspect?"

The aged pirate seemed torn between curiosity and a darker emotion that caused Palmer to sit up straighter.

"Not as such…" he began, hesitantly. "As one of the older pirates, I assumed you would have encountered Roberts… This one, or the others…"

"This Roberts was, I suspect, a recent addition," Nemo interrupted, not sounding entirely placated. "He has shifted his territory away from Asia, where I previously crossed paths with him, concentrating upon the waters about France and Europe."

"Yes, I recall hearing rumors… stories," Palmer nodded. "Something about him… seems… familiar… I can't put my finger on why…?"

With an effort, Captain Nemo got to his feet, and with the two sailors hovering nearby, hobbled over to the tent. After several minutes, he returned.

"It is a distinctive face," he commented, lowering himself down slowly. "There is a hint of nobility about it, but even death has not taken away the arrogance of expression. Unfortunately, it jars no memory."

"So, we know nothing of who he was before he became Roberts," Palmer mused. "No idea if his past life held the reason for his murder… which just leaves us with an island full of suspects, all of whom are working equally hard to keep their own pasts secret… Then, there is only one thing to do…"

"And that would be?" Nemo asked, intrigued.

"A bath," Palmer replied, matter of factly. "I cannot concentrate with the constant itching of this beard."

Soon, dressed in the plain clothes of a common sailor, sporting trimmed hair and mustache, Palmer sat under a palm tree, on the edge of the tent village.

Gunn and Haddock had been assigned to assist in his efforts, and most likely to keep an eye on him.

Gunn was eager to help, as well as seeming interested in Palmer's methods and being involved in the intrigues of the conference.

Haddock slumped nearby, grumbling and taking occasional clandestine sips from a flask.

"Shouldn't we… uh… be… I don't know, searching for clues?" Gunn asked.

He was seated on the sand, but upright and trying to keep following wherever the young detective was looking.

"We are," Palmer replied, absently, watching the population of the pirate conference going about their business. "I have no straight line to follow: suspects and motives are scattered like breadcrumbs for the pigeons. My only hope is to see if I can narrow the focus."

"I feel I should we doing… something," Gunn said.

"Then talk to me, tell me about the conference."

"I'd heard of it, every sailor has heard the stories, but was newly arrived to the *Nautilus* crew. We had practically no inkling that it was our destination. The Captain plays his cards very close to his vest."

Palmer nodded.

"That fellow... the stout Captain in the domino mask...?"

"Captain Mors," Gunn replied. "A German air pirate... surly. Seems constantly peeved that he doesn't have the reputation of Captain Nemo, or even Captain Robur..."

"Ah, yes, the self-proclaimed 'Master of the world'," Palmer mused. "Angry fellow... seems to chafe in Nemo's shadow... Mors... He's kept mostly to Europe... He might have come in conflict with Roberts...?"

He frowned in thought, only to be distracted by several men of Indian appearance. They gave an air of title, but were dressed quite plainly in brown tunics and unadorned, white turbans.

"Crew men?" Palmer asked, inclining his head towards the passing trio.

"They're from the Singh Brotherhood," Gunn replied. "Nasty bunch. The Captain doesn't like or trust them. They operate mostly in Africa."

"So many of you to sort through," Palmer grumbled, stroking his mustache in thought. "It could be anything from a recent grudge to... a hundred years in the past... there are immortals, but what of other... um... pirate dynasties...?"

"What?" Gunn asked, hesitantly.

"You said, you're from an old sailing family, and it seems common knowledge Roberts was a succession of men, rather than actually being immortal... Who else here has a history like that?"

"The Singh," Gunn said, after a few minutes thought. "They are more a... cult than a family, though. The Turner family, though can't say I'm sure there's one in attendance... Same with Sala's band of women... You think it's an old grudge...?"

"At this point, I'm not sure how much actual thinking I am doing," Palmer replied with a cynical smile. "But, there are... hints... little pieces that seem to... I don't know, fit... somehow... That gentleman seems to require our attention?"

"My attention," Gunn corrected, getting to his feet. "Mister Ishmael, the *Nautilus*' first mate. Haddock, pretend to guard Doctor Palmer, I'll be back as soon as I can."

Palmer watched the young sailor jog over to his superior, then glanced over at his remaining guard, who was snoring.

"Makes one feel right secure, doesn't it?" A voice asked.

Palmer turned and gave a slight start, before quickly recovering.

The jungle parted, like a theater curtain and a man emerged, tall and cadaverously thin, with eyes of the sharpest blue, a long cascade of black Charles the Second curls and a pointed mustache. He wore a foppish outfit, a blood red long coat adorned with buttons polished to a shine, stockings and black, buckled shoes. His black hat bore a snow-white ostrich plume. His right hand was missing and in its place, a steel hook.

"Doctor Palmer, I presume?" he asked in a refined purr.

His smile resembled that of an undertaker anticipating a busy season.

"I... uh... yes," Palmer muttered. "And you are...?"

"Captain James Hook, at your service," the pirate said, making an elegant leg.

Feeling at a disadvantage, Palmer stood, dusting sand off his pant legs.

"Ah," he said, feeling quite at a loss as to what to follow it up with.

Every bit as legendary as Nemo, Hook was quite possibly, one of the pirates not pretending to be centuries-old, but still laying claim to actual immortality. Despite his quaint, old world appearance, he had a reputation every bit as fearsome as Blackbeard or the Dread Pirate Roberts.

"So," Hook drawled, studying the detective. "You are Nemo's eye. The hound amongst the hares."

"I rather think that might be the other way round," Palmer said.

"Quite," Hook said, with a bone-dry chuckle. "How goes the deducing, if I may ask?"

"Are you concerned for your own place on the suspect list?" Palmer asked, instead of answering the query.

Hook's chuckle more resembled a sharp cough.

"Lord, no, idle curiosity at best. Killed me own fair share of Roberts. If I'd added one more to the tally, I'd see no need to skulk about. More wishing to judge which way the, shall we say, political wind, is blowing."

Under Hook's gaze, Palmer grew a deeper understanding of what a mouse feels when cornered by a cat, while at the same time, sharply aware that Hook seemed to be leading the conversation somewhere: He had a question that needed answering, or wished to impart some bit of information, but only under his own eccentric, devious terms.

"Are you for continuing the pirate alliance, or are you for war?" Palmer asked, unsure, but thinking that if he kept Hook talking, he'd gain some needed knowledge.

"Oh, it's much of a muchness, as far as I am concerned. I have me own concerns, me own vendettas... This bunch are welcome to scheme and stab as they wish. One likes to keep up on the gossip... bit like attending family dinners at the holidays, that way."

"I see," Palmer frowned, sternly, but still unsure.

He decided to try for a more aggressive stance in this verbal fencing and see where it took the conversation.

"Well, much as I wish I could indulge you, I do have other matters to attend to. If it's merely gossip you seek, might I suggest the kitchen tent?"

Hook's over-done gentlemanly façade cracked for a moment, and the glint in his eyes was decidedly murderous.

"A civil tongue is more likely to stay in one's mouth," he said in a low, dangerous tone.

Palmer realized he had a chance at more honest answers from the legendary pirate, if only he could gain it without also receiving any fatal wounds along the way.

"Yes, I should be more considerate of the feelings of a notorious cutthroat," Palmer countered. "Delicate as a child."

Hook grew slightly pale and leaned back.

"A child!" he muttered, darkly, his hand going for his sword, which in an instant was a mere inch away from Palmer's throat.

"Choose your next words carefully, m'lad," Hook rasped.

Whatever those words were, they were interrupted by a blade sliding along Hooks and James Gunn stepping between the pirate and the detective.

"Sir, I will remind you of the codes of the conference," Gunn said. "As well as reminding you that this man is under Captain Nemo's personal watch."

The two men locked gazes, prepared to spill blood, rather than back down from the other.

After the initial shock, Palmer returned to calmly studying the two swordsmen. Taking in the scene, without any seeming thought to the danger he might be in. He tucked away several interesting crumbs of information, and then turned his mind to extracting himself and his chaperone from the situation without any bloodshed.

"Excuse me," Palmer interrupted. "I have no wish to see violence done. So, allow me: Captain Hook... My words were ill chosen and provocative. My sincere apologies."

Both Captain and sailor seemed caught off guard by the detective's words. After several tense moments, Hook shrugged, sheathed his blade and gave a mocking bow.

"Such gentlemanly conduct is appreciated in this day and age," he drawled. "I accept and apologize for allowing temper to trip me up; most unseemly. Good day to ye both."

As he sauntered off, Gunn kept his blade at the ready, not trusting the Captain's words. Palmer glanced at his sword and then laid a hand on the sailor's wrist.

"Don't worry about him," Palmer said. "Dangerous as he undoubtedly is, I doubt we have any more to fear from Captain James Hook."

"What happened?" Gunn asked, returning his sword to his belt. "What did he want?"

"I'm not entirely sure," Palmer said, stroking his chin. "Nor am I sure if what I've learned is what he intended to impart. Curious fellow."

"That's one way of putting it." Gunn frowned and then gave the sleeping Haddock a kick.

"Huh...what...?" the bearded sailor sputtered.

"Go back to sleep," Gunn muttered, turning back to the detective. "I am sorry for that…"

" Don't be," Palmer said, "Some pieces have come together…"

"Really? Sitting in the dirt and nearly being stabbed tells you who killed Roberts?"

"Missing a few pieces," Palmer nodded, absently. "I need to think… My old accommodations, anyone else occupying them?"

"Um… no."

"Then, I'll go there." Palmer nodded. "Tell Captain Nemo that by morning, I think I may have a solution for him."

Still nodding to himself, deep in contemplation, the young Doctor walked off, returning to his former prison, leaving his guard puzzled and unsure…

Palmer, despite his announcement, felt equally unsure.

He felt certain that he knew who the murderer was, but the why of it was a slender thread of knowledge that he was following through a hurricane of doubt.

His former prison, a sturdy, but otherwise dreary shack, set on a thumb of land jutting off from the main island, offered little comfort, but all the solitude he required. There was a desolate tranquility about the place; nothing but the sand, rolling ocean and sounds of the jungle.

For a moment, he was able to forget he was surrounded by pirates and expecting the arrival of a murderer.

"If I live through this, I shall give serious thought to finding a dull corner of England and never travel to anywhere more exotic then the local pub," he lied, quietly, to himself.

Around the curve of the island, he could hear the faint sounds of the pirate harbor, the noises of any shipyard in the world, mixed with an undercurrent hum of exotic modes of transportation.

He let it swirl around, listening to the sounds of the world changing.

There might always be pirates, rogues and villains in the world, but at this very moment, who they were and how they plied their trade, and made their way across the map, was changing.

It felt oddly concerning and humbling that he was in the middle of it and, perhaps, having some impact on that change. He could only hope that his contribution would prove a positive one.

His slide into maudlin contemplation was halted by a new sound, a nautical sound, coming closer.

In the gathering dusk, the small, black boat had drifted up, practically unto the beach, unnoticed by the detective.

There were two figures in it, one stayed huddled over the oars, while the second jumped onto the beach, and strode across the damp sand, towards the hut.

He was slim, moved with a self-assured ease and dressed in a familiar, all black ensemble.

"The Dread Pirate Roberts, I presume," Palmer said, getting to his feet. "Or would it be more appropriate to say 'A' Dread Pirate Roberts?"

"Doctor Palmer," the man in black replied, in a low voice, giving a slight bow. "I believe you were expecting me?"

"No, Captain Roberts, I was not expecting *you*. On the other hand, Mister Gunn..."

The pirate frowned, then pulled off his mask.

"When did you suspect me?" the young sailor asked.

"You caught my attention quite quickly, not as a murder suspect at first, but merely as someone to keep watch of," Palmer explained. "You were suspiciously helpful, not to mention quite well-informed for a newly-acquired member of Captain Nemo's crew. I, at first, merely assumed, your captain had chosen you as my chaperone to help steer my investigation. It was your defense against Captain Hook that finally helped me connect you to the murder of the previous Roberts."

"How so?"

"Roberts was killed by a precise, single stab wound," Palmer continued. "A single, distinctive wound. I had noticed that very few of the pirates carry swords; I suppose it's gone out of style in these modern times. You are one of the exceptions."

Gunn glanced down at his scabbard, then back up at the detective.

"When you so thoughtfully sprang to my defense, I was able to examine both your and Captain Hook's swords. Not only is your blade of the right design to have made Robert's wound, but I was also able to notice how both of you hold and use your weapons: Hook aims for the throat."

Palmer absently raised a hand across his own throat at the memory of how he'd gained that knowledge.

"You are left-handed, as is the murderer, but also aim for the heart. My dilemma was in piecing together a motive: Were you merely some other pirate's agent, or working on your own?"

"And what did you decide?" Gunn asked intently, tucking his mask into his sword belt.

"It was interesting to me how many times dynasties and families were mentioned when discussing pirate history," Palmer explained. "Several people referenced it when I spoke with them. You, yourself, spoke of your own ancestor. So, it seemed a place to focus. As well as who benefited from the death of Roberts..."

"Von Warteck," Gunn snapped, irritably.

"I'm sorry?"

"He was never Roberts. He was Manfred Von Warteck." Gunn said, darkly, practically spitting the name.

"Von Warteck?" Palmer muttered. "Thank you. The missing piece of the puzzle. That's why he appeared familiar..."

"What?" Gunn said. "Now, I'm confused...?"

"Back when I was first learning to balance my medical practice and my detective practice, I was involved with a case. There was a Von Warteck amongst the suspects... A financier of some sort, and the family resemblance is quite striking."

"They are a vile clan," Gunn said, his brow furrowed. "With aspirations to rival the great criminal brotherhoods of Europe, such as the Black Coats..."

"Was that how Manfred was chosen by the previous Roberts?"

"He wasn't. I was."

Gunn sighed, glanced away, towards the darkening ocean, and then back to Palmer.

"He wished to retire," he continued, "so he approached me, and having the family romantic streak, as well as a notion to see what could be accomplished if the Dread Pirate Roberts was a bit less dread, I accepted. I had to deal with some... personal business, and was to rendezvous and take on my new roll. I arrived to find, my predecessor dead and a new Roberts already installed, along with several key crewmembers. I had no way to fight for my claim..."

"But, you knew of the approaching pirates' conference, and joined the crew of the *Nautilus*!" Palmer interrupted. "Then, taking advantage of the fraudulent Roberts' increased need for secrecy, you were easily able to catch him alone and unaware."

The pirate nodded.

"So, case solved," Palmer said, clasping his hands behind his back. "Except for a remaining loose end—myself."

Gunn looked at the detective, momentarily puzzled, and then breaking out in a smile.

"You? Doctor Palmer, you are my newest, dearest friend and ally!" Gunn chuckled, drawing out and replacing his black mask. "I was stymied, as to how to take my rightful station, as I was unsure how it would be possible to resolve matters without causing grave, political upset... while several of the Captains were displeased with the fraudulent Roberts' recent ambitions, they take the neutrality of the conference very seriously."

"And then Nemo happened upon a detective," Palmer muttered, thoughtfully. "A hare amongst the hounds... interesting."

"You, as a disinterested party, can solve the murder in such a way as to keep what passes for peace amongst the pirate community." Roberts said, crossing his arms and nodding. "You have nothing to fear from me. I couldn't have done it without you!"

He gave an elaborate bow, a jaunty salute and drifted off into the night.

The next morning, Doctor Palmer was trotted out before a gathering of pirates, where he presented his conclusions.

There were dark grumblings from several captains, but how much was caused by doubts over his findings and how much was merely a few disappointed, bloodthirsty souls who had been hoping for a war, was hard to discern.

While he was happy to expose the plans of the Von Warteck family, he was suitably vague concerning the identity of the spurned successor to the title of Dread Pirate Roberts, stating merely that he had acted solely in his own interests, rather than as part of some intrigue against the broader pirate community.

From the dark looks he received, Eric Palmer was aware that he may have gained the favor of Captains Nemo and Roberts, but had also gained the animosity of several other pirates.

He then retreated to the shelter of one of the many tents.

The mystery solved, there was no further need for a detective and the pirates still had business to attend to.

The next morning found him on the beach, watching the numerous ships, submersibles and aircrafts leaving the safe harbor and returning to their various corners of the world.

Palmer stood, watching the surf and sky, pondering what plans the pirates had for the world, and which of them he might cross paths with again, when a sailor came jogging up and tapped his arm.

"Captain wishes a word, sir."

Palmer nodded and strode over to the dock, where Nemo stood.

He leaned heavily on his cane and it caused the detective a mix of emotion: a bit of pride that Nemo judged him worth the effort, and a sadness to see this larger than life man seeming so frail and mortal.

Nemo nodded in greeting, and Palmer returned the nod, feeling the elder pirate should be the one to speak first.

"There is a ship at the end of the beach," Nemo said, gesturing with his free hand. "Its master will take you and young Haddock to a safe harbor."

"Haddock?"

"His weakness for the bottle renders him a poor seaman. Perhaps one day, he will master it, but till then…"

Nemo made a dismissive gesture.

"It seems you have lost several crewmen during this conference," Palmer said. "I hope that won't hamper any plans for future voyages?"

Nemo favored him with a brief flicker of a smile and then turned distant eyes towards the sea.

"This conference was my last, great effort," he said, with quiet dignity. "This world and I have grown tired of each other and will soon part ways."

"Did you know?" Palmer asked.

141

"Know?" Nemo echoed, turning back, slowly to face the detective. "About Roberts? Suspected, or more likely, hoped, his death was a personal vendetta, rather than politically motivated."

"Well, then it was quite lucky you had recently acquired a captive investigator," Palmer mused.

"Yes, quite a fortunate happenstance."

Again the flicker of a smile from the master of the *Nautilus*.

"Circumstances aside, it was an honor to have met you, Captain Nemo," Palmer said, extending his hand.

Nemo stuck his free hand into his longcoat pocket, and Palmer was sure he was about to be snubbed, when the aged explorer brought out his thin, veined hand and offered it to the detective.

He did not actually shake the detective's' offered hand, but rather pressed a folded piece of paper into it.

"With the conference ended, so does its rule of neutrality," Nemo explained, straightening up and squaring his thin shoulders. "The smuggling network you were investigating when you were captured was the Singh Brotherhood attempting to broach an alliance with the Black Coats. I have no interest in that alliance succeeding."

Palmer nodded his thanks, and then stood on the dock, watching Nemo turn, and then walk down the dock, to his submarine and into history.

This story departs from our standard formula, something we are usually reluctant to do. But in this case, it was such a brilliant homage to one of the most famous and memorable characters of French popular genre fiction, Captain Nemo, that it felt "at home" in our anthology. Jean-Pierre Laigle is the nom-de-plume *of a well-known French science fiction writer and essayist. This tale was first published in the French sf magazine* Galaxies #30 *in 2014.*

Jean-Pierre Laigle: *Mobilis in Vacuo*

An Unpublished Chapter of Twenty Thousand Leagues Under The Sea
*by M. Jules Verne Rejected By Its Publisher M. Pierre-Jules Hetzel, Presented As A Gift By The Author In Its Manuscript Form To His Friend
His Excellency The Count Of Paris; Thought Lost, But Recently Rediscovered Among His Personal Papers*

To the spirit of J.M. Troska the first to relaunch Captain Nemo.[8]

"...it suffices that I justify the terrible actions of the Captain because of the provocations of which he is the object. Nemo does not attack ships to sink them; he responds to their attacks. But nowhere, despite what your letter says, have I created a character who kills for the love of killing. He has a generous nature with feelings that are occasionally expressed in the environment in which he lives. His hatred of humanity is sufficiently explained by what he and his own family have suffered..."
Jules Verne's answer to a letter from Pierre-Jules Hetzel (1869).

CHAPTER X: THE PRODIGIOUS ASCENSION
(*to be inserted between the current chapters IX and X of Part II
of the published version*)

Leaving the ruined city in the realm of Neptune, we took off our scubasuits in the changing room. At a gesture from him, I followed Nemo to the library. He offered me a seaweed cigar and waited for me to light it before lighting his. Soon the air of the *Nautilus* improved under the heady clouds of smoke

---

[8] Jan Matzal (1881-1961), a.k.a. J. M. Troska, was a Czech sci-fi writer, who penned four young adult genre novels featuring Captain Nemo: *Nemo's Empire* [Nemova říše, 1939], *Nemo's World* [Nemův svět, 1941], *Commands from the Aether* [Rozkazy z éteru, 1939] and *The Invisible Army* [Neviditelná armada, 1939]. His books were very popular with children and teenagers. *Ed.*

and Captain Nemo broke the solemn silence which had presided over our underwater excursion, when he had traced the name "ATLANTIS" on the basaltic rock:

"Professor Aronnax," he began, "I wanted to be alone with you, for I owe you an explanation.

"Do you? Is that why you didn't invite Ned Land and Conseil to join us?" I asked reproachfully.

"Do you remember that I promised you a strange excursion?"

"It seems to me that you kept your word," I said.

"There is an even stranger story that I'm going to tell you..."

"One that my companions of misfortune could never reveal to the outside world since the *Nautilus* is their prison," I reminded Nemo.

"Professor Aronnax," he replied, with some irritation, "you know that you are not my prisoner. We are both devotees of science. However loyal they may be to you, I can't say as much about your friends. It seemed to me necessary to conceal from them certain secrets, of which you have had only a tiny glimpse. The relics you saw only foretell the fate of our own megalopolises that the Creator, weary of our misuse of knowledge, will someday drown under a second great Flood. Will you believe me if I tell you the full story...?"

"I'm all ears," I encouraged him, sensing his hesitation.

The man who had chosen to live under the waves took a long puff on his cigar and gave a tired look at the crowded bookshelves of the salon before returning his gaze to my modest person. In other circumstances, I would have liked to think of this character who professed to not be a civilized man as endearing, for had he not spared three survivors from an enemy ship? I was impatient to go to bed at this early hour, and was tempted to speak again, but my host shook the ashes from his cigar and began:

"Professor, will you mind if I remind you that I have so far demanded no oath from you or your companions in exchange for free movement aboard my *Nautilus*?"

"So far."

"Yes. I have not made a mystery that all that you have learned here must perish with you, before or at the same time as the *Nautilus* and all its secrets. But that is nothing compared to what I am about to tell you. Disclosing it would provoke catastrophes of a magnitude comparable to the one that sent Atlantis and its brilliant civilization to the bottom of the ocean. So this time, I shall ask you for your solemn word before continuing. Will you give it to me?"

"You have it," I replied without hesitation.

"Very good. Were you not surprised that I only showed you the ruins of Atlantis from afar?"

"Well, thinking back on it, perhaps, yes. Could they be haunted by the same gigantic creatures we saw near the dead forest? In that case, why not sail over them with the *Nautilus*? It is true that you should have locked Mister Land

and my good man Conseil in their cabins if you were so anxious to keep it all a secret."

"Your second observation adequately describes my situation when I first discovered the sunken city. I interrupted the navigation over the ruins. But by so doing, I almost lost my life, those of my companions—and the *Nautilus* itself."

"Ah! I would never have guessed! What danger did you run into? I'm inpatient to find out!"

"All in due course, Professor. I intended to 'land' the *Nautilus* on a unoccupied central space that reminded me of a Roman racecourse in order to better explore the city. But, as we touched the bottom, my ship was struck by an intense light and I felt we were rising. I had ordered the two bay windows of the grand salon opened, confident of the safety of the maneuver. So I stood there, blinded by the light, pressed against the floor by an invincible force, and I lost consciousness.

"When I woke up, my sight had come back to me, but I was floating in the air. Imagine my shock! The paintings adorning the salon's walls were drifting around, as well as all many other objects. A spectral light filtered through the bay windows which were covered by a thick frost. Having reached out to sweep it, I was pulled back abruptly, but not without tearing a bit of skin from the tip of my finger. I realized then how cold it was inside the room.

It soon became clear to me that the *Nautilus* was no longer subject to the effects of gravity. Regrettably, by virtue of the Newtonian principle that an action produces an equal reaction in the opposite direction, I pushed away several canvases and thus propelled myself to the corridor, where multiple other providential objects allowed me to eventually reach the engine room. There, I ordered my crew to activate the powerful sodium batteries that would generate heat and light.

"Slowly, the temperature rose inside the *Nautilus*. I had all the pieces of iron that we could find magnetized. It was enough for a man holding one in each hand to move forward by pressing them alternately against the ship's metallic walls. We passed through the entire ship, informing the rest of the crew of this mode of travel. It took hours, and learning how to do it properly, days. There were fewer wounded men than dead ones, who'd been drained of their blood by the absence of gravity.

"I gathered all my remaining crew and gave the strict orders that were necessary to restore a minimum of efficiency aboard the *Nautilus*. As a matter of priority, it was important to recapture all the objects that were floating freely and constituted obstacles that were both troublesome and even dangerous, now that a means of progression had been found. Most of our strings and ropes were used in the process. As for the drifting liquids, we used all the sponges aboard to absorb them..."

"May I interrupt you? This reminds me of the phenomenon experienced by the three adventurers from the Gun Club when they traveled to the Moon..."

"Indeed! I did not yet have proof, but the *Nautilus* had suddenly left the underwater kingdom of Neptune for the heavenly firmament of Uranus! We were in outer space!"

"But how could it be possible, without a cannon...?"

"Come now, Professor! The Columbiad's cannon could never have launched a craft as massive as my *Nautilus* into outer space. We had spotted no bore holes or titanic tubes suggesting the presence of such artillery in the sunken city. The *Nautilus* had floated for quite a while over the ruins before lowering itself. No, it was a machine based on an unknown scientific principle that I could not explain to you that had sent us there. Pray the gods that it will always escape the attention of our modern scientists!"

"The Atlanteans' science was so powerful? And still operating after all this time...?"

"Undoubtedly. And the how does not matter. Let me continue..."

"At least, I suppose you searched the city for this machine, whatever it is, and reversed its effects, since you are back?"

"Stop, Professor Aronnax! Are you aware of what you're suggesting? Suppose I had managed to find this machine, or others like it, and, worse yet, to decipher their workings. What then? How could have I resisted the temptation to use their power to reshape the destiny of the world? I have already used the considerable power of my *Nautilus* to defend myself from my enemies and occasionally right some wrongs, mostly for my own disenchanted satisfaction. What would have I done with such unimaginable power?"

"Perfect the happiness of humanity!"

"With what accomplices? Think of all the vultures that would not have failed to be drawn by even a tiny fraction of such power! And how many millions of deaths might have been the price of success? Don't most people eventually fall in love with the chains that tyrants have forged to the point of no longer being able to live without them? Most men are born to be enslaved! Only another tyrant could free them! Even humanity would not have deserved such a fate! You, who love men so much, would you have been able to resist such a temptation?"

"Probably not," I admitted.

"So you understand now. Once order had been restored aboard my ship, I had all the machines revised and any parts that had suffered from the gravityless environment replaced. For, you see, in the absence of gravity, parts move and wear faster and lubricants become more volatile. It was necessary to examine them and replace those that might have become dangerous. Even thermometers and dials had become unreliable. Later, we failed to calculate a reliable figure to pinpoint the total duration of our journey."

"Which lasted approximately how long?"

"About twenty-six and a half days. The journey of the Gun Club's adventurers lasted only a dozen. Hence ours was much worse than theirs."

"How so?"

"We were not amateurs like them, but I doubt very much that we would have survived much longer. While food was in ample supply, we could not go to the surface to replenish our air supply. I had calculated that our oxygen reserves would last only two days, three taking into account the deaths we had incurred. Luckily, the *Nautilus* carried equipment that could be retooled in order to break up water into oxygen and hydrogen. Twice this would be our salvation, as you will see later.

"Order having been restored inside the ship, I was now curious to see what was outside. The *Nautilus* appeared trapped inside a giant block of ice; its dark blue color indicated its extreme thickness. Designed to withstand the high pressures of underwater journeys, the hull could withstand the dilation of water well below its freezing point, and I knew that the special glass of the bay windows would hold as well. However, the needles of the thermometric probes remained stuck well above the actual temperature outside.

"We saw only frozen fish and seaweed in that blue ice all around us, at least when it did not darken periodically. To access the ice, I decided to use the exit bay located at the back of the *Nautilus*. To open the airlock, it was necessary to first heat it electrically. When it opened at last, a tumultuous flood of water rushed in and had to be pumped out. My crew and I had donned scuba-suits, but we soon realized the limits of our plan.

My intention had been to drill a tunnel straight to the surface of the ice. We began by using electric lances, but the quantity of water that we produced was such that it quickly filled all the tanks. Midway through, we had to forego the lances and switch to ice picks. The absence of gravity required three members to support a fourth, who did all the digging, but the diving suits became a hindrance, so work proceeded in fur clothing

"While one crew member did the digging, the others were packing up the ice rubble in bags and stashing them outside the *Nautilus*. A mask worn over the mouths prevented the inhalation of ice crystals. Despite the warm air generated by all this activity, the temperature was around minus forty degrees at the end of the tunnel. When the pallor of the ice betrayed its thinness, the temperature became almost unbearable. A light explosive equipped with an electric timer was placed, and a new ice cap was reconstituted just beneath it.

"This new cap was meant to dampen the shock wave against a thick glass porthole we had set in the ice tunnel, held by strong metal brackets. The conditions we were working under made the accuracy of the timer unreliable, so the team of men who had done the work rushed back to the ship as fast as the narrowness and length of the tunnel—about three hundred and forty meters—allowed. A slight vibration indicated that the explosion had happened. I admit that I hesitated for a long time before again opening the airlock..."

"The risk was not too great. The *Columbiad* passengers were successful in expelling an animal without losing their air."

"I'm afraid, Professor Aronnax, that the *Columbiad* crew might have embellished the truth. Had I tried to repeat their so-called experiment, I would not be here to tell you about mine. Know that it didn't take me long to understand the terrifying suction power of the cosmic void. The Nautilus might have lost all its air in a matter of seconds. As for the equally terrifying temperature of outer space, it would have instantly frozen the entire ship if the portion of solidified ocean turned to ice that surrounded us had not attenuated its effects, at least temporarily."

"That will teach me to not take for granted the unreliable reporting of amateur scientists!"

"Detecting no aspiration, I opened the airlock and let the air of the *Nautilus* warm up the tunnel a little. I stepped outside, walking very slowly. My hands, covered with a double thickness of gloves, shook as they held the wooden banister that we had installed along the tunnel. At the end of it, I carefully wiped the fog from the glass of the porthole, and was briefly assailed by the light of the Sun. Then, came a softer light, and I beheld the Earth passing before my eyes, a blue, white and ocher sphere in space.

"The ice covered a third of the porthole, but the center was clear enough and we could see outside. In its protective cocoon of ice, the *Nautilus* was not drifting towards the Moon or another planet. We were in orbit around the Earth. I had beaten the Gun Club to outer space, even though it had never been my intention. The *Nautilus* did not go as far as they did, but it still traveled more leagues in space than under the seas—something that the outside world shall never know."

"Captain, do you realize that your ship is probably what the members of the Gun Club mistook for a second satellite of the Earth?"

"Ha! Then, they'll all be be ridiculed when astronomers become tired of looking for it. That will teach them a lesson!"

"They claim to have almost hit it."

"Well, I did not notice anything, but then, I checked the concordance of the dates. Our improvised satellite was describing an almost circular orbit at 8200 kilometers, about the same as they claimed, but in four hours and fifty minutes instead of the three hours and twenty minutes they reported. We rotated on our axis in twenty-three minutes and twenty seconds. Based on the length of the tunnel we drilled, I estimate our total size to have been eight hundred meters in diameter, assuming that we had a roughly spherical shape."

"We should ask Mr. Barbicane or his companions."

"I have no other sources of information than the newspapers and books that I bring back from the few secret stops I allow myself, in order to keep abreast of the progress of science and the world. But our shape must have been at least roughly spherical, or my calculations to get ourselves of this bad strait would have been seriously incorrect."

"What about the clocks? Were you able to fix them?"

"No. But I knew that the Earth rotates on axis in twenty-three hours fifty-six minutes and four seconds. By taking detailed observations of its surface, and comparing it with what my watch indicated, I could calculate the actual duration of a full turn of its dial. From there, I was able to perform a series of calculations of time, angles, distances, and velocities. I should add that I used an astronomical telescope in addition to my sextant and the books in my library. You would have done the same, wouldn't you, Professor Aronnax?"

"Indeed, captain. So, how did you get back to Earth?"

"My improvised observatory soon proved to be a rather inconvenient place. I stood in what was, in effect, the bottom of a crater, which considerably limited my field of vision. Further, the extreme coldness and the rapid rotation of our satellite made my observations difficult. I concentrated first on other scientific problems directly related to the survival of the *Nautilus* in this hostile environment. Thanks to the digging of a second, much narrower tunnel, I managed to ensure our continued supply of air.

"For lack of a reliable thermometer, I could not accurately measure the frightful temperature of the external vacuum of space, but its proximity allowed me to expose hydrogen and oxygen to it—and the latter liquefied earlier.[9] This difference allowed me to separate the two gases fast enough, using a narrow tunnel created just under the surface of the outer ice. I obtained these gases by performing an electrolysis of water, with soda added. Oxygen regenerated out atmosphere, but I was then faced with what to do with the extra hydrogen, twice as abundant? Can you guess the answer, Professor?"

"Heating the ship to conserve electricity? Hydrogen is highly flammable, but also explosive when compressed..."

"Very well reasoned! You know that the revolution of a celestial body around another is shorter the closer it is to it, until it finally collapses and falls. At a certain distance, called the Roche radius, it can no longer maintain its orbit. I determined that our satellite had to break its orbit definitively and instantly, and not settle on a lower one where we might be stuck forever, and eventually explode. Slowing it down was not enough; I had to convert it into a projectile."

"I see. When the shell of the *Columbiad* tore itself away from the Moon's attraction, it took rockets to increase its speed. So you did the same?"

"In effect, but in reverse. I did not seek to tear ourselves away from the Earth's attraction, but on the contrary get closer to it. I did not have rockets, but hydrogen could give me the same thrust to slow us down. So I had a third tunnel dug, which I filled with liquid hydrogen, adding a little oxygen to help its combustion. I had created a vacuum inside by means of opening it through the surface of the ice, then recapping it. The combustion would be brief, but powerful. We had only one chance."

---

[9] The absolute zero temperature is - 273.15 °; oxygen liquefies at -183 ° and hydrogen at -252.7 °. *Note from the author.*

"You were running the risk of burning on reentry like a meteor and crashing to Earth…"

"But, Professor, the sea occupies nearly three quarters of the Earth's surface. My companions and I had nothing to lose. The thickness of the ice surrounding us protected us from the coldness of space by conserving the heat we generated inside the *Nautilus*. This should have spared the sodium batteries, but the opening of the tunnels had created damaging leaks. It was therefore necessary to close them. In addition, electrolysis consumed far too much electricity. Finally, our supply of soda was going to run out.

"The absence of gravity affected our health, without me being able to explain why. Our strength was declining and we were finding it increasingly difficult to feed ourselves. In the last days, we had had only fish cut out of the ice to eat, and our digestive systems were starting to fail. Digging that last tunnel had been a real martyrdom; I had used half of the crew, the rest being sick. There was nothing left to do, but electrically detonate the hydrogen near the surface.

"The ignition and the orientation of the outside nozzle had been set according to the rotation of our satellite and the most favorable angle to slow our descent towards the Earth. The friction of the atmosphere against our ice shell would be terrible, but its thickness would help absorb the heat as it evaporated, and its decreasing weight would slow our speed. I was hoping, without too much hope, that there would be a little bit of ice left when we hit the water, in order to dampen the shock.

"My calculations proved accurate enough, but the thrust, the descent and the final shock were truly terrifying. As much as we could, we had secured each object aboard with ropes and each man with straps, but our ship shook, rolled and turned in every direction. Its contents were tossed as if by a gigantic storm. We passed out, and when we regained consciousness, we saw that the *Nautilus* was still trapped in a fast melting chunk of ice. But once the propellers were freed, we quickly resurfaced. At last, the good air of Earth filled our lungs and we resumed life as before."

"I'm surprised no one detected the huge steam release coming from such a large meteor?"

"We fell in the middle of the Pacific Ocean. If some natives saw us, they kept it to themselves. There were no inhabitants on the island where we moored to do all the necessary repairs, recharge our batteries and restock food and fresh water. We spent a month there, resting, healing and restoring the forces sapped by our incredible cosmic journey, and also burying our dead. I meditated for a long time on the absolute necessity of keeping what we had experienced secret from the so-called civilized world."

"Do you realize, captain, that by so doing, you took the responsibility of stopping the march of progress?" I could not help saying in a somewhat accusatory tone.

"Professor Aronnax, imagine that a nation, no matter how benevolent, acquires control of the machine that projected the *Nautilus* into space. It would quickly surround the Earth with a ring of artificial satellites. It would be able to bomb its rivals at its leisure, and to enslave and exploit less advanced peoples on the pretext of forcing upon them their own conception of happiness and their own image of the Creator. Do you understand at last why I demanded your solemn promise to not reveal anything about this?"

I nodded silently. Everything had been said. The dawn was well past. Captain Nemo handed me a new cigar and relit his. We observed a long silence punctuated by the puffs of marine tobacco in the library that already contained so many other secrets. Then a drowsiness fell upon us.

To not break my word without disappointing my readers, I falsified the location of Atlantis and its forbidden wonders. Never had the *Nautilus* experienced a more prodigious adventure.

Translation: Jean-Marc Lofficier

Full disclosure: a somewhat different version of this story appeared in The Worlds of Philip José Farmer - Dust and Soul *in 2011, featuring characters created by Mr. Farmer. Here, the main protagonist is the mysterious Count Saint-Germain from the Hexagon Comics universe, and this self-contained tale serves as a prelude, or a sampler, for Volume 1 of Tales of the HexagonVerse, to be released next month, a collection of other stories featuring heroes and villains from that same universe, written by some of France's best authors, and translated by Michael Shreve.*

Jean-Marc Lofficier: *The Legacy of Atlantis*

France, 1952

Like many stories, this one began with a dog.

A dog named "Robot."

(You can't make up details like that!)

It started on September 8, 1940, near the peaceful village of Montignac, in the lush and green Périgord region of Western France. At the time, people there lived a life of quiet, but very real, desperation. France had signed a humiliating Armistice with Nazi Germany in June of that year. Yes, Montignac considered itself lucky not to be in the occupied part of the country, but in truth, the crushing blow of the recent defeat, combined with the dismal aspects of everyday life under the meretricious Petain régime, weighed heavily on every soul.

But perhaps not on Robot's, for he was merely a dog, a handsome setter-terrier mix with a smooth, long brown coat, who remained steadfastly oblivious to his humans' miseries. Robot continued to enjoy his daily routine of running in the hills, digging holes, running some more, chasing after voles and little furry animals, and did we mention the running?

All that he did in the company of his young master, 18-year-old Marcel Ravidat.

Tall and strong, Marcel had been apprenticed as a mechanic to the local Citroen garage. His boss thought him gifted with tools, having a good comprehension of engines, and knew his future would be bright—after the War. (Everything in those days was measured by "After the War.")

Rather shy, but goodhearted, Marcel had been nicknamed the "Convict" by the villagers, not because of any blemish on his character—far from it!—but because of his flattering resemblance to the actor Harry Baur, who had played the burly Jean Valjean in the film version of *Les Misérables*, which had screened with considerable success at the local theater a few years before.

Once, the verdant hills surrounding Montignac had been planted with grapes, but the phylloxera epidemic of 1880 had killed them all, and the locals had chosen to replace them with pines. Then, the pines had been cut down and nature had eventually reclaimed the land, which had returned to wilderness.

Robot liked the wild; it suited him just fine.

That afternoon, Marcel noticed his dog digging more madly and obsessively than usual at the bottom of an excavation. It was a big hole in the ground that had been caused by the uprooting of an old pine that had been struck by lightning.

"What is it, Robot?" said the young man, understandably curious about his dog's manic behavior.

Marcel stepped into the excavation, expecting to find a nest of voles, or perhaps a dead, half-buried bird, the latter being considered a supreme delicacy by Robot. But instead, at the bottom of the excavation, he saw nothing but a hole. Not just a hole, but something that was quite out of place in such an ordinary bit of rural scenery. It was about ten inches in diameter, but deep, and dark, very dark.

It looks like a vent hole from Hell, Marcel couldn't help thinking.

The young man gathered a few pebbles and dropped them into the hole, then listened. It took a long, long time for them to hit the bottom.

There was something down there.

Marcel was nothing if not enterprising, and he had, as the French put it, *de la suite dans les idées*, or follow through. Therefore, he returned four days later, without Robot, this time, but accompanied by three strapping young friends, Georges, Simon and Jacques, all under 17. They were equipped with small pick-axes, and they quickly enlarged the hole enough to let Marcel descend into the pit at the end of a rope, carrying an oil lamp.

And there, Marcel discovered an extraordinary, magical underworld of caves, lakes, stalactites and stalagmites—and fabulous paintings.

Marcel Ravidat had just discovered the prehistoric wonders of the Caves of Lascaux!

Things flash forward to October 1952, when Germany and France had become allies, but Western Europe trembled under the threat of the Cold War—and mutually assured nuclear destruction. Lascaux had been opened to the public "after the War" in 1948 and, for the first time, the contents of those wonderful caves were being probed, poked, catalogued and investigated by serious and dedicated scientists.

No one was more serious and dedicated that François Bordes, a burly man, barely 30, with short-cropped hair and a square face who looked as if it had been chiseled out of stone. Monsieur Bordes was a native of the region, and shared the good common sense and salt of the earth nature of the local peasantry. His parents had scrimped and saved to send him to the University at Bordeaux, and he was working on his doctorate thesis on *Les limons quaternaires*, but had lost none of his genuine attachment for his region and its traditions.

Sometimes, at night, he looked at the sky and wondered—not about the next day's weather, like his fellow Périgordins—but about the cosmos, and in that he was different from them. Remember this, as it will be important later.

As we become acquainted with Monsieur Bordes, we discover him, assisted by an intern from the University, busy selecting and cataloguing tiny samples of rock, wood and coal. Once assembled, he would take this collection to the University of Chicago, where the famous physical chemist Willard Libby had just developed a method for radiocarbon dating. There was much argument at Lascaux between those scientists who thought that the paintings were from the earlier portion of the Upper Paleolithic, and those who favored later years. It was hoped that the new carbon-14 process would settle the controversy once and for all.

As befitted such a delicate scientific task, an eerie silence reigned in the caves, only broken by the scraping and chipping sounds of the tiny geological tools and sample gathering. But, suddenly, there was an ominous sound, not unlike the crack of a whip. The kind of sound no scientist ever wants to hear at his workplace.

"Monsieur Bordes..." stammered the intern.

"What is it, Jérôme?"

"I'm sorry. It just came out in my hands... It fell out by itself, I swear..."

François Bordes saw that the young man was holding a hefty chunk of rock in his hand. This was almost vandalism, since the samples were supposed to be very small. Reports would have to be written; explanations provided. There would be a long night ahead of him. He prepared to berate his young assistant accordingly, when he noticed something protruding from the stone.

Something which had no business being inside a rock.

It was a small piece of metal, the corner of something embedded inside the rock, as if the stone had formed around it like a cyst.

Bordes put his finger to it and gently touched the tiny pyramidal point protruding from the rock. It was indeed metal. The archeologist was familiar with crystals and metal ores and the wonderfully pure geometric shapes they could often take, but he had never seen anything like this. It looked... manufactured.

"Should I call the supervisor?" asked Jérôme the intern, oblivious to Bordes' concerns and far more preoccupied by the fate of his internship if his act of "vandalism" were to be discovered.

"No," said Bordes after a minute of reflection. "This requires more study and analysis. I'll take it to the lab. I think we're finished here for the day."

François Bordes was a pipe smoker. It helped him relax and, more importantly, it helped him think. He had smoked pipe after pipe for several hours, while grappling over what to do about his discovery.

First, he had used his geological tools to delicately expose a little more of the metal artifact inside the rock. But instead of providing answers, this operation had only raised more questions.

The exposed section of the artifact was now an inch wide and half-an-inch thick. It looked like a small metal tablet, perhaps four by five inches in total, judging from the size of the rock. Bordes could not identify the nature of the metal with the equipment at his disposal in Montignac. But what he had literally unearthed had shaken him deeply.

There were rows after rows of microscopic characters engraved with uncanny precision on one side of the tablet!

Bordes had spent a lot of time thinking about that discovery. He could have stopped there and waited for the morning to gather a team of scientists. That would have been the right course of action. But then, they would have taken the tablet to Bordeaux, perhaps even to Paris, and Bordes would have received a cordial but insincere handshake, and his role in the discovery would not guarantee him even a modest footnote in the future academic publications that would no doubt be written.

The man who sometimes looked at the night skies and wondered, finally made up his mind. He sighed and, with a heavy heart, took his rock hammer and brought it down on the rock.

This, at least, he thought, would buy him the footnote.

The stone broke into two, sharp fragments, plus some smaller shards of rock, and released the tablet within. As Bordes had surmised, it was about four by five inches, made of some kind of dark green metal, and engraved with about a hundred lines of tiny characters.

The archeologist cleaned the tablet with a brush and took a magnifying glass to study the markings.

He did not recognize the characters. They looked a little like proto-Basque carvings, but they weren't proto-Basque; if they had been, he would have been able to identify at least a few signs, even though ancient languages were not his specialty.

He went to his reference shelf and returned with a book by Professor Aristide Clairembard, a renowned archeologist from the Collège de France, who had written many authoritative articles about the languages of "lost civilizations," such as Mû and Atlantis. But according to the latest Bulletin de l'Institut Français d'Archéologie, Clairembard was presently on Easter Island, looking for Mûvian remains...

After an hour of study and meticulous comparisons, Bordes found some similarities between certain characters on the tablet and samples recorded in Iceland by Professor Lidenbrock in the 19th century. Clairembard, who was always generous with praise, stated that only one man had been able—and then, only partially—to decipher those writings, one of Clairembard's colleagues, the brilliant Professor Germanus.

A month later, François Bordes found himself crossing the threshold of the Institute, which was housed in a large *hotel particulier* in the oldest section of Paris called Le Marais. It was late November and the archeologist, well acquainted with the subtle currents of academic life, could sense that everyone was already preparing for the holidays.

He was soon introduced to a tall, slender man, with astonishingly piercing grey eyes that seemed to penetrate to the very depths of one's soul. Despite her impeccably cut silver hair, it was hard to estimate his age. Bordes thought he looked a bit like actor Jules Berry.

"Professor Germanus?" he said hesitantly.

"Monsieur Bordes," responded the man warmly, extending his hand. "You're right on time. Who said Meridionals are always late?"

"Someone who doesn't like Meridionals?" replied Bordes, with a smile.

"Well said! Actually, one of your compatriots said it just the other day, when he showed up late for a lecture."

"Really?"

"Yes. We have a distinguished visitor from your region. Doctor Rochemaure from the University of Toulouse. He arrived last week to give a lecture on pre-Akkadian languages."

"I'm afraid that's quite out of my specialty. I wouldn't know anything about it."

"But it is in mine. Rochemaure has quite a few interesting theories. His lecture was truly fascinating. But come with me, I'll introduce you..."

Germanus pushed open the doors of the lecture hall and invited Bordes inside. There was a small gathering of teachers and students talking, or rather listening in awe to a a thin, brown-haired man with a hawkish nose and angular features reminiscent of those of a Roman Emperor.

"Doctor Rochemaure," said Germanus, pushing his way through the small crowd, "there's someone you should meet—from your neck of the woods, no less. François Bordes, one of the archeologists working at the Lascaux site."

Rochemaure spoke with a hint of a regional accent. His smile was warm and genuinely friendly. Bordes knew that he should have liked the man, and yet something deep inside him screamed to not trust him.

"Docteur Rochemaure," he said, shaking the hand proffered to him.

"Monsieur Bordes it is a pleasure... an honor... I'm very familiar with your outstanding work..."

"Thank you, but it's not much," said Bordes, still reluctant to let himself be drawn in by the man's geniality.

"Monsieur Bordes is too modest," interjected Germanus. "We've spoken on the telephone many times and his latest discovery is quite remarkable."

"Ah yes, I remember you mentioning it before, Professor Germanus," said Rochemaure. "Something to do with some archaic writing, possibly Nippurian I believe?"

"That's what I hope to find out," said Germanus. "Monsieur Bordes has brought the tablet with him, and I plan to carefully transcribe every sign starting tomorrow."

"I see. Are you planning to stay in Paris long, Monsieur Bordes?"

"Alas, no. This is only a side-trip for me. I must return to Lascaux soon; we're waiting for all the samples to have been carbon-dated by Professor Libby from Chicago."

"I see," repeated Rochemaure.

For some unfathomable reason, Bordes felt that the other man was not pleased with the news; it was as if he had just told someone his cat, then his dog, had died.

"Well, then, I wish you good luck," said Rochemaure, offering his hand, indicating that the conversation was over. "I will be most eager to read your findings when you publish them."

Bordes thought about an article with his name on it appearing in the Bulletin de l'Institut Français d'Archéologie. That would be such a feather in his cap.

By the time he pulled out of his rêverie, Rochemaure had walked away with his entourage.

"Well, Professor Germanus," he said, "it is time for you to take a look at this tablet."

François Bordes returned to Paris just before Xmas. He fully felt winter's bite as the cold winds of the season roared across the narrow streets of the Marais. He looked at the sky as any Périgordin would have done, and while the climate in this region was unfamiliar to him, he could almost smell the storm approaching.

Raising the fur-lined collar of his leather jacket, the archeologist accelerated his pace and briskly walked the ten blocks to the indoor shooting range where he had been told he could meet Professsor Germanus.

Once inside, he took off his jacket and shook as if, somehow, he could get rid of the penetrating cold that had managed to seep through it. Rubbing his hands, he walked towards the shooting gallery. With its dark wood-lined walls and soft red carpet, the range was a welcome refuge from the outside. For the first time since he had left his home in Bordeaux, Bordes felt truly relaxed.

He almost glided over the three small steps that took him to the shooting gallery. There, he saw Germanus methodically shooting arrows precisely into the center of a target.

"Good afternoon, Professor Germanus," he shouted.

The archeologist put down his bow and smiled at the sight of the newcomer.

"Monsieur Bordes! I didn't expect to see you back so soon. How was your trip?"

"Very successful, thank you." Bordes looked at the target and the narrow grouping of arrows in its center and whistled in admiration. "You are quite a marksman, Professor..."

"Call me Denys, please. Would you like to try?" Germanus said, pointing at the bow on the counter.

Bordes made a self-deprecating grin.

"I'm afraid I've only shot quails and wild boars with an old rifle in the Périgord."

Germanus laughed.

"Come on, François! I've heard tales of the exploits of your maquisards during the War. Now, if I were to ask you to shoot the elephant gun I keep in my office, that would be something else, of course... Anyway, what brings you back so soon?"

"I had to come back to see you, Denys, because, well, something rather unusual has turned up..."

"Let me guess?" said Germanus. "It's about the tablet, isn't it?"

Bordes nodded. During his previous visit, he had left the tablet at the Institute, to be deciphered, taking just a few scrapings for the carbon dating tests.

"I've finished the transcription and I took it to our computer lab," continued Germanus. "They've just received a new Bull computer. I think it will take at least another two weeks to crack it. But the first results have been promising, and I'm confident that..."

"No, it's not that. I don't doubt your abilities as a linguist," interrupted Bordes. "There's no better expert in Ancient Languages than you, but, you see, the carbon dating turned up something very strange..."

"I see. What did they find?"

"That's where it gets odd. The samples were dated to be approximately a hundred million years-old... Now, at that time, there was no civilization on Earth capable of producing such a tablet..."

"Are you sure it's not an elaborate prank by one of your students? They do that all the time here, too. Why, recently, it seems that one of our students has taken to running on the rooftops disguised as a gargoyle... Sooner or later, the police will catch him, of course—just as you'll catch your practical joker."

Bordes looked unconvinced.

"A practical joker capable of devising an ancient language that has even you perplexed, Denys? Is that really possible? Besides, I know it's not a fake. I saw the rock come off the wall... I opened it myself with my own hammer."

Germanus considered the matter for a moment, and shook his head. "I admit you've got a point, François. No one could forge those markings, not to mention the fact that I still don't know how they were actually engraved... I tell

158

you what—let's go and take another look at that tablet. It's in the safe in my office…"

Germanus stepped into his office. It was a small attic room, even by Parisian standards, but cozy, with a nice view of the rooftops—a prized achievement, for which he had had to fight for years. It was furnished with a small mahogany desk, presently half-hidden under a pile of student papers waiting to be graded, a single metal filing cabinet, and a handsome oak bookcase. A collection of Colts, Remingtons and other guns hung over it. Bordes followed his colleague and went to sit in one of the two leather chairs facing the desk.

Germanus took a look around the room, then froze.

"Someone's been in here," he said suddenly.

"How can you tell?" asked Bordes, looking skeptical. "You just told me yourself that you locked your office when you went down to the range, and the key has not left your pocket since."

"I tell you, someone's been in here," repeated Germanus.

He pointed towards a travel bag sitting on top of the filing cabinet.

"See that bag? It was closed before, but now, it no longer is. No, I tell you again, someone was in here—while I was at the range."

"Have you checked the safe?"

"The tablet!"

Germanus rushed to a small portable safe sitting on the bottom shelf of the bookcase between two piles of books in Ancient Greek.

"It looks undisturbed, but we'll soon find out…"

With a few flips of the fingers, he turned the tumblers and the safe opened with a click. Inside were some documents, money, a passport, but—no tablet!

"The tablet's gone!"

"But who could have taken it? And why?" asked Bordes, crestfallen.

Germanus slammed the safe shut, then paced about the room.

"Who knew you'd left it here?" he asked.

"Well, there's Professor Libby in Chicago and my team in Lascaux, but their integrity is beyond question."

"I agree. Anyone else? Did you make a copy of the markings?"

"I did send a rubbing to Professor Clairembard, but he's on Easter Island, on the other side of the world. How could he?…"

"Clairembard, you say? Hmm… That might be a clue… I have an idea. All may not yet be lost. But before we take action, we need to make some preparations…"

The weather had gone from bad to worse, if that was even possible. The storm that François Bordes predicted had arrived, and gales of frigid rain, melted snow really, hit the neighborhood with unabated violence. Fortunately, there was virtually no one in the streets of the Marais to suffer the wrath of the elements, everyone having long before sought refuge inside.

The Institute's computer lab, located in a modest, more modern one-story extension, was ordinarily closed for the night, but Germanus had a key and everyone was used to seeing him work late, when he could grab some free time on the computer to help him decipher the latest cuneiforms from Iran or pre-Minoan writings from Crete.

The rain was falling hard on the skylight just above the desk where Germanus now sat; its surface was lit only by a goose neck lamp. He got up, grabbed a print-out from the jaws of the Bull machine and returned to sit at the desk. He spread the pages of the original transcription he had made of the tablet's microscopic characters and compared them, one line at a time, with the contents of the printout. Behind him, the Bull computer continued chattering, spewing out more data and drowning out the sounds of the gale.

After he finished reading the printout, Germanus remained pensive for a minute, then returned to the computer, took the next batches of pages, and again went back to the desk for more comparisons.

Suddenly, he heard a noise coming from the skylight; it sounded like a pet scratching at the door to let his master know he wants in, but when he looked up and peered into the darkness, he saw nothing and heard only the wind.

Germanus checked his watch. It was now past midnight. Perhaps his intuition had been wrong. Perhaps...

Suddenly, he heard another sound, this time from behind him. It was the click of the door. Someone had entered the room and closed the door behind him. Germanus smiled because he felt he had been right.

The man removed a large hat, soaked by the rain, took off his dripping coat and hung it on a stand by the door.

"Professor Germanus," the newcomer said. "What are you doing here on a night like this?"

"I could ask you the same thing, Doctor Rochemaure," said Germanus, purposefully not extending his hand. "What is our distinguished visiting professor doing hanging around this humble abode at this time of the night?"

"Research for a paper I plan to write..." responded Rochemaure evasively, sounding slightly annoyed.

"If you want the computer to yourself, I'm almost done with it," said Germanus, gathering his papers.

"May I see?" asked Rochemaure, barely hiding his eagerness.

"Certainly," Germanus replied, handing him the sheath of papers.

But, as he got up from behind the desk, he dropped them and the papers fell and spilled across the green linoleum floor.

"Oh, how clumsy of me! I apologize," said Germanus. "Could you give me a hand?"

"Of course."

160

Germanus began picking up the sheets of papers from the floor and handing them to Rochemaure, who straightened them, stacked them, and eventually handed the pile back to Germanus, after leafing through it.

"Any insight, Doctor Rochemaure?" asked Germanus, frowning lightly as if to better study his opponent.

"No, of course not," replied Rochemaure, in all appearance sincere. "How could I?"

"But I understand that you've worked with Professor Clairembard, the only man to have found samples of Mûvian writings. Surely, some of those signs should at least be familiar to you?"

"No, I'm afraid it's all gobbledygook to me. I admire your ability to make sense of it all, Professor Germanus. Have you managed to decipher any of it?"

"Yes, some. But that is not the most interesting thing that I found..."

"Ah?" said Rochemaure, falsely casual.

"Yes. You see, Doctor Rochemaure, these papers are written in an alphabet that no one as yet can identify. Its very origins are a mystery and its significance seems to mostly belong in the realm of myths..."

"I don't see what you're getting at..."

"You will. When I dropped these papers, on purpose, I confess, they were all mixed up. You will note than none of the pages are numbered. Yet, when I gave them to you, one by one, you sorted them out—unconsciously, I presume—and handed them back to me in the right order. So I ask myself: how is Doctor Rochemaure, a man who professes total ignorance of the contents of this document, nevertheless able to read it fluently?"

There was a long silence. Germanus was waiting for Rochemaure to respond, but no answer was forthcoming. He saw the fires of uncontrollable rage and wounded pride burn and grow within the eyes of the man who had called himself Rochemaure but who—he was now certain of it—was, in reality, his arch-enemy, Maleficus!

Strangely, at that moment, he felt an odd kinship, a strange rapport with Maleficus, and he saw in the other man's eyes that he had felt it too. But Maleficus' own moment of uncertainty was short-lived, consumed by the unleashed fury that engulfed him in seconds.

"Mislik! To me!" he shouted to the sky, managing to overpower the sounds of the storm. "Mislik! I, your creator, am summoning you!"

The skylight suddenly broke into a million shards with a shattering sound of broken glass and metal, letting in the gale and the raging rain. A monstrous being made of stone, a living gargoyle, with fiery eyes of electric blue, jumped into the lab. Germanus briefly remembered the reports about a practical joker gallivanting on the rooftops dressed as a gargoyle and smiled bitterly. He also recalled that such reports had coincided with the visit of "Doctor Rochemaure"— and the first call of François Bordes.

"You've come across a secret that doesn't belong to you, Saint-Germain," spat Maleficus, grabbing his coat and making for the door. "The secret of Kera, the ultimate weapon of the Twilight People. Only I am worthy of it! Mislik, kill him and destroy this place. Nothing must remain of it!"

Maleficus then stepped through the door and vanished into the night.

The Mislik, surprisingly fast for a creature made of stone, sprang towards Saint-Germain. Its deadly purpose was all too clear.

"François! Think of it as just another wild boar from the Périgord!" shouted Saint-Germain.

François Bordes came out from behind the Bull computer, where he had been hiding, and fired Saint-Germain's elephant gun. Twice.

The Mislik shattered, exploded into a thousand pieces, but at the same time, spread a lava-like substance, which began to set fire to everything it touched. Bordes thought it looked like Grecian fire. In a matter of minutes, the lab turned into an inferno. Luckily, the two scientists were able to crawl out of the way and find refuge behind the computer's massive cooling unit.

"How do we get out of here before we dry like sausages?" asked Bordes, panting.

Saint-Germain pointed at a huge metal box attached to the wall.

"There, the air conditioning," he explained, already grabbing the box. With Bordes' help, he was able to unseal the heavy machinery. "Watch out for the backdraft!" he said.

They immediately felt a welcome blast of frigid air on their faces, followed by a burst of heat from behind them. The lab was turning into a miniature inferno, but outside, it was still a very frigid December.

Resting his back against the cooling unit, Saint-Germain quickly kicked the metal grate that separated them from the outside, and they both crawled through the opening, feeling the pressure of the raging heat behind them.

By the time they were out, the computer lab was more than halfway to being entirely consumed by the flames. Bordes, who had seen buildings burn to the ground during the war, though that nothing would remain of it.

"Well, this is it then," said Saint-Germain, looking at the conflagration.

"What do you mean?"

"No more tablet, my transcription, the punched cards, the print-out... all gone. We have nothing. And if you want my advice," he added, hearing the sound of the fire engine in the distance, but getting closer, "we're probably better off forgetting this ever happened."

"But what about Maleficus? And this legendary weapon—Kera, was it?"

"The documents that Maleficus stole were only skillful fakes that I had prepared. As for him, I am certain that he and I will meet again soon..."

But they didn't forget, of course. Ever.

After he had returned to Bordeaux, François Bordes launched a discrete investigation into the so-called "Doctor Rochemaure." Professor Clairembard remembered him only as a recent acquaintance he had made at the Collège de France. His credentials were impeccable—but all false. No traces of him could be found anywhere. It was as if he had never existed.

The French archeologist never solved the mystery of the hundred million years-old tablet. He finally convinced himself that it may have been a fake after all, but never looked at the skies and the world around him in quite the same way.

A couple of years later, he became a science fiction writer of some stature under the nom-de-plume of Francis Carsac. In his first novel, *Ceux de Nulle Part* (Those from Nowhere), he wrote about aliens who fought creatures made of stone called "Misliks."

As for Saint-Germain, over the next few months, he experienced a spate of strange, colorful, exotic dreams, filled with creatures of legend, but he never seemed to remember those dreams when he woke up.

The only one who remained truly at peace was Robot, who lies peacefully under the lush and green hills of Périgord, buried one sad morning by his master, having lived a long, happy and well-filled life of running in the hills, digging holes, running some more, chasing after voles (and did we mention the running?), and never knew how close he had come to exposing the legacy of Atlantis.

Nigel Malcom's saga takes place in a dystopian near future where the Nyctalope once again, and very reluctantly, appears to serve the forces of fascism that have overtaken Europe. The first installment in the series was "Tomorrow Belongs to the Nyctalope" in Volume 14, followed by "Enemies of the People" in Volume 15. This third chapter further widens the scope of the series, (re)introducing some new and old characters…

Nigel Malcolm: *Useful Idiots*

New York, the near future.

From the window, Leo Saint-Clair could just about make out the Empire State Building.

He remembered the time when it was brand new, and the tallest in the known world. Nowadays, it was almost hidden in a forest of skyscrapers. The second and third layers of traffic—all those spinners and other flying vehicles—only served to subdue the building even more. Like an entire city of Babel.

The buzzer rang, breaking Saint-Clair's reverie. He went over and pressed the video-com. The small monitor flashed up an unflattering, overlit picture of his British contact.

"Hello, Sexton, come on up," said Saint-Clair, before buzzing him in.

As he lived on the 75th floor, he knew Blake would take a few minutes to get up to him, so he made a pot of tea.

As another long-lifer, Sexton Blake had not aged a day since the early 20th century. The Nyctalope mused over whether he should set up a support group for people like them. A group of people he could imagine as sitting around in chairs, expressing their confusion about j-pads and spinners, and bafflement over the popularity of some vacuous celebrity, and how there aren't any genuinely talented entertainers anymore, like Harry Lauder or Edith Piaf.

To be fair though, Blake seemed to have stayed up to date with all the important developments. While he was still, at his core, a Victorian gentleman, he had made sure he maintained the discipline of lifelong learning and continual adaptation to the times he lived through. In fact, it was one of Blake's more recently acquired skills that Saint-Clair wanted to make use of now.

Saint-Clair warmed the teapot, put in three spoonfuls of loose tea, and poured in the boiling (not boiled!) water. He reflected that he evidently had maintained the regime of lifelong learning himself—given that he had learned how to make tea the way Blake liked it.

Sexton Blake looked tired when Saint-Clair let him into the flat. In many ways, he was unchanged. He still had the V-shaped widow's peak forehead, which he never changed through the years. However, now he consented to wearing a blazer, Oxford shirt and chinos, and looking every inch the Englishman abroad. He had a rucksack over his shoulder.

By the time Saint-Clair had brought in the teapot, cups and saucers, and poured out the tea, Blake had produced what used to be called a laptop. He couldn't quite remember what they were called these days. The Englishman was tapping away on the keyboard, accessing files, and programs. Leo decided to not disturb him while he was doing this.

Then, five minutes later, Blake seemed to relax, sit back and rub his eyes. He noticed the cup of tea, steaming in front of him.

"I'll let you add your own milk," said Saint-Clair.

"Thank you."

"You must have had a tiring journey."

Blake added milk and three sugars.

"Obtaining permits to leave the Fortress Isle is getting harder these days." he replied.

"Even for the UK Government's most trusted Consulting Detective?"

"Absolutely. Things have cooled between them and myself quite considerably. They seem to prefer having other, younger, consultants, whose thinking is more in line with that of the Government's." He took a sip, and enjoyed it. "At this rate, I'll probably have to lower my scale of rates, and start taking on divorce cases again. Do people still get divorced?"

"Yes, they do."

"Still, such are the peaks and troughs of a Consulting Detective's career. One can only hope that this time will soon pass, and we will move once more further along in the cycle."

Saint-Clair poured himself a cup of tea. He just drank it black.

"I appreciate you coming all the way out here to help me," he said.

"I am happy to do my bit," replied Blake.

"I'll pay you," said Saint-Clair, feeling slightly awkward. Then he realized he may have trodden on his friend's pride. "At least, reimburse your flight over."

"Thank you, but no. British Intelligence will be monitoring my bank accounts. Payments from a recognized French 'traitor' would immediately raise the alarm. Officially, I am in America on a mundane case involving a missing person—a person so missing, in fact, that he doesn't exist. I have traced him to New York, and then later on, I will trace him to Texas, where the trail will go cold," said Blake, with a smile.

"Yes, of course," said Leo, knowing where they were both going very soon. "Maybe I'll owe you in future then. If only in kind."

"Perhaps," said Blake, before quickly moving on with the conversation. "Ah! We're almost fully loaded."

"You are sure we cannot be traced?" Saint-Clair had to ask.

"Rest assured, I have become very adept at all this, and I have taken every step necessary to avoid us being traced. Although the sooner we leave this location, and the shorter the time limit we allow ourselves, the better."

Austin, Texas.

Excitement only intensified throughout the civic hall as American success story Gouroull, and his wife Rachael, arrived.

He was a commanding and mesmerizing presence. A hulking giant of a man, with a lumbering gait. He seemed to be the color of orange squash. Cynical, latte-drinking, Capitol Hill types suggested that this was what happens if you apply spray tan to a deadly white skin.

Gouroull and his PR people responded to these gibes by saying that his skin was actually the product of good genes. Also, his yellow eyes were a sign of his 'perceptive genius' and not, as they claimed, high cholesterol. He was boosted by those Deep South Evangelists, who even claimed that he was divinely appointed, and his bright skin was actually glowing with divine radiance.

His wife Rachael also came under unkind scrutiny. With her defiant, enigmatic poise and Californian 'Noir' style of dressing, some conspiracy theorists had even suggested that she wasn't a real woman, but a *replicant*—and a groundbreaking Nexus-7 one at that. There were even online polls asking questions like *Rachael Gouroull—Human or Toaster?* However, these rumors were ignored by the fans of the couple.

Gouroull lumbered through the crowd, pushing supporters to one side as he went. Rachael followed in his wake.

A journalist stepped in front of the billionaire, and held a microphone up to him.

"Mr. Gouroull, are you excited to be here this afternoon?" she asked.

He glowered at her with his unblinking eyes.

"Yes," he said simply.

"How long have you known Mr. Ewing?" the journalist pressed on.

"Six months."

"Six months doesn't seem like a long time to know a candidate."

Gouroull regarded her blankly for a moment. "It's long enough," he said, already turning away from the journalist to walk away.

Still persisting, the journalist scurried after him, almost barging in front of Rachael, and jostling with other members of the crowd.

"So why do you support Ewing for Governor of Texas?" she called out after him.

"He's the best man for the job," Gouroull shouted, not even turning around to face her. He carried on walking to the backstage area.

The journalist carried on following after him, doggedly. And launched her biggest gambit.

"Mr. Gouroull, well done for bouncing back from your bankruptcy with that investment in that gold mine in Hidalgo," she shouted after him.

He stopped. The atmosphere seemed to change instantly. The crowd around them became very quiet. Focused on the two people.

Gouroull slowly turned round and stared at the journalist for a moment.

"Thank you," he responded, cautiously.

He and Rachael turned round to resume their journey to the backstage area. But the journalist pressed on with her new line of questioning.

"Could you tell us how you found that gold mine?"

The Gouroulls ignored the question. The crowd around them was beginning to murmur their annoyance at this woman.

"Mr. Gouroull, how were you able to buy it when you were declared bankrupt at the time?"

The crowd between them were now getting very agitated.

"Who bought the mine for you Mr. Gouroull? Was it in exchange for you funding Ewing's campaign?"

Some were beginning to heckle her.

"Who owns you?" she shouted after the billionaire.

This finally made him stop in his tracks. Like a dog hearing a whistle. Gouroull spun around and charged back to the journalist. Rachael knew him well enough to stand clear, and even pushed someone in the crowd back, to be safely out of his way.

He ran towards the journalist, shoving other members of the crowd aside. He grabbed the journalist's head between his massive hands and crushed it until blood squeezed out between his fingers.

"NO ONE OWNS ME!" he roared. "NO ONE! DO YOU HEAR ME?"

He picked her up by her head and flung her around. Her body flopped at angles it had never done during her life.

"NO ONE!" Gouroull shouted, throwing her across several meters of the room, as the crowd ran out of the way, and still got sprinkled in blood.

Rachael hurried over to him, and carefully took hold of his arm with both her hands. She tenderly calmed him down, and suggested they go backstage, as they were supposed to.

As they walked away, the crowd was clapping, whooping, and cheering him on.

The incident took less than an hour to dominate the news cycle. And later that afternoon, Gouroull was back in Gouroull Tower—a glass and steel monstrosity, piercing Dallas from the ground like a claw from Hell.

He was sitting in his office, in a massive chair ergonomically-designed for him. On the desk in front of him, on a vidscreen, was Pierre Lecoq, scowling back at him.

"It took us ten years to vet and condition this candidate," Lecoq shouted. "You nearly ruined everything! Do you even realize it even takes that much time to arrange the right circumstances?"

"Of course I do! I've arranged many complex schemes in my time!" said Gouroull, defensively.

"Then stop trying to destroy our work!"

Gouroull banged the desk and growled at Lecoq.

"Don't you growl at me!" said Lecoq, "You've met the Marchef. He can kill you. It would be an even match, but he CAN kill you! You wouldn't be the first monster he's killed. He's practically a monster himself."

Gouroull fumed.

"Control yourself," Lecoq snarled. "Just remember that if it wasn't for BlackSpear, you would still be bankrupt. And remember your media training. If a clever journalist tries to confront you with something like this, just deny it. Just say that she is talking rubbish, or fake news. Or attack the TV network."

Gouroull looked surprised by that last comment.

"Not physically! Say they are pumping out Liberal propaganda or something."

"But my popularity ratings go up whenever I attack someone!" said Gouroull, before grinning an evil grin. "They say that I might one day run for President."

"Not if BlackSpear doesn't approve. We don't like elements we can't control." Lecoq paused for a moment. "No more killing journalists, understand?"

Lecoq abruptly terminated the call. The screen went blank. Gouroull just sat there, brooding.

Sexton Blake flew the rental spinner up from the Car Hire lot just near Dallas Bullet Station, and steered it in the direction of the city itself. Saint-Clair sat in the passenger seat.

"Back there, I was expecting you to hire a ground car, under a nom-de-plume," said Saint-Clair.

Blake laughed.

"Well, how better to disguise myself than as myself?" he said. "Those who track my movements electronically would not think anything odd about a private investigator going about his business, tracing a missing boy to Texas."

"Ah, yes of course. Hiding in plain sight."

"Absolutely. Well, almost. I did tell the manager at the rental business that your name was Edouard Cartier."

Saint-Clair looked at Blake.

"Not just for old time's sake," Blake continued, "but the French Government would consider me to be harboring a fugitive, and the British might find that suspicious."

"Yes. I appreciate that," said Saint-Clair.

He looked out through the windscreen in silence for a few minutes. He watched the horizon as the shimmering heat from the ground gave way, and the central cluster of skyscrapers got closer, interrupting the pink and yellow of the twilight. They were gradually aligning with the lit-up freeway. Leo's thoughts turned back to the job in hand.

"So you are absolutely certain that this is the same Gouroull from Switzerland centuries ago? Who was created by Victor Frankenstein and caused terror across Europe?" he asked.

"The evidence is irrefutable. I have been keeping a file on our friend Gouroull since my first encounter with him more than a century ago. Clearly, he eventually came to America, and became a real estate magnate. An unusually sidestep for him perhaps. Or maybe he was trying to live a different life, turn over a new leaf, perhaps. Or maybe he noticed that the sort of killer instinct and ruthlessness he possesses is easier to hide in the world of big business. Either way, He made a success of it, and even got married. But then he went out of business. And then he mysteriously discovered a goldmine in Central America and bounced back to success. And now he finances contenders for office. He is obviously being controlled by someone."

"BlackSpear?"

"Yes. And so Gouroull may well be the link between BlackSpear and the Schasch regime in France."

Half an hour later, Saint-Clair and Blake walked into the reception area of Gouroull Tower.

As he looked around, familiarizing himself with the surroundings, Leo noticed that it seemed to be sparsely populated. Either Gouroull ran a skeleton staff, or the company was not doing as well as the billionaire made it out to be.

They walked up to the reception desk, and Blake led the conversation with the bored-looking woman behind the counter.

"Hello. My name is Sexton Blake, private investigator, and this is my colleague Monsieur Edouard Cartier. We would like to talk to Mr. Gouroull himself please."

He handed the woman his business card. The receptionist stared at it for a split-second and then handed it back.

"Sir, Mr. Gouroull does not meet people unless they have an appointment," she said, in a well-rehearsed, monotone voice.

"Unfortunately, I did not have time to make one. However, it is very urgent," Blake insisted.

"Sir, Mr. Gouroull does not meet people unless they have an appointment."

Blake clearly struggled to keep his patience. Saint-Clair wondered if the receptionist was a replicant.

"Madam, could I speak to your superior?" Blake asked.

Just then, Rachael walked into the reception area, and came up to them. She looked weary.

"Samantha, is there a problem?" she asked.

"These gentlemen want to speak with Mr. Gouroull. I have informed them that they cannot see Mr. Gouroull unless..."

"...Yes, thank you Samantha." Rachael turned to the two men. "Who are you?"

"I am Sexton Blake, and this is my friend and colleague..."

"...Leo Saint-Clair," said the 'friend and colleague'.

The Nyctalope had decided not to let the pretence continue. This situation called for honesty, even if it was a risky move.

"Mr. Gouroull may not be expecting us," he said, "but he does know who we are. We do need to talk to him urgently."

Rachael, too, seemed to know who they were.

"Follow me," she said.

"Thank you," said Blake, as he and Saint-Clair came with her to the elevator.

Rachael led them both up to the top floor, via a long and awkwardly silent elevator journey. She took them into Gouroull's office. There, they were greeted by the vision of the hulking figure slumped in his reinforced chair at the reinforced desk, framed by a metal and glass room with burnt-orange sunshine illuminating it. Even in silhouette, Gouroull looked full of barely suppressed rage.

Saint-Clair looked at Blake, and saw a split-second of hesitancy. He could not blame him for it. He was afraid too, but opted to make the opening gambit himself:

"Gouroull, we come here under a white flag of truce. We merely wish to speak with you."

Gouroull looked up and stared at Saint-Clair.

"You know very well that I do not pay any attention to these'conventions."

Saint-Clair tried again.

"Listen to me. I appeal to you as one artificially engineered man to another. We just want to talk."

Gouroull smirked.

"Is he artificial too?" he said, looking at Blake.

"You can help us," said Blake. "And in return, we can help you."

Gouroull sat up straight. Saint-Clair felt himself flinch and resisted the urge to adopt a defensive posture. But at least, he knew where the exit was.

The monster rose to his feet.

"And what can you do for me?" he said.

"We can help you to leave all this behind. Arrange a new identity. You'd be free to start again somewhere else. Away from BlackSpear," said Blake, who then paused, expecting a strong reaction from Gouroull.

But the Frankenstein Monster didn't react. He just stood there, listening to them and regarding them with his cold, yellow eyes.

"In return, we need you to provide us with information about BlackSpear's control over the US Government," Blake continued, "as well as various European governments, not least the British and French."

Gouroull paused. He regarded the two men, still on the opposite side of the room, with cunning eyes. He turned his back on them, and looked out of his window at the burnt orange panorama outside.

Saint-Clair and Blake both looked at each other.

Gouroull turned around.

"How will you arrange these new identities?" he asked.

"Well, I can get you two e-cards; they contain your new identities. Your old ones will be wiped," said Blake, before glancing at Saint-Clair again, knowing they were about to reveal something big to an enemy. "In approximately ten minutes from now, a virus I placed in the systems of Wall Street will be activated. It will wipe out information about selected individuals—yourself and Rachael included—and also expose all the details of what's going on there. Insider dealings, secret dealings, you name it. The financial world will lapse into chaos—at least for long enough to expose the Stock Market's dark secrets to the world, including to various police forces."

Gouroull listened to this impassively. Saint-Clair couldn't work out if he had registered what had just been said, or if he just wasn't surprised. Or merely concealing his reactions. Then he finally spoke, quietly and clearly:

"BlackSpear keeps hard copies of information about many leading politicians, businesspeople and media people around the world. They use this information to blackmail them into doing their work for them. That is, if they cannot simply bankroll them," he said.

"Where are these hard copies kept?" asked Blake.

"In a secure room in BlackSpear Tower in Paris."

Blake nodded.

"Yes, I thought so, but I had to be sure."

Saint-Clair wondered if Blake really had thought so, or was just pretending to be all-knowing.

Blake took two plastic cards out of his pocket.

"Well, here is my side of the bargain. These cards contain your—and your charming wife's—new identities."

Gouroull grabbed then between his thumb and forefinger. He looked at the two cards, thoughtfully. Blake continued, with a lighter tone in his voice:

"Anyway, so this is goodbye. Good luck in your new life, Gouroull. Try not to go back to your old ways. It is still possible that we might meet again one day; only time will tell. It's not impossible with us long-lifers."

He nodded a farewell, and made for the elevator. Saint-Clair also nodded farewell, and followed Blake.

The two men left the building as swiftly as they could without appearing to hurry, and were back in the hired spinner in the parking lot within ten minutes.

Rachael had seen them go. The fact that they were still alive left her wondering what they had discussed with Gouroull. She went into his office to see how he was.

He was sitting at his desk again, looking at the news on the vidscreen. She walked over and saw what it was. A cyber-attack on Wall Street, causing a stock market crash and the massive exposure of information companies had been keeping secret. Already the police were being called in. It was mayhem.

Gouroull had heard her heels clacking on the smooth floor. He looked up at her. She put her hands onto one of his massive shoulders.

"Were those two men connected to this?" Rachael asked.

"Yes," replied Gouroull.

"Are we affected by this?"

"Yes. We've lost the gold mine. I don't know about the shares or bonds though." He put his hand on top of her hands. "We might not be here long enough to find out. It's all useless, anyway."

Rachael looked worried.

"Will we have to go on the run?"

"I have our new identities here," said Gouroull, showing her the cards Blake had given him. "We will be free of BlackSpear. We can start again."

He then paused, and an element of doubt came into his voice—very rare for him. "Will you run away with me?" he asked.

Rachael was surprised for a moment, before responding:

"Yes. Of course I will!"

Gouroull stood up, and embraced her. As he held her close, she knew he could feel her heart beating inside her android frame, even though she could not feel any heartbeat at all in his strange body.

They stayed like that for a moment or two; and then, with a tenderness that even he didn't know he was capable of, he detached himself.

"Pack only a few things. Meet me by the limo in fifteen minutes."

Rachael looked at him for a moment. Life always seemed to change abruptly and dramatically for her after any long period. She nodded, and hurried off.

The cold, ruthless glint returned to Gouroull's eyes, as he surveyed the office one last time.

Then he picked up the vidscreen and smashed it into the computer. Kicked the desk into two, and threw his chair out of the window.

In the parking lot outside, Blake and Saint-Clair sat in their rental spinner. Blake was looking at his j-pad pensively. Saint-Clair was looking at the building in the same way.

Suddenly, the top floor of Gouroull Tower exploded into a fireball.

A moment later, a Limousine spinner swooped out from behind the building and flew away.

"I wonder if BlackSpear will try and hunt them down?" said Saint-Clair. "It doesn't seem to be worth their time or resources."

Blake put away his j-pad.

"You seem to have answered your own question, Leo. Although Gouroull does have certain skills they would like to make use of, so it is not completely improbable," said Blake. "Then again, they have quite a lot of their plate already. The virus has done its job, and according to the news, the FBI have already been called in to investigate certain financial irregularities that have been exposed. Maybe I should have done this five years ago."

"I wouldn't be so sure. Five years ago might have been the wrong time in other ways. The world might not have been ready for this kind of exposure back then."

"You are quite right. Timing is essential," said Blake. "Speaking of which, we'd better get you back to Paris for the final act."

"It is far from the final act," said Saint-Clair.

Blake started up the engine, and lifted the spinner up into the sky, before turning it round back in the direction of Dallas Bullet Station.

"Look in the glove compartment," said Blake.

Saint-Clair did, and he found two more electronic cards.

"Those are our identities for getting us out of the USA," said Blake. "And we will have flights booked for us at Miami Airport. We'll get there by bullet train, and take a flight to Barcelona. From there, I'm sure you can find a way back into France."

"Yes, that should be fairly straight forward. Organizing it, anyway."

"Would you like me to come in with you? I'm sure my skills would be useful in bringing down a Fascist government," Blake asked.

"I already feel like I've asked a lot of you. But yes, I could certainly use your help," said Saint-Clair.

"Then that's settled," said Blake, with a little too much gusto in his voice for Saint-Clair's liking. "Paris it is then."

And with that he slammed down the accelerator.

Normally, our stories involve at least one character from popular French fic-
tion, but this one does not. (Well, Sâr Dubnotal does get a mention in passing.)
Still, Xavier's notion was seductive enough that it was worth making room for
this short, clever bit of retroactive continuity...

Xavier Mauméjean: *The Replacement*

New York, January 1938

Whenever he visited New York, Bruce Wayne always experienced mixed
feelings. The city was as if it was a missing link between Gotham and Metropolis. It shared a historical background, rich, dark, full of secrets, with the former,
and the steady pace of modernity, the media—newspapers and radios—and live-
ly and witty theater shows with the latter. One factor, however, set New York
apart from the other two megacities: it could count on its heroes.

The young man stayed in the suite he rented permanently at the Waldorf
Astoria. Before it had been converted into a hotel, the splendid building had
consisted of two private residences, belonging to the Astor and Waldorf families. However, although cousins, they could not stand each other. Thomas
Wayne, Bruce's father, had told him that, as a child, he had been invited several
times by one or the other of the two wealthy families. That was a custom
amongst New World aristocrats, and Gotham's Waynes belonged to the elite of
the founding fathers of America. Thomas Wayne had not liked visiting them,
though, because their residences were separated by walls that no one dared
cross.

The ringing of the telephone pulled Bruce out of his reverie. Alfred Pennyworth, his exquisitely mannered English butler, answered the call.

"Miss Lane? Yes... yes... very well... Of course... Thank you, Miss Lane."

The butler placed the handset back on the telephone.

"Lois Lane?" Bruce asked.

Alfred smiled slightly.

"A remarkable deduction, although an inaccurate one. You may want to
continue to practice your detective skills. It wasn't Lois Lane, but her elder sister, Margo."

Margo Lane was the celebrated beauty who ran the Cobalt Club, the most
exclusive nightclub in Manhattan, which belonged to Lamont Cranston, an eccentric millionaire with a rather shady past. During the Great War he had shot
down more than thirty German fighter planes down; he was certainly an "ace"
but one with near suicidal tendencies if his former squad mates were to be believed. By the end of the war, Cranston had disappeared only to resurface in

China in the mid-1920s, as an advisor to the cruel general Cho Tsing. He had gone on to Tibet to follow the esoteric teachings of Marpa Tulku, who had had only one other disciple, the dreaded Shiwan Khan. At least, that was the story Bruce Wayne had put together from more or less reliable bits of gossip. Cranston's identity was fragmented into different personas named Clifford Gage and Kent Allard., not counting that of the Shadow, who, in turn, hadn't failed to notice Bruce Wayne. It was true that the young man was following in the former's footsteps, in many ways...

Officially, Bruce was in New York to launch Wayne Tech, a scientific subsidiary of his family's business empire, which he was planning to expand. For this purpose, he had met a number of great American scientists, such as Howard Stark, who had been lavish with his advice, and Nathaniel Richards, whose young son, Reed, showed promise also being a genius. But unofficially... Like any would-be knight, dark or otherwise, Bruce Wayne wanted to be dubbed. The Heir of the Waynes sought another legacy.

"So our meeting will take place at the Cobalt Club?" he asked his butler.

"No, Master Bruce. At the Empire State Building."

The Rolls Royce Phantom stopped right at the entrance to the skyscraper. Alfred got out, circled the vehicle and opened the right rear door to let Bruce descend. He and his butler walked into the lobby. A man of short stature but massive build, with disproportionately long arms, was waiting for them near a private elevator. Bruce knew that he should not judge him by his ape-like appearance; he was in the presence of one of the world's top chemists. The man smiled, running his thick fingers through his tangled black hair, and invited them to climb into the cabin.

The elevator stopped at the 86th floor. A very special committee was waiting for Bruce, whose heart filled with pride as he recognized each of the doctor's assistants. One of them, slim and elegant in his tailored suit, shared a certain resemblance to Alfred, who, himself a veteran of the Great War, addressed him by his rank of Brigadier General, as if they knew each other. Bruce knew him as a high-profile attorney.

"My dear Bruce," said the man, "last year I chaired a debate competition between graduating students from Yale, Harvard and Gotham's law schools, and I can say that your friend Harvey Dent shows promises to be an outstanding attorney!"

One of the assistants, a tall, extremely thin man with black hair and a large nose, wearing a monocle over a damaged left eye, interrupted the exchanges.

"They're waiting for you."

The plural reassured Bruce, but made him nervous at the same time. The two greatest heroes of New York, and arguably, of America, had responded favorably to his request for an audience. It was now necessary for him to not disappoint them.

Bruce entered a room that was plunged in darkness. His eyes adjusted quickly. He first noticed the master of the house, an Olympian giant, exuding strength and intelligence. Everything about him was remarkable, even his hair, which looked like a bronzed aura around his head. His guest was more difficult to focus on, something deliberately created by the fruit of long training. Bruce fixed his gaze on the features, but failed to discern them; they were fluid like melting wax.

His host began to talk:

"From now on, and throughout this conversation, I propose that we call ourselves by our first names. And as we're likely to meet again in the future, let's adopt this practice. I am Clark."

"Kent," said the shadowy man.

"Bruce."

"Very good," said the doctor. "We know which event motivated your decision. The tragedy of Park Lane."

"Crime Alley," said the shadowy man.

"We can understand it," continued the doctor, "but will only endorse it if your motivation is altruistic."

"Is it revenge?" asked the dark man who seemed to retreat further into the shadows.

"No. Justice," Bruce replied, his throat dry.

The doctor nodded imperceptibly.

"What title will you claim? That of an avenger?" he asked.

"Or of a vigilante?" the dark man said, giving a mournful laugh.

Bruce took his time before answering, thinking of his stay in England, particularly in Sussex, and of the rewarding hours he had spent with the old bee-keeper in his cottage on the South Downs. He answered:

"Detective. I'd prefer to be called Detective."

Both heroes approved.

"You will need a lair," said the doctor, "a kind of secret base for storing your equipment. For my part, I have several warehouses along the Hudson River..."

"And I, all over the city."

Of course, they confessed only to what Bruce had already discovered, and put into practice. The renovation of his "cave" was almost finished.

"Will you be assisted in your mission?"

"No, except for my butler. I prefer to work alone."

The two heroes replied with almost one voice:

"No, you'll need help," said the doctor. "Sooner or later, you will need the support of some reliable people."

"I was like you, at first," said the dark man. "But you will see, experience will change your mind."

There remained one final question, perhaps the most important of all. The doctor asked it:

"How will you neutralize your enemies?"

The shadowy man cuckled his icy laugh again and said:

"Nothing better than a pair of Colt 45s. And if they're really recalcitrant, a good old-fashioned Thompson submachine gun."

"I prefer more sophisticated methods...," began the doctor.

"I will use non-lethal means," Bruce stated.

The two heroes stood up. The doctor held out his hand.

"I speak for Kent as well as myself. Bruce, we knew what to expect from you, but now, we feel certain. You are one of us."

Bruce, deeply moved, felt the energy of the hero when he shook his hand. Then, when he squeezed the other man's bony hand, ringed with a splendid red stone, he felt a dark force. Sensing his trouble, the doctor ended the interview with a lighter note:

"The next time Patricia visits Gotham, I'm counting on you to be her escort!"

"Your charming cousin? It will be my pleasure, Clark!"

Alfred Pennyworth felt an immense joy at seeing his master walk out, smiling unreservedly for the first time in a very long time.

At the elevator, Bruce came face to face with Britt Reid, like him, a wealthy heir, who published the *Daily Sentinel*.

"Bruce, old pal!"

"Britt!"

He was accompanied by his Asian valet who, if one were to believe his uniform, served the same function as Alfred. His name was Kano, or Kato, remembered Bruce. The simian-like man was escorting them out. Bruce smiled as he stepped inside the elevator.

Britt appeared before the two heroes, in the company of Kato, his designated future assistant.

"I saw you at work," said the shadowy man. "You are impressive. You have perfect body control."

"Thank you. Coming from you, I'm quite touched," answered Reid.

"I'm not talking about you, Mr. Reid, but your assistant. Did you, by any chance, spend some time in Tibet following the teaching of Sâr Dubnotal?"

Translation: Jean-Marc Lofficier

Christofer Nigro has already written a series of tales featuring Paul Féval, fils' creation, Felifax the Tiger-Man (available from Black Coat Press, ISBN 978-1-932983-88-0), as well as his half-brother Felanthus. They are "Eye of the Tiger-Man," published in The Shadow of Judex, *then "The Privilege of Adonis" (in Vol. 10), "The Noble Freak" (Vol. 11), "Justice and the Beast" (Vol. 12), "Kindred Beasts" (Vol. 14) and "The Anti-Adonis Alliance" (Vol. 15). This is the latest installment...*

Christofer Nigro: *Clash of the Jungle Lords*

A small private airfield on the outskirts of Paris, mid-1937

Felanthus the Man-Tiger rushed across the darkened airfield as fast as his enhanced limbs could carry him. He made certain to use all four of his limbs, which increased his already great running speed. The object he sought, a large private cargo aircraft, was quietly situated several hundred yards across the runway. The felinoid was aware he would have to sneak on board when the workmen loading it for the next morning's flight were away from the open hatch.

The Man-Tiger's combination of speed and natural alacrity for stealth had already served him well this evening. It took much surreptitious spying within the Parisian city limits to learn when an aircraft of precisely the type he required was due to take off the following morning. And it couldn't just be heading anywhere; it needed to be *en route* to Benares, India. That much Felanthus understood.

Upon leaving the verdant sanctuary of the Bois de Boulogne for the final time after securing one last large meal of ducks, Felanthus had traipsed through the great city streets in the middle of the night. He made certain to keep to as many secluded streets as he could until reaching the Gare d'Auteuil station. He was seen by no one, save for a busy street sweeper who was getting an early start on his job. The man caught a quick glimpse of a large, hirsute figure as Felanthus rushed past him. His only reaction was to shake his head and continue working.

After hitching a ride on the sprawling Parisian train network, Felanthus, doing a good job of keeping to the shadows, arrived at the airport of Villacoublay, located to the south-west of Paris, and recently expanded to accommodate the French airforce. It was there that, in 1897, French engineer Clément Ader had been the first man in the world to take off the ground in his *avion* (he had invented the word), but this feat had gone unrecorded, because the genial inventor had foreseen from the start the military possibilities of his invention, and had sought to preserve the secrecy of his tests.

Having jumped off the train after Velizy, Felanthus sped towards the airfield, the location of which he had memorized during his sporadic nighttime forays into the city. Only two farmers coming home late in the evening after a day of hard labor in the fields saw him rush by.

"Doux Jésus!" one of them exclaimed. "Did you see the size of that... dog, was it?"

"I could not tell what it was, as it moved so fast!" replied the other man. "But what would a dog be doing here?"

"Chasing rabbits, perhaps? How the hell should I know! I just hope we never see it again! There was something... unnatural about it."

After a short time, Felanthus found the airfield. There, he ran onto a cargo plane on its way to the Middle-East without being noticed, hiding behind several large wooden crates piled atop each other in the back of the vessel. The Man-Tiger then lay still, slowed his breathing, patiently waiting until dawn when the aircraft would leave for Athens, Beirut, Baghdad, Karachi, Calcutta, Bangkok and, finally, Saigon. From Calcutta, he planned to travel to Varanasi (Benares) and enter the jungle in search of his sibling, Prince Rama, a.k.a., Felifax the Tiger-Man.

A recent personal loss had devastated him[10], and he was determined to reunite with the more human-looking brother he once had briefly met and fought alongside before the capricious whims of fate cruelly had separated them.

Felanthus would soon be off from the woodlands of France to the jungles of India.

It was mid-afternoon of the following morning when Felifax the Tiger-Man, who was visiting Paris for its 1937 World Exposition, stood in that same airfield. And that was most unfortunate for airport security officer Brosseau, whom the Hindu jungle lord held against the hull of a different cargo plane by the collar of his uniform.

"What do you mean *that* cargo plane took off hours ago?" the angry Prince Rama bellowed. "I spent all morning locating and tracking my brother's scent, starting in the Bois de Boulogne and through your needlessly complicated rail network, and his spoor led me to this very spot on your airfield. And now, you tell me this is the wrong plane?"

"Yes, Prince Rama, that is what I just said!" Brosseau replied. "Now, please remove your hand from my person this instant!"

Rama's stalwart friend and bodyguard Baber was also present, and he grabbed the jungle lord's wrist in an attempt to extricate it from Brosseau's collar. The Hindu prince's grip proved too strong to wrest from the officer in that fashion, so he next resorted to calm words.

---

[10] See *Kindred Beasts*.

"You should comply with the officer's request, Rama," Baber said. "We both understand why you are so frustrated, my friend, but let us not direct it towards an innocent target."

Rama turned and glared in his friend's countenance with gritted teeth. The bottom of his incisors looked sharpened, and Baber knew this did not bode well. However, the man's faith in the prince was soon justified when Felifax calmed and released Brosseau.

"Please forgive me for my behavior," the Tiger-Man said with sincerity. "I am simply very distraught over the search for my brother's whereabouts. Doing so has been a painstaking and distressing procedure, and I thought the trail would end here."

Felifax's level of despondency actually touched Brosseau's usually iron heart. "It is... understandable, Monsieur. I wish there was more I could do for you, but..."

"No need to fret, Prince Rama, because I *can* do something for you," an unfamiliar voice from behind interjected.

Rama and Baber turned to see the firm visage of Detective Cocantin, a dedicated ally to the cloaked Parisian vigilante Judex—an alliance that went back to the former's childhood, when the resourceful waif had carried the street name of the Licorice Kid.

At first assuming that the policeman was there to arrest Felifax, Baber attempted to smooth things over. "Please do forgive Prince Rama for acting out of turn, Monsieur. As he said, he is simply very upset right now."

"*Naturellement,* I know who your friend is, Monsieur Baber, since it is my job to know these things, and I am no dummy," Cocantin interrupted. "And when I said I could do something, I meant actual assistance and not an ironic way of implying I was going to throw him in prison for his assault against Officer Brosseau."

Rama stepped forward and put his hand on Baber's shoulder to indicate that he wanted his friend to stand back and let him handle this affair.

"Detective, what assistance do you offer?" the Tiger-Man asked the shorter Cocantin.

"First off, you should know that I am a friend of Judex," Cocantin said.

Felifax scoffed as his teeth again began to lengthen. "Damn that vigilante! I told him I didn't want his assistance in this matter!"

"Indeed," Cocantin replied, "which is why he asked me to step in and make the offer in his stead—which is partly because, unlike him, I do have the law on my side, and I will throw you in prison if you attempt to raise a hand to me out of misplaced anger. That will give you pause against starting a pointless scuffle, as you may have done with him. Your princely status would undoubtedly prevent you from staying in our prisons for long, but it would cost you precious time. So, I urge you to accept this generous offer."

Felifax again gnashed his teeth, and clenched his right fist. Then he forced himself to calm down, determined that the man should remain in control of the tiger, whose genetic code he shared.

"Again, I ask: what type of assistance?"

"Judex is a man of many resources," the former Licorice Kid replied, "and he has hired the pilot of a private aircraft to return you to India much faster than could be expected of the transport you and your entourage used to come here for the Exposition. That plane ready to go on the other side of this airfield as we speak."

Now it was Baber's turn to place a hand on Felifax's shoulder.

"Please abandon that mistrust of yours, Rama, and take this gracious offer. I shall remain here in Paris and handle the matter of your entourage's planned departure for India in a few days."

Cocantin seemed to grin.

"Well, what'll it be, Prince Rama? Pride, prison, or pursuit?"

The Tiger-Man sighed.

"Very well. I can brook no further delays in tracking my brother's journey back to India."

"That's the spirit, my Prince!" Baber said with a smile.

"I will take you to the craft that will swiftly get you out of my hair," Cocantin said as he headed in that direction and motioned for Felifax to follow.

India, mid-1937

Within a week, Felifax found himself trekking back through the steamy verdure of the Indian jungle outside of Varanasi. It was home ground, yet he realized that finding his quarry would still be difficult. For the jungles of India were vast, and though the Tiger-Man was the unquestioned lord of the tropical wilderness surrounding Varanasi, there were more distant regions where he was not so hailed.

Such was the mysterious Seeonee hills section, which included the large body of water known as the Waingunga River. The people and animals who dwelled in that region recognize another man (if a man he truly was) as lord; one who was spoken of in hushed whispers throughout India, much like that other jungle lord who ruled portions of the African jungle. Only, unlike the African jungle lord, whose legends said he had been raised by apes, the Indian jungle lord of the Seeonee had reputedly been raised by wolves.

Prince Rama had avoided approaching Seeonee throughout his reign in the Benares area out of respect for that other legend (and had been extended the same courtesy in return). After all, he was more than content with the huge slice of wilderness that was his to rule. Now, however, circumstances were such that he could no longer stay out of that portion of the jungle.

Upon his return home, Felifax had checked the records at the British-controlled airfields to learn that the French cargo plane on which his brother Felanthus had stowed away had indeed landed in Delhi several days previous. A fracas involving a "beast-man" of some sort was reported to have ensued when, after a successful landing, this creature had escaped from the airfield. The reports continued to describe this "strange beast-man" racing at great speed toward Benares, where "it" had been sighted by several Brahmans who resided within the many Hindu temples dotting the city. Its trek had reportedly taken the unknown animal into the jungle, where it had promptly vanished from sight.

You are not an "unknown" to me, my brother, Felifax thought. *I will find you, wherever your spoor may lead. And I swear that any who attempt to bar my way shall suffer the wrath of Kali.*

The acolyte of the multi-armed Hindu goddess of destruction knew this was no hypothetical allusion, since after finally picking up the trail of his brother, he realized that it led towards the Seeonee hills. Uncharted territory for Felifax, and a domain claimed by another jungle lord. How his journey there would turn out was anyone's guess, but Felifax knew he must be prepared for anything.

Felifax realized his odyssey into the Seeonee region was not one he should undertake alone. And with Baber busy for the time being back in Paris, the Tiger-Man knew of only two others who would be loyal and formidable enough to accompany him.

To this end, he stopped at the Hindu temple he had built years earlier in the middle of the jungle. This imposing, vine-encrusted residence served as a home to Rama, his wife Grace, his surrogate little sister Djina, and her husband, the explorer and former big game hunter Matt Challenger. And always nearby were the two whose assistance he sought: the twin Bengal tigers Rudra the man-eater and Durgane the crusher—the progeny of the previous tigers to hold these respective names who had served as Felifax's constant companions and allies in decades past.

"Rama, you have returned!" an excited Djina yelled as she ran from her wing of the jungle temple of Kali.

She stopped and cut short the intended embrace for her brother when she found him entwined in the arms of his wife, Grace Palmer.

"Oh, my apologies," Djina said with a smile as she took a few steps back. "I presume I will get my turn at showing you affection after Grace is finished with hers. Eventually."

"If so, then you'll be waiting 'til the sun goes down, luv," came Matt Challenger's scruffy voice from behind. "But not to worry, I'll gladly give you some of what Rama is giving to Grace while you wait."

Djina smiled and gave her husband of a year and a half a hefty hug and kiss of her own. She knew that would get the attention of her brother, who had always disapproved of her choice of spouse due to his unsavory past as a poacher. The fact that he was the grandson of famed British explorer George Challenger, and that he felt he had redeemed himself by turning on his former partners-in-crime and saving Djina's life, still meant for nothing in Felifax's eyes.

"I see your hands must always be either on a rifle or my sister's body, Challenger," Rama commented, his face now turned away from his wife's lips.

"She does happen to be my wife, oh haughty jungle lord," Matt retorted. "That's what husbands and wives do, which you and blondie there are apt to demonstrate at any moment."

"Matt…" Djina grumbled.

"Begging my pardon, luv," her husband replied, "but that Tiger-Man bloke has a double standard in place here. He continues not to like me no matter what I do to make up for my sordid past."

Felifax's retort was predictably harsh. "Forgive me for believing I may be worthy of Grace's love, while you fall far short of that honor regarding a fine woman like my sister."

Matt gritted his teeth. "Sod off, Felix!"

Rama stepped away from his golden-trussed wife. "What did you call me, Mr. Poachman?"

"Surely a man with tiger blood isn't hard of hearing," Matt said as he took a few steps towards his brother-in-law.

Djina grasped her husband's arm. "Matthew, that will be quite enough!"

Grace likewise grabbed her husband. "Your sister is right, Rama. This constant fighting between you two needs to stop. He is part of the family now, and he has saved Djina's life and tried hard to make up for the mistakes he made prior to meeting us."

"Thank you, Gracie!" Matt exclaimed. "Teach your husband a thing or two about forgiveness."

"No, Grace, you should teach me nothing on his behalf," Rama insisted. "Did he not insult you as well by calling you 'blondie'?"

"Well," Grace responded, "I am blonde, am I not? But Matt is no longer a poacher, and you, my dear, are not… well, whatever 'Felix' is, I'm sure. So, you two need to refrain from riling each other with unjust name-calling."

"I told you, hun, I'm willing to bury the hatchet," Matt offered with extended arms.

"Most likely in the skull of a helpless animal, preferably of an endangered species," Rama remarked.

"Oh, what the bloody hell! I give up here!" Matt threw up his arms and turned to leave.

"Sweetheart, you really need to put aside this animosity," Grace suggested.

"What I really need to do right now," Felifax said, "is to gather up Rudra and Durgane and head for the Seeonee. My brother is lost in the far reaches of this jungle searching for me, and I must find him."

"Rama, it is dangerous in that region of the jungle!" Djina proclaimed with concern. "Even for one such as you. Even with the twins at your side."

"It is also reportedly under the jurisdiction of… another protector," Grace added. "It may be taken as a sign of great disrespect if you breach the unwritten treaty by invading that region."

"Nevertheless," Felifax said, "I must go there. As we speak, my brother Felanthus, as formidable as he may be, is now facing unknown dangers alone. I must be off in a moment."

"You're out of your bloody mind, Tiger-bloke!" Matt protested. "Let me get my rifle and I'll come with you."

"I think not!" Rama angrily lamented.

"I do not want either of you to go!" Djina pleaded. "But… I understand the brother you told us of is in peril. I would rather you two go together than either of you to go alone. Please put your bad feelings for my love aside, brother, and let him accompany you."

"Please, listen to your sister," Grace pleaded in a soft, impassioned tone.

It was accompanied by a tear glistening in the corner of her eye that Felifax could not overlook.

"Very well," he said. "I do want to return to you and Djina with my brother, and if my pride is an impediment to that, I must overcome it."

"In other words," Matt interjected, "let's get moving, old chap."

The expert hunter/adventurer stood prepared with his modified .50 caliber Mauser rifle that included a razor-sharp bayonet tied tightly to the barrel. He was garbed in his patented olive-green safari outfit and matching pith helmet.

"Do your best to keep up with me," Felifax said, "as I have no time to waste."

"Wait a minute now…" Matt hollered as the Tiger-Man took off into the jungle with speed far surpassing that of the most experienced hunter.

Rudra and Durgane followed and managed to keep pace, a feat which Matt Challenger could not hope to match.

The great tiger known as Shere Khan, the Big One, sniffed the air around him. His keen olfactory senses caught a strange scent—one that was undeniably human, but with an odd taint reminiscent of the tiger's own species. This intrigued the vicious predator, one whose unusual constitution had enabled him to live and retain the vitality of a considerably younger Bengal much longer than he should have.

Could it be? Could this strange scent be that of the man I have heard of in the place called Benares? Could he at long last be leaving his claimed territory for the one here, the one claimed by the hated man cub Mowgli? Could he be violating the Law of the Jungle that compelled him to so long obey the boundaries he now crosses?

Shere Khan sniffed the air again, this time with more effort. He detected other scents moving in alignment with the approaching Felifax, who was still over two miles from the Seeonee hills at this point. Khan discerned a pair alongside the Tiger-Man, these being entirely of his own species. It was clear, based on their proximity to Felifax, along with the rumors he had heard, that these two tigers were under his control. If they hailed from outside the Seeonee region, however, they were almost certainly of the standard Bengal type, not the truly intelligent variant that Shere Khan belonged to. The animals of Khan's type were native to few areas beyond the one he and his fellow beasts thrived within.

Thus, did Shere Khan's sinister mind begin hatching a scheme that would take advantage of this rare situation. One that may eliminate his hated enemy Mowgli once and for all by bringing him into direct conflict with Felifax, the interloping jungle lord from Benares.

Mowgli stood looking at the mangled bodies of two Waingunga villagers, a mother and young daughter. His dark eyes had an expression that evoked both great despondency and unbridled anger. These two had gone to the river to collect some water, as indicated by the wooden baskets and milkmaid yokes which lay on the verdant ground a few feet away from their bodies. They were ambushed and torn to pieces by something that bore the distinct mark of Bengal tigers. Obviously more than one, which was rather strange, as tigers tended to hunt alone.

Even more strange and disturbing was the fact that the killing had occurred at all. The Law of the Jungle which the intelligent animals of the Seeonee rigidly adhered to forbade the slaughter of humans, as well as their cattle, to prevent mass retaliation from mankind's firearms. Of the striped big cats in Seeonee, only the vile Shere Khan had become an eater of men, but he had sworn off this behavior over twenty years past. Had he started his profane eating habits again? And who was the other of his kind that was apparently his partner-in-manslaughter?

"I saw who did this foul deed," came the voice of Tabaqui from a few yards behind Mowgli.

The jungle lord boldly turned to face the sly one. Now an adult, he stood at over six feet in height, and his brown skin rippled with the imposing musculature that lay beneath. His long, black bushy hair hung down past his shoulder blades, and he still looked quite young. The dark eyes of his handsome face glared with unspoken warning at the brown-coated jackal before him. Mowgli's right hand was clasped over the hilt of the dagger kept in a leather sheathe sewn into his loincloth shorts, ready to draw and use it at a second's notice.

"Tell me what you saw, Tabaqui," Mowgli demanded.

"Another jungle lord from beyond the Seeonee hath come to this land of ours. He is a man like you, but also bearing the traits of a tiger. With him are two true striped ones, which he ordered to kill these village females. He covets

185

this land of ours and would challenge thee for it. He would, in fact, challenge all the peoples of the Waingunga for it."

Mowgli cocked his head. "Why should I believe you, Tabaqui? You who hath deceived all the jungle peoples before and are prone to fits of madness. You who hath aligned thyself with Shere Khan in past days, though not recent ones."

"I bear no respect for the Big One any longer, man cub. That is known to all the peoples who dwell here. I warn you of this because the challenge of the outsider jungle man and his striped servants is one that extends to all in the Seeonee. Only you among us can stop him, and I gave thee the warning to enable this."

"Very well. What you say rings true, but I remain with caution. I do detect this outsider's unfamiliar and strange scent, so that is in your favor. Keep your eyes and nose to the jungle and seek me out should more knowledge come your way."

"Aye, my lord."

With that, Mowgli, lord of the Seeonee section of the Indian jungle, took off in search of the outsider he believed responsible for two senseless killings and the apparent determination to commit more of them. With his greater familiarity of this region, it would not be long before Mowgli found the rival jungle lord he was determined to kill for the good of his land.

Approximately one mile away, Felifax moved through the unfamiliar terrain with admirable speed and stealth, two things very difficult to carry out in tandem. Close behind were Rudra and Durgane, the progeny of the originals that stalked about the jungle floor with equal surreptitiousness. All three sniffed the air about them, doing their best to lock onto the scent of Felanthus, who appeared to have already passed completely through the region.

Felifax barely heard the thud of a fellow human jumping out of a short tree and landing on the dirt a few feet behind him. He turned in a prepared stance a split second later, where he found himself confronted by no less than the jungle lord of the Seeonee region. Mowgli stood almost as tall as Rama himself, his skin a darker brown, his muscles every bit as intimidating to behold.

"You would be Mowgli," Felifax said in English, after hearing that his fellow jungle lord had since learned the language from British missionaries. "Can you understand the language I use?"

"I can," Mowgli replied curtly in the same lingo. "And you would be the despicable Felifax, the Hindu lord of the tigers. Challenger of my station. Murderer of the peaceful people under my protection."

Felifax's handsome features took on a look of incredulity as he refined his prepared stance. "I fail to understand what you say, my fellow jungle warrior. Wanton murder is not something I have ever done, nor do I challenge anyone for reasons related to pride."

"Is that so? The innocent mother and daughter whom I found torn to pieces were mauled by two tigers. Much like those two that accompanied you here to Seeonee."

Mowgli pointed to Rudra and Durgane, who both lay close to the ground in preparation to spring as soon as trouble reared its head.

"Rudra and Durgane are not man-killers. Nor am I."

"Then why, murderous one, did you journey past the boundaries we had both always recognized in the past? How did I come to find those slaughtered villagers at the same time you arrived here?"

That is a good question, and a serious mystery. But it does not change the matter of our innocence, nor the urgency of my mission.

"I know how this must look, great Mowgli. But I came to your land not to challenge you, or any of the villagers who call it home. I am searching for a brother of mine who journeyed here in search of me, not knowing exactly where in the jungle I reside. He is not familiar enough with me to have memorized my scent, though I did pick up his back in Paris."

Mowgli laughed derisively. "Entertaining story, killer. But hardly likely." Mowgli unsheathed his blade. "Now prepare to meet whatever spirits you may worship."

"I have no time for this!"

Saying that, Felifax issued a hand signal to his companions. Rudra and Durgane ran towards Mowgli and snarled at him, giving the jungle warrior pause.

"You leave me no choice but to have Rudra and Durgane hold you at bay while I search for my brother. They shall not hurt you so long as you make no move on them or attempt to follow me. I swear to our innocence of the crime which you accused us of, and I also swear to leave here forever after I find my brother."

Mowgli grinned again. "You say you have no time for me? You shall *make* the time, then!"

The child of the wolves cupped his free hand over his mouth and released a loud hoot. It served as a signal, and within seconds a sleek black panther and an older but still rugged-looking bear emerged from the surrounding foliage. Bagheera and Baloo had once again come to Mowgli's side.

"So, this is that other jungle lord," Bagheera noted to Mowgli and Baloo using a form of ultra-sound to roughly simulate language.

"A killer of mankind is what he is," Baloo added. "He and these two striped ones, who are from outside Seeonee and lack the special gifts of our peoples. But they are no less deadly for that."

"What will be shall be, then," Felifax said in acquiescence. "Rudra? Durgane? Hold those beasts at bay while I deal with Mowgli! You will pay for forcing my hand like this!"

Rudra charged Bagheera, and the two big cats spat and clawed each other to a standstill. Durgane sprang at Baloo, who managed to fend the savage Bengal off with the great strength and fearsome claws of his forelimbs—but for how long?

"Now!" Mowgli yelled as he raised his blade and ran to meet Felifax's attack.

The Tiger-Man was startled, however, as the rival jungle lord's charge proved to be a feint. Mowgli stopped short his attack mid-way, made a remarkable leap straight up, and grasped onto a low-hanging tree branch. He then swung his legs forward and double-kicked Felifax in the chin with the soles of his feet. The Tiger-Man was truly taken off guard and the mighty blow sent him sprawling onto his back. His own blade fell from his hand and was lost in the nearby shrubbery.

Impressive, Felifax mused to himself as he shook off the stars in front of his eyes. *But could I expect anything less from one who earned such a legend?*

Mowgli then released his hold on the branch and fell five feet back to the ground, landing skillfully on his bare feet. He brandished his blade and resumed his attack on Felifax, who was still on the ground. The battle was not to end as Mowgli hoped, however, as his own inspiring prowess was easily matched by the Tiger-Man, who caught his foe's wrist during its downward plunge. The blade thus failed to sink into its target's flesh, and Mowgli found his wrist caught in a painful grip of steel.

Several feet away, Bagheera and Rudra rolled around in the greenery, each unsuccessfully attempting to land a crippling strike or bite upon the other. Baloo had managed to continue fending off Durgane's rushing attacks, but the latter's strength and speed looked as if they would soon get past the mighty old ursine's defenses.

Mowgli was startled as Felifax's visage now bore yellow, feline eyes and pronounced incisors. The tan skin on his torso and back suddenly developed darker brown stripes resembling those of the tiger whose genetic stock he shared. His anger triggered the transformation, and Mowgli suddenly realized what he was truly up against. Not that this put an end to his determination to take retribution, however.

As the now quasi-feral Felifax snarled at the opponent, he held fast in his grip, Mowgli's trapped wrist dropped the blade. Then, in a blur of motion, he partially bent down and caught the knife with his free hand. Mowgli swiftly swiped the blade at the Tiger-Man, slashing a bloody gash across the flesh of his sternum. As Felifax howled in pain and released the grip that was crushing Mowgli's wrist, the latter swiped the blade at his enemy again. This time the Tiger-Man's enhanced reflexes enabled him to bend backwards and avoid being cut. However, Mowgli dashed forward with unexpected speed and delivered a haymaker to Felifax's jaw before he could regain his posture.

The punch was strong enough to send the Tiger-Man reeling... but he remained on his feet. Mowgli then leapt at his striped adversary with his blade ready to pierce his heart. Unfortunately, Felifax was wise to such attacks even in his feral state. He caught Mowgli in his powerful clutch and hurled him almost twenty feet away.

The lord of Seeonee was stunned when he hit the ground. He then focused his indomitable will into getting back on his feet before Felifax could pounce on him. It was a noble but futile effort, as a mere three seconds later Mowgli found himself struggling to keep the enraged rival jungle lord from sinking his incisors into his throat. At the same time, he furiously endeavored to push his stronger foe upwards so he could sink the dagger he held into his opponent's muscular throat.

This battle may have yielded a tragic end for all the noble personages involved if not for Bagheera's ultra-keen senses detecting a most familiar presence as he and Rudra circled each other with fangs mutually bared.

"Hold!" the ebony big cat shouted to Mowgli and Baloo. "'Tis the scent of Shere Khan in the air! I would know it any time it took to the winds!"

Baloo swatted the attacking Durgane aside as best he could and sniffed the air himself. "From whence does it come?"

"From there, on yonder hill!" Bagheera shouted as he moved his head to indicate the proper direction.

Baloo looked and finally caught sight of the Big One attempting to camouflage himself in a hedge of shrubbery just up a nearby hill. The scent of several wolves that stood close behind him then became evident to the great jungle duo.

"We need to make these two understand!" Baloo decreed. "And stop those other two from killing one another!"

"Aye!" Bagheera concurred. "Follow my lead to do exactly that!"

Bagheera turned away from the growling Rudra and ran towards the struggling jungle lords at amazing speed. Baloo went down on all fours and followed suit, doing his best to match speed with his quicker ally. Rudra and Durgane followed, believing the two they had fought would attempt to bushwhack Felifax.

Instead, Bagheera suddenly turned and swatted all four paws at Rudra, causing her to jump back. Baloo then reached Felifax, stood on two legs, and used his mighty forelegs to grasp and lift the fighting-mad Tiger-Man off Mowgli.

Seeing this accomplished, Bagheera turned and leapt atop his longtime human friend to deliver an important message.

"Mowgli, methinks this jungle man and his striped friends are innocent! Shere Khan is nearby watching with many wolves at his side. I would wager a week's kill that it is they who are the true killers of yon villagers!"

"What a fool I was!" Mowgli yelled as he rolled from underneath Bagheera.

He then ran towards Felifax, who was still endeavoring to break free from Baloo's powerful, well, bear hug. The ursine was skillfully positioning himself so Durgane risked slashing his own master if he launched an attack. Mowgli did his best to talk his enraged foe back to full cognizance. This was something he had to accomplish with due haste as he was unaware of the full measure of the Tiger-Man's strength while in "wild" mode, and thus was uncertain how long Baloo would be able to hold him.

"Felifax! Listen to me! I now know you are innocent! Forgive me for my foolishness and let us join together against the true evil!"

Within moments, as Bagheera still did his best to hold off Rudra without getting seriously injured or worse in the process, Felifax stopped his animalistic snarling. His eyes promptly regained their normal hazel irises, and his teeth seemed to lose their sharpened points.

"Please call off your striped companions," Mowgli pleaded. "Baloo is only restraining you, not inflicting harm. Call them off and I promise Baloo will release you, and I will talk to thee in peace."

"Rudra! Durgane!" Felifax shouted, along with another command spoken in Hindi. The two tigers immediately calmed and sat down as if in "attention."

Bagheera and Baloo did the same, and Mowgli ceased all hostilities as promised. He approached his fellow jungle lord and inspected the gash across his chest.

"Forgive me for this," Mowgli said. "I acted out of ignorance. I will get you some plants whose inner moisture has great healing properties. Then we shall talk, and I will start by telling you who was responsible for both those murders and for tricking me into thinking it was you."

"How are the animals in this region so intelligent?" Felifax queried his new ally while the restorative sap of the greens now affixed to his chest wound did their miraculous work.

"There is a legend that many moons ago," Mowgli explained, "a strange rock from the sky fell in the Seeonee hills. I believe men of science from Britain would refer to it as a 'meteor.'

"The rock gave off strange energies that seemed to affect both man and animal of this land. The few people exposed to it, including my human parents' grandsires, gave birth to children who grew to display some fantastic traits. I am said to be one of those, which is how after being abandoned I could grow and thrive among a pack of wolves and learn both their own language and that of men very quickly, and eventually learn to read. The children of those affected also seem to live much longer than normal, which is why many moons have passed for me, yet I remain as fit as the day I first reached manhood.

"As for the many animals who came across that strange rock? Their spawn were also changed. They were much smarter than normal animals, to the point of being able to duplicate 'language' by use of strange sounds that seemed to work on what the British people call a 'psychic' level.[11] They still live much as those of their species always have, but their ability to communicate with each other and to develop an understanding of the world around them in ways ordinary animals cannot has set them apart from those outside of Seeonee. They have a level of culture and organization that in some ways mirrors that of men.

"They do not create art or use numbers, and their lack of hands prevent them from building any type of technology. Only the monkeys have that, but they use the ruins of past civilizations as homes rather than building their own, and still only use the simplest of tools.

"Of course, the animals here also tend to live much longer than the ordinary ones beyond this land. This is good, as I still have Bagheera and Baloo with me after all this time. But, unfortunately, I also still have Shere Khan."

"Fascinating," Felifax replied. "This sounds much like other such meteors, including the one which landed in Wold Newton so long ago. And I, too, communicate with tigers and at times other animals of the jungle. But it is strictly on an empathic level, and the animals I know cannot use strange sounds in the way those you grew alongside do."

"Can you understand *this*, jungle man?" came a sneering "voice" from behind them.

The parties of the two jungle lords turned to see Shere Khan standing there in all his arrogant glory. Surrounding him was a pack of dangerous Seeonee wolves with which he had long ago built an alliance.

"I *did* understand this tiger," Felifax confirmed. "As if he was 'speaking' to me. I would imagine my empathic abilities allow me this communication with your animals. I also imagine this is the Shere Khan you spoke of, the one who will dearly pay for his evil tricks."

"Yes, it is he," Mowgli said through gritted teeth and clenched fists. "And yes, he will pay."

"So, thou hast seen through my trickery, jungle lords," Shere Khan glowered. "Because of that fool Bagheera. But it matters not. If you searched for me, you would find me in time. Thus, my decision to approach you first with my howling brothers in full force. Now, not only will I get my long overdue meal of thee, Mowgli, but we shall take Seeonee as our own. And after we kill this other jungle man, we shall take his land of Benares as well!"

"Please do try!" Baloo shouted as he stood on two legs and prepared for battle.

---

[11] Modern scientists have recently begun to learn how animals, including tigers, utilize ultra-sound for various purposes. The intelligent mutant animals of Seeonee obviously learned to use it for even more impressive feats, including communication to the point of actually simulating a variety of "languages." Mowgli's status as a human meteor mutant enabled him to likewise learn to use and understand the "language" of his animal peers. *Note from the Author.*

And the skirmish was joined. The wolf pack surpassed the jungle lords' entourage in number, and they were fearsome to behold. But the combined strength, claws, and fangs of Rudra, Durgane, Bagheera, and Baloo fought back savagely and proved themselves forces to be reckoned with in their own right.

Felifax's dreaded rage was triggered and he quickly metamorphosed into his primal mode. His strength, speed, and savagery now increased, and several wolves found themselves with ripped throats and a broken back or limbs at his hands and teeth. Mowgli's speed and skill with his blade proved true, and several wolves fell before him despite the many severe bites he took.

The Tiger-Man had just finished slamming an attacking wolf to the ground and crushing its spine when a particularly large lupine rushed at him from behind. It leapt to sink its deadly teeth into his throat… only to have its skull explode in a spray of blood and brain matter alongside a thunderous boom. Felifax turned to find that saving blast was courtesy of Matt Challenger's Mauser rifle.

"Sorry I'm late for the party, mate," the hunter quipped, "but you did run ahead of me, and you're a major chore to catch up with. Be thankful my tracking skills are what they are, and that smarty-pants tiger didn't pick up my scent since I was lagging so far behind you."

"Watch out!" Felifax cried past his feral psyche.

Matt swung around and blasted another wolf's head off as it attempted to pounce on him from behind. "Much obliged, guv!"

Felifax and Baloo rushed in front of Matt to shield him from further wolf attacks so that he had time to reload. They continued to fight on, and with Matt's rifle power added to their roster, the tide began to turn against Shere Khan's forces. Numerous bleeding and dismembered wolf carcasses were strewn across the verdant fields and none of them managed to inflict wounds serious enough to debilitate a single member of the jungle lords' combined teams.

Shere Khan's vertical feline pupils gleamed with rage as he watched the melee before him. *Even if I fail to win, I shall not fail completely. I will take the life of Mowgli. I will feast upon the man cub's flesh. He has slowed from the many wounds he has taken, and his attention is stolen; I shall rip into him from behind! The others on his side are too busy to take notice!*

The tiger tyrant ran towards the unwary Mowgli, and each of his allies were indeed too occupied with the last of Shere Khan's wolfen allies to notice. The brutal Bengal leapt many yards through the air with his front claws extended, ready to rip into the jungle warrior's flesh as the tiger's incredible weight crushed him into oblivion.

However, Shere Khan suddenly found his powerful form suspended in mid-air with a choking sensation besieging his throat.

"Look hence, Mowgli!" came a hissing "voice" from just above the tree line.

This occurred at the same time Matt dispatched the wolf Mowgli was fighting with a gunshot that blasted open its rib cage. The jungle warrior then turned and looked up, only to see Shere Kahn caught in a choke hold by a mighty and familiar python.

"Kaa!" Mowgli shouted. "Rarely have I been pleased to find thee in my presence. But this is most certainly one of those times!"

"Yes," Kaa replied. "I followed the Big One here quietly, to see what he was up to. So, I thought, why not help thee now as I have before? But only because I owed Bagheera for that tasty boar he recently brought me."

Shere Khan writhed and kicked his powerful limbs in a desperate attempt to shake himself free, but Kaa had all the advantage here. The tiger was helpless with his throat caught in the serpent's deadly coils. The python slithered his front portion down until his scaly face was close to Khan's massive orange head.

"Remember that I could have killed thee here. Remember that should you be foolish enough to seek vengeance."

Kaa swung his massive tubular form and hurled the gagging Shere Khan over fifty feet away. The tiger struck a thick tree in that distance and fell to the ground with a resounding thud. If he was able to get up again soon, he did nothing save retreat from the area, as he would realize his lupine allies would by then be slain.

"In case you should wonder, this is how Shere Khan made the attack on those villagers. He did it with the help of his wolf allies, and in such a skillful manner as to make it seem to be the work of two tigers instead of one tiger and several wolves. Of course, he convinced that jackal to lie for him, as they are secretly on good relations once more. Do not be angered by my failure to stop them then, as I was truly outnumbered."

Mowgli sighed before collapsing to the ground to nurse his wounds. The last of Khan's wolfen forces were killed within moments, and his allies ran to his side.

"You have taken many bites," Bagheera noted.

"Now that I can understand your animal friends' 'speech,'" Felifax added, "I must agree. Tell me where I can find some of those healing plants, and I will bring many handfuls of them to you."

"I think we will all need some of those," Baloo opined. "Save for Kaa, of course."

If the python was capable of smiling, he would have done so then.

Many hours later, Mowgli's already hardy constitution was healing nicely from the sap of the restorative plants his body was covered with. The others made use of them as required, including Matt Challenger, whose lower left leg was torn open by one of the wolves.

"Good thing I was able to sink my bayonet into that blighter's neck," the hunter complained. "When it jumped on me, I thought I was a goner for sure."

"Your help was... appreciated, Challenger," Felifax forced himself to say.

"Was it now?" Matt replied with a smile. "I wish I could get that in writing from you, mate."

He did come through as he promised. And he did take a vicious wound while defending me. He also fought our foes valiantly. I need to convince myself to take that into consideration the next time I disapprove of Djina's choice for a husband.

"Can you at least tell me how you talk to these bloody animals?" Matt queried.

"It was an honor making your acquaintance, despite the circumstances of how we met," Felifax said to Mowgli as he stroked the fur of Rudra and Durgane while they sat on each side of him. "When dawn breaks, however, I must be off. I need to locate my brother before he finds himself in danger that is too great for him to overcome on his own."

"I should be mostly healed up by sunrise," Mowgli noted. "I will get a good sleep to quicken the process, and I will accompany you to find your brother. Bagheera, Baloo, and Kaa will watch the village while I am gone."

"Many thanks, my friend, but this is a personal matter that does not involve you."

"Do keep in mind that I know this part of the jungle very well, while you do not. Also, your situation occurring here on my land has made it my concern."

Felifax smiled. "Very well. It will be an honor to have you at my side as I seek Felanthus."

The two jungle lords shook hands, and a great new alliance was formed.

"Are you going to tell me how you and the long-haired chappie talk to those animals now?" Matt inquired once again to complete the evening festivities.

*John Peel's imagination is a bottomless pool of wonders! This year, the re-
nowned Doctor Who author takes us on a on from the heart of Africa to the
peaks of Tibet. The indomitable Doc Ardan (well known to our readers) teams
up with Tarzan's Jane to investigate the disappearances of famous scientists.
John's stories always contain that "sense of wonder" so much appreciated by
the classic authors from the 40s and 50s, and once again he doesn't disappoint
with this rollercoaster ride...*

John Peel: *The Eye of the Hawk*

French Equatorial Africa, 1934

The streets of Brazzaville were difficult to navigate, even for someone as
skilled as Doctor Francis Ardan. There were the inevitable street traders, offering a vast variety of fruits, vegetables and meat, and who sprawled across the
pavements and into the streets. These stalls attracted crowds, who seemed
blithely unaware—or simply uninterested—in motorized traffic. Added to this,
there were workers and construction equipment still engaged in activities on the
newly-opened Congo-Ocean Railway and its sparkling new station. Mixed in
with this were cattle, pigs and the occasional sheep that were being driven, either to be fed or to be slaughtered. Steering his rented car—which appeared to
have been kept, unmaintained and rarely used, in a jungle clearing for the past
decade—was a lot more arduous than Doc had expected. Still, somehow he
managed to make his way to the buildings of the *Institut Pasteur* eventually. The
directions he'd been given had proven to be mostly accurate. Once there, he
parked next to an impeccably maintained silver-colored Rolls Royce Phantom,
whose chauffeur lounged nearby, smoking a *gauloise* with an aloof indifference
to his surroundings.

Doc hurried inside the building, paused for a second to get his bearings,
and then followed the instructions he'd been given to end in a smallish laboratory. There was a French police officer and a bored Sergeant taking their leave of
the room's other two inhabitants. The officer snapped off a crisp salute to Doc
as he passed—obviously just in case Doc was someone whom he *should* salute—and the policemen hurried off. Doc raised an eyebrow, and then entered
the room.

The man he knew; the woman he did not.

"Doc!" Fred exclaimed, his weathered face breaking into a relieved smile
as he hurried forward to clasp Ardan's hand. "I can't tell you how glad I am that
you're here! Thank you for coming so promptly."

"Were the police any help?" Doc asked.

"This is the French Congo," the woman said carefully. Her accent was a mixture of Boston American and British upper class, with a touch of something Doc couldn't identify thrown in. "Are the police *ever* helpful here?"

Fred shrugged. "Uh, oh, this is Lady Jane Clayton," he said, apologetically.

The name was vaguely familiar, but Doc couldn't place it.

"Lady Clayton," he acknowledged, politely.

"Doctor Ardan," she replied.

She'd clearly been briefed by Fred, then.

"Can you tell me precisely what happened?" he asked Fred.

"Doctor Omega has been kidnapped."

"I was hoping for a few more details," Doc said gently.

"There really isn't much more to it than that," Fred said.

He was a large man—as large as Doc, and almost as muscular. He looked as though he wasn't overly bright, but that was a misconception—he was actually a fine mechanical engineer and a superb chef.

"The Doctor and I came here a week or so ago" he continued. "He'd been asked to help out with some research being conducted here."

"The same research I was invited here to assist with?" Doc asked.

"I imagine," Fred replied. "Not my field, really—something to do with uranium extraction is all I know."

Doc nodded, and Fred continued:

"Well, we arrived this morning early—you know how the Doctor is when he gets his mind set on a subject, all eager and raring to go. I went to see about breakfast and ran into three men down by the kitchen. One of them had a gun and shot me." He produced a two-inch long feathered dart. "Some kind of fast-acting knockout drug. I was out like a light. It must have been about an hour later that I awoke. I immediately ran back here to check up on the Doctor, but he had vanished. I presume he was their target, and that they used the same gun on him." He shrugged. "That is all."

"Not quite," Doc murmured. "You saw no other vehicles here when you arrived?"

"None," Fred stated. "I had been given a key—we arrived before anyone else, around five a.m. That's why nobody found me while I... slept. Nobody else arrived until after I had discovered that the Doctor was gone. I'm afraid there was nobody else here to see anything. I promptly called the police, and then you."

Doc had given Fred his hotel number when he had arrived the previous evening. He had planned to confer with Doctor Omega this morning on the uranium processing; there hadn't seemed to be any great urgency in the matter, and he had been quite exhausted by his journey. Sleep had seemed to be the most important thing. But now...

"I assume that this whole business is about the uranium," Fred added.

"Never make blanket assumptions," the beautiful young woman said, rather languidly.

Doc eyed her curiously. "May I ask why you are here?"

"You may," she replied, as if giving away a favor. "I am here because I expected this to happen. I wished to confirm my theories." She gave him a dazzling smile. "Now that I have, I'll be on my way."

"If you wouldn't mind," Doc said quietly, "would you enlighten us about those theories before you leave?"

She shrugged her shapely shoulders. "Fred has been telling me about your reputation as a genius," she said, a slight hint of mockery in her voice. "Do you *really* need to be informed?"

"Perhaps not," Doc said. "But, if you would be so kind…"

She raised an eyebrow. "Why not? Doctor Omega is not the first scientist to disappear under rather mysterious circumstances. There have been two other such cases in the past week."

"Four," Doc corrected her. "Two of them have gone unreported in the press—at my request."

The eyebrow rose again. "Four? That is interesting—and significant. Thank you. When I was informed that Doctor Omega had been invited here, I was certain he would be the next victim. The previous two cases that I knew of were north of here, and both men had also been recently invited into the country. And the other two…?" she prompted.

"Also in the north," Doc confirmed. "I learned of the second of those yesterday in Casablanca—from a contact at Rick's Café." He smiled without humor. "It is said that everyone goes to Rick's. I, too, realized that Doctor Omega was likely to be the next victim. I simply didn't realize how swiftly the kidnappers would work. I hurried here yesterday, thinking I had beaten them here. Obviously, I underestimated them."

"They appear to be remarkably efficient," Lady Jane observed. "And, I must confess, a trifle puzzling."

"In what way?" Fred asked, annoyed. "They've kidnapped Doctor Omega, and we have to get him back!"

"From where?" she replied. "They don't appear to have left a single clue at any kidnapping site. Unless…?" She glanced at Doc.

He shook his head. "There was nothing I could find at the other two strikes. And you are quite correct—their purpose in these attacks is difficult to see."

"They're probably after the uranium," Fred growled. "That's why the Doctor was here, after all."

"But the other four scientists have nothing to do with uranium," Doc commented. "One is a nutritionist, one a marine biologist, one an astronomer and the last a physicist. And Doctor Omega isn't really noted as a specialist in radioactivity, is he? He's far more occupied with space flight, and was only here as a favor to a friend. No, none of the men so far have more than a single thing in common."

The eyebrow rose again. "And that would be?" she prompted.

"That they are the pre-eminent specialists in their particular fields," Doc replied.

Fred scowled. "Then why haven't they kidnapped—oh, Einstein, say? Or Schrödinger?"

"I am not certain," Doc admitted. "But they may have some specific purpose in mind concerning their chosen victims. They appear to be concentrating on practical scientists rather than theoreticians."

"You think that there will be other victims?" Lady Jane asked.

"I fear so," Ardan replied. "Having taking four prominent men, I can't see why they would not go on to a fifth—or sixth."

"I would agree," she said. "And I rather fear I know who the next victim will be—the man I came to this country to see. Abner Perry."

"Perry is here?" Doc asked, surprised.

"Who's Perry?" Fred asked.

"A great mechanical engineer," Lady Jane answered. "And a very good friend of my late father's—Professor Archimedes Q. Porter. I aim to protect him."

Fred eyed her with open incredulity. "I don't see how you can possibly do that," he commented.

"I'm sure you don't," she agreed.

She glanced around the room.

"Well, I don't think I can learn anything further here, gentlemen, so if you'll excuse me..."

Doc held up a hand. "One moment." He glanced at Fred. "My friend here may have been a trifle blunt, but he *does* have a point. Whoever is behind these kidnappings is well-organized and clearly powerful. I think you may have trouble in store."

She gave a delightful laugh at the thought. "Oh, I'm quite certain of that," she admitted. "Good day."

She started to move around him.

"It might make more sense if you simply told me where Dr. Perry is," Doc suggested. "I can offer him more protection than you. And if we can arrive *before* any assailants, we may be able to recover the previous victims."

Lady Jane slowly looked him over.

"Doctor Ardan," she finally said. "I will make a bargain with you—if you can keep up with me, you may accompany me. But this is a matter of some urgency, and Perry is a family friend. I will not wait for you."

Her attitude, frankly, astonished Doc. He wondered for a brief moment if she was crazy—the heat and the tropics could do that to some people. But he realized that she appeared to be in earnest.

"I should not wish to be encumbered by you," he said, frankly. "If you were there, I would be worried about protecting you."

She didn't quite roll her eyes. "How remarkably condescending of you," she said, cheerfully. "I was, frankly, thinking much the same about *you*."

Fred scowled again. "You obviously don't know who you're talking to," he snapped. "Doc is more than capable of handling himself."

"I may live most of my life here in Africa," she replied, "but we *do* get some news. I've heard of Doctor Francis Ardan and his exploits—which is the only reason I agreed he could accompany me." She gave Fred a frank stare. "*You* are not invited. You're big and strong, but you'd be clumsy in the jungle, and I don't have the time to look after you."

"Hey!" Fred looked furious. "I'm coming! It's my job to look after the Doctor."

"He does have a point," Doc stated. "And my plane is only a two-seater. Surely you can see that it would be best if you simply told me where Perry is, and allow us to go alone?"

This time she did roll her eyes. "You wouldn't be able to get to within a dozen miles of him in your plane," she said. "He's quite deep in the jungle. Frankly, I'm not sure either of you have the ability to reach him in time to do him any good."

"And yet *you* can?" Doc asked.

"Don't sound so amazed," she snapped. "I've spent a good deal of my life here in the wilds, and I have had the best possible teachers." Her face softened. "On the other hand, your plane *would* save us a great deal of time... Very well, let us both proceed *together*." She glanced at Fred. "You—stay here." From her tone, it was quite clear that she was used to giving orders—and for them to be obeyed.

"I'm not..."

"Two-seater," she said, firmly. "She pointed to Doc. "One." And then herself. "Two. End of discussion." She turned to Doc. "Come along, Doctor—my chauffeur will drive us to the airport."

"I have my own car."

"But he is used to the traffic here," she replied, gently. "Shall we dispense with the rivalry and choose the more sensible arrangements?"

Fred glanced from one of them to the other, his face twisted in agonized indecision. Doc reached out and clasped his shoulder.

"I promise that we shall do all we can to rescue the Doctor," he said, gently. "But Lady Jane is right—you must stay here."

"I should go instead of her," Fred muttered.

"You don't know how to reach Abner's cabin," she pointed out. "And you would not be able to make the trek as swiftly as I—" She glanced at Doc. "*We* can." With compassion in her eyes, she assured him: "You know that you can trust us to do our best, Fred. Please don't argue further." She turned back to Doc. "Shall we go?"

This was clearly a young woman who knew how to get her own way. She gave orders with self-assurance and suggestions as if they were velvet-gloved orders. A typical member of the English aristocracy—even if she had been born in America. Doc had a feeling that this was going to be a very sticky partnership. He was never very comfortable with women—his odd upbringing had been carried out in isolation, at the hands of strictly male scientists—and Lady Jane was clearly no mere woman. He hoped he would not be forced to leave her to fend for herself.

Fred offered no further protests, but he looked like a boy whose puppy had been stolen. Doc ignored this, as there was nothing more he could do to reassure the man. He followed Lady Jane out to her car.

The lazing chauffeur sprang to life, flicking aside his partially-smoked cigarette and holding the rear door for them. She swept in, and Doc followed.

"The airport," she ordered, and then sat back. "Swiftly."

Doc was impressed with how relaxed she appeared to be, especially considering the appalling speed of their journey. Somehow their driver managed not to hit any person, animal or structure, though he did slaughter several fruits. He drove on the road and the pavement with equal indifference, skidding around corners and whipping down the crowded streets as though they were empty. Doc was alternately impressed and appalled by his recklessness. But he managed to get the car to the airport in astonishing time, and with nothing more than fruit juices staining it.

He pulled up next to Doc's plane—not as surprising as it might have been, since it was the only non-military aircraft there. The chauffeur leapt from the barely-halted car and held the door open for Lady Jane.

Completely unaffected by their hectic trip, she stepped lightly from the car. "Thank you," she said, smiling cheerily. "I'll let you know when I need you again."

"Yes, m'lady," the man acknowledged.

As soon as Doc was out of the car, the driver leaped back inside and sped off.

"A remarkable chauffeur," Doc commented.

"He has a lot of… interesting skills," Lady Jane replied. She glanced at Doc's aircraft. "I don't believe I know this model."

"It's my own design," he replied, trying not to sound as if he was boasting. "Rather experimental, so not commercially available."

"Well, as long as it flies and lands with speed and safety, I shall be happy," she said. "Can I see your local maps?"

He pulled them from the cockpit. She studied them briefly as he started up the engine and made the pre-flight checks. When he was ready, she slipped into the seat beside him and spread the map out.

"You can follow the Congo down to here," she said, tapping the relevant spot. "There's a very rudimentary airstrip there, used by mail planes. I hope this experiment of yours doesn't need a long strip."

"No," he replied. "If airmail planes can land, we certainly can."

"Good. From that point on, we're in the jungle, I'm afraid."

"I shall manage."

He glanced at her pointedly. All he got in return was a dazzling smile—and no reassurance.

They were in the air moments later, and Doc took the craft up to a thousand feet. He could see the river heading roughly eastwards, and followed it.

"Why is Abner Perry out here?" he asked her.

The engine he had designed for this craft was quieter than any commercial model, so they could converse with ease.

"Was he lured here, as Doctor Omega was?"

"No." She chuckled softly. "Abner's an odd bird—a mechanical genius, but he's frowned upon by a lot of conventional scientists. He's a firm believer in the hollow Earth theory. I take it you've heard of that?"

"The idea that the interior of the globe is hollow and may contain another world almost as large as our own? It's not an accepted theory."

"No. Well, Abner has never been one for accepting things without proof. He believes that the crust of the Earth is thinnest below the jungle out here, and he's been experimenting with what he calls an iron mole."

"I am afraid he may well be disappointed in the results," Doc commented.

Lady Jane's lips twitched a bit, but all she said was: "He's used to disappointment. But I think you'd agree he is likely to be the next victim of these kidnappers."

"Considering the fact that they lured Doctor Omega so close to Perry, I would concur." He considered for a moment. "If there is no closer landing place to his location, then we cannot be far behind the kidnappers." He frowned slightly. "Then how did Perry get his iron mole into the jungle?"

"By river," she replied. "In pieces. He's been reassembling it for weeks now. It took several trips for him to get to this stage. The last message I got from him said he'd be ready to attempt his next experiment in about a week's time, so he's bound to be at his compound at this moment."

"Unless our opponents have reached him first," Doc observed.

He flew on steadily, as the miles of river and jungle passed below them. Eventually, Lady Jane gestured.

"The landing zone is down there," she said, pointing to what looked like impenetrable jungle. "You may want to do a fly-over first to get the lay of the land."

It was a sensible suggestion, and he took the plane lower. At about 300 feet, he finally made out a narrow area of cleared brush. He kept descending, cutting his air speed.

She had been correct—this wasn't much of a landing strip. It ran vaguely northwards from the river for several hundred yards, and ended abruptly in a wall of trees. It was literally a dirt strip, with no facilities of any kind.

"Do you think you can manage it?" There was the first hint of uncertainty in her voice.

For an answer, Doc banked and came in for a landing. Wheels touched earth a dozen feet from the river's edge, and he brought the craft to a halt about a hundred yards before the jungle reasserted its claim on the land.

"Nicely done," Lady Jane said, sincerely. "Not everyone is that good."

He could see that there were bits of aircraft on the edge of the jungle to back up her comment.

Doc was never good with being praised—especially by young women—and he tried to shrug off the pleasure he felt. He clambered from the plane, and turned to help his companion, but she leaped nimbly down before he could. He eyed her clothing critically.

"Perhaps you should simply point me in the right direction," he suggested. "You're not exactly dressed for jungle travel."

Lady Jane glanced down at her long, floral dress and high heels. "You're quite right," she agreed, cheerfully, and kicked off her shoes. When she started to unbutton the dress, Doc looked at her in alarm.

"What are you doing?" He had to fight to keep his voice level.

"Dressing for jungle travel," she replied.

"It looks more like you're *un*-dressing."

She gave a delighted laugh. "Don't look so shocked," she advised him. "I'm wearing my travel clothes under my dress."

She finished unbuttoning it and threw it back into the plane. She stood ready, cocking her head slightly. She now wore—well, barely anything. It looked mostly like a single-piece bathing suit made of antelope leather. It stretched from half-way down her breasts to considerably higher than half-way up her long, muscular thighs.

"That's *dressed*?" he enquired.

She held up a finger. "You're quite right," she agreed.

She reached into her overly large traveling bag and pulled out a knife on a belt, a bow and a quiver of arrows. "*Now* I'm dressed."

The knife was a good foot long, and the bow was a man's bow, and not a smaller woman's model. Judging from her very visible arm muscles, she was used to using this weapon.

And then, finally, he remembered where he had heard her name before. "Lady Jane," he mused. "Lady Jane *Greystoke*."

"The same," she agreed.

He managed to avoid blushing at how foolish his comments must have seemed to her.

"Isn't this more your husband's field—so to speak?"

She laughed again. "Yes, but he taught me everything I know. Not quite everything *he* knows, though."

"I don't suppose he's around?"

"No," she replied. "He's off investigating another of those endless lost cities he always manages to stumble across. We probably shan't see him for a couple of months." She gave another of those delightful grins. "He does so enjoy his work." Then she turned serious. "It doesn't look like there has been any other plane here for at least a month."

"I agree," he replied. "Which means that we may be ahead of the kidnappers."

"Or dear old Abner isn't their next target." She gestured at the trees. "If we're ahead of them now, let's stay that way, shall we?" She grinned again. "This time, it may be *you* who isn't dressed for jungle travel."

She ran lightly ahead, and he followed.

Despite popular belief, the jungle wasn't wall-to-wall trees, underbrush and thorns. Animals cleared pathways for their own needs, so there was frequently a simple path to follow. It was also cooler than the clearing, as the trees tended to intersect about twenty feet into the air, providing shade and cover. Because there was less light reaching the ground, the undergrowth was thinner and more scrub than thick bushes. There were plenty of animal tracks, but certainly no human footprints. It looked to Doc as if they were way ahead of their quarry. They should be in time to keep Perry safe.

Her bare feet didn't slow Lady Jane down at all. He understood why, of course—she and her husband had achieved almost legendary status in Africa. He was, of course, the more noted, but he had clearly chosen his mate extremely well. She showed no signs of tiring as they raced along the jungle paths. Doc was in extremely good shape, but even he was finding it hard to stay with her.

The voices of the jungle hushed as they traveled, but were loud and vocal ahead and behind them. From time to time, he caught glimpses of birds—sometimes with startlingly bright plumage—and at others small creatures drifting through the background. There were none of the larger cats, of course, as this profusion of trees was not conducive to their hunting style; they preferred the open savannah, as did the larger antelopes, zebras and other beasts. This was the home of the smaller, shyer creatures, the largest of which was likely to be that forest ghost, the okapi—and they had such good camouflage that they might even now be being observed by one that was practically invisible.

They moved swiftly through the forest. His companion didn't hesitate, somehow following a trail or memory that he couldn't see. They paused only once, by a small steam, from which they drank.

"About another fifteen minutes," she announced, "and we should reach the compound."

He nodded. "I've seen no signs of other people so far, Lady Jane."

She grinned again. "Call me Jane," she said. "Titles seem so pointless in the jungles, don't they?"

He smiled back. "Call me Doc."

She cocked her head slightly and studied him. "You don't like people getting close to you, do you?" She shrugged. "None of my business, of course—Doc." Then she was on her feet again. "Enough lazing about—come on."

And she set off again.

He followed, wondering if he should attempt to explain his motivations. In his line of work, it was important to act without being affected by emotion. Getting too close to others made one vulnerable.

Of course, *not* getting close to people made one lonely…

Now was not the time for an analysis of his motivations. There was a job that had to be done. And she was, after all, another man's wife.

They reached the compound in the time Jane had predicted. It was a small affair—three buildings and an outdoor cooking area—with several natives milling about. It was surrounded by a thorn *boma*, the entrance of which was open.

One of the men spotted the new arrivals and let out a cry. The rest immediately became alert, raising spears and shields and grouping together. Jane called out in some language he didn't recognize—there were far too many local tongues in Africa for him to have even a smattering knowledge of more than a few. One of the men called back, and Jane walked slowly forwards, her hands spread to show that she was unarmed. Doc followed suit.

The natives relaxed, lowering their weapons. Their leader continued to speak with Jane, whose face fell.

"We're too late," she informed Doc. "The kidnappers have already struck, and have taken Abner."

He felt a moment of anger, and then puzzlement. "How could they have reached here ahead of us? We saw no sign of them."

"I know."

Jane went back to talking with the spokesman. Doc couldn't help there, so he glanced around the compound. Two of the structures were clearly for resting, and that meant the third had to be where Perry had worked.

He crossed to it and entered the hut, which was of wooden posts covered with woven reeds. He saw that his guess had been correct, and that inside was an almost completed machine that had to be Perry's iron mole. It was about fifteen feet long and ten high. There was a large drill at the front, and an open door in the side. He was itching to examine it, but his curiosity would have to wait. There were open hatches all over the outside of the vehicle, showing it to be a work still in progress. Tools were scattered about, which could be a result of Perry being messy or because he'd been attacked whilst utilizing them.

There was one odd thing that he noticed. On the ground by the entrance was a pure white silken scarf. He picked it up to examine it, and recognized what it was almost immediately. Odd…

One of the natives had followed him, talking rapidly in his incomprehensible language. He gripped Doc's arm and then pointed to the roof excitedly. Doc glanced up, but saw nothing remarkable. The man pulled on Doc's arm, leading him outside, and then pointing at the sky.

Jane came over. "The head man says that the attackers came from the sky," she informed him. "There were about a dozen of them, and they walked down to the ground. They had guns, but only fired them at the ground. They captured Abner and then walked back into the sky. Then they were taken away by the eye of the hawk."

"Some kind of dirigible, then," Doc guessed.

"That's what it sounds like to me," Jane agreed. "But—how could a zeppelin have beaten us here? Your plane is much faster than any dirigible I've ever seen."

"Indeed," Doc agreed.

He could see now in the dirt the marks where rope ladders must have dragged, and several sets of shod footprints. The natives were all bare-foot.

"If this *was* an airship of some kind, it must have been a very sophisticated one—as well as very swift."

"Unless these were not the men who kidnapped Doctor Omega?" Jane suggested. "Perhaps there are *two* sets of assailants, working together?"

"It's possible," Doc agreed. "But the existence of this unknown aerial device suggests we are dealing with an uncommon foe."

"And we have no real leads," Jane said, soberly. "The zeppelin flew off to the east—but there's a lot of Africa to the east."

Doc managed a slight smile. "Even one or two of those lost kingdoms your husband enjoys so much?"

"You think that *that* is where they might have gone?"

"I don't believe they are heading anywhere in Africa," he informed her. He held up the silk scarf. "I discovered this in Perry's work hut."

She frowned slightly. "It doesn't look like anything Abner would wear. He's not what you'd call dressy."

"It isn't," Doc informed her. "I suspect it was left by one of his attackers. It's a ritual scarf, and comes from Tibet. They are used as gifts for visitors to lamaseries. Each lamasery makes their own, so they are all slightly different."

"So you can tell where that came from?" she asked, surprised.

His mouth twitched. "I do know a good deal of useful information," he admitted. "But I've never felt the need to study silk weaving in the past. However, I *do* know someone who can help us out here."

"Excellent. And where would that person be?"

"Tibet," he replied. "Which would appear to be my next port of call."

"*Ours*," Jane said, firmly. "Abner is my friend, after all. And if John is off having fun in a lost city, I think I deserve a trip to a Tibetan monastery."

He looked down at her. "You do realize that this is a trap, of course?"

"Obviously," she agreed. "They've kidnapped five previous victims and never left a clue before—it would be unrealistic to expect this to have been left by chance." Her pretty forehead furrowed slightly. "Logically, *you* are their next target, and they're politely inviting you to your own kidnapping."

"Quite." He hesitated slightly. "I am afraid that they may not have any use for you, though—so if you accompany me, you may be placing yourself in severe danger."

She laughed. "Like I said, I don't see why John should have all of the fun in the family."

Doc had to admire her calm resolve. He could see why the so-called Lord of the Jungle had picked her as his mate: she wasn't unrealistically hopeful, but determined and focused.

"I'm not sure that this could be called *fun*," he said.

"If it's not fun," she asked. "Then why do you do it?" She grinned again. "What's our next step?"

"Back to Brazzaville," he replied. "My plane isn't able to take us to Tibet—it would need to refuel too frequently—so we'll need an alternate form of transport, which I can arrange for us back in Brazzaville."

"Right," she agreed, cheerfully. "Race you back to the plane!"

Once they reached the airport in Brazzaville again, Doc made arrangements quickly to store his plane and for an alternative one that was able to travel longer distances. Jane called Fred to update him, and he joined them at the airport by the time their new flight was ready.

"This time, I go along," he said, firmly. "The Doctor will be relying on me."

"It's a larger craft," Doc agreed. "You're more than welcome."

He knew of Fred's abilities from the past, and the large man would be very helpful. Jane, not knowing Fred, was more dubious.

"What can you offer?" she asked.

Fred looked her over. "Aside from my strength and mechanical abilities? What sort of a cook are you?"

She grinned. "I can field-dress and cook an antelope as required," she said. "But I do prefer a nice restaurant."

"I'm a gourmet chef."

"Welcome aboard, partner," she replied.

Doc was the pilot again, and he had the craft in the air quickly. Fred was in the co-pilot's seat, and Jane behind them both. The airplane was a freighter, but the rest of it was empty—which would help keep the fuel consumption down.

Jane had to shout to be heard over the howl of the engines. "What's the plan?"

"Casablanca first, and then on to Alexandria. Our next ride should meet us there."

"Our next ride?"

"This crate will never be able to stand the rarified air in Tibet," Doc explained. "We need something a little better equipped. A friend of mine will meet us in Alexandria with my latest dirigible." He frowned slightly. "It will delay us getting to Tibet, but we can't meet it any closer, since it's coming from Europe. We'll need it to ascend into the mountains."

"I don't think the Doctor and the other victims are in any immediate danger," Fred said. "Nobody would go to all this trouble in kidnapping them merely to harm them."

Jane agreed. "Nobody would benefit by harming Abner, so they must be attempting to pick his brains. Doc, is there any connection between the victims?"

"Aside from their technical skills and intelligence?" he asked. "No, they all work in different fields. They're all excellent people, but at least two of them are unknown to the general public. Whoever has kidnapped these men has chosen carefully and wisely. But—to what end?" He shrugged. "I'm afraid I simply cannot see, at present."

They touched down at Casablanca to refuel, and then again at Tripoli. There was a telegram awaiting him there, and it made him smile slightly.

"The dirigible is well on the way, and will be awaiting us in Alexandria," he announced.

"That's good news."

Jane had retrieved her normal clothes earlier (Doc was rather relieved she'd covered up her rather attractive legs; he didn't need that kind of distraction), but she gestured at her dress.

"Will we have a chance to stop for a little shopping? I'm not exactly dressed for the snows. Come to that, neither are either of you."

"We'll have all of the equipment we'll need about the ship," Doc assured her. "I'm sure you'll be able to find something appropriate."

"Yes, but will it be fashionable?" she asked. Then she laughed at his worried expression. "I'm joking," she explained. "I'm sure it will be fine. And, like all women, I do love furs…"

Doc was wondering whether he'd made a mistake in allowing her to accompany him; she had a rather disconcerting habit of unnerving him. Then again, he suspected that if he'd refused to allow her to come along, she'd have found some way of making it alone… At least, this way he could keep an eye open for her safety.

He hadn't been exaggerating earlier when he'd worried about her chances—so far, nobody had been killed during the kidnappings, but the villains behind this plot wouldn't have much use for her. As likable and skillful as she was, she had absolutely no scientific training. They might simply see her as unnecessary—and if she knew where their base was, then she might move from *unnecessary* to *disposable*...

He did not need the extra worry of keeping her safe; it might interfere with resolving this issue. But, honestly, what other choice did he have? He would have to deal with the problem if it arose.

She surprised him again when she offered to spell him. It turned out that she was a licensed pilot, and did indeed know what she was doing. Being honest with himself, he was getting tired after the day's flights, and so he accepted her offer. He had the ability to fall asleep almost instantly.

Dawn was breaking on the horizon when he awoke. Fred was sleeping in the co-pilot's seat, but Jane was focused on her task. Somehow, even over the noise of the engine, she heard him stirring and glanced back.

"Alexandria in about an hour," she estimated. "Good thing, too—it'll be light when we arrive, and we're getting low on fuel." She moved aside to allow him to retake the controls. "What are the facilities like on this dirigible of yours?"

"Fairly primitive, I'm afraid," he informed her. "There's a small galley, and a couple of cabins for sleeping, but it was built for scientific exploration and not luxury."

She laughed. "I live in the jungle most of the time. I'm used to primitive, believe you me. But I do enjoy a nice luxurious bath when I can get one. Will we have the time for that?"

He briefly considered lying to her and telling her that they would, so that he could leave her behind. But he couldn't bring himself to commit such a deception. "I rather fear not."

She sighed. "Oh, well, something to anticipate, then. Rescue first, bathing later."

Alexandria was a large and bustling city beside the Mediterranean, but the airport was definitely an afterthought. It lay on the edge of the desert and on the outskirts of the ancient city itself. That was fine, as far as Doc was concerned—it made landing simpler, and meant there were less crowds about. Sunlight glittered in the distance on the spires of mosques and ancient churches, and he could see the bustling port as they approached the city. There were no other aircraft aloft, so landing was simple and swift.

As he taxied from the field, he was pleased to see that his dirigible was tied to a makeshift mast. Fred had woken up for the landing, and he grinned when he saw the airship.

"No waiting for the transfer, then," he observed.

"It *is* a bit small," Jane commented.

"It's experimental," Doc reminded her, slightly offended by her remark.

"Of course," she agreed. "I didn't mean to criticize. But it's a good job we're all friends."

Doc cut the engine as they neared the dirigible, and they jumped out. The only person in sight appeared to be fast asleep in the shade of the craft. Jane ambled across and dug the toe of her shoe into his side.

"Up, you lazy creature," she said, with a smile.

His eyes opened and he grinned up at her.

"Say—I like the local sights." He jumped to his feet and grinned at Doc. "All ready and provisioned," he said. "We can be off in half an hour."

"Good." Doc turned to Jane and Fred. "Allow me to introduce our pilot—James Bigglesworth."

"Everyone calls me Biggles," the pilot added, shaking hands.

"Are you the entire crew?" Jane asked, surprised. "I thought these things needed dozens of men."

"With Doc, yes. I fly, Doc fixes things. It works out pretty well. Doc designed this ship, so much of it is automated." He gave a broad grin. "It's a sweet little thing. Can't compare to a Sopwith Camel, of course, but she has her uses."

"It sounds intriguing," Jane confessed. "Pipe us aboard, will you?"

"With the greatest of pleasure, ma'am," he replied. "Local services are a bit primitive, so..." He gestured at the rope ladder that hung from the gondola. "Up you go."

Doc smiled secretively at Biggles' surprise at how swiftly Jane ascended. Biggles followed her with considerably less speed and grace. Fred followed, and Doc brought up the rear.

By the time he reached the cabin and hauled in the ladder, Biggles had fired up the ship's engines, and Jane had vanished into the interior of the gondola—no doubt checking out just how primitive the facilities were.

Fred stood to one side, trying not to get in the way as Doc joined Biggles as they prepared the ship for flight. Below them, two Arabs had materialized from somewhere and were standing by the fore and aft moorings.

Fred went to the forward hatch to prepare to receive the mooring line. Doc was about to go aft to do the same when he saw that Jane was already there and waiting. She flashed him a grin, and he realized he'd misjudged her again. It seemed to be becoming a habit.

At Biggles' signal, the men below cast off the ropes, and Fred and Jane hauled them aboard and sealed the hatches. Jane and Fred then joined them in the cabin as Biggles throttled up the engines and their flight began.

"Top speed's about a hundred and fifty," Biggles announced. "It's about 24 hours to our destination if we fly continually. But we'll need to make a couple of stops for fuel and provisions, so let's say a day and a half."

Jane's eyebrows rose. "That's pretty good time."

"Doc builds well," Biggles said.

"You'll have lots of time to teach me how to pilot this."

Biggles frowned. "It's a bit hard for a girl."

She gave him an insincere smile. "*I'm* a bit hard for a girl."

Doc took pity on him. "You may as well give in now," he advised. "It will save you a good deal of effort."

Biggles looked a little sheepish. Like Doc, he wasn't too used to women. He'd basically grown up in the fledgling Royal Air Force in France in World War I, and thus was a part of an exclusive all-boys club. When most 16 year-olds were learning how to socialize, Biggles had been soaring through the skies after German fighters. He'd become one of England's top aces, and since then gone into the air transport business—with occasional forays into intelligence work. He'd rarely had to socialize with women, and felt rather uncomfortable around them. Doc could empathize.

Jane was, of course, quite relentless. She simply brushed aside Biggles' mild protests—she may not have been born into British nobility, but she had taken easily to the role. She simply assumed that people would do as she wished, and they very often did.

"Main airbag is 150 feet long," Biggles explained, on firmer ground when talking of things mechanical. "Helium, rather than hydrogen."

"It won't produce as much lift," Jane commented.

"No, but the risk of fire is a good deal lower. With Doc's structural improvements, that offsets the loss of lift. Four engines, all to Doc's design, and with wizard efficiency. Low running temperature, so a lot fewer breakdowns."

"It sounds wonderful," Jane said, clearly in admiration. "And 150 miles an hour steady air speed?"

"A bit higher, actually," Biggles replied. "We average 150 when you factor in the wind."

"Marvelous." Then her eyes crinkled, and Doc realized she was going to say something to prick any pomposity. "But the facilities aboard are a bit primitive, I gather?"

"As I said, it's an experimental ship," Doc said, mildly annoyed. "It's not designed for comfort—or the aristocracy."

She grinned widely. "Let me know when the mark two is available. I may want to buy one—if I can install a bathtub."

"The weight factor..." he began, before he realized she was teasing him.

"Maybe a shower?" she suggested, innocently.

"I'll consider it," he said, flatly.

"What *do* we have aboard for comfort?" she asked Biggles.

"One cabin, so we'll have to take it in turns to rest. A small galley, but plenty of food and drinking water for a day's flying. And a small w.c. Very small, sorry."

"Understandable. Right—now, what do these controls do?"

They flew on, following the Egyptian coast. Fred took a turn sleeping, and then whipped up some very tasty omelets. Doc took a short rest, leaving Biggles to field Jane's endless questions.

By the time he awoke, night had fallen. He returned to the cockpit, and took over the controls from Biggles, who was next for the small bed. Jane was a lot more silent now, watching the occasional light in the darkness below them.

"We're over Sinai now," she informed him. "Coming up on the coast." After a pause, she added, "This really is a rather nice little craft. I can see it will have a lot of uses."

"Thank you." He was uncomfortable with praise, especially when it was as sincere as hers. "I have a lot of modifications still to make."

"Improving on perfection, eh?"

"I try."

They flew on. It was barely possible to tell when they had passed over the shore and onto the sea. There was no moon, but the stars were incomparable, and the Milky Way slashed across the night sky.

"It's a bit like the jungle," Jane observed. "Only with engine noise instead of animal sounds. But the view is much the same—spectacular."

"You love Africa?" he asked.

"Very much so. My life has become so much richer since I met John."

"Do you miss him when he's away?"

"Of course I do, you idiot," she said, but good-naturedly. "But he's a wild creature, and there are times he simply has to be off on his own. He makes up for it when he returns. Besides," she grinned, "I do have some interesting adventures of my own, so I can't complain."

"Don't you miss civilization?"

She regarded him with her head cocked on one side. "I can take it or leave it. When I *want* it, John and I can head to England. The rest of the time, we vastly prefer the jungle. It's not the life for everyone, but it's the life we choose. A bit like you and yours," she added. "It's what fulfills us, isn't it?"

He found her comments perhaps a little too understandable. He tended to think of women as flighty creatures or impulse and whim, but Jane was clearly nothing of the sort. He didn't know whether this was because Jane was extraordinary or because he didn't have sufficient experience with the fairer sex. The latter, he suspected.

He was a lot more comfortable, though, when Biggles reappeared and Jane went to rest.

The sun arose as they neared the Indian subcontinent. They had passed over Arabia and were approaching the northern shores of India now. From here on, they would have to rise, as they approached the mountain chains that laced across the region. First, though, they would stop to refuel in Jamnagar in Gujaret Province. It would give the engines a short while to cool off, and the four of them a chance to stretch their legs.

Land was a sliver, and then a wall on the ocean. In a short while, they were passing over forests and fields, with small villages and towns far below them. They pressed on. He kept an eye on the fuel gauge, and saw that his calculations had been virtually correct. There had been a little head wind in the night, but not enough to slow their progress substantially.

They reached the airfield at Jamnagar in mid-morning. Doc had cabled ahead from Alexandria, and everything was prepared for them. He oversaw the refueling while Jane and Fred walked to the newly-built admin building. Biggles—as fastidious as ever with his craft—checked over the engines. From his expression, all was fine, though he had several long conversations with some of the Indian workers. He finally came over to where Doc was supervising the disconnections of the fuel hoses.

"The locals tell me that they have seen a huge hawk that overflew the field at daybreak," he reported. "It can't be anything other than our quarry, old chap."

"Indeed," Doc agreed, thoughtfully. "So we are only a few hours behind them, then." He eyed the horizon speculatively. "We may be able to catch up with them before we reach Tibet..."

Within the hour, they had cast off and were heading north east again, towards Rajasthan. The longest stretch would be over Uttar Pradesh, and then they would reach Napal and the Roof Of The World...

The view below was spectacular. There were small clearings around villages and the occasional town, but a good deal of the countryside was jungle. Jane eyed the view wistfully.

"Rather different from my usual haunts," she said. "But..."

"Still appealing, eh?" Fred suggested. "There's lots of talk about man-eating tigers..."

"There's lots of talk about all manner of things," Jane answered. "Including over-sized hawks. That doesn't make it true."

"Bit of a coincidence that both your native friends and the locals here describe it the same way, though," Biggles observed from the helm.

"True," she agreed. "But that doesn't mean it *is* a giant hawk—merely that it *looks* like a giant hawk." She glanced at Doc. "It has to be some sort of dirigible, correct?"

"That's one possibility," Doc agreed. "And a strong one. But if it is a dirigible, then it would have to be more advanced than this one."

Jane laughed. "And you're too modest to suggest that nobody could build a better airship than you?"

"That's not precisely what I meant," he replied, a little annoyed. "Merely that it would take a very sophisticated engineer—and none springs to mind. At least, none living..."

He refused to elaborate on this, preferring to keep his suspicions to himself until he had some evidence.

They flew on, admiring the sights below, for several hours. They passed the only major city, Lucknow, too far to the north to see it. There were trade roads winding through the hills below them, as the land began to rise toward the Himalayas. As they neared Napal, the sun sank towards the horizon.

"We will stay the night in Kathmandu," Doc announced. "We can't chance flying into the mountains in the darkness—it is far too dangerous. We'll recommence our journey first thing in the morning."

"Mmmm…" Jane said, dreamily. "Real beds and a bath…"

Fred laughed. "I thought you liked sleeping in trees and bathing in rivers?"

"Oh, I do," she laughed back. "But I do enjoy my comforts from time to time… I know a good hotel here, and I'm sure I can get us rooms for the night."

"I for one won't complain," Biggles announced. "A good night's sleep will set us up for the final leg tomorrow, chaps."

Doc concurred. He guided the airship into the bowl-shaped valley. The sprawling city lay within the bowl, with palaces, temples and vast gardens spread below them as they came into the small area selected as a rudimentary airfield. Virtually nobody flew into the area, so it saw little traffic.

Except the locals all reported seeing a giant hawk fly over a few hours earlier… Doc had been hoping—though with no great expectations—that their quarry might have paused also before heading into Tibet. It was more than likely that they had flown this route before, though, and were more comfortable than he with a night journey.

"These kidnappers seem to be going out of their way to ensure that they are observed," Biggles remarked.

"They don't want to lose us," Jane agreed.

"No," Doc added. "They clearly know these skies, but they're been careful not to be observed in the past. Their current activities can only be designed to ensure that we know where to follow them."

"Come into my parlor…" Fred commented.

"Well, I hope they've got the tea on when we arrive," Biggles said.

They rented a car and driver to take them to the hotel Jane knew. A few words with the manager and she had obtained rooms for them. "I have first dibs on the bath," she informed her companions. "Then we'll eat."

Doc could work and rest anywhere, but he had to admit that he did enjoy a touch of luxury from time to time.

The hotel was small, but very well equipped, obviously catering to upper-class visitors. The manager fawned over "Lady Greystoke", and graciously included the men in his subservient attitude. He undoubtedly thought them her retainers, but was taking no chances on possibly offending her.

Their rooms were small but extremely comfortable, and their meal was a vast improvement over the rations aboard the airship. Even Fred was impressed with the chicken and goat dishes, and wandered off to chat with their cook, undoubtedly seeking the recipes.

Despite the appeal of their beds, all of them were up early, ate a light breakfast and then hurried back to the airfield. In a very short while, they were in the air again, and continuing on the flight towards the north-east.

They were well into the mountains now. Jagged peaks pushed upwards from the plateaus below them. Kathmandu was situated at 4,600 feet above sea level, so they were flying at about 5,000 feet now. Fred had broken out the furs, and they were all dressed in the heavy outfits. Jane's was a little on the large size, and Fred's a trifle tight, but both would be able to manage. Below were mountains, rocks and snowfield. Ahead and behind were mountains, rocks and snowfields. There were occasional small villages, isolated temples and cairns of the weathered stones. But, mainly, there was raw, rugged nature.

"We're not going to find many people around here to tell us where the great hawk flew," Biggles remarked. "Are you sure we can find our way from here?"

Doc held up the scarf. "This is our map," he said. "We simply need to talk to the man who can read it." He pointed slightly to the north. "There is a small, isolated monastery ahead; the lama we seek lives there. He will be able to give us the final directions we need. We are very close now, my friends."

They flew on for about another fifteen minutes. Doc had only been here once before, but he knew that his memory was accurate. Then ahead, spread over the side of the mountain, he saw the gray stone walls of the Det-sen Monastery.

He pointed it out to his companions, and guided the dirigible in as close as he could make it before handing over the controls to Biggles.

"Close down the engines as soon as we're moored," he ordered.

Then he threw the rolled-up rope ladder from the doorway. Gripping the end of the mooring rope, he descended rapidly. He fastened it to a gatepost, and heard the engines above whine down.

He glanced around and saw that several of the monks were watching him placidly, as if the arrival of an airship was something they witnessed on a daily basis. There were a couple of novices also, who were having trouble controlling their reactions—a mixture of surprise, awe and a little fear. The only outsiders they usually saw were the occasional (very occasional!) travelers. Despite their interest, though, the novices stayed back. They had learned discipline as the first requirement of their calling.

Doc knew a smattering of Tibetan, learned from his previous visit to the monastery during his own training period, almost twenty years earlier.

"Is Sapan to be found?" he enquired.

One of the monks bowed slightly. "Master Sapan would be pleased to see his former pupil again," the man said serenely.

"I look forward to the reunion."

He glanced back and upwards as Jane descended the rope ladder quite rapidly. Fred followed her, but Biggles remained in the airship to keep an eye on things. It was probably only their training that prevented the monks from commenting on Jane. The novices had a harder time controlling their curiosity. None of them had seen a woman since they had joined the monastery, and none of them would ever have seen anyone quite like *this* woman before. Jane was tall and lithe, even in the bulky furs, quite unlike the shorter, stockier native females.

The monk who had spoken didn't even blink. "You are our guests," he said in a gentle voice. "If you will accompany me, there will be tea while I inform Master Sapan of your arrival."

"We would be honored to share tea with you," Doc replied.

The monk gestured towards two of the novices. One bowed deeply, and then moved off at an impatiently sedate pace. The other indicated a doorway, and led them through.

It was much warmer inside the building, out of the biting winds. Doc, Jane and Fred followed their guide to a reception room. Here were cushions on the floor surrounding a low wooden table. The novice gestured for them to sit, and the novice that had left earlier now returned, bearing three yellow scarves. He solemnly hung one around each of their necks, bowed and then both youngsters withdrew.

"As I mentioned, the gifting of a scarf is an important matter to the lamas," Doc explained.

Jane examined hers. "It's exquisite workmanship."

"They take great—I almost said *pride*, but that would be incorrect; perhaps *care* would be more appropriate." Doc touched his. "It is a symbol of the honor they hold visitors in."

Then one of the monks appeared, bearing a tray, on which were bowls containing rich, yellow liquid. "Please," he said. "Be welcome." He handed each of them a steaming bowl.

"Should I ask what this is?" Jane enquired. "Or are we supposed to simply drink it?"

"You should drink it," Doc replied. "It's simply tea, with butter melted in it. Yak butter. It's quite delicious, and another of their formal greetings."

Jane sipped hers and smiled politely at the monk. "You're right, it's very tasty. And quite welcome in this cold. Could you tell our host so for me?"

"There's no need," Doc informed her. "This is Padme—he speaks quite excellent English, and so already knows of your pleasure. We are old friends." He bowed his head. "It is most pleasant to see you again."

"It is also a pleasure to me, Francis," Padme answered. "I am glad that you have returned. You are following the flight of the hawk?"

"We are," Doc agreed.

"It passed over here a few hours ago," Padme said. "When your own vessel was observed, I was certain the hawk was the cause of your journey."

Doc nodded. "You were always most perceptive." He took the scarf they had found from his pocket and showed it to the monk. "This is our guide to their destination."

Padme inclined his head slightly. "Sapan will know what it means."

"Indeed." Doc finished his drink and glanced at Jane and Fred, who followed his lead in draining their bowls. "Is it possible to see him now?"

"He looks forward with much pleasure to speaking with you again, Francis. If you would all please follow me?" He glanced at Jane. "Women are not usually allowed into the heart of the lamasery," he said. "But you will be allowed as you accompany our good friend. But, please, I ask you—do not attempt to speak to any of the monks or novices. It may prove... disruptive."

Doc was expecting an outburst at this request, but Jane surprised him by smiling slightly. "I've been accused of a lot worse," she said. "Oh, sorry, shouldn't I have spoken to *you*?"

Padme merely inclined his head, and then moved to leave the room. Doc, Jane and Fred followed after him. Despite the passage of time, every step of their way was still firm in Doc's memory. The corridors were mostly bare, save for an occasional statue or prayer wheel. Rooms led off, most of them for prayer or contemplation. They saw monks from time to time, all of whom bowed slightly but otherwise ignored the visitors. Deeper into the complex they passed.

They reached the small room that served as Sapan's meeting place. The elderly monk was seated there on the floor, awaiting them as they arrived. Doc bowed respectfully, and his companions followed his lead.

"Greetings, Master Sapan."

"You are welcome here, as always," Sapan replied, indicating that they join him on the floor. "Knowing the path you have taken in your life, I imagine that there is some urgent need for this visit?"

Doc nodded and explained briefly. "So we are following the kidnappers, who left us this clue."

He passed over the prayer scarf. Sapan glanced at it.

"Clearly an invitation to step into a trap."

"Clearly."

"And yet you follow?"

"It would seem to be the simplest way to find those we seek—and the reason that they have been taken."

Sapan smiled slightly. "Your path would appear to lead you to the Shining Way monastery," he said. "This scarf is one of theirs—and one I had not expected to see again."

"Why is that?"

"Because the monastery has been closed for almost thirty years," Sapan explained. "It is high in the mountains, and the snows have made it all but inaccessible."

"That would be logical," Fred said, eagerly. "It makes a nice hideaway if the locals can't even reach it."

"But the great hawk can," Sapan commented. "It has flown and returned to the Shining Way three times in the past month."

"Three?" Doc was slightly surprised. "Everyone we have spoken to until now have only seen the hawk the one time."

"You should know by now, my friend, that there are ways and ways of seeing." Sapan handed back the scarf. "If those at the monastery were Tibetan—or simply Buddhist—then I would remind you that this scarf would be a safe conduct. But as they are not..."

"All bets are off," Fred muttered.

Sapan smiled slightly. "Indeed."

Doc could see that Jane was itching to speak, but he glared at her and she subsided. "Can you show us the path we must take to the Shining Way?"

"Padme will guide you," Sapan replied. He smiled again. "I imagine you will wish to be on your way."

"With your blessing."

"You have it, of course." Sapan glanced at Jane. "You are unusually silent for a woman."

Jane glared back at Doc. "I was... advised."

"Ah." He shook his head slightly. "A pity—it has been a while since I have spoken with a lady. Perhaps you would call again?"

"I should like that."

Jane bowed slightly and then gave Doc a very fake smile. As they followed Padme from the audience room, she muttered:

"Don't speak, eh?"

Doc shrugged. "Buddhist monks are not supposed to speak with women. You must have impressed Sapan somehow."

"Well, it wasn't my sparkling conversation."

Outside in the courtyard, Padme pointed to a tallish mountain in the distance. "The monastery you seek is about two-thirds of the way up the eastern side," he said. "I trust you will be careful."

"So do I," Doc agreed.

They took their leave of the monks, and rejoined Biggles in the airship.

"We have our target."

Biggles nodded, and started the motors up to full throttle.

Below them, the various novices and even some of the monks had gathered to watch them depart. It was clearly a great deal for any sort of external activity in this remote place. The air was thinner than at ground level, and it took a moment for the engines to fully fire. Two of the novices cast off the lines, which Fred and Jane reeled in, and Biggles turned the helm toward their destination.

Jane joined Doc. "You know, there's a lot of snow on that slope," she observed. "We don't all have to go in through the front door..."

"We would not be able to pause to drop anyone off," Doc replied. "This close to their lair, I am sure we are being kept under observation."

"If we were low enough, I could drop down into the snow without harm."

"That could prove very dangerous."

She shrugged. "If one didn't know what one was doing," she agreed. "I, however, do know what I'm doing."

Doc considered her suggestion. He believed her claim—while she wasn't exactly modest about her skills, neither did she overestimate them. And having a second string to his bow might prove to be very handy. On the other hand... he still couldn't quite wrap his mind around the idea of a young woman on her own being of any real use—even one as talented as Jane Clayton.

"Would it do me any good to reject the idea?" he finally asked.

She laughed. "That's a point you might want to discuss with my husband sometime," she suggested. "I'll go and get ready."

He had no idea what she had in mind, but he was clearly going to have to trust that she knew what she was doing. Biggles gave him a slightly nervous grin.

"She's a hard one to say no to."

"She does seem used to getting her own way," Doc agreed. "Do you think you could bring us fairly close to the ground at some point close by the monastery?"

Biggles judged the air flow. This high in the mountains, the winds were unpredictable.

"I can manage about thirty feet," he finally decided. "Any lower and we might find ourselves pushed down ourselves. Even though the gas bags are filled with helium and not hydrogen, a crash wouldn't do us any good." He scowled. "Do you think she can make it from that height?"

"We will have to trust her judgment," Doc replied. "While she takes risks, I don't think that they are uncalculated. She's got too good a head for that."

"Right-ho."

Biggles paid his attention to their course. Doc could see that he was unhappy, and shared that feeling. But Jane did have a point, that a second approach to the monastery would be helpful. He glanced at Fred, wondering if he might suggest that either he or Biggles join in Jane's attempt. But she had the skill for this, and they did not. Neither Fred nor Biggles were clumsy, but drooping thirty feet into a snowbank was outside their skill set.

He just hoped that she really *did* know what she was doing.

When she returned, he could discern no change in her at all. Whatever "get ready" meant, it wasn't obvious. But she didn't appear to be at all nervous. When Biggles mentioned she'd have to drop thirty feet, she simply nodded.

"Somewhere over there, I'd suggest," Biggles told her, gesturing. "That outcropping will shield us from view of the monastery for a few moments."

"That's good," she agreed.

As they approached, she grinned cheerfully at the others. "See you later."

And she simply stepped out of the cabin and dropped to the ground. When Doc looked back, she was nowhere to be seen.

"She'll make it," Fred said. "She's a heck of a woman."

"Now for our part," Doc replied, trying not to think what might happen to Jane. "With any luck, we may not need her assistance."

Their target was ahead of them now, as they flew slowly up the slope toward the rambling building. It might have been deserted years before, but it had been built to endure, and it would seem to be completely intact. Doc trained binoculars on the place, and caught some glimpses of movement, but no signs that they had even been seen. He didn't believe that this was the case for a moment.

"Doc," Biggles said, urgently. "Here's our quarry."

Moving around the slope of the mountain was the giant hawk that the witnesses had attempted to describe. It was above them, and clearly aiming to force them to commit to a landing. Doc watched it with a professional eye, and had to admire it.

It was slightly shorter than the dirigible—perhaps a hundred and twenty feet in all—but clearly constructed from some sort of metal. It did have the appearance of a hawk—a slender body and large outstretched wings—and there was some sort of windows where the eyes on a real bird would be. It moved slowly through the air, though he could see neither a gas bag nor engines that held it up or powered it. Whatever they were facing was sophisticated to the extreme. Whatever science powered it, it was one with which he was completely unfamiliar.

And now there was motion clearly visible at the monastery. The large gates had been thrown open, and a force of men was moving about. Several of them held rifles, though fairly casually, and none were aimed at the approaching airship. Yet. The hawk slipped through the sky until it was directly above the dirigible, and then it dropped a dozen feet.

The message was perfectly clear, and Doc nodded at Biggles to follow the order to land.

As they dropped, several people moved out, hands raised, and Fred dropped the mooring ropes to them. The workers gripped the ropes and fastened them to the uprights beside the main gates. These had probably been built to hold yaks, but they would suffice to keep the airship moored safely.

Biggles, with a sigh, shut down the engines. Fred threw out the rope ladder, and they clambered down to join the people below.

Some of them were obviously locals, but there were mostly Europeans in the small crowd. Four men with rifles moved forward. They held their weapons at the ready, but didn't actually point them at Doc and the others.

"Where's the girl?" their leader asked.

"We dropped her off," Biggles said—with reasonable honesty. "You didn't think we'd bring a woman into this, did you?"

The man scowled, and then shrugged.

"Right, follow me. The boss wants to see you, and he doesn't like to be kept waiting."

Either he'd accepted Biggles' story, or he simply didn't care. Doc thought this an interesting attitude.

The people who had gathered to see them arrive now began to disperse again. Doc noticed that two of the armed men stayed by the mooring ropes, clearly to ensure Doc and his friends didn't make a break for it. He glanced at the people in the small crowd. None of them seemed to be hostile, and a couple were even grinning. None of the kidnapped scientists were visible, though.

"It's obviously quite an operation, Doc," Fred muttered softly.

"Indeed," Doc agreed.

What puzzled him slightly was that none of these men—not even the ones with rifles—looked like criminals of any kind. Doc had, over the course of his career, discovered that most criminals had a feral look about themselves, as if they were constantly picturing what they could steal from other people. Most of the faces in this crowd looked like ones you could find in the streets of any town in Europe or America. Most were clearly workers, some with their bearings suggesting that they were overseers. It was quite puzzling.

They entered the monastery, which looked pretty much like Det-sen—a sprawling, grey stone complex built into the side of the mountain. There were no prayer wheels or statues here, though—it was mostly bare surfaces, with a few mats on the floors. There were other people in the buildings, including a number of women. Again, a few were obviously locals, but most of them were not. The people they passed had only the vaguest interest in the newcomers, and were clearly occupied in their own affairs—whatever they might happen to be.

Again, it was more puzzling than enlightening. Their armed guides didn't seem to be particularly alert, and didn't point their weapons anywhere near Doc, Fred and Biggles. Doc could have taken them out in seconds, had he wished to. This was the oddest captivity he'd ever been in. He was looking forward to discovering the answers to all of his questions, as they were clearly being taken to somebody in charge.

"What do you make of this, Doc?" Fred asked under his breath.

"I'm not sure yet," Doc admitted. "But I imagine we're on our way to the answers."

He was rather surprised that they weren't ordered to be silent. A very strange captivity indeed.

They had climbed a couple of hundred feet in the passageways by now, and they were ushered into a room.

"You'll be met shortly," their guide informed them, and left the three of them alone.

Doc glanced around. The room had several large pillows scattered about, and a table with an urn of steaming tea and several delicate china cups. It was some twenty feet square, and the far wall was a large window looking out onto the slopes below. Doc could see their airship and the still-hovering hawk down there. There were drapes hanging from ceiling to floor in several places about the remaining three walls.

"Doc," Biggles called.

When he had Doc's attention, he opened the door into the corridor.

"No locks, no guards..." he said. "What kind of prisoners are we?"

Doc shook his head. It was puzzling—and more than a little disturbing.

Fred snorted. "We're half-way up a mountain, there are no other buildings around and they have the dirigible. We don't have exactly very far to go, do we?"

"You are quite missing the point," a fresh voice broke in from the far side of the room.

Doc turned—there had been a door hidden behind one of the wall hangings. Holding back the drapes as he entered into the room was a quite imposing figure. He was tall and muscular, and appeared to be in his early fifties. His neat, dark beard was speckled with grey, as were the edges of his temples. He looked to be very fit, and had penetrating, hooded eyes. There was something of the hawk about this man.

"You are our captor, I take it?" Doc asked.

"My dear Doctor—no. I am your liberator."

"You'll forgive me if I find that... difficult to accept?"

The man laughed. "Of course," he agreed, readily. "But—do come and sit. It's so much more civilized to discuss matters over a pot of tea, don't you find?"

He lowered himself, cross-legged, onto one of the cushions and started to pour tea for them all from the urn.

"Introductions first," he said, handing the tea around. "You are Doctor Francis Ardan—I have long admired your work, my friend. And you are James Bigglesworth, but I do hope you allow me to call you Biggles."

He handed over a cup of tea. Biggles glanced at Doc, who had settled onto one of the cushions, and then followed suit. Finally, the man smiled at the suspicious Fred.

"And you are Fred. I'm afraid I don't know your last name."

Not many people did, as Fred never informed anyone of it.

"And you would be...?" Doc prompted.

"I am Robur."

Doc raised an eyebrow. "I find that difficult to accept. Robur died in 1903. If he had somehow survived, and you were he, then you would be about eighty years-old."

"That was my father," Robur replied. "He did indeed perish in the wreckage of his *Terror*."

"I see."

221

Things were starting to make sense to Doc now. Robur had once been the most brilliant of inventors, initially creating an unprecedented airship—the *Albatross*—powered by electricity, and capable of staying aloft almost indefinitely. After this was destroyed, he had created the *Terror*, a super-vessel that travelled on land, sea and in the air at amazing speeds. Neither vessel had been duplicated, even to this day. But Robur's brilliance had been matched by bouts of insanity, and he had taken the *Terror* to its destruction in one such fit, challenging the powers of nature—and losing.

"And that hawk-ship down below?"

"My modification of his original concepts," the younger Robur explained. "My father was a brilliant inventor, but his mind was more than a trifle unstable. Possessed by his plans to remake this world, he had abandoned my mother and I in one of his fits. When he regained his senses for a while, he contacted us, and left directions for us to meet with him again. Sadly, his illness recurred, and he perished before we could be reunited. But we were able to make our way to his hidden workshops, which were filled with half-developed wonders. I am—in some ways—my father's son, and I was able to complete some of his visions. Including the *Hawk* below, yes." He smiled. "I look forward to showing you how it operates; I am certain you will find it most fascinating."

"This is an odd way to treat your prisoners," Biggles commented.

"Prisoners?" Robur shook his head. "My dear sir, you are mistaken—you are not prisoners." He gestured to the door. "That is not locked, and no one will stop you if you choose to leave. Have I or any of my men threatened you, or offered any kind of compulsion to you at all? No, you are invited guests who followed my little challenge—quite neatly, I might add."

"And what about Doctor Omega and Abner Perry?" Fred demanded. "They were certainly not offered any choice about accompanying you."

Robur looked a trifle embarrassed. "Ah, well, there you have me," he confessed. "I am being driven by the needs of time, and didn't have the luxury of explaining to them why they were required. But they will be offered the same choice that I give to you."

"And that is?" Doc asked.

"Hear my plans and then decide whether or not to join me in my crusade."

Doc didn't need to consider the offer for a moment—it was clear that Robur wished them willingly to join him in whatever his scheme was, and that the man preferred persuasion over imprisonment.

"Very well," he agreed. "We will listen. Feel free to explain."

Robur hesitated. "If you're agreeable, I should prefer to do so over dinner in a few hours. Your missing friends will be present, and I can explain to you all at the same time, and then you can confer together."

Doc nodded. "That seems reasonable," he agreed.

Robur stood up and extended his hand to shake Doc's. "Until dinner, then," he said. "Incidentally, I understand that Lady Greystoke is no longer with your party?"

"No."

He shook his head. "A pity. Our men do outnumber our women by a considerable margin, and she would have been a useful as well as attractive addition to our numbers."

Biggles smiled slightly. "She is a married lady," he said. "And appears to take her marital vows quite seriously. Perhaps she wouldn't have been quite as useful as you imagined."

"We do not subscribe to conventional morality in our refuge," Robur replied. "She might have found the attention... appealing."

He nodded and then left the room.

"She might not."

It was Jane's voice, from behind the window drapes. She jumped lithely to the floor, grinning.

"If you ask me, his father wasn't the only batty one in the family."

Doc was relieved to see that she was obviously well, but he kept his delight private. "I'm reserving judgment on that matter until I have further information."

Jane poured herself a cup of tea. "It's rather cool outside." She hugged the cup comfortingly. "Not the place, really, for a jungle girl." She grinned again. "It's good to see you chaps again."

"Likewise," Biggles said. "Did you hear all of that, then?"

"Most of it. It took me a while to climb the outside walls. I'm not used to doing everything wearing furs." She opened her coat. "Mind you, it's quite warm in this place, so I might be able to discard it for the time being. So, what are your plans, Doc?"

"Dinner," he said, firmly. "Robur junior has promised that Doctor Omega and Abner Perry will be present, so that will save us from having to seek them out. Besides, I confess a desire to hear what our non-captor has in mind."

"He sounds as nutty as a fruitcake to me, Doc," Biggles admitted. "His plans may not make a lot of sense."

"Well, we'll find out later," Doc said.

"Meanwhile," Jane added, "I'll stay hidden—just in case—and back up whatever play you may need to make." She frowned slightly. "Me—after attention! Perish the thought. As if anyone here could match John..." She glanced up. "Ah, no insult implied, chaps."

"And none taken," Doc assured her.

In fact, he was rather relieved that she was so obviously devoted to her husband. If she had taken a shine to any of the three of them, it could have been a serious problem...

As there was nothing they could do for the moment, they all rested and waited. Doc considered testing the limits to Robur's promises by exploring the monastery, but decided against it. It seemed to be more fruitful simply to wait and see if Robur would provide the revelations that he had promised.

It was some three hours later that there was a gentle rapping on the door. Jane bolted behind the drapes, and Fred opened the door. There was a young woman there, dressed in local clothing, although she was clearly an American by her accent.

"Time for chow," she announced.

Doc, Fred and Biggles followed her as she led them back through the way they had come before turning off into a corridor that led to a fairly sizeable hall. Doc guessed that it had been the monks' dining hall when this had still been a monastery. Now it served a similar function, though with a mixed group. As Robur had mentioned, the men outnumbered the women quite substantially.

It was clear that they were from many different countries. There was a preponderance of Westerners, but there were also a fair number of Asians and a lesser number of Africans. All appeared to be of equal status, though, with those seated and those waiting on the tables being similarly of mixed races. There was a strong scent of stew and the delightful scent of freshly baked bread, which proved to be the main courses.

Doc and his friends were led to a large table that was headed by Robur.

"Fred!"

Doctor Omega leaped to his feet, grinning, and clasped his friend's hand.

"And Doc Ardan! A pleasure to see you both. Indeed, a pleasure! And do introduce me to your young friend."

While Fred introduced Biggles, Doc saw that there was another elderly scientist beside Doctor Omega, and recognized him as Abner Perry.

Doc greeted the old man, who seemed somewhat bemused by what was happening. The other missing scientists were nowhere to be seen, however, which worried Doc somewhat.

Beside their host was a stocky, muscular man in his late thirties. Like Robur, he was neatly bearded, and had deep-set eyes. Other than that, there was no resemblance between the two men.

Robur gestured to him.

"Permit me to introduce Sergei Zattan—my invaluable right-hand man."

Doc nodded, and Sergei nodded back.

"Now, sit and eat—yak stew, a local specialty. Our cooks prepare it remarkably well, I assure you."

Doc followed the invitation and discovered that Robur was correct—the food was delicious. He hadn't realized how hungry he had been until he started to eat. The bread was fresh and doughy, absolutely splendid. To drink he was offered spring water or yak milk, which was thick and buttery.

"You did promise us an explanation," he finally reminded their host.

"Indeed I did," Robur agreed, laughing. "Look about you, my friend—do you find this scene convivial?"

"It appears most egalitarian," Doc answered.

Robur nodded. "Nice and no-committal. To be expected. Yes, everyone here is equal."

"But some are more equal than others?" Biggles asked.

"We are not communists," Robur replied. "Yes, some of us have positions of authority, but that is because we have specific skills in certain fields, and not because we are inherently any better than our fellow men." He waved his hand. "What you see here is a model of what we wish the world to become."

"A utopian society?" Biggles inquired. "It has been tried before, you know—and found lacking."

"I understand and accept your skepticism, my friend," Robur said, equably. "But—you are all realists. Take a look around this room—is it not something to be desired in the world at large? Here the color of a man's skin is not as important as the content of his heart, and what is in his mind is the most important thing of all."

"You both make good points," Doc said. "But I would prefer to learn why you have been kidnapping scientific minds."

"I am coming to that," their host/captor answered. "I am sure you all have looked at the societies you live in with equal attention. And I am certain that you must see that we are heading into another war—one that will be more terrible, more lethal and more destructive than the so-called Great War of 1914 to 1918."

"There are good people seeking to prevent another such devastation from occurring," Doctor Omega pointed out.

"And what sort of a chance do they stand?" Robur enquired. "Germany is rebuilding its armed forces, and it is inching towards totalitarianism. As my friend Sergei here can tell you, Russia, too, is preparing to expand its borders through warfare. Britain is occupied with increasing the size of its armed forces, and America is constructing a fleet to be loosed in the Pacific Ocean. Japan occupies Korea and Manchuria. Need I go on? It doesn't take a soothsayer to realize that the world is heading for war. Yes, I grant you that there are men of goodwill and peace—but they are out-matched by those who favor war. I tell you, a greater conflagration is on the horizon."

"Perhaps so," Doc agreed, uneasily. "But—even if we grant you the possibility of another war—what has this to do with kidnappings?"

"Because the next war will be one that will involve the entire planet. Greedy men in charge of so many countries wish for fresh territories, resources and power. They will band together to attack those they feel are weaker and susceptible to conquest. And these men at war are developing more numerous and devastating weapons. As a result, the next war will wipe out many millions, and lay waste to huge sectors of the world. I can even foresee that there is the possibility of weapons of almost infinite force being utilized. Several of the great minds I have gathered say that it may one day be possible to harness the very energies that bind atoms and molecules together in forces of such destruction as to terrify even the bravest of men."

"The power of the atom?" Doc nodded. "I have heard speculation on that concept from a man called Jimgrim..."

"You're a well-educated man, Ardan," Robur said. "No doubt you have heard that such atomic fires could ignite the very atmosphere about our planet, and burn this planet to a cinder?"

"Of course—but that is merely supposition."

"Are you willing to game the future of the human race on the belief that is may *not* happen?" Robur shook his head. "No, I say that we have to act as though this were the inevitable outcome of such a destructive force. So that the human race might not perish from this universe of ours, we *have* to take the threat seriously."

Doc paused. "If we do, then we have to admit that the human race would be burned from the face of this planet."

Robur's face was filled with ecstasy. "Precisely! *From the face of this planet*! But not necessarily from the *depths* of this planet."

"What do you mean?"

Robur flung his arms wide. "Why do you imagine I chose *this* place for my life's work?" he asked. "The ancients called this place *The Roof of the World* because almost every human being on this planet lives at lower altitudes." He gestured around again. "I propose to dig a refuge for the chosen few out of the solid rock of these ancient mountains—to burrow down and seal ourselves within. Then, when the atomic conflagration strikes, it will burn over the surface of the world, but leave us untouched in the depths."

He turned to Abner Perry.

"You see why we need you, then? With your Iron Mole, you can do the burrowing for us, open up the inside of the mountain for us."

He turned to Doctor Omega.

"And your invention of the amazing substance stellite will also prove to be invaluable. Its ability to shield us from space and time will enable us to accumulate the light and energy we will need to stay buried until such time as the Earth above us has recovered, and we—or our children—may emerge and reclaim the surface of our world once more."

Doc stared at the man. "It is an audacious plan," he admitted. "But one that may be completely unnecessary."

"It *may*," Robur admitted. "But would you gamble with the future—the very existence—of the human race on that word *may*?" He shook his head. "I am not willing to take such a chance. Neither are my friends assembled here. We will be the stock from which the human race may be rebuilt. And you are all invited to join us in this venture. You are a scientist and engineer almost without peer, and would be of great assistance to us. And your two friends are coura-geous and would be most welcome. So, I beg you all—agree to work with us in order to save the human race from its premature extinction. What do you all have to say, then?"

Abner Perry coughed into his hand. "I—ah, well—I'm afraid that I have to say no. It's not that I don't think your aims are admirable," he added hastily. "It's simply that I have urgent business elsewhere that I cannot ignore."

Robur stared at him in surprise. "More important than saving the human race? What could possibly be more important?"

Perry shook his head. "That I cannot tell you," he replied. "But—believe me—even if this super-weapon you describe does somehow annihilate the sur-face of our world—it will not destroy the human race. And that is all that I can tell you."

Robur was clearly shaken by this, but he turned, pleading, to Doctor Ome-ga. "You, at least, will join us in this endeavor, surely?"

"My dear fellow," the Doctor answered, "you really have no idea of the dangers that are posed by attempting to harness the power of stellite. One small slip, one slight miscalculation, and your band of survivors could easily be wiped out. I have abandoned using the material myself because of the frightful danger it poses. No, my friend, you must look elsewhere for your power source."

His face a mask of worry and confusion, Robur turned to Doc. "And what of you and your friends?"

"What you propose is admirable," Doc said slowly. "But it is not my way to retreat and hide from an upcoming battle. War is inevitable, you say? I fear that you may well be correct in your analysis of the world situation. But I cannot bring myself to believe that the optimal solution is to build a retreat *from* the world, but to attempt to *save* that world. I must face the situation as it is, and do my best to ameliorate it."

Biggles nodded. "My loyalty is to England," he said. "If she's in danger, then I have to stand ready to help out."

"But this cause is far greater than mere nationalism," Robur protested. "It is for all of humanity."

"It seems to me," Fred said, "that the best way to help the whole of human-ity is to help whatever small portion of it we can. Like Biggles here, my loyalty is to my native France first."

Robur looked from one to the other in despair, and then finally shook his head in bewilderment. "I had expected better of you all," he confessed. "I thought that you would be able to see the strength of my vision, and its utter ne-cessity. But if you cannot... Then you are free to leave. I shall have to attempt a different solution."

"No!" Sergei cried, springing to his feet. "Robur, these men are absolutely necessary to our plans. We cannot save humanity without them. They cannot be simply allowed to desert us." His eyes narrowed. "Besides, what is to prevent them from telling everyone of our plans? The governments of their petty, insular countries would never allow our project to go forward—they would see it as a revolution against their corrupt and warlike regimes."

"My friend, we cannot compel them to remain." Robur shook his head. "If we did that, we would be no better than those foul governments."

"Robur, this is about *survival*!" Sergei exclaimed. "We cannot back down from this."

Their host shook his head again. "No, my friend, we will not employ brutality and slavery to achieve our goals. What you suggest goes against everything that we believe in. Men must be free to make their own decisions—even when we disagree with their conclusions."

"This is not a polite debating society," Sergei snapped. "We are facing the extinction of mankind, and that I will not allow. Nothing—not even your high ideals—will matter if the human race is wiped out. After we survive, we can discuss what the fresh world will be like. But we *must* survive."

"Everyone must be free to follow the dictates of their consciences," Robur insisted. "It may be that these men may come to see the errors of their ways before the inevitable end. They may then return to aid us."

"*May*?" Sergei shook his head. "Oh, no, Robur—we cannot stake the very future of humanity on such a small, powerless word. For the sake of survival, we must impose out will."

"I will not allow it," Robur replied, angrily.

"Then you, too, must be compelled."

Sergei Zattan drew a revolver from his pocket, and pointed it at Robur. More than two dozen men sprang to their feet also, each of them holding pistols or rifles. Doc realized that e Russian had planned ahead for this moment.

"What is the meaning of this?" Robur exclaimed in shock. "Put those guns down immediately."

"We are no longer following your path," Sergei replied. "For the sake of humanity, we do what we must."

"The mark of all tyrants at any time in history," Doctor Omega stated. "When you allow your goals to outstrip your morality, you simply replace one evil with another."

"Be silent," Sergei ordered. "You are hereby conscripted into the army of the future. You are to work to ensure the survival of the human race."

"You may be able to compel us to remain using those weapons," Perry said. "But you cannot force us to work for you. What will you do—shoot us? But you *need* us."

Sergei shook his head. "We do not need *all* of you. If you do not agree to work for us, we are quite prepared to kill the superfluous amongst you."

"Sergei, come to your senses!" Robur pleaded. "This is no way to ensure the future we envisioned."

"It is the *only* way," Sergei answered coldly. "And you had better come to see that, Robur, for you have placed yourself amongst the disposable."

"You would turn against me, after all our time together?"

"You have left me no choice," Sergei answered. "To preserve our plan, this is the only way forward."

He turned back to face Doc and the others again.

"Will you join us willingly, or shall I be forced to compel you all?"

Doc considered the possibility of jumping the man, but he knew that it would be pointless. Even if he could take Sergei out, the other armed men wouldn't simply stand by.

"You are making a grave error," he stated. "Robur is correct—you cannot build a good society on bad foundations."

Sergei sighed. "Then you force me to use compulsion," he stated.

He turned his revolver towards Biggles. "You are the least valuable to us, I think…"

He raised the weapon to fire.

And gasped slightly. There was suddenly an arrow buried deep into his breast. He looked down at it in bewilderment, as his life-blood pumped from his split heart, and then he crashed down, dead.

The suddenness of this had shocked his companions for an instant. Another started to aim his pistol, and went down with a second arrow directly through his heart.

Doc glanced at Biggles and Fred, and the three of them went into action. The main body of the men and women in the room had been sitting, confused and undecided by what had been occurring, but they now understood that their lives were in danger. Most panicked, crashing to their feet and heading for the nearest exits. The men with guns were ignored, and even battered aside by the fleeing people. Doc and his companions waded into them, punching and disarming the men. Some of the gunmen, seeing the bodies of Sergei and the other man, threw down their weapons and fled with the general throng.

Out of the corner of his eye, Doc caught a glimpse of Jane, dressed in her hunting gear, her bow in hand and an arrow nocked and ready to fire should it be needed. But the gunmen were demoralized and leaderless. More went down to well-placed blows, and the final few simply threw aside their guns and raised their hands in surrender.

It was all over in a few short minutes. Doc, Fred and Biggles collected the discarded weapons and tossed them into a pile on one of the tables beside a still-steaming pot of stew. Jane slipped the arrow back into its quiver and the bow over her shoulder as she joined them.

"Thank you for your assistance," Doc said.

"I'll say!" Biggles agreed, enthusiastically. "But aren't you cold, dressed like that?"

"Just watching you lads fight warmed my heart," she replied, grinning. "Though I shall have to find my furs soon, I think."

"Jane!" Abner Perry said, happily. "It is so good to see you again."

He gave her a huge hug, and she laughed.

"Try not to crush me," she suggested.

"I think you're far too tough for an old man like me to injure."

Biggles tapped Doc's arm, and pointed to where Robur was still seated, looking confused and dejected.

"What are we going to do with him?" he asked.

"Do?" Doc shook his head. "Nothing. He is not really a villain, is he?"

"No, but he's had a rude awakening."

"Yes, quite." Doc went over to the would-be savior of the world. "What will you do now?" he asked, gently.

"Do?" Robur shook his head. "What is there *to* do?" He gestured at the fallen. "Men I thought believed in my plans attempted to overthrow and perhaps even kill me. My plans are in ruins. I am a fool and a knave."

"You, young man," Doctor Omega put in, "are an idealist—and you've run head-first into reality." He chuckled. "But that doesn't mean that your vision is entirely mistaken, you know. The vast majority of your people appear to support your ideals, you know. They will be back."

"You may need to rethink and recalculate a little," Doc added, "but I am sure that you will think of a different way ahead. And there will be those who will be just as inspired by your vision. I am truly sorry that we don't share it— but, as you said, it may be that you will be proven ultimate correct, and that we are wrong."

"You think so?" Robur looked hopeful.

"I do," Doc said. "Stay here and work for your vision. It may prove to be essential to this world. Meanwhile, my companions and I will go out into the world again to fight for what we believe in." He held out his hand. "Goodbye— friend."

"And the best of British luck," Biggles added.

Robur reached out and grasped the offered hand. "Will you be able to reach civilization again?"

"I think we can, even with a few extra passengers." He raised his voice slightly. "Come along, friends—we'd better get started back."

Jane laughed. "I'd better get my furs again," she said. "You know, I can't tell you how much I am looking forward to getting back to the jungle again."

She smiled at Robur. "No offense, but you can keep your snows and hawk's nest; I'm going after the sun."

Frank Schildiner relaunched the character of sword master and Paris Morgue Director Jean-Pierre Séverin, initially created by Paul Féval in The Vampire Countess, *in his series* Napoleon's Vampire Hunters, *to which this story is a prequel of sorts. Centered around the Louisiana Purchase, this tale sees the dour but indomitable Frenchman tackle one of the most famous vampires in literary history...*

Frank Schildiner: *Vampire Diplomacy*

Paris and New Orleans, 1803

The vampire was an idiot, this much was apparent. He appeared every evening, his too-pale face peeking out from the crowd, his movements demonstrating inhuman celerity. Every evening without fail, leading up to the final ceremonies.

The diplomats' ball was a minor social event, though one possessing a rather exclusive list. Dignitaries from France, Spain, and the United States were the guests of honor. Wealthy residents of Louisiana and the city of St. Louis attended, dressed in finery that clearly outshined the diplomats and other government employees.

No wonder Bonaparte requested my presence, Jean-Pierre Séverin thought.

He sighed, remembering his meeting with the new Master of France.

The First Consul was a self-assured man. Standing in his massive office, dressed in a simple army uniform, he radiated calm and control as he waved his attendants from the room. They left without a murmur, closing the thick doors without looking back.

"Maestro," Napoleon Bonaparte said while staring down at his seated guest. "Or would Morgue Director be more appropriate?"

Jean-Pierre Séverin, newly-promoted director of the Paris Morgue, shrugged without much interest. A tall man with broad shoulders, graying hair and a saturnine face, he resembled an aging prelate to the eyes of most who viewed him close or afar.

"It matters not, Excellency," he said. "Address me in any manner you choose."

Bonaparte frowned, having heard Séverin address him in a royal manner once before. The man was serious then, and appeared so now.

"Maestro," the First Consul said, taking a paper from his desk, "you are an expert on the creatures known as vampires."

The Morgue Director nodded slowly and replied, "As much as anyone can be of such a subject, I suppose."

"How would you react if I told you that three agents of France died by the bite of vampires while serving in the Americas?" Bonaparte asked.

"I would say that this is odd. Vampires are rarely so discerning in their attacks. To most, humans are merely food, or an inconvenience they must overcome. Occasionally, the undead attack for personal reasons. Usually this involves the encroaching upon their territory."

Napoleon Bonaparte slapped the page down upon the table and smiled without warmth.

"My thought exactly! We cannot tolerate this attack upon France's sovereignty. Our ambassadors shall travel to the territory we sold to the United States and complete the transfer. If these damned creatures dwell in those lands, they may disrupt the final ceremonies. You must go there in our name, Maestro, and prevent any disturbance. Let those monsters be a problem for Jefferson and the Americans..."

He used the royal we that day, Jean-Pierre Séverin thought, as the vampire vanished from the crowd once again.

Glancing about, he spotted the undead imbecile again, standing on his own in a patch of darkness. The shadows did not hide the vampire's fine clothing, long, curling blonde hair, handsome alabaster face, and long, sharp, glassine fingernails. He was pretty, if dissolute in appearance, with a petulant mouth and barely hidden sharp incisors.

"*C'est n'importe quoi*, vampire," the Morgue Director whispered, smiling as he advanced towards the undead creature.

The vampire's face twisted in a quick expression of demoniac fury. His oversized fangs extruded from his mouth and his eyes narrowed as he gazed in Séverin's direction. He pulled his head back and hunched his shoulders, hooding himself like a cobra preparing for a vicious strike.

Suddenly, a hand appeared on the enraged vampire's shoulder, a pale extremity with equally long, glassine talons. A second undead man had appeared, seemingly from nowhere, his dark hair blurring for a moment as his inhuman speed brought him close to his vampiric brother.

This one was also quite handsome, with dark hair, high cheekbones and the serious expression of a scholar. He had a long face that reminded Séverin of an aristocrat—the type who died first when the Reign of Terror had begun in France.

The dark-haired vampire whispered several words into the ear of his blond friend, who shook him off. They exchanged a few more words and the blond vampire straightened, his face suddenly calmer.

The two vampires approached Jean-Pierre Séverin, their movements languid and falsely human. They spoke again to each other and smiled, hiding their pointed teeth by remaining tight lipped during the discussion.

They were not handsome men, these vampires, but could easily be called beautiful. Both men were clean-limbed and their faces bore the debauched loveliness of ancient nobility. Séverin admired their inhuman perfection with the same clinical details one used when examining a work of art.

"Who are you?" the blond vampire asked, in a slightly archaic sounding form of French.

Séverin raised an eyebrow, his dour face taking on an expression of amusement.

"Excuse me? I think proper manners require you to introduce yourself before issuing demands for my identity."

The blond vampire looked murderous, but his friend stepped forward and bowed his head an inch.

"You are, of course, quite right. My... friend... is Lestat de Lioncourt and I am Louis de Pointe du Lac. You name, if you please?"

"I am Jean-Pierre Séverin, a servant of the First Consul and a republican agent sent here to assist in the transfer of sovereignty of these lands to the United States of America," he said, looking at the vampire Lestat, "Are you the one who killed the French agents?"

Lestat sneered his direction and rolled his light-colored eyes.

"Who are you to question me?"

"Ah, I thought as much," Séverin said.

He slapped the vampire across the face with his training glove.

"Consider that my challenge."

Lestat looked momentarily stunned by the slap. He stepped forward while touching his unmarked cheek. He then straightened and laughed, shaking his head and giggling like a madman.

"You challenge me? You? Do you know who I am?"

"You both are vampires. You do not fear the cross or holy symbols, yet the light of the Sun will burn you like dry wood in a fireplace. You are, like most undead, strong, fast, arrogant and fairly foolish. Based on your behavior, I would estimate your age at under one hundred years, and your family was once noble. Do I wrong you in any way, Monsieur Lestat de Lioncourt?"

Lestat's sneer fell away and an angry expression crossed his face. His pale gray eyes turned stormy as the Morgue Director's recitation continued and, by the end, he frowned deeply.

"Who are you?" he repeated.

Jean-Pierre Séverin shrugged slowly in a Gallic manner and replied:

"My name, you already know, as well as my position in this delegation. As to the rest, I am a student of your kind. Now, shall we meet tomorrow at sundown? I shall provide the dueling blades."

Both vampires appeared confused for a moment and Lestat giggled again.

"Yes, fine. Louis shall direct you a park we know. There I shall carve you into tiny pieces, mortal!"

Séverin shrugged again, his resolute face denoting no anger or interest at the vampire's boasts.

"Perhaps you shall, perhaps not. We shall find out tomorrow night, *non*?"

Jean-Pierre Séverin sat upon a stump and watched as three vampires strolled through the park and stopped at his location. The park was a small one, a tiny square of land with four trees, a pair of wooden benches, and a small stream that slowly bubbled behind the trees and ran into a large creek that the locals used for drawing water.

Séverin frowned upon spotting the third vampire, disliking what he viewed. She was tiny, the size of a small child, with golden ringlets framing a petite, delicate face. Her clothing resembled that of an idealized child, one who behaved perfectly and never acted in a manner that spoiled her sweet image. This vampire resembled a porcelain doll and his heart broke at her fate.

"A child? You converted a child?" he asked, surprised by the outrage in his voice.

"Yes, we did, what of it?" Lestat asked, his eyes heavily lidded as he glanced in Séverin's direction.

"We are a family, Monsieur," the tiny, child vampire said.

Her voice was musical, like a tiny bell, but her words held the firmness of an older woman. Her tiny, lovely eyes looked up at him and the depths within them added to Séverin's sadness.

A child vampire, he thought. *They grow up and resent all life for trapping them in the body that never ages. They become demons of the worst and most sadistic sort.*

Knowing that telling this truth would not penetrate the undead minds of these fiends, Jean-Pierre Séverin simply stood and extended both swords to Louis.

"As his second, you may examine and choose your weapon."

Louis took both rapiers, studied the blades for a moment, and frowned.

"I could not tell you if either weapon is good or not. My knowledge of swords was limited to some small training from my family."

"A swordsmith in England forged these blades personally," the Morgue Director said. "His family designed swords and other fine weapons for King Charles II of that country. You shall not find finer blades in the New World. Shall we begin?"

"Yes!" Lestat said, his voice echoing through the deserted park.

Seizing a proffered weapon, he slashed the air with theatrical skill and intensity, though lacking in any artistry or skill. To an observer, he was the very image of a young hero. His pale, lovely face and curling blonde hair that flowed freely across his shoulders would cause sighs in many women—or men.

Séverin appeared unmoved as he stripped off his jacket and hung the garment across a tree bough. He stopped several feet from the vampire and raised his blade in salute, taking up a fighting stance after his opponent responded.

"*En Garde!*" he said, and parried a lightning fast lunge from Lestat.

The vampire giggled and stabbed again, his hand moving with blurring speed. Séverin blocked the attacks with movements that stopped the wicked blade point mere inches from his chest, face, and legs.

Lestat pulled back and shook his head, smiling and flashing his vicious fangs.

"You are a fool, human. I used the least of my power and you barely survived. You have courage, for all your stupidity. You may withdraw."

"Prometheus heretofore went up to Heaven, and stole fire from thence. Have not I as much Boldness as he?" Jean-Pierre Séverin said, resuming his fighting stance.

"What are you babbling? Have you gone insane, Republican?" Lestat asked.

Séverin rolled his eyes and sighed.

"For all your false immortality, you are naught by a child, Lestat the vampire. I quoted the great Cyrano de Bergerac—soldier, playwright, novelist, and, in his time, the finest duelist in France. His sword style was the first I mastered in my youth."

"The first?" Louis asked.

Séverin's mouth twitched slightly with amusement.

"Did I not mention my profession as a maestro of the sword?"

"You did not!" Lestat said, slashing the air with vicious strokes.

Waiting for the end of the whistling cuts, the Morgue Director continued:

"Well, I do apologize for my failure. I also serve as a hunter of evil, like many swordmasters throughout the world. Now, shall we begin again? You may withdraw, but you must leave this city immediately if you do so…"

Lestat's pale, pretty countenance twisted with unconcealed rage. Once again, he pulled his head back and stared back at Séverin with the bestial fury of a enraged predator.

"No," he whispered back.

The Morgue Director resumed his stance and said, "Please begin when you are ready."

Lestat exploded forward and veered quickly left and right, his movements' mere blurs in the growing darkness. He attacked the swordmaster's left and right side almost simultaneously, though no strikes touched the older man's body.

After the third such assault, Lestat appeared a short distance away and shook his head.

"You are not human! No man can match the speed of a vampire!"

Jean-Pierre Séverin snorted and shook his head.

"Lestat de Lioncourt, you are young and silly. Vampires possess great speed and inhuman strength, greater than that of any human. Nevertheless, what does that matter? Bears and lions are greater than man... Yet we find methods of defeating them for our survival. Vampires are little more than such beasts and humans shall always triumph in the face of such enemies."

"Not today!" the vampire said and attacked.

His slashes, slices, stabs, and lunges were even faster than before. Yet the motions were that of a spoiled child swinging a sword they'd picked up for the first time. Séverin found himself hard pressed, grateful that this creature's arrogance had prevented him from gaining anything but the crudest skills with weapons.

As Lestat pulled back and thought of his next move, Séverin attacked. His rapier moved with nearly equal speed to the undead man, but with greater precision. Backing the vampire up, he stabbed the creature in the right arm and left leg.

The attacks were mere scratches, ones that would not cripple a man, nor a vampire. However, the expression of Lestat's face slowly shifted to confusion, followed by a trace of fear.

Jean-Pierre Séverin then slashed twice across the vampire's chest and stomach, missing the alabaster flesh with each attack. Lestat looked amused for a moment—an expression that changed when his red silk shirt fell from his body in tatters.

The vampire Lestat stared as his garments dropped from his body, his expression as dumbfounded as a bull in an abattoir. That was when Séverin struck.

Kicking out in a swift movement, the Frenchman swept the vampire's legs. Lestat fell backwards, his narrow torso landing on the tree stump. The Morgue Director stabbed downward with his blade, piercing the creature's undead heart. The blade sunk deep into the old wood, pinning Lestat de Lioncourt like a butterfly in a collector's glass.

Lestat cursed for a moment and then spoke in a rasping, yet amused tone.

"You win, Republican. The duel is yours, but not the day. I shall free myself and hunt you down."

Séverin stepped away and removed an object from his hanging jacket. He stopped by Lestat's side, facing the vampire Louis and the child vampire Claudia. Opening his large, scarred hand, he revealed a glass vial, one filled with a murky liquid.

"Holy water or oil? Are you planning on anointing me in the church, human?" Lestat asked and managed a weak smile.

Shaking his head, the Morgue Director carefully removed the cork stopper:

"Not oil or water, vampire, but vitriol. Acid," he said.

"Acid?" Louis asked in a tremulous voice.

Jean-Pierre Séverin nodded once and locked his gaze upon that of the prone vampire.

"This is a particularly vicious mixture. My first teacher, a lovely Neapolitan agent of the Church, demonstrated the power of this mixture on the head of a vampire named Alucard. It burned the flesh from his skull, and then destroyed the bone beneath. His final death was slow, painful, and terrible."

"No!" Claudia said and surged forward.

Louis caught her by the shoulders and pulled her in a tight embrace.

"*Non, ma chérie*, we mustn't intervene. The code does not allow it!"

Claudia shrieked and wailed, burying her angelic face in Louis's stomach. He stroked her hair and back and made soothing noises, though his eyes glittered with malice.

"Why then," Lestat asked, "are you waiting?"

Séverin bowed slightly, saluting the bravery of the helpless undead monster.

"I could—but then, I would immediately face the wrath of your two companions. Both at the same time may overcome me... A child vampire is a terrible creature. One nearly killed me in Sweden, and I only survived by chance. She shall live many years, I should imagine..."

Shaking his head and ending the reverie of the child vampire named Eli, he looked down upon Lestat.

"I offer you a compromise. I shall remove the sword and let you go. I care not why you hate the French transfer of this land to the United States, but it shall happen despite your attacks. You and your companions shall leave this city immediately and live anywhere you wish. I shall not follow you unless you behave foolishly again."

"Your word of honor? As a maestro of the sword?" Louis asked with a hopeful tone in his voice.

"Yes, so long as I have yours, Lestat de Lioncourt," the Morgue Director said.

Lestat's eyes narrowed and he asked:

"How can I be sure you shall not violate your promise?"

Jean-Pierre Séverin raised his hands—one open and empty, one holding the vial of acid.

"I extend to you two hands, Monsieur le Vampire. It is your choice which you shall take."

Lestat thought for a moment and nodded.

"Agreed. We shall leave this rat-filled excuse for a city tonight."

Séverin studied the vampire for a heartbeat and then reached for his sword. With a harsh twist, he pulled the weapon free and stepped away. He kept his sword pointed at Lestat, though he did not move forward.

Lestat stood up slowly and touched his wounded chest, staring with angry eyes towards the Morgue Director.

"I will have my revenge upon you, Republican."

Jean-Pierre Séverin shook his head.

"I doubt it, vampire. I believe you shall hide for a time and nurse your wounded pride. Then you shall debauch to your black heart's content. By the time that ends, I shall already be dead of old age or some other calamity. However, please consider a piece of advice…"

"What?" Lestat asked as he backed towards Louis and Claudia.

"Avoid politics and human affairs. Your kind do not possess the skills necessary for such delicate affairs. If you must join such activities, battle for the position of ruler of your kind. That is a simple affair of strength that lacks the subtlety in which humans excel."

The vampire Lestat did not reply but fell into Louis's arms and limped slowly away. Within a moment, they vanished from sight.

Pulling out a handkerchief, Jean-Pierre Séverin cleaned the rapiers of the vampire ichor and placed them in his case. He returned the acid bottle to his pocket and headed away.

It still amazes me how vampires will believe that silly tale of Alucard. Imagine the legendary undead prince using such a silly name as an alias! he thought and strolled away into the dark.

A new Tales of the Shadowmen *would not be complete without a story featuring that wonderful rogue, Arsène Lupin, and we can always count on David Vineyard to provide one. The following tale takes place rather late in Lupin's career, but focuses mostly on the dark occult doings of John Silence and the Duke de Richleau; it is also a sequel of sorts to "The Moon of the White Wolf" published in our Volume 13...*

David L. Vineyard: *The Stone of Solomon*

Paris, 1935

"Nonsense, there is no such thing as this Stone of Solomon," pronounced George Gurdjieff as he cracked his three minute egg in a gold rimmed china cup set on a tray across his lap in the immense bed where the great mystic had been forced by exhaustion.

"That may be," psychic detective John Silence said sitting beside the bed of the famous guru in his lavish suite at the Ritz-Carlton in Paris, "but the fact remains that Crowley..."

"Crowley!" Gurdjieff roared. "That pretender, that clown, *do what thou wilt*... That man is a charlatan, a pornographer, a joke... and all too dangerous to any fool who follows him. Let him pursue this nonexistent relic of ancient magics. Like all the others, he will find nothing but phantoms."

Silence had been prepared for the great man's response to the mention of Crowley's name. Aleister Crowley was the most notorious of modern adepts, and all the things Gurdjieff said of him, his reputation and his followers, were altogether correct. But Gurdjieff himself was one part guru, one part philosopher, and one part white mage. A giant contradiction larger than life or legend.

"As I was about to say," Silence continued, "Crowley believes in it, enough that one of his pupils is convinced it is somewhere in Paris, and plans this very night to conjure it up at a black mass. Even then, I wouldn't be concerned, but his pupil, in this case, is one Mocata, and his reputation well exceeds even that of his master when it comes to evil. Mocata is a most dangerous man—an adept with real power."

Gurdjieff paused in his morning meal and nodded.

"Mocata—now, that is another matter, John. A case of the student far exceeding the teacher. I sensed a disturbance nearby, but I never considered the presence of another adept. In fact, when I saw you this morning, I assumed it was your presence that I'd detected."

"I'm no adept, Master. I merely delve in some of the darker aspects of the human psyche. I have at best only the smallest of gifts."

"If you insist, but truthfully, the disturbance I sensed was greater than a benign adept would cause. Mocata, well, he is another matter... What makes you think he hopes to conjure the Stone of Solomon, though? You seem to have much more than a vague suspicion."

Silence sat back and took a sip of coffee from the cup the Mage had offered.

"I was in London three days ago," he explained. "There, I was approached by an odd duck by the name of Klaw—Morris Klaw. He claims to be a dream detective, and admittedly, he has had some success in his chosen profession. He consulted with me at my residence and revealed that he had dreamed that a young woman was in some real danger. He was busy on a case of his own, but revealed the young woman's name to me, and told me that she was part of Crowley's inner circle. He specifically saw her on a sacrificial altar, while Mocata was conjuring something abominable from the outer realms. The object he described –a diamond set in the open mouth of a roaring lion—could only be the Solomon Stone of legend.

"With only that to go on, I turned to a private detective of my acquaintance, one George Gregory Gordon Green, called Gees by his friends. He has had some successful run-ins with the supernatural, and was open to looking into the matter for me with some of his more colorful informants. It was he who confirmed that there was indeed such a young woman just as Klaw had described, who was tied in with Crowley's lot, and particularly with this man Mocata.

"The young lady in question is of good family, so I hesitate to use her name. Both she and Mocata took the night train to Paris. As I said, Gees was unfortunately tied up in another matter, leaving me to follow the trail all by myself. Sir John Meredith of Scotland Yard informed me that he couldn't act on so little evidence, and I was told pretty much the same thing this morning by Commissioner Maigret. Both were sympathetic, but their hands were tied. No actual crime had been committed, or even hinted at, and the law could only act if I had more than a dream to go on.

"Sad to say, there is no time for me to seek out anyone less cautious about the law and well versed in the mystic arts. Sâr Dubnotal is in Tibet somewhere, Carnacki is, of course, retired, and Madame Palmyre appears to have vanished... Then, I saw that you were in Paris..."

"And found me abed, weak and in no shape to help you," Gurdjieff said nodding. "I do see your dilemma, my friend. Fortunately, I may have just the right man for you. Only this morning, minutes after your card was presented to me, I received a request for an audience from a most remarkable man, a white mage of some untested but real power, a man with what you most need—nerves of steel, the Duc de Richleau."

"Richleau," Silence said. "Of course, I recognize his name. There was that business in the Soviet Union... but I hadn't heard that he was interested in the occult."

"He is a man who keeps his interests to himself, but I'm sure that I can persuade him to listen to you. I'm supposed to see him at one. If you could join me..."

"I'd be most grateful," Silence said. "At this point, even the unknown is a lifeline."

"Good," Gurdjieff stated. "Then, we will meet here for lunch and make a plan. No doubt, such a game with improve our appetite—and your mood, my dour friend. There is yet hope. Remember that. There is always hope where there is belief."

Silence spent an uneasy and fruitless morning after leaving Gurdjieff. When one o'clock came, he was visibly nervous to even the most casual observer. He felt as if it took hours for the elevator to climb to Gurdjieff's floor. He knocked at the suite's door and Gurdjieff's man met him there, ushering him into the salon where he found the mage, still in pajamas and robe ,seated in a large chair across from a tall, slender man, dressed in formal day wear with a wildflower in his lapel. He might have been a younger Don Quixote, handsome, elegant, and whipcord-lean as a sword.

As John Silence entered, the man rose from his seat, offering his hand, which was lean and brown and belied the gray hair at his temples. His eyes were frank and his expression welcoming, but guarded. All in all, he was a most impressive fellow.

"Doctor Silence," he said, gripping the others hand. "It is a pleasure. I've read your papers and followed some of your less standard treatises. It's always good to meet someone with such a clear head and mind in an area that, all too easily, attracts those simple of mind and prone to dangerous flirtations with the darkness."

As Silence shook the firm hand, he was reminded of someone, though he could not quite place who. Perhaps it was only because Richleau was so open that he felt as if he had known him before.

Gurdjieff intervened before Silence could reply to the compliments.

"Be seated, gentlemen. Ivan, a drink for Doctor Silence. We have a fine cognac currently..."

With no further introduction, Silence found himself seated and, in due course, presented with a snifter of a more than passable cognac as Gurdjieff led the conversation.

"I've explained what you told me this morning to Monsieur de Richleau, and he seems to feel the same urgency that you expressed. Perhaps even more so. It would appear that he has had Mocata in his sights for some time, and knows more about the Solomon Stone than I suspected."

241

"I confess," Silence said, "that my knowledge of the Stone is fairly incomplete. I know it is supposed to be a diamond set in a gold lion's mouth and rumored to have belonged to the Mage-King Solomon, but beyond that, and its obvious symbolism, I fear I am at a loss..."

"No reason to apologize, Doctor," said Richleau. "The Stone is one of the most guarded ritual objects in occult lore, not merely a trinket that is alleged to have belonged to Solomon, but one which is said to be infused with his own magical powers. Legend says it was mined in the depths of ancient Ophir, and that its powers were legendary long before Solomon came to own it. The Queen of Sheba herself is said to have sent for the Stone, and forced her own mage to surrender it. Then she had it set in the roaring mouth of a golden lion in ring form. It was her gift to her lover, Solomon, if you believe such things, and after learning of its true power, the King then traveled to Endor, where the famed Witch helped him transfer the essence of his own magic into the ring which, on his deathbed, he had returned to Ophir to be buried and lost forever.

"But, as is too often the case, the men entrusted with the ring were not to be trusted. They traveled nowhere near Ophir and instead tried to harness the power of the Stone for themselves. Of course, for anyone but the most gifted adept, such an attempt was doomed. They only succeeded in destroying themselves. The ring then fell into the hands of others, who only saw its monetary value. Over the ages, it passed through many hands, some who knew what it truly was, and many more who had no idea. Some say mad Caligula possessed it; some that the great Saladin mastered it for a time, but found it too dangerous to keep...

"What I do know is that Leonardo da Vinci seems to have come into possession of the ring shortly before he left Italy for France. It then remained in some secret drawer in some neglected piece of furniture for centuries until sometime late in the Eighteenth Century, Joseph Balsamo, the notorious Cagliostro, came into possession of it—resulting, some say, in the Revolution and its bloody aftermath, because he didn't understand how to wield it power.

"Perhaps his daughter would have had better luck, but again the ring went missing. That was until some months ago, when a pupil of Crowley's who had seen pictures of the ring in some esoteric book saw it for sale at a small pawn shop in Marseilles. He bought it, hoping to impress their Master, but made the mistake of showing it first to Mocata, who, I suspect, cut his throat, or had it cut, and now plans to reveal it to a stunned audience at this Black Mass you uncovered."

Silence listened patiently.

"But why holding a Black Mass if he already has the ring?" he asked. "What's the point of invoking demons when he already has them potentially at his beck and call?"

"I think I can answer that," Gurdjieff said. "The Ring, as it stands now, has no provenance. No one, not even Crowley, is going to believe that Mocata could have come by a talisman of such power by nothing more than a follower spying it in a pawn shop, and slitting the fellow's throat for it. But if he conjures up the ring during a Black Mass, in front of witnesses, ah, then no one will question his possession of one of the most famous talismans of all time! Mocata knows that no talisman, however great, can reach its full power if it does not have the faith of human adepts behind it. Mocata could never hope to wield its full power if his acolytes failed to believe in its absolute authenticity."

"So our only choice now is to find where they are having their Black Mass," said Silence," infiltrate the guest list, and..."

"Oh," de Richleau said, "I don't think it will be at all difficult. This afternoon, you and I, Doctor Silence, have an appointment in Montmartre with a most attractive young lady and a certain Englishman. I can assure you that they will be able to get us into the Black Mass."

"Adepts?"

"Indeed. The young lady is, in fact, to be guest of honor at this night's sacrifice—the lamb to be slaughtered."

After that, Gurdjieff's man returned to announce that lunch was now ready. They adjourned to another room, where the repast had been laid out, and one of those long, leisurely French lunches proceeded. Silence ate little despite being told by the others that he should increase his strength for the ordeal ahead.

It was nearly three in the afternoon when they left the hotel and, although traffic would not be too bad at this time of day, Richleau wanted to be certain they arrived in time for their appointment.

The Duc decided against taking his Rolls Royce, thinking it would be better for them to arrive in Montmartre in a taxi, even though he humorously suggested that a Parisian taxi might be a greater risk to life and limb than the very demons they might well face that evening.

Silence, who knew something of Richleau's background, half-expected that they would be joined by his friends, two Englishmen and an American whom he had heard were the man's companions in adventure, but no mention of them was made. So the Doctor decided they were on their own, other than the young woman they were to meet and the mysterious Englishman Richleau had mentioned.

Their destination was in one of the seedier sections of Montmartre, away from the Sacré-Coeur and the famous nightclubs that made it the brightest spot in the Parisian nightlife. Tenements—and these houses were little more than tenements—were much the same whatever the language of those living in them.

They arrived at a small hotel, with the rather elegant name *Grand Hôtel Royal*, a misnomer if there ever was one. Silence and Richleau entered the rundown establishment, replete with faded red velvet cushions, stained satin wall paper from an earlier century, gaslights rather the newer electric lights, and a lift that looked as if it would strain at carrying a frail old woman, even less two hardy men.

They agreed with a mutual nod to take the stairs after being informed by a balding turtle-like clerk that the person they sought resided on the fourth floor.

The room, they were informed, was a suite, although not the Royal suite. Silence assumed that, in a place like this, a suite meant that it was adjacent to what passed for a bathroom.

They knocked at the door discreetly and heard footsteps. The door opened.

At first, Silence was sure they were done for. A tall man had answered the door, and he was himself the very definition of devilish. Tall, dark, his hair falling in a wave over half of his face, a thin scar bisecting an eye, the fellow was saturnine to the point of danger, but when he smiled, his face changed.

Silence recognized an English gentleman in both his well cut clothes and sudden transformation.

"Richleau!" the man said in a deep distinguished voice. "And you must be Doctor Silence. Come in, gentlemen! It doesn't do to hang about in the corridors in a place like this."

As the man turned to let them in the room, Silence opinion of him took another turn when he spied the German Luger the man wore in shoulder holster under his jacket.

Once they were inside, the man looked back down the corridor then shut and locked the door.

"Dr. Silence, " Richleau said, "this is Mr. Gregory Sallust, who is something of a journalist, with a penchant for other things."

Sallust and Silence shook hands.

"Phryne with be with us in a moment gentlemen," Sallust said. "She prefers simply to be referred to as Phryne. We are, of course, using another name than her own, but she would rather not risk her family being embarrassed by this business. She'll explain her part in this shortly. As for my own, as the Duc said, I am something of a journalist. I was investigating our friend Mocata, from the inside so to speak, when Phryne came along. I recognized a cool head and, after a time, she confessed to me she had her own reasons for looking into Mocata.

"How the Duc found us out, I won't hazard to guess, but last night, he managed to meet with us, and we decided that a third party equal to Mocata in all ways would make a good ally. I must say, this magical mumbo jumbo is a bit out of my area of expertise. I'm much more comfortable with more down to earth villains than warlocks and wizards, a gun rather than a wand."

As if to punctuate the end of his sentence, Sallust paused to light a Sullivan, after offering one to Silence and Richleau. In the dim room, the glow from the match emphasized his handsome Satanic features.

"We might have use for both tonight," Richleau said. Then noting a door opening, "Ah, the fair Miss Phryne. We delight in your company, I assure you."

A slender young woman with dark hair cut short in the way of the actress Louise Brooks, wearing silk lounging pajamas, entered the room. She was beautiful, her features like something out of a magazine illustration, with her large dark eyes frank and open.

She extended a hand which Richleau kissed and Silence took, happy to discover a strong and steady grip. She then sat on a faded white chair and gestured for them to sit across from her. Sallust, remained standing, the man of action, eyeing the door as if, any moment, men might burst in, guns blazing.

Though it was quiet afternoon in a seedy but otherwise safe neighborhood, in a rundown but still respectable hotel, Silence felt the same tension himself. The air was palpable with it.

"Mr. Sallust assures me we aren't being closely watched by Mocata's men, so I think we are safe here, gentlemen," Phryne said in a soft, clearly upper crust, English-accented voice. "He is far too sure of himself for that. He cannot imagine his will might be resisted. He is a loathsome man in many things, but not the least in his absolute certainty that he is the most devastating, the most accomplished, and the strongest man in any room. How he and Crowley manage to be in the same house, much less the same room at the same time, is a wonder. Two such egos are draining on anyone else in their presence. Even if I did not believe him to be the essence of evil, I would still find his company as welcome as snake's."

"You don't strike me as a mere adventuress," Silence said. "I have to ask how you came to be involved in this business, and why you sit here being so blasé when you must know that your life is to be sacrificed tonight at Mocata's Black Mass."

"That is quite simple Doctor Silence. While I may lie upon the altar, I hardly need to worry. When Mocata raises his knife, it will be for the last time. Mr. Sallust here is going to shoot him, saving me and ending the threat Mocata poses. A just end for an evil man. A fair revenge. And in saving my life, a mostly legal execution. I would happily execute the man myself, but I fear my costume, or lack of it, makes concealing a weapon impossible."

It the modern young woman's frankness bothered the older Frenchman, he showed no sign of it.

"You do not strike me as a bloodthirsty young woman," Richleau said, hardly taken aback by her confession of planned murder. "I take it there is more to this than you are letting on?"

There was evidently more to the Duc than being a mere dabbler in the occult arts. Silence wondered again, not for the first time, what he had gotten himself into when Morris Klaw had come to his office.

"You have me there," Phryne said, raising one long silk trousered leg on the chair, with her knee raised as she stretched the other out beside it. "Nor am I usually vengeful in nature or spirit, but I saw and learned a great deal during the war driving an ambulance, and I am not the innocent woman I once was. About a year ago, a young Englishwoman of my acquaintance became involved with Crowley and his circle. Dorothy—I won't share her last name to protect her family—was an innocent, but like many of us after the war, she sought something, anything, to replace what had been lost—our youth, our innocence, our belief in the future...

"Crowley's obscenities, in the form of magic rituals, gave her structure. The illegal drugs he offered helped her escape from her own mind and conscience, and Crowley, and particularly Mocata, took a special interest in her because of her natural beauty and vivacity.

"What she experienced, what she went through I can't know. When I next heard from her, she was in a low hostel outside London, her beauty and her health both destroyed. I took her to the best doctors I could find, Reggie Fortune, Dr. Haley, but they all agreed there was no road back for her. Her will to live had been destroyed as much as her ability. They made her as comfortable as they could, but day by day, hour by hour, sometimes visibly minute by minute, her body was dying. Mocata had made her into his particular favorite, molded her, used her up, and thrown her life away.

"I buried her on a cold wet December day and swore then that I would avenge her. I have friends in certain low circles and, despite their warnings, I convinced them to introduce me to Crowley. I admit the foul man has a certain bestial charm, the way you feel attracted to a caged beast and it raw power. Mocata, well, even more so. Crowley is at least something of a clown and con man, and well aware of it. He no more believes in his obscenities than a flim flam man does in his patent medicine, but Mocata... Mocata is a monster, a true believer, and all the more powerful for it.

"I have no esoteric knowledge, gentlemen. I have read certain texts, but I am far more interested in the real world than the occult one. However, I am sure, as sure as I breathe, that this Stone of Solomon mustn't fall in Mocata's hands."

"You are risking much for this friend," Richleau said softly.

"If you mean my soul, I can well take care of it," Phryne said. "If you mean my life... Well, I have risked it before. In any case, I have Mr. Sallust, and now the two of you. I should assure you that Mocata and I have rehearsed tonight's little drama. He has assured me there will be no true Black Mass. A false dagger, a good deal of bad lighting, flickering candles, weird music, and sheep's blood are the order for this evening's gala. The altar is supposed to be a stage magician's table. As the dagger rises, I will be dropped into a recess and a dummy made to resemble me will take my place, Mocata driving his dagger into a bladder inflated with sheep's blood."

"And you trust him?" Silence asked.

"No," Sallust said. "Neither she nor I trust that devil. That's why when he raises the dagger, whether Phryne is recessed beneath the altar or not, I intend to kill the bastard."

Richleau looked at the dark young man. "And what is your role in this deadly game, Mr. Sallust? I know you are an independent journalist, but I have heard rumors you played other games during the Great War? You appear to be of that breed that has arisen since—the gentleman adventurer, but a somewhat darker, less jovial, branch of that family tree than the fellow they call the Saint. Both of you, bright as you are, brave and capable as you are, are still in over your heads in this business. You have no real idea of the forces at play, or what Mocata is actually capable of. So, I ask again, what brings you into this game, Mr. Sallust?"

Sallust smiled that devilish smile. "Fair enough. I am, as you say, a freelance journalist, and when the mood strikes sometimes, something more. Like Phryne here, I came into this through a casual friend. An old school chum. I can't say I care much for the whole Old Boy business, or that I fit particularly well in that society, but Frank was a friend, and when a mutual friend, a writer of cheap thrillers, asked me to look Frank up, I naturally did.

"Unlike Phryne I arrived far too late. Frank was already hanging from a rafter—suicide, I made certain of that, asked my friend Bill Ironsides of the Yard to look into it—but he'd left behind more than a note. He wrote an extensive journal that detailed how Mocata had recruited him in this damnable business, perverted him, indoctrinated him in foul occult practice, and ultimately left any man with half a soul and a tiny spark of decency no choice but to destroy himself.

"Like a good reporter, I began to dig in to Mocata and Crowley and the whole obscene lot. I interviewed people who had escaped from the cult, a few on the outskirts. All the time, I kept a low profile, knowing all along that the only way to deal with this sort was to beard them in their own den. I knew I would have to move in their circles, appear to be one of them. With the help of Lucius Leffing—I believe you may know him, Doctor Silence, he dabbles in the same game you do—I was able to appear as a limited but attractively gifted adept, certain to draw the attention of Mocata.

"Not long after, I was brought into the edges of the elite and I met Phryne. I recognized a kindred soul and, in due time, though not without some fencing on both our parts, we joined forces."

"And decided to murder Mocata?" Richleau asked.

"Essentially," Phryne said. "You disapprove?"

"Of murder, almost always. Of ridding the world of Mocata, less so. But there is far more happening tonight than whether a would-be wizard is killed or not. I warn you, there will be forces afoot tonight that you can only imagine. The Stone of Solomon is an object of great power. There will be presences tonight, unseen, but quite real, working against all of us, and if we act precipitously, if we think mere violence will serve us, we all risk losing far more than our lives.

"I recognize you two young people have no real idea what is at risk, but both Doctor Silence and I have seen things that would shake you to your very soul. I warn you that tonight, it will take all my skills to protect us, all my knowledge of the esoteric arts to bring us out alive and in possession of the Stone. Merely assassinating Mocata is the least of the goals we need to pursue. I promise you, Mocata is on a path that will destroy him in ways no mere human bullet could. If you will put yourself in my hands, if you will trust me, I can assure you that we have a fighting chance; if not, you might as well turn up the gas and stretch out on this chair right now and end your lives comfortably."

Richleau was still seated, but he seemed to have grown in stature like some ancient Biblical prophet come to life. Even Sallust seemed impressed.

"Then what do we need to do?" Phryne asked.

The Duc smiled. "There are certain preparations for us to make. We must purify ourselves before tonight in mind and body, and prepare for the ordeal. Tonight, you will hear and see things you have only imagined, nightmares from the darkest corners of the universe. Tonight, you dance with the Devil and cavort with demons, so you must be prepared."

"Amen," Silence said.

"Exactly, my friend," Richleau said, one hand idly fiddling with the wild flower in his lapel. "Prayer is not the least of the tools we will need tonight."

The afternoon and early evening were spent with the purification rituals Richleau had discussed. Sallust was clearly a bit bemused by them, and Phryne fascinated, but unconvinced; still, both followed through in the arcane matters. The Duc then suggested a light repast and rest until almost ten p.m., when they prepared to leave.

Richleau claimed there were matters that must be attended to, and it was decided that Phryne would go alone to meet with Mocata, while Sallust and Silence would waylay two acolytes known to be attending the meeting that night so that no more than thirteen would be present for the Black Mass—the magical number needed.

Luckily, Sallust knew two men who were planning to attend and wasn't bothered in the least by talking his way into their hotel room, and then, at gunpoint, trussing them up and gagging them while taking their hooded robes. Richleau has assured them he had his own robes and means of reaching the site of the ritual.

The Black Mass was to be held at a chateau owned by one of Crowley's French acolytes, in the family graveyard, using a stone crypt located inside a small chapel. Sallust and Silence took Richleau's Rolls since one of the men had owned a Rolls, and, as the hour approached, at 11:30 p.m., they found themselves turning down a narrow country path and parking some ways from the small private graveyard and chapel.

They had donned their robes before they left the car, so there was no question of being recognized. As they entered the small graveyard, they saw a path lit by smoking oily torches flickering weirdly among the ancient stones, so that shadows and imperceptible movements appeared animated on the white marble. The path was littered by upside down crosses and other defilements, more silly than threatening in Silence's eye.

He had seen glimpses of much higher realms, of madness and of things outside the ken of most men. This studied obscenity was aimed at the immature mind, the dilettante, with no understanding of what might lie beyond the boundaries of reality. These superstitious and weak acolytes sought demons and devils out of children's book, saw the face of evil not for what it was, but as the poet's tragic fallen angel, accompanied by his riot of blasphemy and obscenity and childlike defiance.

They had no idea what madness lay beyond the thin veil of our world, the cosmic horror, the terror of the soul, the face of something greater, something man's mind was incapable of grasping—the true face of the unknown.

They passed several large men who were dressed solemnly, but obviously not acolytes. Mocata's bodyguards were there, if something went wrong, like the police showing up at the door. Seeing them, Silence felt relief Sallust was armed and ready to use his Luger if need be. Whatever happened in the chapel, they might well have to shoot their way out, and he was a man of the mind, not a brawler, though he was fit enough.

A bit of low ground fog had formed as the night cooled, and it added to the atmosphere. If Silence didn't know better, he would have imagined Mocata had ordered up the weather to fit this night's activities.

They walked up broad stone steps before the chapel door. Two of Mocata's thugs stood on either side of the door. Once the ritual began, they would close the doors and lock everyone in at Mocata's orders. Again Silence felt gratitude that Sallust looked as if he would have no problem blasting their way out. For that matter, he suspected Richleau to be armed himself, too.

As yet, he had seen no one among the black-robed and hooded acolytes that might be the Frenchman. He wasn't really sure if the Duc was even here; that was only a matter of faith. In fact, this whole business was a matter of faith.

They passed inside the chapel doors and into madness.

Great heavy scarlet hangings of some crepe material draped the walls, and huge black satin curtains blocked the light from the leaded windows. A great number of oily torches made the room uncomfortably warm, and heavy incense hung in the air, one that Silence suspected had been mixed with opium or some other kind of mind-altering drug. Among the scents, he recognized were hashish and certain rare Arabic perfumes said to alter consciousness. As Richleau had suggested, he and Sallust positioned themselves nearest to the door and what little fresh air was available from it.

The scarlet hangings were, Silence observed, decorated with strange figures, the signs of the Zodiac, but exaggerated and bordering on the obscene, along with figures out of Bosch, or the illustrations of Von Struck, but weaved with curious glittering thread treated with some cunning chemical so that in the smoky, incense-heavy room, they seemed to move, dance, and cavort in a dark, unholy ballet.

At the end of the now-crowded room stood a raised platform and a stone crypt decorated with blood-red and white drapes upon which, like the walls, crawled strange figures whose movements and actions were best not described. Surrounding the altar were the usual inverted crosses, black-candled menorah, and, mounted behind it, the goat-headed face of the Satan of the Black Mass. Also on the elevated platform, one man, robed in white, with scarlet and gold trim and inverted crosses front and back, stood, hooded, holding the sacrificial dagger, a great curved *kris* that seemed to reflect the strange lights evilly.

Now the midnight hour approached, and the jabbering nervous noises made by the acolytes was replaced with a low ominous hum that seemed to rise up Silence's spine and chilled his sweat-dampened skin under the heavy robes.

Somewhere strange music played, Pan's pipes, low and tempting, swaying in the mind like a cobra before it strikes. Silence felt himself almost swaying to the suggestive music that, no doubt, would be part of the orgy that would follow the human sacrifice, when the acolytes would throw off their robes and clothing and would couple in a frenzy in the blood of the victim, while Mocata would watch from his narrow serpentine eyes, holding the newly-consecrated Stone of Solomon like a third eye above the crowd, bathed in the light and shadows.

Silence was grateful Richleau had kept them from eating heavily. Even with only the lightest repast resting on his stomach, he still fought down his impulse to vomit.

Now the chapel doors opened and Phryne stood, silhouetted in the light. Though she was clothed from neck to foot, the white virginal gown fit so close to her body as to show every shadow, every movement. Her head held high— Silence strove in vain to determine if her eyes reflected that she had been drugged—she advanced toward the altar with a slow swaying step, looking only straight ahead, not glancing to one side or the other.

Silence heard a soft groan escape Sallust's lips.

The pipes had become riotous, madly picking up the pace, racing to a climax, maddeningly out of step with Phryne's languorous progress to the altar.

Somewhere along the way, Mocata had entered and stood at the altar, his hand extended toward Phryne. It was impossible not to envision a groom welcoming his bride to their bower. A thin smile played on his lips.

Silence was not a violent man, but it took all his nerve not to rip Sallust's Luger from the younger man and empty it into that self-satisfied smiling leer of conquest.

At the moment Mocata's fingertips touched Phryne's, there was absolute silence. It seemed as if every soul in the room held its breath, as if nature itself held her breath. Phryne stepped lightly up on the raised platform before the altar and stood for a moment with her magnificent back to the room; then she turned to face the crowded chapel.

Some sort of spotlight had been rigged to focus on the altar. All the torches were suddenly extinguished and the only light in the room was that focused on the altar, Phryne, Mocata, and the mysterious figure in white with the sacrificial dagger.

Phryne, still immobile and staring into space, made no movement as Mocata raised his hand and undid a pen at her throat. The white sheath slid from her body and pooled at her bare feet. There was an audible gasp from the acolytes, hunger and lust, and a taste for blood in a single breath.

Mocata took Phryne's hand and led her to the altar. She seated herself on the edge and then swung her slim legs up before, still helped by Mocata, laying back, the light of the black candles playing on her body.

A sound that could only be a gong was heard. Mocata turned toward the acolytes, flung his arms up, and shouted something in Latin, too loudly to be heard clearly. Then, still in Latin, he began to invoke his satanic lord, to bless this sacrifice to his lord, and beg a boon from his Luciferian majesty—the Stone of Solomon no doubt hidden in some pocket of his robes.

Silence well knew the ritualized blasphemy of the Black Mass. The Lord's Prayer read backwards, the curses and calculated childish mumbo jumbo of the minds of dirty children. For all the modern world around them, they might as well have been in a cave worshiping ancient pagan gods. The world had turned backwards into darkness, into the fear-based madness of early man, the sick, violent crocodile brain, let loose without regard for morality or sanity.

There was a sing-song hypnotic quality to Mocata's incantation, rising and falling in mockery of a Catholic liturgy. The acolytes swung back and forth with Mocata's tone and the movement of his body.

There was no mistaking the sexual nature of the ordeal. No pretending this was not structured to resemble some bizarre imitation of coitus, and surely, with each intonation and gesture, Mocata was building to its climax, the great curved blade plunged into Phryne's breast to cut out her still-beating heart.

There was no question of stage magician's trickery. Mocata was going to slaughter her. He reached out for the dagger. The white-robed figure proffered it with both hands. Mocata took it, raised it with his left hand, let the acolytes stare as the curious light flickering and playing along the blade. Many in the audience sighed, some half cried out in anticipation.

Then, Mocata gripped the dagger in both hands, and now the room trembled.

Silence heard Sallust cocking the Luger, saw the barrel rise from under the sleeve of his robe.

No one breathed.

Mocata drove the dagger down.

And throwing back the hood of his white robes, the Duc de Richleau's lean muscled arms shot out and caught Mocata by the wrist!

As if the warlock was a mere child, he was thrown backward, halfway across the room.

In a voice that might have been that of an Old Testament's prophet, Richleau began to chant in Hebrew and Latin, mixing ancient texts and words of religious faith.

Mocata, clearly enraged, leaped to his feet, screaming like an animal. If he had had a clear shot, Sallust would have done for him in that moment. But in his rage, Mocata fell against one of the black menorahs, and it struck the drapes hanging behind the altar.

With a whoosh, the wall burst into flame.

In a moment, the room became a literal inferno.

Silence threw back his robe, and, with all the pent of emotion and rage of the last few moments, drove a fist into the soft belly of the nearest acolyte. Sallust threw back his robes, too ,and with a roar, fired two rounds above the crowd's heads.

Panic ensued; a stampede of flesh crowded the door, trampling anyone too weak to stay on their feet.

Sallust and Silence made for the altar. Richleau was covering Phryne, who seemed drugged. Sallust swept her up in his arms.

"Get her out of here. Kill if you have to," Richleau commanded. "Get back to my Rolls and leave. I still have business with Mocata. Hurry! For God's sake, hurry!"

That was that. They met little resistance exiting the graveyard. By the time they reached the Rolls, Phryne had come around, enough to want to stand on her own feet. The flames from the burning chapel enveloped the night and wrapped the dark moon in smoke and red glow.

They did not hear from the Duc de Richleau. Nothing of Mocata, and nothing about the Stone of Solomon. Even Gurdjieff knew nothing useful.

Eventually John Silence returned to his practice in London and tried to put the business of that night out of his mind by plunging himself back into his work.

Some months had passed when he received a note from Sallust asking if he would meet him and Phryne at Sallust's flat for drinks. Though he was reluctant to relive that awful night, Silence agreed. There were too many unanswered questions.

He arrived at 8 p.m. as instructed, and was met by Sallust, wearing formal wear. While Sallust was taking his coat, Phryne appeared, restored to her full youth and beauty, decked out in a Chinese-themed outfit.

After a hug, she said:

"We have a surprise. A true surprise—and a bit of a mystery we hope to unravel."

They escorted him into the salon, where he saw a tall man, also in formal wear, standing with his back to him by the fireplace. It was impossible not to recognize him—it was the Duc de Richleau!

"Well, well," Silence said, "I had been wondering what became of you..."

He stepped forward to shake the Frenchman's hand as he turned towards him... then, with his hand still offered, he stopped still.

It was Richleau—and yet, it was not Richleau, not the man he had met in Paris, not the man who had led their foray into madness.

"I don't...?" said Silence, looking at Phryne and Sallust.

"Doctor Silence, may I present the real Duc de Richleau. Sir, this is Doctor John Silence."

Richleau took Silence's hand. "I have heard great things about you and your work, Doctor. I am surprised we haven't met before."

"I'm afraid I don't..."

After a stiff drink, with all being seated, it was Sallust who began:

"A few days ago, I happened to read in the papers that the Duc was going to be in London, and I thought, why not see if he can fill me in on what went on after we separated. I happened to call Phryne and she asked to join me. The Duc graciously agreed to meet with us, and of course, as you just discovered, we realized he wasn't our Duc at all.

"We told the Duc our stories, and then we decided to call you to see if you could add anything we might have missed since you spent more time with him than we did."

"Yes, Doctor," added the Duc. "Please fill me in on how you met my double and every detail you can recall, no matter how small."

Silence, head still spinning, did as the Duc asked, gratefully sipping the straight whiskey Sallust had offered. He could not help but feel almost as dizzy as that night in the chapel.

When he had finished, the three of them sat forward on their chairs as Richleau sat back, his hands steepled over his chest in deepest thought.

"I must say my doppelganger behaved as I hope I would have, and I am impressed that he did well enough to fool even Gurdjieff, whom I actually know. Whoever this fellow is, he is damned clever. I might have been less forgiving of that monster Mocata, but a young friend of mine is involved with him, and I may yet find myself fighting that man."

"Who was our false Duc would seem to be the question," Phryne said.

"We must not let this mystery overwhelm us," Richleau said. "The human mind tends to complicate things, and I think the answer here may be far simpler and more direct than we expect. Two elements strike me as key. The first being the value and fame of the Solomon Stone. I think we make a mistake by relegating it to a mere supporting role in our story. It is, after all, a legendary talisman, and also, since the days of Leonardo da Vinci, one of the royal treasures of France."

Something began to tickle at the back of Silence's mind, a nagging memory that he couldn't quite grasp.

"Another factor strikes me as odd," Richleau continued. "Each of you mentioned a rather odd fact... I can't help but think it is vital here."

"I'm a fair sleuth myself," Phryne said, "but I can't imagine what it is."

"A flower," Richleau said.

"What?" Sallust asked.

But Silence felt the blood drain from his face.

"The wild flower in your *faux* Richleau's lapel," explained the Duc. "I sometimes wear a carnation, on Armistice Day, perhaps a red poppy, but I have never worn a wild flower in my lapel. The only question is, what kind of wild flower was our false Duc wearing."

Sallust paused.

"It's quite common.... What do they call the damn things..."

"Wolfsbane, wasn't it?" Phryne said. "I recall thinking it was an odd choice, Why would anyone wear..."

"My God," Silence said, sighing. "I know him and yet, I never recognized him... You may have read about that gypsy business on the Talbot estate not too long ago... I spent several days with him, but he seemed younger, taller, I don't know, different... It can't have been *him*?"

"Who else could it have been, Doctor?" Richleau asked. "It was certainly not me. And who else would be so interested in a royal relic of French history. They have been something of an obsession throughout his career, and who better to act as guardian to the ring of the greatest King of Israel than the self-styled protector of the treasures of the Kings of France..."

Sallust still look perplexed, but a light seemed to illuminate Phryne's face.

"Of course," she said. " It's only wolfsbane here, but in France, it's called...

Silence took pity on Sallust, and said with some resignation:

"A lupin. There, it's known as a lupin."

And then he knocked back a very stiff whiskey in a single swallow.

Credits

The Peculiar Cats of the Sea of Dreams

Starring:	Created by:
Madame Palmyre	Renée Dunan
Renée	Renée Dunan
Victoria Custer	Edgar Rice Burroughs
Mademoiselle Kephra	Jack Mann
Ishmeddin	E. Hoffman Price
The Dreamer	E. Hoffman Price
Randolph Carter	H.P. Lovecraft
Nu of the Nicene	Edgar Rice Burroughs
The Rabbi's Cat	Joann Sfar
The Men from Leng	H.P. Lovecraft
The Moon Beasts	H.P. Lovecraft
Co-Starring:	
Baal	Renée Dunan
Cthulhu	H.P. Lovecraft
Azathoth	H.P. Lovecraft
Mana Yood Suchai	Lord Dunsany
The Al Azif	H.P. Lovecraft
Nath-Horthath	H.P. Lovecraft
Also Starring:	
Zuang Zi	*Historical*
Bast	*Mythological*
Sekhmet	*Mythological*
And:	
Atlanaät	E. Hoffman Price
Celephaïs	H.P. Lovecraft
R'leyh	H.P. Lovecraft
Dylath Leen	H.P. Lovecraft
Astral and Astarral Co-ordination and Interference	William Hope Hodgson
The Black Tome of Alsophocus	H.P. Lovecraft & Martin S. Warnes
The Seven Cryptical Books of Hsan	H.P. Lovecraft
The Necronomicon	H.P. Lovecraft
The Black Galleys	H.P. Lovecraft

| Shantak birds | H.P. Lovecraft |
| The Catbus | Hayao Miyazaki |

Matthew BAUGH is the author of oodles and oodles of short stories and several novels, who aspires to keep writing until there are no more stories left to tell. He is represented by Rebecca Angus of the Golden Wheat agency and lives and writes in Torrance, CA. In his spare time he is an ordained pastor and serves the Manhattan Beach Community Church. He is also the author of *The Vampire Count of Monte-Cristo*, and a regular contributor to *Tales of the Shadowmen*.

Rage of Terror

Starring:	Created by:
Coffin Ed Johnson	Chester Himes
Grave Digger Jones	Chester Himes
Theo Kojak	Abby Mann
Ellen Patrick (The Domino Lady)	Lars Anderson
The Black Bat	Norman A. Daniels
Fantômas	Pierre Souvestre
	& Marcel Allain
Lt. Anderson	Chester Himes

Nathan CABANISS is a writer based in Atlanta, GA, where he lives a life consisting primarily of danger, intrigue and Netflix. His stories have appeared in various publications, in both English and French. 2016 saw the release of his first collection of short fiction, *Mares in the Night*, and in 2018 his short novel *The Mummy's Hand At the Center of the Universe* was released by Pro Se Press. He is a regular contributor to *Tales of the Shadowmen*.

Dwelling in the Dark

Starring:	Created by:
Peyton Westlake (Darkman)	Sam Raimi
Frank White	Nicholas St. John
Joey Dalesio	Nicholas St. John
The Black Coats	Paul Féval
Gordon Gekko	Oliver Stone
Colonel Bozzo-Corona	Paul Féval
The Marchef	Paul Féval
Co-Starring:	
Robert Durant	Sam Raimi
Marsellus Wallace	Quentin Tarentino

Keyzser Söze	Christopher McQuarrie
Carl Kolchak	Jeff Rice
Julie Hastings	Sam Raimi
Leo Saint-Clair (The Nyctalope)	Jean de La Hire

Matthew DENNION lives in South Jersey with his beautiful wife and daughters. He currently works as a teacher of students with autism at a Special Services School. Matthew writes giant monster stories for *G-Fan* magazine and he has recently published three giant monster novels, *Chimera: Scourge of the Gods*, *Operation R.O.C.: A Kaiju Thriller* and *Atomic Rex*. He is a regular contributor to *Tales of the Shadowmen*.

The Vampire President

Starring:	**Created by:**
Boris Liatoukine	Marie Nizet
Natasha Rostova (aka Polly	Leo Tolstoy / Paul Féval /
Bird, aka Irma Vep)	Louis Feuillade
Countess Irina Petrovski	based on Arnaud d'Usseau
	& Julian Zimet
Baron Vordenberg	based on Sheridan Le Fanu
Lady Ruthven	based on John William Polidori
Kirill Bezukhov	based on Leo Tolstoy
Vasily Juragin	based on Leo Tolstoy
Boris Dubretsky	based on Leo Tolstoy
Father Joseph	Brian Gallagher
Karl	Brian Gallagher
Co-Starring:	
Von Bork	Arthur Conan Doyle

Brian GALLAGHER has a BA in Politics and Society and lives in London. He works in the media and for many years has written on the politics, economics and many other aspects of Croatia and has been quoted in Croatian and international media. In relation to that he has written extensively on Croatian-related cases at the International Criminal Tribunal for the Former Yugoslavia. He has always been interested in science fiction, classic horror, comics and is proud to be a lifelong *Doctor Who* fan. He is a regular contributor to *Tales of the Shadowmen*.

Rouletabille and the House of Despair (2)

Starring:	Created by:
Joseph Rouletabille	Gaston Leroux
Harry Dickson	*Anonymous*
Dr. Rupert Grierson	Martin Gately
Klaus Eschmann	Martin Gately
Stanley Hopkins	Arthur Conan Doyle
Mrs. Bardell	William Murray Graydon
Oliver Treadwell	Martin Gately
The Munros	Martin Gately
The Hainings	Martin Gately
Co-Starring:	
Judith Fraser (Vinegar Judy)	Martin Gately
Solar Pons	August Derleth
Sherlock Holmes	Arthur Conan Doyle
Sexton Blake	Harry Blyth
Seaton Begg	Michael Moorcock
Victor Drago	Chris Lowder & Roy Preston
Also Starring:	
Alfred Hitchcock	*Historical*

Martin GATELY is the author of the official prequel to Philip José Farmer's first novel, *The Green Odyssey (Samdroo and the Grassman* in *The Worlds of Philip José Farmer 4—Voyages to Strange Days)*. His writing career commenced in 1988 when he wrote for D C Thomson's legendary *Starblazer* comic book. He is also a contributor to the UK's journal of strange phenomena *Fortean Times*. For Black Coat Press, he has provided stories for the following anthologies: *Night of the Nyctalope, Harry Dickson Vs. The Spider* and *The Vampire Almanac Vol. 1.* His latest work is an adaptation of Edgar Rice Burroughs' *Pirate Blood* into comic strip form—drawn by Anthony Summey and available on the official Edgar Rice Burroughs website. He is a regular contributor to *Tales of the Shadowmen.*

The Other Vampires of Paris

Starring:	Created by:
The Shadowman (aka The Faceless Man aka Fantômas)	Georges Franju & Jacques Champreux / Pierre Souvestre & Marcel Allain / André Hunebelle,

	Jean Halain
	& Pierre Foucaud
Tom Lawrence (Second Falcon)	Michael Arlen
	/ Stuart Palmer
	& Craig Rice
Boris Williams aka The Grandmaster	Claude Barma
	& Jacques Armand
	/ Jean Rollin
Stéphanie Hiquet	Claude Barma
	& Jacques Armand
Ellen Patrick (The Domino Lady)	Lars Anderson
Solange	Jean Rollin
Gay Lawrence (First Falcon)	Michael Arlen
Companions of Baal	Jacques Champreux
Co-Starring:	
Laurence Borel (Belphegor)	Claude Barma
	& Jacques Armand
The Vampires	Louis Feuillade
	/ Jean Rollin
Venenos	Louis Feuillade
Irma Vep	Louis Feuillade
And:	
The Jetty at Orly Airport	Chris Marker

Joseph GIBSON is a wealthy playboy and amateur criminologist based out of Austin, Texas. His interests regularly take him to every corner of the globe but it is the secret chamber in an undisclosed location (rumored to be at the top of the University of Texas clocktower) that he calls home. In his spare time he enjoys target shooting, chemical experiments, and honing his mind and body through the practice of a martial art so ancient its true name is no longer known to any living human being. This is his first contribution to *Tales of the Shadowmen*.

A Pirate's Life

Starring:	Created by:
Doctor Eric Palmer	Paul Féval, *fils*
Captain Nemo	Jules Verne
Captain Robur	Jules Verne
James Gunn	Robert-Louis Stevenson
Archibald Haddock	Hergé
Dread Pirate Roberts	William Goldman
Kapitan Mors	*Anonymous*
Singh Brotherhood	Lee Falk

Ishmael	Herman Melville
Captain James Hook	James Barrie
Manfred Von Warteck	based on Jean de La Hire
Co-Starring:	
The Turners	Ted Elliott & Terry Rossio
Sala	Lee Falk
The Black Coats	Paul Féval

Travis HILTZ started making up stories at a young age. Years later, he began writing them down. In high school, he discovered that some writers actually got paid and decided to give it a try. He has since gathered a modest collection of rejection letters and a shelf full of books with his name on them. Travis lives in the wilds of New Hampshire with his very loving and tolerant wife and a staggering amount of comic books and *Doctor Who* novels. He is a regular contributor to *Tales of the Shadowmen*.

Mobilis in Vacuo

Starring:	**Created by:**
Captain Nemo and other characters from *Twenty Thousand Leagues Under The Sea* and *From the Earth to the Moon*	Jules Verne

Jean-Pierre LAIGLE, born in 1947 in Toulon, is a writer, translator, essayist, editor, publisher and science fiction scholar. He founded the critically acclaimed sci-fi magazine *Antares*, and won the second prize in the *Visions du Futur* 2000 contest for a story published in *Présences d'Esprit*. This is his first contribution to *Tales of the Shadowmen*.

The Legacy of Atlantis

Starring:	**Created by:**
Count Saint-Germain (aka Professor Germanus)	Pier Carpi & Luciano Bernasconi
Maleficus (aka Doctor Rochemaure)	Pier Carpi & Luciano Bernasconi based on Maurice Magre
Mislik	Francis Carsac
Co-Starring:	
Professor Aristide Clérambard	Henri Vernes
Otto Lidenbrock	Jules Verne

Also Starring:
François Bordes (aka Francis   *Historical*
Carsac)

Jean-Marc LOFFICIER, the editor of *Tales of the Shadowmen*, has collaborated with his wife **Randy** on five screenplays, a dozen books and numerous translations, including *Arsène Lupin, Doc Ardan, Doctor Omega, The Phantom of the Opera* and *Rouletabille*. Their latest novels include *Edgar Allan Poe on Mars, The Katrina Protocol* and *Return of the Nyctalope*. They have written a number of animation teleplays, including episodes of *Duck Tales* and *The Real Ghostbusters*, and in comics, such popular heroes as *Superman* and *Doctor Strange*. Randy is a member of the Writers Guild of America, West and Mystery Writers of America.

Useful Idiots

Starring:	**Created by:**
Leo Saint-Clair (The Nyctalope)	Jean de La Hire
Sexton Blake	Harry Blyth
Gouroull (The Frankenstein Monster)	Jean-Claude Carrière based on Mary Shelley
Rachael	Hampton Fancher & David Peoples based on Philip K. Dick
Pierre Lecoq	based on Paul Féval
Co-Starring :	
BlackSpear Holdings	Jean-Marc Lofficier based on Paul Féval
The Marchef	Paul Féval
Victor Frankenstein	Mary Shelley
Schasch Régime	based on Vladimir Volkoff
And:	
The Replicants	Philip K. Dick
Hidalgo	Lester Dent

Nigel MALCOLM lives in Kent, England. He works as a Teacher of English as a Foreign Language. He is a long-term *Doctor Who, Star Trek* and *Prisoner* fan - long before all the new-fangled versions came along. As well as being a regular contributor to *Tales of the Shadowmen,* he is working on various novels and audio plays

The Replacement

Starring:	Created by:
Bruce Wayne	Bob Kane & Bill Finger
Alfred Pennyworth	Bob Kane & Bill Finger
Andrew "Monk" Mayfair	Lester Dent
Theodore Marley "Ham" Brooks	Lester Dent
William Harper Littlejohn	Lester Dent
Doctor Clark Savage, Jr.	Lester Dent
Kent Allard (aka Lamont Cranston)	Walter Gibson
Britt Reid	George W. Trendle & Frank Striker
Kato	George W. Trendle & Frank Striker

Co-Starring :	
Howard Stark	Archie Goodwin & Don Heck
Nathaniel Richards	John Byrne
Reed Richards	Stan Lee & Jack Kirby
Lois Lane	Jerry Siegel & Joe Shuster
Margo Lane	Walter Gibson
Shiwan Khan	Walter Gibson
Harvey Dent	Bob Kane & Bill Finger
Sherlock Holmes	Arthur Conan Doyle
Patricia Savage	Lester Dent
Sâr Dubnotal	Norbert Sevestre

Xavier MAUMÉJEAN won the renowned Gerardmer Award in 2000 for his psychological thriller *The Memoirs of the Elephant Man*. His other works include *Gotham*, another thriller, *The League of Heroes*, which won the 2003 Imaginaire Award of the City of Brussels and was translated by Black Coat Press in 2005, and the recent *La Vénus Anatomique*, which won the 2005 Rosny Award. Xavier has a diploma in philosophy and the science of religions and works as a teacher in the North of France, where he resides, with his wife and his daughter, Zelda.

Clash of the Jungle Lords

Starring:	Created by:
Felanthus	Christofer Nigro based on Paul Féval, *fils*
Felifax	Paul Féval, *fils*

Baber	Paul Féval, *fils*
Cocantin (Licorice Kid)	Arthur Bernède & Louis Feuillade
Grace Palmer	Paul Féval, *fils*
Djina	Paul Féval, *fils*
Matthew Challenger	based on Arthur Conan Doyle
Rudra	Paul Féval, *fils*
Durgane	Paul Féval, *fils*
Shere Khan	Rudyard Kipling
Mowgli	Rudyard Kipling
Tabaqui	Rudyard Kipling
Bagheera	Rudyard Kipling
Baloo	Rudyard Kipling
Kaa	Rudyard Kipling
Co-Starring:	
Judex	Arthur Bernède & Louis Feuillade
Tarzan	Edgar Rice Burroughs
George Challenger	Arthur Conan Doyle
And:	
Waigunga	Rudyard Kipling
Seeonee	Rudyard Kipling
Wold Newton meteor	Philip José Farmer

Christofer NIGRO is a writer of both fiction and non-fiction with a strong interest in pulps, comic books and fantastic cinema, and a regular contributor to *Tales of the Shadowmen*. He may be known to some by his websites *The Godzilla Saga* and *The Warrenverse*, as he is an authority on the subject of *dai kaiju eiga* (the sub-genre of cinema specializing in giant monsters), and the characters featured in the comic magazines published by Warren. He has recently revived and expanded Chuck Loridans' classic site MONSTAAH, and has since been published in the anthologies *Aliens Among Us* and *Carnage: After the Fall*. He is a regular contributor to *Tales of the Shadowmen*.

The Eye of the Hawk

Starring:	**Created by:**
Doctor Francis Ardan	Guy d'Armen
Fred	Arnould Galopin
Jane Clayton	Edgar Rice Burroughs
James Bigglesworth (Biggles)	W.E. Johns
Sapan	Mervyn Haisman
	& Henry Lincoln
Padme	Mervyn Haisman
	& Henry Lincoln

Robur	based on Jules Verne
Doctor Omega	Arnould Galopin
Abner Perry	Edgar Rice Burroughs
Sergei Zattan	based on Jean de La Hire
Co-Starring:	
Archimedes Q. Porter	Edgar Rice Burroughs
Lord Greystoke (Tarzan)	Edgar Rice Burroughs
Jimgrim	Talbot Mundy
And:	
Rick's Café	Murray Burnett
	& Joan Alison
Det-Sen Monastery	Mervyn Haisman
	& Henry Lincoln

John PEEL was born in Nottingham, England, and started writing stories at age 10. John moved to the U.S. in 1981 to marry his pen-pal. He, his wife ("Mrs. Peel") and their 13 dogs now live on Long Island, New York. John has written just over 100 books to date, mostly for young adults. He is the only author to have written novels based on both *Doctor Who* and *Star Trek*. His most popular work is *Diadem*, a fantasy series; he has written ten volumes to date. He is a regular contributor to *Tales of the Shadowmen*.

Vampire Diplomacy

Starring:	**Created by:**
Jean-Pierre Séverin	Paul Féval
Lestat de Lioncourt	Anne Rice
Louis de Pointe du Lac	Anne Rice
Claudia	Anne Rice
Co-Starring:	
Alucard	Robert & Curt Siodmak
Eli	John Ajvide Lindqvist
Also Starring:	
Napoléon Bonaparte	*Historical*

Frank SCHILDINER has been a pulp fan since a friend gave him a gift of Philip Jose Farmer's *Tarzan Alive*. Since that time he has written *The Quest of Frankenstein, The Triumph of Frankenstein, The Spells of Frankenstein, Napoleon's Vampire Hunters* and *The Devil Plague of Naples* for Black Coat Press. Frank has been published in many other anthologies. FranHek works as a martial arts instructor at Amorosi's Mixed Martial Arts. He resides in New Jersey with his wife Gail who is his top supporter. He is a regular contributor to *Tales of the Shadowmen*.

The Stone of Solomon

Starring:	Created by:
John Silence	Algernon Blackwood
Duc de Richleau	Dennis Wheatley
Gregory Sallust	Dennis Wheatley
Phryne Fisher	Kerry Greenwood
Mocata	Dennis Wheatley
Arsène Lupin	Maurice Leblanc
Co-Starring:	
Morris Klaw	Sax Rohmer
George Gregory Gordon Green	Charles Vivian
(Gees)	(as Jack Mann)
Sir John Meredith	Francis Gerard
Jules Maigret	Georges Simenon
Sâr Dubnotal	Norbert Sevestre
Thomas Carnacki	William Hope Hodgson
Madame Palmyre	Renée Dunan
Reggie Fortune	H.C. Bailey
Dr. Eustace Haley	Anthony Wynne
Simon Templar (The Saint)	Leslie Charteris
Bill Ironsides	Victor Gunn
Lucius Leffing	Joseph Payne Brennan
Joséphine Balsamo	Maurice Leblanc
Also Starring:	
George Gurdjieff	*Historical*
Aleister Crowley	*Historical*
King Solomon	*Historical*
Queen of Sheba	*Historical*
Witch of Endor	*Historical*
Leonardo da Vinci	*Historical*
Cagliostro	*Historical*

David L. VINEYARD is a fifth generation Texan (named for his gunfighter/Texas Ranger great grand-father) currently living in Oklahoma City, OK, where the tornadoes come sweeping down the plains. He has useless degrees in history, politics, and economics, and is the author of several tales about Buenos Aires private eye Johnny Sleep, two novels, several short stories, some journalism, and various non-fiction. He is currently working on several ideas while battling with a three month old kitten for household dominance and the keyboard of his PC. He is a regular contributor to *Tales of the Shadowmen*.

Index of Authors

Aiken, Jason Scott: Ardan at the Pole (#12), Galazi in the Enchanted City (#13).
Alhadeff, Daniel: The Vertigo (#15).
Altairac, Joseph & Rivera, Jean-Luc: The Butterfly Files (#3).

Barreiro, Roberto Lionel: Secrets (#7).
Baugh, Matthew: Mask of the Monster (#1), Ex Calce Liberatus (#2), The Heart of the Moon (#3), Captain Future and the Lunar Peril (#4), The Way of the Crane (#5), The Scorpion and the Fox (with Harris, Micah) (#6), What Rough Beast (#7), Don Camillo and the Secret Weapon (#8), Tournament of the Treasure (#9), Quest of the Vourdalaki (#10), Gilgamesh Revisited (#11), The Lament of the Duke and the King (#12), A Dollar's Worth of Fists (#13), The Lights on Haint Mountain (#14), High Noon of the Living Dead (#15). The Peculiar Cats of the Sea of Dreams (#16).
Bezecny, Atom: The Revelation of the Yeti (#12), Harry's Homecoming (#13), The Curse of Orlac (#14), A Bug's Life (#15).
Bosch, Thierry: A Waltz in Norbury (#15).
Boving, Nicholas: The Elfberg Red (#8), Wings of Fear (#9), The Green Eye (#10), The Evil Among Us (#12), The Aquila Curse (#13).
Brannan, Thom: What Doesn't Die (#7).

Cabaniss, Nathan: The Great Ape Caper (#10), The Darkness in the Woods (#11), The House of El Hombre Loco (#12), From Paris with Hate (#13), Hero of Two Worlds (#14), Rage of Terror (#16).
Cardno, Anthony R.: So Much Loss (#10).
Carey, Christopher Paul: Iron and Bronze (with Eckert, Win Scott) (#5), Caesar's Children (#6).
Castelli, Alfredo: Long Live Fantômas! (#3).
Colin, Christophe: Of Beasts and Men (#12).
Cunningham, Bill: Cadavres Exquis (#1), Trauma (#2), Next! (#3), Fool Me Once... (#4).

Darnaudet, François: Au Vent Mauvais... (#3).
Darvel, Robert: The Man With the Double Heart (#9).
Dennion, Matthew: Faces of Fear (#7), The Most Dreadful Monster (#8), The Treasure of Everlasting Life (#9), He Who Laughs Last (#10), Don't Judge a Book by its Title (#11), Turning Point (#12), A Purpose in Life (#13), A Case of

Mistaken Identity (#14), The Crater of the Dead (#15), Dwelling in the Dark (#16).
Dicks, Terrance: When Lemmy Met Jules (#1).
Di Filippo, Paul: Return to the 20th Century (#3).

Eckert, Win Scott: The Vanishing Devil (#1), The Eye of Oran (#2), Les Lèvres Rouges (#3), The Atomos Affair (#4), Iron and Bronze (with Carey, Christopher Paul) (#5), Is He in Hell? (#6), Nadine's Invitation (#7), Marguerite's Tears (#8), Violet's Lament (#9).
Etrivert, Viviane: The Three Jewish Horsemen (#1).

Friend, David: Doctor Omega and the Future Museum (#15).

Gabbani, Peter: A Bond between Gentlemen (#12).
Gallagher, Brian: City of the Nosferatu (#10), The Trial of Van Helsing (#11), The Stake and the Sickle (#12), The Berlin Vampire (#13), The Death of Von Bork (#14), The Skull of Boris Liatoukine (#15), The Vampire President (#16).
Gallagher, John: The Books of Shadows (#8), Last of the Kaiju (#10), Princes of the Universe (#14).
Gately, Martin: Leviathan Creek (#8), Wolf at the Door of Time (#9), Rouletabille vs. The Cat (#10), Rouletabille and the New World Order (#11), Rouletabille on Mysterious Island (#12), Rouletabille Rides the Horror Express (#13), Rouletabille at the Old Bailey (#14), Rouletabille in the House of Despair (#15, #16).
Gibson, Joseph: The Other Vampires of Paris (#16).
Gick, G.L.: The Werewolf of Rutherford Grange (#1, #2), Beware the Beasts (#3), Tros Must Be Crazy! (#5).
Gorlier, Emmanuel: Out of Time (#6), Fiat Lux! (#7), The Brotherhood of Mercy (#10), Once More, the Nyctalope (#11).

Harris, Micah: The Ape Gigans (#3), The Anti-Pope of Avignon (#4), May the Ground Not Consume Thee... (#5), The Scorpion and the Fox (with Baugh, Matthew) (#6), Slouching Towards Camulodunum (#7, #8). The Frequency of Fear (#10), Meeting with the Mir Beg (with Wallace, Loston) (#11), The Goat of Saint Elster (#13), Beneath the Mount of Divination (#14).
Hiltz, Travis: A Dance of Night and Death (#3), Three Men, A Martian and a Baby (#4), The Treasure of the Ubasti (#6), The Robots of Metropolis (#7), In the Caves of the Serpent (#8), What Lurks in Romney Marsh? (#9), The Next Omega (#10), All Roads Lead to Mars (#11), The Case of the Curious Cadaver (#12), The Island of Exodus (#13), The Case of the Remains to be seen (#14), The Robots of Valencia (#15), A Pirate's Life (#16).

Hugli, Paul: Death to the Heretic! (#7), Sleep No More! (#8), As Time Goes By (#9), Piercing the Veil of Isis (#10), Dream's End (#11), As Easy as 1, 2, 3... (#13), The Night of the Dazzling Sun (#14), Night of the Craven Raven (#15).

Ilseman Matthew: Guided Tours of Famous Secret Places (#14).

Joby, Gulzar: Science outraged, Science murdered! (#15).
Jounieaux, Vincent: The Necropolis of Silence (#15).

Kane, Tom: The Knave of Diamonds (#5).
Kindzierski, Lovern: Perils Over Paris (#5).

Lai, Rick: The Last Vendetta (#1), Dr. Cerral's Patient (#2), The Lady in the Black Gloves (#3), Corridors of Deceit (#4), All Predators Great and Small (#5), Incident in the Boer War (#6), Will There Be Sunlight? (#7), Vampire Renaissance (#8), Gods of the Underworld (#9), The Mark of a Woman (#10), Shadows Reborn (#11), The Tomb of the Veiled Prophet (#12), Eve of Destruction (#13), Phantom Masquerade (#14).
Laigle, Jean-Pierre: Mobilis in Vacuo (#16).
Lamere, Joseph: Satan's Signature (#8).
Lanuque, Jean-Guillaume: Lucretius' Maze (#15).
Leary, Roman: The Evils Against Which We Strive (#4), The Heart of a Man (#5), The Children of Heracles (#6)
Le Bussy, Alain: The Sainte-Geneviève Caper(#1), A Matter without Gravity (#5).
Legrand, Olivier: Lost in Averoigne (#8), The Last Tale (#10).
Lehman, Serge: The Mystery of the Yellow Renault (#2), The Melons of Trafalmadore (#2).
Lofficier, Jean-Marc: Journey to the Center of Chaos (#1), Arsène Lupin's Christmas (#2), Figaro's Children (#2), The Tarot of Fantômas (#2), The Star Prince (#2), Marguerite (#2), Lost and Found (#2), The Murder of Randolph Carter (#3), Madame Atomos' Xmas (#4), Madame Atomos' Holidays (#5), J.C. in Alphaville (#6), The Sincerest Form of Flattery (#7), The Affair of the Necklace Revisited (#8), Dad (#9), Christmas at Schönbrunn (#10), Bertie of the Jungle (#15), The Legacy of Atlantis (#16).
Lofficier, Randy: The Reluctant Princess (#4), The English Gentleman's Ball (#5), The Spear of Destiny (#6).
Lorin, Patrick: Troubled Waters (#10).

McDonald, David: Catspaw (#8), Diplomatic Freeze (#9), The Lesser of Two Evils (#10).
McDonnell, David: Big Little Man (#7).
McIntee, David A.: Bullets Over Bombay (#3).

Malcolm, Nigel: To Dust and Ashes, in its Heat Consuming (#9), Von Bork's Priorities (#10), A Fistful of Judexes (#11), The Adventure of the Orcival Rain (#12), Maximum Speed (#13), Tomorrow belongs to the Nyctalope (#14), Enemies of the People (#15), Useful Idiots (#16).

Mauméjean, Xavier: Be Seeing You! (#2), A Day in the Life of Madame Atomos (#3), A Wooster Xmas (#4), The Most Exciting Game (#5), The Man for the Job (#6), My Femmes Fatales (#7), The Wayne Memos (#10), The Replacement (#16).

Maynard, William P.: Yes Virginia There is a Fantômas (#6).

Mengel, Brad: All's Fair... (#3), The Apprentice (#7).

Miller, Sylvie: The Vanishing Diamonds (with Ward, Philippe) (#2).

Moorcock, Michael: The Affair of the Bassin des Hivers (#3), The Icon Crackdown (#10).

Mouiller, Jean-Marc: Behind the Mask of the Ripper (#12).

Nevins, Jess: A Jest, To Pass The Time (#2), : Red in Tooth and Claw (#4), A Root That Beareth Gall and Worms (#5).

Newman, Kim: Angels of Music (#2), The Mark of Kane (#4).

Newman, Sharan: The Beast Without (#7).

Nigro, Christofer: Patricide (#8), Death of a Dream (#9), The Privilege of Adonis (#10), The Noble Freak (#11), Justice and the Beast (#12), Bad Alchemy (#13), Kindred Beasts (#14), The Anti-Adonis Alliance (#15), Clash of the Jungle Lords (#16).

Payne, Samuel T.: Lacunal Visions (#1).

Peel, John: The Kind-Hearted Torturer (#1), The Incomplete Assassin (#2), The Successful Failure (#3), Twenty Thousand Years Under the Sea (#4), The Dynamics of an Asteroid (#5). The Biggest Guns (#6), More Imaginative Sins (#8), The Benevolent Burglar (#9), Return to the Center of the Earth (#10, #11), Time to Kill (#13**), The Gutter God (#15), The Eye of the Hawk (#16).**

Penswick, Neil: The Vampire Murders (#6), Legacy of Evil (#7), The Conspiracy of Silence (#9).

Power, Dennis E.: No Good Deed (#6), Passing through the Hands of Steel (#8).

Rawlik, Pete: The Masquerade in Exile (#7), Before the War, Five Dragons Roar (#8), Professor Peaslee Plays Paris (#9), Revenge of the Reanimator (#10), The Ylourgne Accord (#11).

Reynolds, Joshua: The Carolingian Stone (#8), Nestor Burma Goes West (#9), The Swine of Gerasene (#10).

Rival, Pierrick: The Inn of the First Voyage (#12).

Roberson, Chris: Penumbra (#1), Annus Mirabilis (#2), The Famous Ape (#3).

Robinson, Robert L., Jr.: Two Hunters (#3).

Roman, Steven A.: Night's Children (#4).

Schildiner, Frank: The Smoking Mirror (#5), Laurels for the Toff (#6), The Tiny Destroyer (#7), The Death Bird (#8), The True Cost of Doing Business (#9), The Blood of Frankenstein (#10), Saint and Sinners (#11), Ancient Space Lizards and Other Visitors (#12), The Taking of Frankenstein (#13), Dice, Pearl and Sword (#14), Irma Vep and the Cottage of Doom (#15), Vampire Diplomacy (#16).
Sheckley, Robert: The Paris-Ganymede Clock (#1).
Shiffman, Stuart: The Milkman Cometh(#5), Grim Days (#7), True Believers (#10).
Shirley, John: Cyrano and the Two Plumes (#4).
Shook, Sam: A Professional Matter (#11), The Eldritch Stones (#12), Bringer of the Outer Dark (#13).
Sinor, Bradley H.: Where the Shadows Began... (#6), The Screeching of Two Ravens (#7), The Silence (#9).
Stableford, Brian: The Titan Unwrecked (#1), The Grey Men (#2), The Child-Stealers(#3), The Return of Frankenstein (#4), The Vampire in Paris (#5), Where Zombies Armies Clash by Night (#6), The Necromancers of London (#7), Malbrough s'en va-t-en-guerre (#10).
Stéphan, Michel: The Red Silk Scarf (#6), The Three Lives of Maddalena (#7), With the Compliments of Nestor Burma! (#8), Vampire in the Fist (#9), Nestor Burma in New York (#10), The Submarine "Le Rouge" (#12), One Summer Night at Holy Cross (#13), The Odyssey of Madame Atomos (#14), Madame Atomos Likes Her Music (#15).

Trudel, Jean-Louis: Legacies (#2).

Unbekannt Artikel: Leonox Meets Mephista (#12), The Yellow Peril (#14).

Vannereux, Michel: The Warlord of Vaha (#8).
Vineyard, David L.: The Jade Buddha (#5), The Children's Crusade (#6), The Mysterious Island of Dr. Antekirtt (#7), Interview with a Nyctalope (#10), The Legacy of Arsène Lupin (#11), The White Star of Atlantis (#12), The Moon of the White Wolf (#13), The Third Eye of Osiris (#14), The Theft of the Golden Asp (#15), The Stone of Solomon (#16).

Wallace, Loston: Meeting with the Mir Beg (with Harris, Micah) (#11).
Ward, Philippe: The Vanishing Diamonds (with Miller, Sylvie) (#2).
Welch, Jared: The Vampire of New Orleans (#10), The Revolutionary and the Brigand (#11), The Piano Maidens (#12), Styrian Rhapsody (#13).

Index of Stories

Bug's Life, a (#15)
Bullets Over Bombay (#3)
Butterfly Files, The (#3)

Cadavres Exquis (#1)
Caesar's Children (#6)
Captain Future and the Lunar Peril (#4)
Carolingian Stone, The (#8)
Case of Mistaken Identity, A (#14)
Case of the Curious Cadaver, The (#12)
Case of the Remains to be seen, The (#14)
Catspaw (#8)
Children of Heracles, The (#6)
Children's Crusade, The (#6)
Child-Stealers, The (#3)
Christmas at Schönbrunn (#10)
City of the Nosferatu (#10)
Clash of the Jungle Lords (#16)
Conspiracy of Silence, The (#9)
Corridors of Deceit (#4)
Crater of the Dead, The (#15)
Curse of Orlac, The (#14)
Cyrano and the Two Plumes (#4)

Dad (#9)
Dance of Night and Death, A (#3)
Darkness in the Woods, The (#11)
Day in the Life of Madame Atomos, A (#3)
Death Bird, The (#8)
Death of a Dream (#9)
Death of Von Bork, The (#14)
Death to the Heretic! (#7)
Dice, Pearl and Sword (#14)
Diplomatic Freeze (#9)
Doctor Cerral's Patient (#2)
Doctor Omega and the Future Museum (#15)
Dollar's Worth of Fists, A (#13)
Don Camillo and the Secret Weapon (#8)
Don't Judge a Book by its Title (#11)
Dream's End (#11)
Dwelling in the Dark (#16)
Dynamics of an Asteroid, The (#5)

Eldritch Stones, The (#12)
Elfberg Red, The (#8)
Enemies of the People (#15)
English Gentleman's Ball, The (#5)
Eve of Destruction (#13)
Evil Among Us, The (#12)
Evils Against Which We Strive, The (#4)
Ex Calce Liberatus (#2),
Eye of Oran, The (#2)
Eye of the Hawk, The (#16)

Faces of Fear (#7)
Famous Ape, The (#3).
Fiat Lux! (#7)
Figaro's Children (#2)
Fistful of Judexes, A (#11)
Fool Me Once... (#4)
Frequency of Fear, The (#10)
From Paris with Hate (#13)

Galazi in the Enchanted City (#13)
Gilgamesh Revisited (#11)
Goat of Saint Elster, The (#13)
Gods of the Underworld (#9)
Great Ape Caper, The (#10)
Green Eye. The (#10)
Grey Men, The (#2),
Grim Days (#7)
Guided Tours of Famous Secret Places (#14)
Gutter God, The (#15)

Harry's Homecoming (#13)
He Who Laughs Last (#10)
Heart of a Man, The (#5)
Heart of the Moon, The (#3)
Hero of Two Worlds (#14)
High Noon of the Living Dead (#15)
House of El Hombre Loco, The (#12)

Icon Crackdown The (#10).
In the Caves of the Serpent (#8)
Incident in the Boer War (#6)
Incomplete Assassin, The (#2)

Paris-Ganymede Clock, The (#1).
Passing through the Hands of Steel (#8)
Patricide (#8)
Peculiar Cats of the Sea of Dreams, The (#16)
Penumbra (#1)
Perils Over Paris (#5)
Phantom Masquerade (#14)
Piano Maidens, The (#12)
Piercing the Veil of Isis (#10)
Pirate's Life, A (#16)
Princes of the Universe (#14)
Privilege of Adonis, The (#10)
Professional Matter, A (#11)
Professor Peaslee Plays Paris (#9)
Purpose in Life, A (#13)

Quest of the Vourdalaki (#10)

Rage of Terror (#16)
Red in Tooth and Claw (#4)
Red Silk Scarf, The (#6)
Reluctant Princess, The (#4)
Replacement, The (#16).
Return of Frankenstein, The (#4)
Return to the 20th Century (#3)
Return to the Center of the Earth (#10, #11)
Revelation of the Yeti, The (#12)
Revenge of the Reanimator (#10)
Revolutionary and the Brigand, The (#11)
Robots of Metropolis, The (#7)
Robots of Valencia, The (#15)
Root That Beareth Gall and Worms, A (#5)
Rouletabille and the New World Order (#11)
Rouletabille at the Old Bailey (#14)
Rouletabille in the House of Despair (#15, #16)
Rouletabille on Mysterious Island (#12)
Rouletabille Rides the Horror Express (#13)
Rouletabille vs. The Cat (#10)

Saint and Sinners (#11)
Sainte-Geneviève Caper, The (#1)
Satan's Signature (#8).
Science outraged, Science murdered! (#15)

Twenty Thousand Years Under the Sea (#4)
Two Hunters (#3)

Useful Idiots (#16)

Vampire Diplomacy (#16)
Vampire in Paris, The (#5)
Vampire in the Fist (#9)
Vampire Murders, The (#6)
Vampire of New Orleans, The (#10)
Vampire President, The (#16)
Vampire Renaissance (#8)
Vanishing Devil, The (#1)
Vanishing Diamonds The (#2)
Vertigo, The (#15)
Violet's Lament (#9).
Virginia There is a Fantômas (#6)
Von Bork's Priorities (#10)

Waltz in Norbury, A (#15)
Warlord of Vaha, The (#8)
Way of the Crane, The (#5)
Wayne Memos, The (#10)
Werewolf of Rutherford Grange, The (#1, #2)
What Doesn't Die (#7)
What Lurks in Romney Marsh? (#9)
What Rough Beast (#7)
When Lemmy Met Jules (#1)
Where the Shadows Began... (#6)
Where Zombies Armies Clash by Night (#6)
White Star of Atlantis, The (#12)
Will There Be Sunlight? (#7)
Wings of Fear (#9)
With the Compliments of Nestor Burma! (#8)
Wolf at the Door of Time (#9)
Wooster Xmas, A (#4)

Yellow Peril, The (#14)
Ylourgne Accord, The (#11)

WATCH OUT FOR

TALES OF THE
SHADOWMEN
VOLUME 17: NOBLESSE OBLIGE
TO BE RELEASED DECEMBER 2020

www.ingramcontent.com/pod-product-compliance
Lightning Source LLC
Chambersburg PA
CBHW030356020726
47493CB00003B/842